Rivers S om Stanford
University comparative
studies in nd holds an
MFA in f e Michener
Ce om
the m-
bri d-
nes

An Unkindness of GHOSTS

Rivers Solomon

BROOKLYN, NEW YORK, USA
BALLYDEHOB, CO. CORK, IRELAND

This is a work of fiction. All names, characters, places, and incidents are the product of the author's imagination or are used fictitiously. Any resemblance to real events or persons, living or dead, is entirely coincidental.

©2017 Rivers Solomon
ISBN: 978-1-61775-588-0
Library of Congress Control Number: 2017936119

Cover design: TG Design.
Cover art: re_bekka/Shutterstock.com (female figure) and Derek R. Audette/Shutterstock.com (space).

Akashic Books
Brooklyn, New York, USA
Ballydehob, Co. Cork, Ireland
Twitter: @AkashicBooks
Facebook: AkashicBooks
E-mail: info@akashicbooks.com
Website: www.akashicbooks.com

To my mother
and her mother
all the way back to Eve

PART 1

THERMODYNAMICS

1

*A*ster removed two scalpels from her med-kit to soak in a solution of disinfectant. Her fingers trembled from the cold, and the tools slipped from her grasp, plopping ungracefully into the sanitizer. In ten minutes' time, she'd be amputating a child's gangrenous foot. This shaking and carrying on would not do.

Was this winter?

Dim light—chemiluminescent reactions of peroxide, orange dye, and ester—suffused the makeshift operating room. *Starjars*, the T-deckers called their improvised lanterns. Aster wondered where they'd gotten the peroxide to work them, let alone the phenyl oxalate ester.

"All you got to do is give one of them a shake and the stuff inside gets all mixed up," said Flick, rotted foot propped atop two stacked trunks. "Look! You looking?"

Of course Aster was looking. Couldn't Flick see her eyes?

A pile of faded comics lay next to the child on a flipped-over wicker basket, *The Reign of Night Empress #19* on top. Its cover depicted a woman named Mariam Santi in a beige trench coat carrying a cylindrical device made of metal and wood. When she pulled its tiny lever with her index finger, a silver ball shot out of the tube, wounding her enemy.

"Rifle," Aster whispered, her lips splitting at the corners where the cold had pasted them shut. As a child, she'd called them *ripples* for the way they had of changing everything in a story. And because she'd misread the word the first time around, finding that *f*'s and *p*'s looked similar to her untrained eyes.

Issue 19 of *Night Empress* had been one of Aster's favorites when she was a girl, and she'd read it along with every other Mariam Santi adventure available aboard *Matilda*. Old comics circulated wing to wing, deck to deck.

"Look how it blows up inside when I jostle it! *Boom! Boom! Boom!*" said Flick as she—he—no, *they*—shook the starjar. Aster regretted the error. She was used to the style of her own deck where all children were referred to with feminine pronouns. Here, it was *they*. She'd do well to remember. "Explode! Explode!" Flick continued, tossing the starjar into the air before catching it. "Except not really. If it was a explosion there'd be fire, and if there was fire it'd be hot." They spoke in that matter-of-fact tone native to children who believed they knew everything. "My great-grandmeema say there was blackouts before too, but they was just passing through. After one week they stopped, and lowdeckers never even had to have no energy rations to stop them. No cold," said Flick, dark-brown skin lit bronze under the meek glow of the starjars.

If there was a chance he'd respond—and there wasn't—Aster would radio the Surgeon. He'd write her a pass to transport Flick up to his clinic on G deck or somewhere else warm. He'd sign it in his looping cursive and stamp it with his fancy gold seal. Aster didn't know every guard on *Matilda*, but the ones she did wouldn't dare deny a pass issued by Heavens' Hands Made Flesh.

As it was, the Surgeon hadn't spoken to Aster in three and a half weeks, not since the start of the blackouts. No Surgeon, no access to *Matilda*'s upperdecks. No upperdeck access, no heat.

"It's like a star, see?" Flick said, shaking another lantern, setting off its chemical show.

Aster looked at the lantern, then at Flick, then at the lantern again. "I'm afraid I don't."

"A star's a bunch of little things coming together to make light, yeah? Chemicals and all that. And our little special jars here is a bunch of little things coming together to make light too. Also chemicals. Agree or disagree?"

"Agree," said Aster, familiar with the basic chemistry from studies in astromatics.

"So, they the same. Chemicals plus more chemicals makes magic," Flick said, tongue sticking out.

Aster admired the child's sureness if not their utter wrongness. "Your model lacks specificity and is therefore useless," she said, speaking more harshly than intended. This close to the end of the day, she lost the ability to modulate her naturally abrupt manner for the comfort of others. "According to such a theory, a suitcase would be no different than a bomb. Sugars and synthase react to make the cotton of the luggage. Oxygen oxidizes gunpowder to make an explosion. *Chemicals plus more chemicals makes magic* describes both scenarios rather well, but, of course, we know a suitcase is nothing like a bomb."

Flick blinked obstinately, and Aster searched for a child-appropriate explanation.

"You're arguing that a person is identical to a dog because they've both got bones and blood."

"Guards be calling Tarlanders dogs all the time," Flick said, hand on hip.

Aster twitched at the sound of the familiar word; she hadn't heard it in ages, but it still stirred a sense of belonging. Tarlanders were the inhabitants of P, Q, R, S, and T decks, and it was as close to a nation as anything on *Matilda*.

"The guards are hardly a compass by which to measure right and wrong," said Aster.

Flick's eyes flashed open in what was presumably mock shock. "You gonna get struck down for saying that, woman. Don't you know that Sovereign Nicolaeus is the Heavens' chosen ruler? And that the guards are Nicolaeus's soldiers and, by extension, soldiers of the Heavens? A spurn to them is a spurn to the Heavens direct," Flick said in a high-pitched voice.

"Well, let's hope the Heavens exact vengeance *after* I've amputated your foot. I wouldn't want you—righteous defender of the moral order that you are—negatively affected by my sacrilege." Without meaning to, Aster smiled.

"How about if you promise to do my surgery up good, I'll write a letter to the Guard begging they spare you? I been practicing my vocabulary and I already know what I'm gonna say. Want to hear?" Mischief drew Flick's face into a sly grin.

"*Dear Sirs,*" Flick began before loudly inhaling, "*On account of there being no heat down here on account of there being no electricity on account of the brand-new energy rations so thoughtfully and nobly and honorably imposed on the steerage decks by Sovereign Nicolaeus on account of the blackouts—Aster fell prey to a brief fit of hypothermia-induced de-lirium and spoke out against you in her maddery. She's healed up now so you don't have to worry about it happening again. Yours humbly, deferen-tially, meekly, and respectfully, Flor 'Flicker' Samuels.*" Flick erupted in laughter and took a bow. "Opinions?"

"Your sarcasm reveals clear disregard for the sanctity of the Sovereign's Guard, which I appreciate," Aster said, blowing into her cupped palms before vigorously rubbing them to-gether. As much as she enjoyed the banter, their conversation proved a distraction against resolving the matter of the cold.

"You can have my mittens if you want," said Flick. They set down the starjar they'd been holding and showed off their wrapped hands. "They'll warm you up good so you can cut, cut, cut me up, no problem. Slice into me like a festival ham if you want."

Aster's eyes made uncertain contact with Flick's. "I can-not discern whether or not your offer is in earnest. It should be obvious I cannot perform an amputation in mittens. Are you joking again?"

"Aye," Flick said, having the decency to look a little bashful about making fun. "But they *is* warm. Lined with rabbit fur. My great-meema skint it herself back when there was rabbits aboard *Matilda*. Real rabbits. When was the last time anybody saw one of those?"

Aster assumed the question was rhetorical, as she couldn't very well ascertain when the last time in the entirety of the universe someone had seen a rabbit. "I didn't think the moments preceding an operation were particularly well-suited to humor, but it's characterized a large portion of our interaction," she said. Aster was always memorizing new ways of being with people.

Flick shrugged, the gesture causing the blanket wrapped about their shoulders to fall. "I like to do the exact opposite of what's suited. We got a saying here in Tide Wing: *Should* is for weaklings. Why would we care about such a thing when already nothing is how it should be on this cursed ship? *Should* won't make it so you don't got to cut off my foot, will it? It sure won't turn the heat back on, or kill the man who thought to turn it off in the first place. *Should* disappeared three hundred years ago when our old home went gone. There's no such thing as *supposed to* in space. Didn't your meema never teach you that?"

Breaths glided like exorcized ghosts from Flick's mouth. Aster recognized the puffs for what they were, condensed molecules of H_2O, but she reached out to touch one of the vagabond forms anyway. She imagined each foggy sheaf as an Ancestor, even though the Ancestors were dead, swallowed into the past alongside the Great Lifehouse from which *Matilda* had fled.

"My mother killed herself the day I was born," Aster said. "Though it's possible she attempted to impart a distaste for *should* in me before passing, newborn infants lack the neurocapacity to process language or form memories, so if she did, I don't recall."

The way Flick pursed their lips, they looked on the verge of whistling. "My great-meema says I'm always stirring up old wounds. Forgive me," they said, eyes intent on Aster. Yet the wound of Lune Grey felt quite fresh and untended, no stirring from Flick required.

Aster blamed the blackouts. The last time *Matilda* experienced ship-wide power outages was twenty-five years ago, and every conversation she overheard seemed to revolve around that sum. I *thought they fixed this twenty-five years ago,* someone said, and, It *may have been twenty-five years but I remember it good as yesterday,* or, *Twenty-five years. Couldn't they have bought* Matilda *more time than that?*

These grievances were innocent enough on their own, but to Aster they were reminders. Twenty-five years her mother had been dead.

"Talk about a woman with no care for *should*," said Flick, "leaving her baby 'fore it had a first sip of milk."

"What?" Aster replied, aware Flick had spoken, but clueless as to what they said. Thoughts of Lune had increased to the point of distraction, interfering with her work. She gulped her tea, hopeful the bitterness would focus her enough to deal with this cold. "Do you have isopropyl alcohol?" she asked.

Flick scrunched their brow, poked out their plump lips. "Great-meema!" they called, then louder, "Great-meema!"

A woman appeared after Flick's fifth call. "What?" she asked, hand clamped around a fabric idol. She'd been praying.

"Ole girl say she need alcohol," said Flick.

The woman, young to be the mother of a mother of a mother, turned to Aster. "We don't got nothing pure, *yo'wa*," she said, and it took Aster a minute to parse that particular form of address. Where Aster lived, folks said *yongwa*. Soft *o*, then a *g* sound. It meant *young one* in the language of the Tarlands. "I do got something that might do. One moment," the woman added.

Flick read *The Reign of Night Empress* as they waited for their great-meema to return. Aster saw it was the same copy she herself had owned fifteen years earlier. The lemon curd she'd spilled on it as a child still smeared the top left corner. There was more on page eleven, covering the tip of Night Empress's rifle.

"This good?" the woman asked as she returned, handing over a jar.

Aster unscrewed the lid, flecks of orange rust peeling from the age-softened metal. She gagged upon smelling the contents and slammed the lid back on. "Booze?" she asked.

"More or less," said the woman. "What you need it for? I suppose if you have a drink it'll warm you from the inside. I wouldn't recommend it. Couldn't pay me a new pair of shoes to drink that piss." She pinched Aster's cold-nipped ears, but they were too numb, and Aster didn't feel the pressure.

"It is fuel. For the stove I'm going to build. I'll need that can too," said Aster, pointing to the large cylinder in the corner of the cabin labeled:

> MAMA LOU'S BAKED BEANS
> BROWN SUGAR, MAPLE, BACON
> FAMILY-SIZE 6lbs 5oz

Aster emptied the odds and ends from inside. A few thimbles, a spool of thread, buttons, two packets of poppyserum, razor. "Now socks, shirts, anything," she said. Two other women hustled to gather the materials, stuffing them into the can as Aster directed. When it was sufficiently packed, Aster poured in the entirety of the jar of rotgut Flick's great-grandmeema had procured.

A teenager pointed to the lighter in Aster's hand. "Can I do it?" they asked.

"Go ahead," said Aster, handing over the lighter. Smiling,

the girl grabbed it and held it to the can, the alcohol igniting.

"How long will this burn for?"

"Several hours," Aster said, surprised that the same women who rigged the starjars had never built an alcohol stove. It was *Matilda*'s geography, she supposed. What people had known for two generations on R deck had yet to be discovered on V, and so on. Twenty thousand lowdeckers and almost half as many different ways of life. That was the nature of a ship divided by metal, language, and armed guards. Even in decks as linked as the Tarlands, information had a way of staying put.

"How come there's no smoke? I never seen fire with no smoke," said a woman wrapped in a small afghan.

"Alcohol's good fuel." Aster didn't have time to elaborate and returned to the operating area. There, Flick already sat, their great-grandmother next to them. "Lay on your side for me," Aster said. "I am going to lift your nightgown for just a moment. Acceptable?"

Flick lifted the gown themself. Aster scrubbed their back with a sponge, pinching the skin where she'd insert the needle. Not necessary, but she'd picked up the habit from times she'd watched the Surgeon. She'd learned most body-cutting craft from other Q deck healers, but the Surgeon's tricks stuck with her most. "You'll feel a small nip," she said, then injected local anesthetic into the child's intervertebra. Flick whimpered and grabbed their great-meema's hands. "You'll feel heavy pressure in three . . . two . . . one." Aster inserted the larger needle into Flick's spine. Then she dragged her stool down to the bottom of the cot and pinched the gangrenous skin above Flick's metatarsals.

"Is it gonna hurt much once that stuff you put in my back wears out?" asked Flick.

"Yes."

A tear formed in the corner of Flick's eye, but they wiped

it away with the collar of their shirt before it could fall.

Aster pressed her stethoscope to Flick's talus bone and listened. The steady pulsing of blood signaled viable vessels and circulation, and she drew a line in ink where she planned to make the incision. Preserving the anklebone would make fitting a prosthesis easier.

"It feels good," said Flick.

"Hmm?"

"The cabin," Flick clarified. "It's like being on the Field Decks, Baby Sun on my back." They squeezed their eyes shut, and for the tenth time this week, Aster thought of her mother. This time, it was the talk of Baby that summoned her. Lune had worked as a mechanic on the miniature star that sourced *Matilda*'s power.

"Are you certain this is the only way?" Flick's great-meema asked. "I heard you make potions, medicines so strong they regrow skin. They say you got a secret lab with tinctures that cure anything." She squeezed her left hand with her right, kissed each knuckle prayerfully.

"I don't have a secret laboratory," Aster lied. "But if I did, and it had the cures you speak of, I wouldn't keep it from you. This is the only way."

Aster took her scalpel and made a decisive slice into Flick's epidermis, through to the muscle, a line going all the way around, creating a flap of skin that she would later suture to form a nub over the bone.

"May retribution come to those responsible for this," said Flick's great-meema, fists balled into her apron.

Aster cut away the rotted flesh and muscle of Flick's foot, gratified by the falling off of blackened and corrupted limb, shiny white bone revealing itself underneath. There was no sense mourning that which no longer nourished.

By the time Aster finished, Flick's arteries sufficiently ligated, skin repatched, it was only a little over an hour to curfew. She placed the foot into a cooler. She had to hurry if she wanted to deposit it in her botanarium—or secret laboratory, in Flick's great-grandmeema's words—before retiring to her quarters for the night.

"It's true what people say—you're a good physic," Flick said, eyes fluttering drowsily. "Good as the Surgeon herself, and they say her powers came from the Heavens themselves."

Aster didn't correct Flick's reflexive use of the pronoun *her*. They'd only forget again.

Flick's great-meema stroked the side of her pinkie against Flick's knee.

"Here," Aster said, handing her a brown bottle, fourteen pills inside. "Once daily at first-meal."

Aster injected a slow-release pain suppressant into Flick's veins, so when the anesthesia waned, there'd be no immediate suffering. Flick whined, then pulled themselves up onto their elbows, wobbly and sedated. They squinted their eyes as they looked down and moved their hips, trying to jostle their legs, the paralytic still in effect. "It's all gone," they said, and finally—finally—succumbed to tears. As they wept, their great-meema held them close.

11

On the subject of amputations—

Seventy years into *Matilda*'s voyage, days after the disaster that claimed the bulk of the Guard's high-ranking members, a scientist named Frederick Hauser proposed a solution to the problem of the Tarlands' declining population.

It was wasteful, he declared, to recycle the Tarlanders' defective bodies into *Matilda* when the steady pulse of an electrical current could reanimate them as perfect, obedient workers. It didn't matter that the genetic anomaly endemic to their people might lead to their extinction if their spiritless cadavers could hoe fields effectively. No productivity loss.

The few who'd survived the disaster crinkled their brows at Hauser's scheme. They argued that every being in the Heavens' creations deserved the dignity of death.

According to Hauser, however, Tarlanders were not of the Heavens. Even beasts of the field were made male and female, were they not? So they might multiply and spread the Heavens' bounty. Tarlanders did not come male and female— everything but.

In his speech to the Guard's remaining members, preserved forever in a phonograph cylinder, Hauser explained that Tarlanders came from the Realm of Chaos—the world that existed before the Heavens overruled it, replacing nonsense with divine structure. Their demon forms could not conform to the Holy Order set forth by the Heavens.

(Aster knew he referred to what the Surgeon once called

hereditary suprarenal dysregula. Due to a broad range of hormonal disturbances, Tarlander bodies did not always present as clearly male and female as the Guard supposed they ought. This explained Aster's hairiness and muscular build despite being born without the external organs that produced testosterone.)

The man who'd taken the role as interim sovereign cleared his throat and, judging by the sound of a clinking glass on the recording, drank from a glass of water. He said that he could not allow the degradation of a creature in the Heavens' realm, whether that creature came from somewhere else or not.

Hauser countered with a compromise. Via amputation, he could use body parts rather than the body whole. Electrified arms to pull rakes. Electrified hands for sewing.

The Interim Sovereign asked Hauser to leave, but the meeting carried on after his departure. They debated the merits of the scientist's idea. The recent disaster meant *Matilda* was in turmoil. Such a program might reify the supremacy of the Sovereign and his Holy Order of the Guard.

Ultimately, however, they decided the plan required too many resources and too much manpower to implement, especially with their depleted ranks. Their meeting moved on to other business before the phonograph recording cut off abruptly.

Aster had asked the Surgeon if any of the record cylinders explained the event that had weakened them so substantially. He shook his head. Most recordings of the transitional Guard's meetings had been destroyed.

Aster carried that knowledge inside her. These men had the means and opportunity to destroy evidence, to protect their legacy, but not one of them thought earnest discussion of reanimating a person's limbs for the purpose of manual labor warranted deletion from their official record. Forget the horrifying cruelty—the incompetent science of it all.

* * *

"Wait, now, *yo'wa*, not so quick," said Flick's great-grandmeema. She tugged Aster's suspenders and dragged her back through the cabin hatch. "Take this." She held out a large gray cloak.

"I should be—" Aster started, but stopped herself when she remembered Flick's anti-*should* tirade. "I have to be going."

"See if it fits. Won't take but a second to try it on," Flick's great-grandmeema said, reminding Aster of her Aint Melusine. The woman who raised Aster had similar levels of persistence.

Flick's great-meema smiled, revealing intermittent metal teeth, sloppily rooted. Whoever had installed the implants neglected to perform a sinus augmentation and gum graft on the decayed gingiva and posterior maxilla.

Aster set down her medicine bag and took hold of the offering. Curled sheep's wool lined the inside, off-white and dirt-stamped.

"It's been in my family since before *Matilda*, I reckon," the old woman said. "I never had much use for it before these energy rations, except for those early-born babies who couldn't keep their temperature up. I've washed out all the spit-up. It's yours now. You like it?"

Aster squeezed the soft lining. "It's too dear."

The woman snorted and waved a hand. "I'd say it's a pretty fair trade for the stove, no? We got quite the bargain."

In the corridor, a guard shouted orders, and Aster moved to the side where she couldn't be seen in the cabin. "But you supplied the materials for the stove," she said.

"Materials are meaningless without knowledge, which is what you gave us. A cloak for a stove, that's the trade."

Aster slipped her hand into her left trouser pocket to check her watch. If she wanted time in her botanarium before returning home to Q deck, she needed to leave now. "Really, it was nothing. I must go."

"How can you call such a gift nothing? If we'd known how to make one of those things two weeks ago, Flick might never got frostbite, certainly not bad enough to turn to gangrene. That stove could've saved my little one's foot," Flick's great-meema said, dark face stern. "If we can get our hands on more alcohol—and believe me, we can; we Tide Wing women can get our hands on anything—when we do, we can save another from my great-grandbaby's fate." She tightened the loose-knit shawl around her neck before continuing: "You're a smart one. You know as good as me and as good as Flick that there is no Promised Land. *Matilda*'s an orphan, a daughter of dead gods. But the Ancestors is real and their spirits are at work. Baby Sun giving out is how they making a fuss. Tryna tell us it's time to move, to act. They gave us the same message twenty-five years ago, but we didn't listen. So they had to make their message louder, break Baby Sun even more. You hear me?"

Aster didn't know if the woman meant *hear* literally or as a euphemism for *understand*. Depending on which it was, Aster's answer would be different.

"We got to help each other survive long enough to find out what the spirits have in store. That means not dying of cold. Please, try on the cloak."

Aster unstrapped her rucksack from her back and set it down next to the cooler and medicine bag. "Fine," she said, then slid on the cloak.

"Magnificent," Flick's great-meema observed. "Do you like it?"

The fabric weighed six or seven pounds, and it pressed down on Aster's body. "I do. It is warm and pleasingly heavy. My sincerest gratitude, *eldwa*."

The woman tilted her head, squinted her eyes. "You have a harsh accent," she said. "It's *elwa*. Not *eldwa*. Elwa. See how much better that sounds? Soft like syrup. Though I prefer you not call me that at all. Who wants to be reminded they are old? Call me *he'lawa*. I am a healer, like you. Well, not quite like you. You're a little off, aren't you?" The woman grabbed Aster's chin, turning her face so they were forced eye to eye. "You're one of those who has to tune the world out and focus on one thing at a time. We have a word for that down here, women like you. *Insiwa*. Inside one. It means you live inside your head and to step out of it hurts like a caning."

Aster had been called worse: *simple, dumb, defective, half-witted dog, get on all fours and spread. Not all there.*

But Aster was all there. She felt herself existing. Perhaps the derogative referred to her motherlessness. A part of each person lay in their past, in their parentage and grandparentage, and if that history was missing, were said people incomplete?

"I'll return to examine Flick as soon as I'm able," Aster said, and bade goodbye once again. She felt thankful that the woman let her go this time.

Two guards stood at either side of the corridor. Aster had a pass to be away from her home deck but she kept her head down, not wishing to draw attention to herself. Pass or not, they might have a mind to start trouble.

A shaved-headed teenager sold blankets in the middle of the corridor, and patrons lined up to barter. They carried bars of soap, swaths of cotton, ivory combs.

Subfreezing temperatures weakened what were already not particularly robust immune systems, and people hobbled to their quarters, wrapped in knit scarves that provided little barrier. Aster thought she should give her new cloak to one of them, but it felt too good around her.

An elderly woman shouted at three children, and they cried. Tears made the charcoal circled about their eyes run down their cheeks in watercolor swirls. They did that here on T deck—smudged black onto their faces in thick, wide circles. *Rakkun eyes*, they called it, after the scavenging animal; for they descended from a scavenging people.

So they said. So they told themselves. So their stories went. This far from the past, no one could truly know their history.

The children were siblings, going by the look of them. All three shared the same murky gray irises, the color near identical to the ashy swells beneath their eyes. She'd seen them before on the Field Decks during one of her shifts. They didn't work near her, of course, being from different decks, but she'd noticed them in passing.

The elderly woman pointed a bony finger at them, and they ran away, right into Aster. They scurried past her without an apology, patting their pockets to make sure nothing had fallen out during the bump.

Lowdeckers, Aster included, hoarded. Pockets got new life as homes for various and sundry collectibles—poppyserum, antibiotics, seeds, thread, screws, thimbles. Aster had stolen whole stalks of corn from the fields before. Slid them up her trouser leg.

"Watch where you're going," one of the children called over their shoulder, and she did. After Tide Wing came Tributary Wing. Aster took the staircase downward, leaving T deck for her botanarium. There, at least, there was some kind of quiet.

Xylem Wing, like all X deck, smelled of decay. *You can't expect the dead to wear perfume,* Aster's Aint Melusine had said. She'd guided Aster through the abandoned deck as a child. *No one but ghosts is here, child. Do what you want with it.* What had once been a mess hall was now Aster's botanarium.

She returned there now, desperate for the sanctuary of her private garden and laboratory. She spun the handwheel and opened the hatch, eyes closed reverently. Pungent florals scented the air.

"Finally," said Giselle, rifling through a pile of papers. "It's almost curfew. I was starting to think you weren't gonna come here to—whatever it is you say you got to do every night. De-brief or decompose."

Giselle knew very well the word was *decompress.* Aster dropped her medicine bag on the floor, set the ice chest with Flick's foot by the hatch. She'd only been away since this morning, but she'd missed the botanarium's moss-covered walls, the vine-strangled support beams. Rows and rows of her botanical progeny welcomed Aster with their familiar order.

"What are you doing here?" she asked, in no mood to deal with Giselle. After her shift in the Field Decks, she'd had only a brief break for supper before going to tend to Flick. She needed quiet and she needed solitude.

Aster undid the straps of her rucksack, wiggling her shoulders and arms out of them. As she did, the brass radiolabe clipped to her right trouser pocket slipped out. Tarnished and dented, it didn't make for particularly fine jewelry, but Aster wore it daily because it had belonged to her mother. It was the tool she'd used to detect radiation levels as one of Baby Sun's mechanics.

"Because I like it here," Giselle finally replied. "Didn't you say I was always welcome?"

"I said that you were welcome as long as I was here. I would argue that last bit is a rather important addendum."

Giselle shrugged, head bent over Aster's papers. She'd cut her hair today. The curls poked out from her head unevenly, unsure of their place. "You got no more right to this space than I do. Far as I'm concerned, it's my botanarium too. It's warm in here, actually warm. I'm so tired of being cold. I got just as much right to be warm as you."

Aster's radiolabe bounced rhythmically against her as she walked the twelve feet to her desk. She squeezed it hard, hard enough to make a dimple in the soft metal with her finger pads. There was no harm she could do to something already so broken. As a child, she'd done everything she could to get it working, sneaking it to the parts of the ship highest in radiation. She'd even tried it down here on X deck, thought maybe the reason it didn't work was because she'd been using it wrong. Maybe Aster's meema hadn't meant for the device to sense normal types of radiation, the ones from the natural world, but rather the types from the other world. Ghosts. Nine years old and still prone to childish flights of fancy, Aster had traipsed X deck's supposedly haunted corridors, radiolabe held out in front of her. If there were spirits there like her Aint Melusine said, surely the radiolabe would beep.

It didn't. She tried it in all of *Matilda*'s secret passages because she liked to unearth abandoned things.

"Are you listening to me at all?" asked Giselle.

Aster's thoughts had wandered off but she had the presence of mind not to tell Giselle that. "I am listening," she said.

"It feels safe down here." Giselle looked up from the scattered papers to stare at Aster. "Can't trust nowhere else on this ship. I swear, even the walls are alive. Every time I think I've found a good spot, an abandoned closet, there's things lurking just round the way. Guards, mostly. They got a special eye on me. It's something in my blood they smell."

Giselle wrapped skinny arms around her middle and hugged herself. "Here I can be practically naked," she continued, standing, kicking off her boots, pulling down her tights. "It's so gloriously hot. And safe." She hopped up onto the counter to sit, thighs spread, her buttocks squashing and crinkling the papers she'd just been reading. "The heat, it's like—it feels like energy from someone doing conjure."

Aster felt it hypocritical to chastise Giselle's magical thinking when moments ago she'd recalled childhood attempts to spy ghosts with her mother's radiation detector, but she still felt the need to set Giselle straight. "The warmth here has nothing to do with conjure or magic. It's heat lamps powered by energy siphoned from Baby Sun. Simple."

"If it's so simple, why don't you do it to the rest of the lowdecks, huh?" said Giselle.

"The amount of energy required to heat one large cabin does not compare to that necessary to heat the whole of ten lowdecks. Someone monitoring Matilda's electrical grid would notice."

"And while you're at it, why don't you *unheat* the upperdecks?" Giselle grinned wildly, ignoring Aster's explanation of unfeasibility. "You can get your precious Surgeon to help. He'll write you a pass to the Nexus like he writes you a pass to everything, and you can switch off they heat like they switched off ours. And I'm a good person. I'm not even asking you to ice up their modest little bajillion-mile mansions. Heavens forbid! Just the sporting fields and the meadows," she said, her tone growing more serious, like she thought this an actual option.

"The average upperdeck estate is 9,300 square feet," said Aster. "Not a bajillion miles."

Giselle rolled her eyes. "The point is . . ." she began, but Aster knew what the point was. Cutting off heat to the lowdecks when there were woods, lakes, beaches, and game fields in the upperdecks didn't make sense if the actual goal was conserving energy.

We must protect the wildlife sanctuaries. Like Giselle, Aster had read the newspaper article on the importance of preserving the upperdecks' nature spaces.

"If I could switch our fates with theirs, I would," said Aster. She happily imagined two updeck men navigating the A deck hedge maze one fine Matildan afternoon. They'd feel suddenly underdressed, then downright chill. Lost in the maze, they'd huddle together for warmth before eventually dying of hypothermia. "I'd do it in a second."

Giselle stilled her swinging legs from her seat atop the counter. "Would you? Would you really do it? Sometimes I don't think you're any different from one of them . . . how you talk. How you strut about this ship like some sort of god— and why? Lots of us is doctors and healers down here, and we managed it without help from the Surgeon. You ain't special just cause you got all your stupid passes."

Aster scraped her nail along the outer thread of her trouser pocket, working the frayed stitches loose. She agreed that she wasn't special, not in the colloquial sense that implied one's difference was praiseworthy. Rather, she was plain-old strange. Always had been.

At nine years old, she used to outfit a tiny wooden doll in a cardigan and navy corduroys. Giselle had sewn the clothes out of fabric stolen from the wardrobes of upperdeckers, using her thumb as a dress form.

Aster pretended the smartly dressed figurine was a clever, important scientist, and the doll-woman's bunkmates had seen fit to host a ball in her honor, because they liked her, because they valued her, because they didn't think her odd or unpleasant to be around.

Aster had placed the doll in front of a spool of thread, which was to be the doll-woman's podium. *As a result of Dr. Doll's research and expert mastery of astromatics, the HSS Matilda has found a habitable planet. No longer are we to wander the Heavens homeless,* said another doll wearing a plaid skirt, introducing Dr. Doll.

You're so stupid, Giselle had said.

I don't care if you think I'm stupid. I will continue to do what I want to do without consideration for your opinion, said Aster.

Giselle had sat down, legs crossed, elbows upon her knees. *Fine, I'll play your boring game . . . Who can I be?* She picked up one of the wooden figurines, thumbed its juts and curves. *How about I be your rival? Professor Doll believes your Dr. Doll is stupid if she thinks anybody is ever getting off this ship. She plans to set off a bomb at your stupid ball and blow everyone up just like Night Empress did that one time.* Giselle scurried away and then returned with a matchbox. *Explosives,* she explained.

If Professor Doll bombs the ball she will no doubt destroy all of Matilda, Aster had said.

Good. Matilda *is shit.* Giselle had rummaged through a shoe box to find a suitable outfit for Professor Doll. She chose a sparkling red dress that left much of the wood on the figurine exposed.

Your Professor Doll does not seem appropriately dressed for the function in question. The guard dolls will notice her attire and realize something is amiss, thwarting your plans, said Aster.

Professor Doll will distract them with her doll tits.

These dolls have no tits, nor any external anatomy in line with the human form, said Aster, running her pointer finger along one of the sexless wood figures. *They do not even have mouths.*

Professor Doll had set the bomb off, Giselle simulating the explosion by throwing little doll parts everywhere. Aster saw Dr. Doll fly into the air, dead as a thing that never lived could be, and it was fine because Dr. Doll liked space and didn't mind so much being hurtled forever into the cold, especially if it meant *Matilda* was gone.

It had been a fun game, one they repeated (though with some variations) several times, most notably when Aster decided to carry out the mock explosion in a guard's office, with a real bomb she'd made as a test of her knowledge of alchematics.

She had committed several more acts of arson, never caught, stopping only when Giselle begged her to, certain she'd get them both in trouble with the Guard. Had Aster kept going all those years ago, she might very well have blown up all the ship, given the chance.

"My commitment to the destruction of *Matilda*'s ruling order is well documented," Aster said, bringing her eyes to Giselle's unblinking gaze. "Please don't doubt that if I could get rid of the cold, I would, or that if it was in my power to kill each and every upperdecker, I'd do that as well."

Giselle smiled quietly, bounced her heels against the cabinet again. She turned her eyes down in a rare show of retreat. "I know. I know you. I'm sick of it, is all. I want to always feel as warm as it feels in here. Warmer than that. I want to be like fire because fire is the only true thing. Or I want to be like one of them cast-iron spider pots you throw into the fire pit—in the morning, the iron remains, shiny like silver serving ware, and all the crust and bad parts is burned out of existence." Giselle scratched an exposed knobby wrist, picking at an invisible scab. She'd withered to skin and bones this past year. "I want to burn up and be burned and explode."

"Would you like medicine to calm your thoughts?" Aster asked when she noticed Giselle pressing her hand to her chest, her heart no doubt racing.

Next to Giselle sat a glass spray bottle, the one Aster used to water the more sensitive of her seedlings. Giselle picked it up and threw it across the cabin. "I don't want your medicine. Your pills or your syrups or your poisons. I don't want you near me at all. I don't even know why I came here."

Aster didn't startle at the outburst. She was always on edge with Giselle and therefore always adequately braced for contact. "I only offered pills because you've requested them in times past. Would you please sweep that up?" She pointed to the broken bottle.

Giselle slid off the counter and walked over to the shattered glass, stepped barefoot over the jagged pieces. She leaned down and used one hand to sweep the shards into the cup of her other hand. "All clean."

Aster watched as Giselle threw the broken glass into a can, then sat down again on the counter, the bottoms of her feet now bleeding. The blood blended seamlessly into the grate floor, droplets of red indistinguishable from flecks of rust.

"You happy now?" Giselle asked.

Aster didn't know what response Giselle wanted, needed, expected. Increasingly, their interactions felt like an aptitude test for which she'd not sufficiently prepared.

"No," said Aster.

"Good!" Giselle shouted. "Neither am I!"

"I fail to see how that's good." Aster fetched a pair of tweezers from across the room as well as a stool and the ice chest she left by the door. She sat down on the stool and used the cooler to prop up Giselle's bloodied foot.

"So disrespectful," Giselle said.

"What?"

"That's that child's foot in there, ain't it? Using that container like it's a ottoman, for fuck's sake. Are you going to bury it in the Field Decks?"

"I've not yet decided what do with it. Would it be proper to bury it? The Surgeon usually burns them, and so that's the practice I've taken." She lifted Giselle's foot onto her knee, preparing to pluck out each piece of glass embedded in her skin. "None of these fragments have slid in particularly deep, but there will still be pain."

"I don't mind it. I like it," Giselle said. "Makes me walk faster. Keeps me alert."

Aster removed the splinters quickly and efficiently. When she was done, she instructed Giselle to rinse off her feet in soapy warm water so she could bandage them. Giselle, for once, obeyed. Aster used the time to update her notebook. She flipped to the page where today's to-do list was and crossed out the items she'd successfully completed:

eat breakfast
clean body (use soap and the scrub brush today)
clean teeth
find out where the Surgeon has been
reread nineteenth chapter of clinical pharmacology
check old woman on S deck for recurrence
amputate Flick's foot

Giselle snatched the notebook from Aster's hand, ink smearing as Aster crossed out the last item. "I can't believe you got to make a list to remind yourself to wash your ass," she said, squinting as she read. Aster's handwriting resembled something a particularly adept two-year-old might muster. Giselle was the only person who could read any of it at all.

"I like to have a written record of all that I do," said Aster. *Documenting,* her Aint Melusine called it. *Recordkeeping. Memorating.*

Giselle tore the page from the pad, scrunched it into a ball. "Do you have a lighter?"

"No."

"Are you lying?"

Aster did not reply.

"Has it got juju?"

Again, Aster did not reply.

"Show it to me," Giselle said, hands on her hips. Aster reached into her pocket and removed the lighter.

"Whatever you are planning, I am sure it is a waste," said Aster. It would cost her several grams of poppyserum to buy more butane, but her poppies were not yet in bloom.

"It's not a waste. Let me burn it. It'll feel good."

"I don't understand how burning something I find valuable will feel good," said Aster.

"It'll all go to dust one day anyway. The sooner you know that, the better. Whether it's today, tomorrow, a million years from now. Why do you want so bad to be remembered? And by who? They won't ever know you. Not as good as I know you."

"I have a system," said Aster. "When an item on the list does not get crossed out, it goes on tomorrow's list. If an item has been on the list for fourteen consecutive days, I examine why I have been neglecting the task, then devote that day to completing it."

Giselle tossed the crumpled to-do list into a pot of soil. But instead of leaving the matter alone—which was not in Giselle's nature—she limped over to the shelf and grabbed another of Aster's notebooks and began flipping through it. "I don't think I've read this one yet," she said. "Or this one." She fumbled through the documents in a folder, loose papers, tanned with age, kiting to the floor. Remnants of Aster's mother. Her journals, notes, sketches.

Aster caught a glimpse of the handwritten formulas, diagrams, and equations in dark-blue ink, the penmanship precise and evenly blocked, nothing like her own. Giselle had stumbled onto a folder detailing one of Lune Grey's more eccentric ramblings. Aster knew the journal entry by heart.

> *A colleague of mine by the name of Zachary West asked me today—why a rat? Of all creatures, why would I wish to change into that lowly beast? I gave him some smart answer, like, "Why <u>not</u> a rat?" But the real reason is because I aspire to be as they are. I like the idea of squeezing through cracks, traveling everywhere as they do, even the places Matilda doesn't want me to go, no one ever able to catch me. Portside, stern, fifty steps that way, down and down more, portward. It's not impossible to change the course of something's destiny. To transmutate. Nothing is as it once was. Nothing as it is now will be that way much longer.*

Aster didn't understand her mother's ravings, no single entry related to another. The handwriting in the journals all came from one person but otherwise could've been written by a hundred different people. She seemed to have suffered some form of early-onset dementia.

"No need to get possessive. I was organizing them is all," said Giselle, perhaps the only person to know the materials as well as Aster, certainly the only other Q-decker to know the language used in the journals.

A Y deck woman, Lune was as much an enigma for her foreignness as she was for her unexplained suicide. She had Y deck customs and Y deck manners, Y deck notions about life and death and the Heavens. She had a Y deck sense of humor, a Y deck palate, and most relevant to Aster, a Y deck way of talking. Lune wrote in a tongue Aster had never seen or heard before when she'd tried reading her meema's journals for the first time at ten years old.

Aster learned her mother's language the same way she

learned the language of the upperdeckers: through disparate reading material and tutors. Aint Melusine had nannied an E deck child who'd had a playmate whose nanny was a W-decker, who had a distant relative on Y, a Ms. Beeker.

Ms. Beeker thought it a shame that the Guard placed Aster on Q when her mother had been a Y-decker, and believed it her duty to teach Aster how to speak and read her true ancestral tongue. Aster didn't particularly want the lessons, and she argued with Aint Melusine over it, said Q was as much her true ancestral tongue as Y.

She'd grown up there, so it was the language her body would always go to first—and wasn't ancestry all about what lived in the body? Further, the reason the Guard had placed her there was because they believed, given the peculiarities of Aster's physiology, that her other parent was a Tarlander.

Aint Melusine made her take the lessons regardless, friended-up the right guards so she could smuggle Aster down to Y deck after curfew. Aster pouted about it, but there were some good things: she could use her radiolabe there, thinking it might finally work now that she was where her mother had been. While traipsing through random corridors, she found a secret wall and the secret shaft that went up, up, up forever, higher than she could possibly climb. As a child, she had believed it a chute to the Heavens, but even in that hallowed passageway, her radiolabe didn't beep. She remembered Giselle batting it out of her hands as it fell down the shaft. *Stop obsessing over that stupid thing. It don't work.*

Though the radiolabe remained unusable, Aster did learn to read and speak her mother's tongue, and by twelve years old she could read Lune's notes proficiently. Giselle learned Y's language later but faster than Aster, using Lune's journals as her reading material.

Aster now walked to the shelf with her mother's volumes and touched her fingers to the spines of the accordion folders, binders, and envelopes. She stopped at the last folder, the thin cardstock the same shade as the tan of her own fingernails, which were bitten to nubs. She turned from the shelf to Giselle, wiped her hand across her mouth. As she did so, she smelled her palm, still thick with the scent of latex from the gloves she'd worn when amputating Flick.

"Sometimes I think the answer to why your meema offed herself is in here somewhere, and I'm gonna find it. Reading her journals is like reading a good detective novel, but better because it's real." Giselle turned brusquely toward the hatch and her whole manner changed from excitedly curious to terrified. "I hear footsteps," she explained, then slid off the counter and bolted across the botanarium, fox-quick, hiding behind a row of greenery.

Aster remained calm; she knew who it was. Though there was no reason to expect him, only one person besides Giselle and Aint Melusine knew of Aster's botanarium.

She went to the hatch and let the Surgeon in.

He looked haggard and worn down. Though he carried himself with the same grace he always did, Aster could see the effort behind the impeccable posture. His seams had come undone, and she recognized his poise for what it was: manufactured. Extreme self-consciousness.

"Surgeon," Aster said, immediately sorry for using his official address when she saw how he chafed at it.

"Aster," he replied, his face a mess of briefly flashing microexpressions. He looked paler than usual, and she wondered if this was somehow intentional, his self-protective instincts finally taking the lead. The blackouts had thrust the ship into upheaval, which the Guard could not tolerate. After upheaval came uproar, and after uproar came uprising. They'd doubled down, and if ever there was a time for rigid conformity . . .

The Surgeon didn't have white skin—whitish, but not white. It was close enough that plausible deniability had allowed him to keep his status when his true ancestry came to prominence during puberty. An upperdeck father, a lowdeck mother. Such children belonged, as Aster had heard a C deck woman once say, downstairs. Light tan darkened into true brown when the Surgeon spent more than an hour in the Field Decks, and his jet-black hair had a definite wave. His nose and lips were wider than Aster's.

"You don't look well," Aster said, noting the redness in his eyes. She'd been so worried when he'd disappeared. It now appeared as if she'd had reason to be. "Go, sit," she said, pointing to one of the botanarium's more comfortable chairs. It had been his once. Anything Aster had of value had once been his.

"May I?" he asked, and reached out an arm to wrap around Aster's shoulder. She nodded acceptance, helping to support his weight as they walked to the chair. He collapsed into it and the bottoms of his trousers rode up. She could see an inch of his mechatronic prosthetic. Connected seamlessly at the knee, it had the shape of a shin and calf, an ankle, a foot. The only difference between this and the good leg was that it was made of metal and not skin, muscle, and bone. It was nothing like the prosthetic Flick would get.

Aster went to one of the cabinets to get him the opianus he'd presumably come here for. It had the pain-suppressing effects of poppyserum but remained in the body longer, had no associated euphoria, and worked particularly well on the deep pain that afflicted the Surgeon in his lower limbs and joints. Only Aster had it because she synthesized it herself.

"Coat off," Aster said.

Instead, the Surgeon pushed up his sleeve. Aster flushed the IV embedded in his wrist, then injected the opianus.

"Would you like the injections for the weakness?" she asked.

"Please."

"You're getting worse," she said, retrieving the shots. She didn't know why he hadn't come to her when he'd run out of his previous dosage, and he obviously had no interest in telling her. Today the Surgeon was all business. "The next time you go so long without seeing me, it'd be in your best interest to take the conventional steroids available to you updeck." Postpolio syndrome didn't have to be as hard on his body as he made it.

"As I've told you numerous times before—no." The Surgeon refused any steroids but the ones Aster made especially for him. Unlike those more widely available, the cocktail of drugs she gave him allowed the testosterone derivative to only target the affected muscles.

"Here," she said, knowing he liked to administer the shots himself in private. "If this was all you wanted, I would've been happy to have this delivered to you. You can rest here the night so you don't have to make the upward journey," she offered, "but I must leave soon. Curfew. I can come back for you tomorrow. We can have breakfast."

"I can't stay," he said, and Aster turned her face from him so he couldn't see signs of her disappointment. "The real reason I've come here is because I need your help. Sovereign Nicolaeus is gravely ill, and I've been entrusted with his care." He clasped his fingers neatly together. Aster could see the brands on the backs of his hands, pink and puckered. They were sigils sealing him to God. "His condition worsens hourly. Without intervention, he will die in days. A fortnight at the very most. That's why I've come to you."

Aster peered across the botanarium to where Giselle was hiding. Soon, the automated rain-simulator would turn on and she'd get sprayed with a light mist. "I don't remember inquiring after Sovereign Nicolaeus's health," Aster said, all her softness for Theo suddenly nowhere to be found. She'd thought the Surgeon had been the one who was ill or that he'd finally been imprisoned for one of his many transgressions against the Guard. Yet all this time he'd been tending to a tyrant.

"You need to help me heal him," he said, the rims of his eyes swollen. "If there's an antidote, I know you're the one who's got it."

Mention of an antidote did, admittedly, win her attention. "Sovereign Nicolaeus was poisoned?" Aster asked, walking to her desk. She wanted to hide her face from his once again, uncertain of what her expression might reveal. "If you inform me who is responsible, I will pass along to them my accolades."

The Surgeon's high cheekbones gave him a beauteous sternness, and he looked at her gravely, skin drawn tightly over his jaw. "Now isn't a time for jest."

"I didn't mean it in jest," Aster responded, though she had. She was taking a cue from Flick: jest whenever the mood struck, regardless of appropriateness.

"Then do you know what ails him?" the Surgeon asked. He seemed on the verge of coming closer to her, touching her in that soft way he sometimes did. Like he was afraid he might hurt her. Everyone else touched her as though they were afraid she might hurt them.

"Until now I didn't know Sovereign Nicolaeus was ill."

"I know—believe me, I know—how tempting it is to seek Nicolaeus's death, but the man slated to succeed him is leagues and leagues worse. Do you think his death accomplishes anything?" Aster had never seen him this disheveled before.

"I should think his death an end unto itself," she said, but found herself taking the bait. "Who will succeed him?"

"I don't think it'd be wise to tell you."

"Then I see no reason why I should help you." Aster returned the pens she'd left out on her desk to their cases, straightened a stack of lab notes.

"Please!" he said, rubbing the sides of his fists against his bloodshot eyes. "Trust me. Have I ever once over the course of our acquaintance done anything but aid and protect you?"

"You have done many things other than aid and protect me over the course of our—*acquaintance*," Aster said, stuttering over the word. She didn't know why it hurt to hear their relationship reduced to something so small.

"What have I done but keep you safe?" he asked.

"Do the meals you take keep me safe? Your baths? The books you read?" she countered, more bewildered than enraged. "I'm sorry, I'm afraid I don't understand."

The Surgeon's face softened and he bowed his head. "I didn't mean literally everything. I should have specified. Let me restate: over the course of our acquaintance, I have done nothing but aid and protect you in matters that involve you, in matters that relate directly to you and your livelihood."

Aster pulled her feet up onto the stool she was sitting on so that her whole body was scrunched into a ball. "I see," she said. She'd thought she'd trained her mind out of its predisposition toward excessive literalism, but there it was, persistent as ever, making a fool of her.

"It was a ridiculous thing to say," the Surgeon went on. "Hyperbolic and, even when not taken literally, probably an exaggeration."

Aster let her grip on her body slacken, but kept her feet up on the stool. "Tell me who will succeed Sovereign Nicolaeus. I have no reason to help you prevent his death otherwise."

The Surgeon wasn't usually given to fidgeting, but Aster knew no other word to describe the way he dug his hands through pomaded hair, tapped his foot. "Uncle," he said, exhaling deeply. "It is my uncle."

Aster tried to swallow away the sick feeling in her stomach though only managed to relocate the dull cramping from upper digestive tract to lower. "How long have you kept this from me?"

"I didn't want to burden you with thoughts of him," he said, but he should have known by now that she was always burdened with thoughts of that man.

"That is not an adequate answer, and I don't believe you."

"I don't know," the Surgeon said in a cracked voice. "I was afraid of what you might do when you found out. Hurt him or hurt—I don't know. My goal was to cure Nicolaeus so that it would never be an issue, so please trust me. Help me help him, and we'll never have to give a thought to my uncle again."

"How can I help a patient I'm not treating? Who I've never really seen?" Aster could tell the Surgeon thought she was being stubborn, yet she meant what she said. Good as Aster was, she couldn't provide the antidote for a poison unless she knew what that poison was. "Tell me his symptoms, at least."

"Cluster headaches. Auditory and visual hallucinations, but no fever. None of that's anything I haven't seen before—except the last thing. The last thing is why I've come to you. His eyes, Aster. His eyes have changed."

The scientist in Aster couldn't feign disinterest, no matter how much she wanted to. Thoroughly entranced, she urged him to continue: "Changed in what way? What do you mean? Changed color?"

She'd only seen Nicolaeus once before. The Surgeon had taken her to his chambers to show her how to perform a colectomy. He had plain eyes, and she couldn't recall the shape or set of them. At the time, they'd held no interest to Aster compared to what hung above the mantel of his fireplace. A rifle, just like Night Empress's. The only one she'd ever seen in real life, and as far as she knew, the only one on the ship.

The Surgeon stared over Aster's head, searching for the

words to explain. "His irises have become jagged. Misshapen," he said, suppressing a shiver. "Like the blade of a serrated knife but more irregular. It's twisted, polygonal."

It sounded like something from one of Aster's nightmares. She'd never heard of such a thing.

"As a result, his vision comes and goes. The pain he's in, it's unimaginable. I've become intimately familiar with the sounds of his screams."

The Surgeon glanced up at her. She supposed he was looking for a reaction. He would find none. Sovereign Nicolaeus's suffering was of no concern to her.

"I've used electromagnetic imaging to peek into his brain. There are bulges everywhere. I suspect whatever is disrupting the cells in his irises is also weakening the walls of the blood vessels in his brain. It's a matter of time before an aneurism kills him. I've clipped off some of them but I can't keep up with the rate they form."

The symptoms the Surgeon described didn't speak to any poison Aster knew. Sounded more heavenly than that. Sounded like retribution. Sounded like when Aint Melusine played a record and it got to the good part. Inexplicable, painful death seemed a fitting magnum opus to Sovereign Nicolaeus's career as *Matilda*'s head.

"I can't help you," Aster said. The Surgeon closed his eyes. Maybe he was praying. "If you no longer have use for me, you may go. Farewell, Surgeon," she said, more stern with him than she'd been in years.

"You know I don't like it when you call me that."

She heard the plea in his voice, a hiccup in the steady, deep tones. "Farewell, then, Theo." Aster supposed the half-centimeter tilt of his chin could be called a grateful nod.

"I'm sorry I've had to be gone from you for so long."

"It's no matter," said Aster. They were only acquaintances. With help from Aster, he stood up and headed to the door. "Uncle's the one who instituted the lowdeck energy rations, in case you hadn't already figured that out," Theo said. She had. "As Sovereign, he will have the power to inflict more suffering than that, and believe me, he wants to. He would have the power to hurt you, to continue his petty and malicious vendetta against you. If you can tell me anything, anything at all that would allow me to heal Nicolaeus, I beg you to tell me. It is only concern for you that makes me ask."

If he was so concerned, he might have bothered to ask after her. She knew well the suffering his uncle caused. It was her, not Theo, who'd just cut off a child's foot.

"Until next time," she said, and he finally gave up, beginning to make his way down the corridor. "Theo. Wait."

He turned back to her, eyes expectant, hopeful—like she might just lay her forgiveness upon him as easily as one bestows a goodnight kiss upon a child's cheek.

"God save the Sovereign," she called out, then let the hatch door slam shut.

Once upon a time, Theo removed Aster's uterus. He made her breathe air that wasn't air. When she awoke, all that remained of her womb was a ghost. This was what she'd prayed to the Ancestors for.

What Theo did violated the oath he'd made when, as a boy of thirteen, he'd joined the Sovereignty's Holy Order of the Guard. Doctors had examined Aster's genitals and reproductive tract and determined she was one of the few females of "this poorly racial stock" capable of carrying offspring. Next to her name in *Matilda*'s manifest was a stamp that read, *Fit to Breed*.

There were less drastic measures of contraception, but Aster liked the decisiveness of a hysterectomy. Cut it out like a cancer.

When her infertility became apparent, Theo had the doctors who were going to reexamine her expelled from the Guard. He then proceeded to chemically castrate all the upperdeck men listed in the records of the ship's reproduction programs. *Routine vaccinations*, he'd explained.

The Guard confronted him about his obvious campaign, and though he didn't confess, he did say he'd received divine providence that the Heavens found *Matilda*'s breeding programs a disgrace. Until they stopped, the plague of impotency would spread to the rest of *Matilda*'s upperdeck men. He was, despite everything, quite fearless. The following morning, Sovereign Nicolaeus issued an edict banning "interference with the natural reproductive order."

Aster supposed that was what the Surgeon meant when he said that over the course of his and Aster's relationship, he'd done nothing but aid and protect her. His sudden disregard for her was unlike him.

"You never told me he knew about this place," said Giselle, emerging from her hiding spot, damp from auto rain. "Who else knows, Aster?"

"Aint Melusine. Him. You. No one else."

"And are you all right?" Giselle asked. "I mean, about the Surgeon's uncle? Lieutenant? That's his name, right?"

"Yes. I am fine."

It was a lie she couldn't sell. Giselle knew as well as Theo how Lieutenant singled Aster out for a startling array of abuses. Not so much in recent years, but as a teen she'd endured daily humiliations. He had given her name to several guards, so though she rarely faced him in person, she frequently experienced his wrath by proxy.

There was the time she'd developed a bacteriophage to treat an antibiotic-resistant staph infection plaguing Q deck, which a guard confiscated because such a thing must obviously contain contraband. He'd ripped IV needles from Aster's patients, gleefully informing her that this was ordered by Lieutenant.

When she'd responded by switching them to a course of medical-grade honey known for its bactericidal properties, he poisoned her remaining beehives. Two of her seven patients died.

Lieutenant was the one who'd had Aster declared fit to procreate before Theo intervened. For a year, he'd made her wear the lowdeck uniform long since discontinued. Perhaps no single thing was particularly significant, but they were small pains that had reduced her fortitude bit by bit.

"To me, a sovereign's a sovereign, but I suppose if I had to pick I'd take Nicolaeus over your Lieutenant any day. The better solution is to kill them both," said Giselle, treading back and forth between Aster's desk and the shelves. She balled her fists into her hair and pulled. Aster watched from a distance as she leaned against the hatch. "Has the Surgeon read your meema's stuff? Her notebooks and things?"

Aster wrinkled her brow, surprised by the change in topic. Giselle's thoughts moved in unpredictable patterns. "No," she replied.

Giselle nodded sharply twice. "That's good at least. Wouldn't want him picking up on the similarities between what's happening to Nicolaeus and what was happening to your meema—then he'd *really* think you had a cure," she said before walking to the shelf holding Aster's mother's papers. She pulled out various folders, let the ones she wasn't looking for fall to the ground. Three she kept. "What she had was more mild then what's happening to the old boy, but it's got to be the same poison that caused it, right, Aster?"

Aster had no answer because she couldn't suss the question. Her mother's journals mentioned nothing about being poisoned or being ill. There was certainly no description of specific symptoms.

"If what was happening to her was going to get as bad as it is for Sovereign Nicolaeus, maybe that's why she self-murdered. She mercy-killed herself," Giselle speculated. "Went out with some dignity." She sat on the floor and began flipping through pages of the notebooks in the folders.

Aster joined her, wrapped an arm around Giselle's waist to try to steady her. "I'm not sure you and I are perceiving the same reality," she said, which is what she always said to Giselle when she seemed in the midst of one of these episodes.

"This isn't madness, Aster—look." She pointed to a passage in one of Lune Grey's notebooks:

Maintenance required in various L deck systems. The speakers blare static despite a lack of sonic input. Happens sporadically but still worth further investigation.

Giselle had pointed to one of the few journal entries that made sense. Lune Grey was a mechanic. Her old bunkmates had verified that much. The radiolabe verified it further. It wasn't surprising she'd made note of something that needed fixing.

"And look at this here," said Giselle, skipping to another passage:

There are some obvious issues in L deck's wiring, I suspect severing its connection with the electrical grid. The speaker static continues. Additionally, the light and heat sensors are shot, showing incorrect readings. So far, not a maintenance priority, but to be looked at in more depth.

"See?" Giselle said. "That's just the beginning."

"I don't understand how my mother's discussion of ship maintenance has anything to do with Sovereign Nicolaeus's poisoning," said Aster.

Laughing, Giselle picked up another of the notebooks. "Are you having a bit of fun at my expense?" she asked, then turned serious. Aster didn't know what she was talking about. "You mean, after all this time you never realized your mother's notes was in code?"

IV

If Aster told a story it'd go like this:

Once upon a time, a mama had a baby, a dark-brown squirming thing, unwieldy and small. The mama named the baby Aster for the genus of florae, and for the ancient word meaning star, and for the way you had to reach to the back of your throat to form that soft *A* sound. Not a name to be trifled with. Not a name for someone immaterial. Not a name you gave a baby you planned to leave in a closet to die.

In Aster's telling, there's no suicide note written in pretty cursive, stashed inside Lune's radiolabe: *Aster, dear. Achingly, sorrowfully, tearfully, regretfully, angrily, I leave you. I am sorry.* And the mama doesn't take a knife to her throat.

Yes, if Aster told a story, it'd go like that. But she wouldn't tell a story.

The precisionist in her hated oral history and memory and that flimsy, haphazard way people spoke about the past.

Back then.

A long time ago.

In that land before this great ship Matilda.

Aster eschewed these ambiguous prefixal and suffixal phrases because they were an affront to the investigative process. They offered summary and conclusion where there were none, by grouping data that should not necessarily be grouped. *That was the year everything changed,* someone might say—to which Aster asked, *Changed how?* What precise unfolding of events? Was it really *that* year, or the year before? Or one event then, and another event several years later, with 1,018 tiny indications in the in-between?

That had been one of her early lessons from the Surgeon: *Do not assign meaning where there is none.* In their first year working together, when Aster was fifteen and still so fresh that the thought of incising a skull to remove meningioma made her nauseous, he took her to see a little blond upperdeck girl whose nose would not cease bleeding for days and days. That, and she had bruises everywhere.

"Hemophilia," Aster had said. She knew this story; she was an expert at patterns. A mild allergic reaction irritated and inflamed the vessels in her nose, but the blood was unable to clot. The bruises were the logical result of the life of play and pleasure allowed upperdeck children. What would be a minor case of internal hemorrhage in someone without the disease, invisible and never forming contusions, was drastic in the hemophiliac. Every bit of contact leaving a bath of blood beneath the skin.

"You are wrong, of course," Theo had said. He spoke with the authority of someone who'd lived many lifetimes, but he was only five years her senior.

"Of course she got it wrong. She's one of them," said the little blond-headed girl, a handkerchief pressed to her reddened nostrils. "She smells."

"She doesn't," the Surgeon had responded in such a tone that the little girl offered no protest. Aster thought to break the girl's nasal bones, give her a real reason to bleed, but the Surgeon treated the child with detached kindness, the way he treated everyone, the way he treated Aster. He placed two tablets beneath the child's tongue and let them dissolve, and in seconds she became woozy.

It had not been necessary, in Aster's opinion, to sedate the girl before cauterizing her blood vessels with silver nitrate. A painful procedure, perhaps, but Aster had endured worse. She was beginning to see how he coddled his patients.

Later, back in his study, the Surgeon explained the girl's condition: "You guessed hemophilia because you assumed the bruises and bleed are connected. They are not. The nosebleed is the result of hereditary disease and the bruises are the result of abuse."

Aster nodded as she digested this new information, wondering if she should allocate some sympathy to that little child, ultimately deciding against it. "Had you given me more details, I would have come to your same conclusion."

"The point is what you do when you don't have the details. Do you interrogate? Do you examine? Or do you settle for the obvious answer?"

With history, with memory, with retellings, people often settled for the obvious answer. Aster wondered if that was what she'd done with her mother's journals: written Lune off as mad instead of investigating obvious clues.

Or maybe she had been right all along about her meema, and it was Giselle being silly. She'd fallen into the trap of inserting narrative where there wasn't any. Any random assortment of dots could be connected into a picture, whether there was an actual picture there or not.

Aster turned with a start at the sound of banging. "Cabin search," a guard announced, his voice muffled through the metal. Though she knew it was unlikely, she wondered if it was one of Lieutenant's men.

The hatch did not yield when the guard tried to push inside, and Giselle squeaked a laugh at his failed entry. Vivian, who was in the bunk above her, did the same.

"Be silent," said Aster in a whisper, tossing a pair of balled-up socks at her bunkmates. The sweat-damp cotton had become frosty and stiff sometime in the night and left an icy, moist residue on Aster's palm.

"Hatch won't open," the guard called out from the corridor, slurring.

Aster had wedged a pipe beneath the handwheel every night for the past several weeks, a countermeasure against such middle-of-the-night intrusions.

"You don't open this hatch right now, I'll wait here till morning and arrest you one by one."

Aster's cabinmates turned toward her, the whites of their eyes glowing.

"Open this goddamn door right now."

Aster pulled off blankets and tiptoed to the hatch, removed the metal bar, then scurried back to bed.

At least they were awake. At least they were prepared. Better that then waking with the point of a baton pushing into your temple, or ice water poured onto your face.

The guard stumbled inside, his boots making all manner of racket. "Wake up!" he ordered, his speech booze-slick. He clicked on his flashlight, and the beam glided over each of the six bunked cots, stopping only upon the last one, where two women, Mabel and Pippi, lay on a single mattress, embracing tightly.

"You two. Up. Out of bed. I see what you're doing," he said. When at first they didn't stir, he jostled them by their shoulders, afghans and quilts falling off their bodies onto the floor.

"We weren't doing anything sinful. Promise, sir, only trying to keep warm," said Mabel. A half lie. It was a reason. Not the only. Mabel searched around for her glasses and coughed as she confronted the guard.

"You sin more by lying to cover up your nastiness. I said get up!" This time the guard swung his baton against the frame of the cot.

Aster watched her bunkmates scramble from the bed before squeezing her eyes shut and pressing her face into the mattress. She pressed her palms over her ears to blot out the noise, but it was no use. She knew these sounds by heart. The metal clink of a guard undoing his belt buckle, the swoosh as he tore it from the loops, then finally, the loud smack of leather against skin.

Both women cried. Aster imagined Mabel's glasses fogging up. Every few smacks, another fit of coughs overtook her.

"Get back in your own beds," he said when it was over, his breaths heavy. "You should thank me."

Aster knew where this was going, one of those Sovereignty speeches about redemption and justice. How beatings were good. How each strike undid one sin. If Aster's eyes weren't forced shut, she'd be rolling them. Why guards quoted this nonsense to justify themselves was beyond her. The whole point of occupying a position of power was that you got to do what you wanted with impunity. It seemed a waste of time to bother with rationalizations.

"You," the guard said. His light flashed over to Aster. She pretended to sleep, bit the dirty cotton of her pillowcase to still her shaking body. "I said *you*." The guard jammed his baton into her ribs, twisting it between numbers six and seven. He stank of ale.

Aster covered her eyes with the back of her hand to block out the glare of white light, and she heard him click it up a notch, the beam brightening painfully.

"Why are you intruding?" she asked, turning her head toward him and squinting. "It's the middle of the night, and we must be well rested for our work shifts tomorrow." The pudginess of the guard's face gave away his youth. Aster guessed he was a few years younger than herself. Twenty. Twenty-one.

Aster sat up, pulling the blanket to her shoulders. She flicked on an oil lamp and found her leather medicine bag, removed the pass she'd used to get access to T deck for Flick's amputation. The guard snatched it from her, squinted as he read: *This badge allows Aster Grey, Q deck, Quarry Wing, Q-10010, assistant to Surgeon General Theophilus Smith, free passage to Tide Wing for the purpose of collecting blood samples for Smith's research.* She had one for every lowdeck. The guard shined his light on the symbol on the card, then to the identical inked mark on Aster's neck, confirming her identity.

Aster grabbed the pass from his hand and slid it back into her bag. She stood, creating a shield between him and her bunkmates. "The Surgeon wouldn't like it if something were to happen to any of us. I will not report you at this juncture, but if you don't leave, I will. What are you? A junior inspector, if that? He outranks you." Aster didn't know if the Surgeon would actually support her in this matter. According to their exchange earlier, she and the Surgeon were acquaintances. One didn't pull strings for acquaintances.

The guard pulled his hand back to strike her, but Aster grabbed his wrist before he could swing. She held on tight, adrenaline feeding her muscles. "You don't do that again," she said. Her cabinmates gasped, and the sound of their shock emboldened her. She liked to impress them. She liked to show them her gall. Earlier, Giselle had doubted her commitment to rebellion. Let her doubt it now.

"Enough," said Mabel with another cough, but Aster did not heed the warning. She would tussle with this man if she had to. She could smell the liquor on him. It made him foolish and weak. She couldn't win a fight against Lieutenant, but this man she could beat.

He went for her with his free hand and she blocked it. He was able to wrestle her down into the bed, but she got enough leverage to knee him in his lower abdomen. As he groaned, she rolled him from atop her and down onto the floor. "You are drunk and worthless. Get out," she said.

He stumbled to get up then vomited onto his own shoes. "I'll tell—"

"And I will tell the Surgeon," she cut him off. "You saw the pass yourself. I've known him for ten years. Even if I were just his pet rat—*ten* years—don't you think I'm maybe worth something to him?"

"Daft animal," he responded, looking pathetic with his belt loose.

"Indeed. Now leave," she said.

Aster didn't know what it was that made her feel so brave. The ghost of her mother, enraged for having been misunderstood for so long, possessing her temporarily?. Flick's insistence that she was weak?

"I won't forget your face, your cabin number," said the guard.

"You will." She pushed him into the corridor, shut the hatch behind as he faltered forward on his feet. She hoped she was right, that he would forget. She hadn't seen him before. He'd probably gotten drunk after his shift and stumbled to the wrong corridor, perhaps the wrong deck altogether.

"Aster, you are without a doubt completely and utterly unhinged," said Mabel, her tears dried but her bronchial distress evident. Clutching her chest, she wheezed and hiccupped.

"Come on, stand up," Pippi told her. "Walking will help." She was dark and graceful, where Mabel was stubby, anxious, and bespectacled. Splotches of eczema roughened her skin. Matted tangles turned her curls into a beehive.

Pippi led Mabel in a slow pace back and forth across the cabin. They both limped, raw from the guard's belt. Aster tossed off her blanket and got up.

"Where are you going?" asked Giselle.

"Move," Aster said, and pushed past her to the cabin's sink basin. Mabel needed oxygen. "Come." She gestured for Pippi to lead Mabel over to the wooden stool. "Go get the face mask I made." She handed Pippi the key to her trunk.

After the sink basin filled, Aster emptied a box of powdered soda inside. There were two more packs in the crate, and she hoped it'd be enough to keep the water conductive.

"Here's the battery you made," said Giselle, a 100-volt in her hand.

"I can't breathe!" Mabel cried out as Pippi returned with the oxygen mask from Aster's trunk, pulled it over her nose and mouth, and adjusted the strap around the thick bundle of her hair. She reached for the tube connected to Mabel's mask and fixed it up next to the basin.

Aster tore the battery from Giselle's grip, used a node to feed the current down into the sink. "There we are," she said, the water starting to bubble. Electricity sliced the oxygens right off from the hydrogens, funneled them into a tube that went straight to Mabel's mask. If they kept the water running, they'd get a decent amount of air out of it.

"Feel it, hon?" Pippi asked. Mabel wheezed assent. "She's getting worse and worse."

Aster nodded and went to her trunk to retrieve the cloak that Flick's great-grandmeema had given her. She wrapped it around Mabel. "It's the cold."

"I keep thinking God's going to fix it," Pippi said.

A sharp gurgle tumbled from Giselle's throat like a laugh. "The Sovereignty's God. Guards are God. So unless you think one of them is going to fix it, you're calling on the wrong folk. They ain't gonna turn it back on."

"It's not a *they*," said Aster, eyeing the bubbles in the sink. She wanted to swish her fingers through the water as it electrolyzed, so her heart would pump hot as lightning.

"What are you talking about?" asked Pippi.

"Hmm?" Aster said.

"You said *not they* just now. What's that supposed to mean?"

Aster took a seat next to Mabel to monitor the rise and fall of her chest before explaining herself. "Giselle said that they weren't going to turn the heat back on. I am saying that it is not a *they*; it is a *he*—a specific man behind the energy rations. And while it's true he represents a larger power, wherein a plural subject would be appropriate, I think—"

Pippi, one arm still around Mabel, raised her hand to interrupt. "Stop. Please, stop," she said, her voice breaking like she might start sobbing again. It was late. They were tired. It was too cold to sleep.

"You sought clarification," said Aster.

"I know," said Pippi. "It was my own fault for asking. Your version of clarifying never actually clarifies a thing."

Mabel pulled the mask away from her lips. "So if it's one he, one person, who is it?" she asked.

Aster didn't say Lieutenant's name out loud. Doing so might summon him. Instead, she shrugged.

"Can't y'all go back to sleep?" Vivian asked.

"Too awake," Giselle said. She walked to Aster's cot and flopped down. Once Mabel was stable, Aster joined her there.

"I'd like . . . I would like to talk to you," Aster said. She and Giselle didn't have a chance to discuss matters earlier. They'd had to leave the botanarium in a hurry to make curfew, then there was headcount. When their bunkmates fell asleep, it seemed rude to stay up chattering.

"Of course you'd like to talk to me. You want to know about Lune's code." Giselle smiled and slid off the mattress, ran to her bunk to grab the notebooks she'd taken from Aster's botanarium. She lifted the oil lantern from the trunk it had been sitting on and set it on the bed so they could read.

"L deck refers to your meema, of course," Giselle explained, sitting cross-legged next to Aster. "I suppose she picked it for *Lune*. Kind of obvious if you ask me. I'd've chosen something a little less recognizable and explicit. A cipher, you know."

"That's it?" Aster replied. "That's all you've got to go on? L is for *Lune*? That's your entire basis for this fabled code?"

"Honestly, it just didn't make sense how bad L deck was. It's a middeck. I can imagine there'd be occasional issues, but every other day something was wrong with it. So I reviewed all the entries and notes that mentioned L deck and organized them by date. Seemed odd that precisely every twenty-nine days there was a leak in Laurel Wing's pipes that she always fixed five days later."

Aster pressed her hands into her mattress, grasping the sheets and squeezing the fabric tight. "You believe my mother was referring to menstruation?"

"I didn't know it for sure until one entry, marked nine days after when the so-called pipe should've leaked, she says Laurel Wing's pipes had strangely sorted themselves out for the time being."

Aster didn't understand.

"She was pregnant with you, nitwit. The date of that entry is thirty-eight weeks before your birthday, Aster. Really, I thought you knew all this. How could you not know? Your mother wasn't even assigned to L deck. She worked on Baby, right? In the Nexus?"

Aster had noticed the discrepancy before but hadn't thought much of it. The Guard shifted workers around quite regularly.

"L deck refers to your mother generally. It's what she says instead of I. Sometimes, she'll use specific wings for particular topics. Laurel Wing is always about her blood cycle, sex, her pregnancy. Leaf Wing is about her work—her *actual* work on Baby."

Then Aster saw how Giselle saw. "The clock! It's Baby!"

Giselle smiled. "Yes." Lune wrote of a beautiful clock that sat on the mantelpiece of a Leaf Winger. Whenever its gear work malfunctioned, she'd been charged with sorting it.

Aster didn't know how she'd missed such obvious clues.

She grabbed one of the notebooks and reread the passages
Giselle had shown her earlier with new eyes:

> *Maintenance required in various L deck systems. The speakers
> blare static despite a lack of sonic input. Happens sporadically but
> still worth further investigation.*

> *There are some obvious issues in L deck's wiring, I suspect sever-
> ing its connection with the electrical grid. The speaker static con-
> tinues. Additionally, the light and heat sensors are shot, showing
> incorrect readings. So far, not a maintenance priority, but to be
> looked at in more depth.*

Aster could see why Giselle thought Nicolaeus's symptoms resembled the issues Lune had described. The blaring
speakers without sonic input: auditory hallucinations. The
sensor malfunctioning with incorrect readings: visual hallucinations. In a later entry, she discussed peculiarities in L deck's
light fixtures—a tiny, barely perceivable divot in the metal of
one, and a more noticeable W-shaped cut in the bottom of the
other: the botched-up irises. Were it just the hallucinations,
Aster might've thought it a reach, but the description of the
fixtures felt more conclusive.

All this time, Lune had been talking to Aster, trying to
tell her something important. She kept notes as obsessively
as Aster did. They were a record of who she was and what
she'd done, and Giselle was right. Somewhere inside was the
reason she'd killed herself.

"Notes on Lake Wing is more personal stuff. How she's
feeling. How her day's been," said Giselle, pointing to the
last few pages of one of these notebooks. "At least, I think so.
There's a lot I still don't understand. Sometimes it doesn't
make sense until I hear or see something. Like what happened
earlier with the Surgeon. When he was saying all those things

about Nicolaeus, that entry just came to me."

Aster read Lune's commentary on Lake Wing. It wasn't that difficult to make sense of once she understood how it worked. Lune had been anxious, stressed, and worried in her last few entries, but more than anything, encouraged. Her notes exuded optimism. She'd found something that gave her tangible excitement. Aster could feel the enthusiasm sloughing off the pages: *I don't know if it will work, but if it does, hallelujah, one thousand hallelujahs!* A sentiment at great odds with her suicide note.

The obvious answer to the question of her suicide was that her plans hadn't worked out—but what could be so calamitous a failure that she'd commit the act of self-murder over it?

Aster had ignored her mother's attempts at communication for so long, and here it was, another chance. Sovereign Nicolaeus's illness was a sign. She didn't believe in the supernatural the way other Q-deckers did. If there was another world where Ancestors walked freely, that was all well and good, but what did it have to do with her? She couldn't see it. She couldn't interact with it. The Spirit World was as much a myth as a planet or a real star.

Signs, however, didn't rely on the existence of the supernatural. History wanted to be remembered. Evidence hated having to live in dark, hidden places and devoted itself to resurfacing. Truth was messy. The natural order of an entropic universe was to tend toward it.

That's what ghosts really are, Aint Melusine had said, *the past refusing to be forgot.* She'd been helping Aster scrub down X deck with ammonia and bleach, a failed attempt to rub out the stink of what had happened there. *Ghosts is smells, stains, scars. Everything is ruins. Everything is a clue. It wants you to know its story. Ancestors are everywhere if you are looking.*

Lune's ghost was pointing Aster to Sovereign Nicolaeus

now. She knew his illness was something hidden trying to show itself, desperate to be seen.

Aster smiled as she remembered another sign—Flick holding the starjar. *Look*, they'd said. *You looking?*

Yes, Aster was looking. Couldn't Lune see her eyes?

V

Aster and Giselle huddled together on the cabin floor, Lune's notebooks and papers spread out before them. They'd spent the last few nights up until dawn studying on a pallet made of cardboard, newspaper, quilts, and afghans. The fort of blankets tenting them reminded Aster of adolescence. Sleepless nights accompanied by comic books and stolen jars of preserves.

"Watch it," Aster said as quietly as she could for the sake of her slumbering bunkmates. Morning bell and headcount were in a quarter of an hour. She wanted Mabel and Pippi to enjoy their last fifteen minutes of rest.

"What is it?" asked Giselle.

Aster pointed to the oil lantern on the verge of toppling. It sat on a corner of blanket and moved every time Giselle stirred. Aster wished to avoid a repeat of last night. A whole notebook ruined. The flame hadn't caught but hot oil blurred the ink into incomprehensible smudges. The two of them had already decrypted most of the notes but Aster hated how easily the reference material had been blotted out of existence.

"Doesn't matter no way," Giselle said, wide awake despite having been up the whole night through. Her eyes, enflamed from oil, smoke, and wear, bulged as she scanned a page of chemical equations that were not actually chemical equations, but schedules of guard shifts. "Everything burns up some time or another, even God Herself. That's how She made the Heavens. She a phoenix. Like me." To prove her point, Giselle ripped off a piece of her nightgown and held it over the uncovered flame until it came alight. The fire spat onto her hands as she cupped the burning fabric. Not once did she cry out or flinch from the pain. She reveled in the spiky peaks of flame.

"Enough," said Aster, and used the edge of the wool blanket to snuff out the flame in Giselle's hand.

"You killed it. It was alive and you killed it." Giselle walked over to Aster's medicine bag and helped herself to some burn cream, displacing and orphaning everything else inside, casting jars and vials to the floor and Aster's mattress. The leather folding case with the scalpels to Pippi's trunk.

"I'm sorry," said Aster, folding up the large sheet of graph paper she'd been examining. Across the cabin Mabel and Pippi groaned and then turned. The bed frame strained and creaked under their combined weight.

"You can't just go killing my babies like that," said Giselle, massaging the healing paste into her palms.

"I don't like to watch you hurt yourself. It's your right to do it, but please, not in front of me." Aster drew her finger along the lines of text in one of Lune's lab notebooks. Carefully documented experiments represented how-tos and directions. The one Aster scanned now was a manual on how Baby connected to the grid and distributed power throughout *Matilda*, all disguised as a detailed drawing of a dissected fish. The heart: Baby. The circulatory system: the grid.

Aster thought the electricity held a clue. The blackouts timed perfectly with the onset of Sovereign Nicolaeus's illness, and the blackouts twenty-five years ago lined up with Lune's milder version of the sickness. Unlikely to be a coincidence.

Giselle huffed heavy breaths, arms crossed over her chest.

Aster glanced away again, back at the lab notebook. "Perhaps you think it's no small thing for you to burn away, but it would mean a great deal to me to lose you. I don't like to see you chip away at your body, especially when you're doing so at a rate faster than it can replenish itself. I don't like watching you die."

Giselle shook her head, then began to pace the room. "I won't die. I can't die."

Sighing, Aster slammed down Lune's lab notebook and slid it across the floor. "You said just two minutes ago everything burns away! Are you now so deluded you think you exist outside the category of *everything*?"

Giselle stilled. Without turning her head to Aster, she spoke in a soft, cool tone: "That was not a kind thing to say."

Aster didn't mean it. As much as it frustrated her, she understood the logic of Giselle's psychosis. Everything dies, so exert control by burning it away yourself. Everything will be born again anyway. There's no such thing as creation, merely a shuffling of parts. All birth is rebirth in disguise.

"You think something's wrong with me. With my mind," said Giselle, squeezing her blistered hands into fists. "But I'm the one who understood what your meema was trying to say. I'm the one who gets her."

Aster stacked Lune's papers into piles to hide in her trunk. Morning bell would be ringing soon, and guards would then follow for headcount.

"How you think her spirit feels? That her own daughter missed what a complete stranger found so clear?" said Giselle. "You're the one who's got something wrong with her."

All Aster's life she'd been looking for Lune. She hoped her mother knew that. Forgave her incompetence. Understood Aster's moments of foolish rejection. "I need to get dressed," she said, and climbed into her cot as the four o'clock Reveille bell rang.

Aster's mind wasn't as cursed by voices and visions as Giselle's, but she knew madness well. Nightmares that plagued whether asleep or awake. Bouts of mutism. Bouts of the very opposite: raving and raving and endless raving.

She shouldn't have snapped at Giselle.

Aster sat in her bunk under blankets, brown legs open. She slicked her fingers up with salve then placed them inside and around herself to distribute ointment. Yarrow root, selivine, and coca leaves numbed the thin skin of her vulva.

She'd stolen a jar of mango butter from Ainy ages ago, mortared-and-pestled the verdure into the creamy, sweet-smelling fat. In addition to its anesthetic component, the concoction provided lubrication for what was—in the words of someone who was not Aster—an uncooperative vagina, should a guard overcome her.

There was no system to their violence, but that didn't stop Aster from trying to devise a formula, a graphical extrapolation based on where she stood in her cycle, pheromones emitted, how well the wheat/amaranth/maize/rice/tea crop fared, the morale of the Guard, and the details of previous abuses: strength, force, duration (all variables affecting the formula). Like any scientific hypothesis in its early stages, there were unexpected outcomes. The discord caused by the blackouts and the rising threat of Lieutenant complicated the calculations further. Best to spread on the salve daily, iron out the formula in the meantime.

"Oy, Aster! You up there rubbing one out?" her bunkmate Vivian shouted as she dressed. The others tilted their heads over groggily.

Giselle laughed, eyes firm on Aster. She'd declared sides. Aster wished she hadn't spoken so harshly about her delusions.

"I'm not rubbing one out," answered Aster to no real end. It would've been better to ignore Vivian.

"Don't be embarrassed. Prudes do it too," Vivian said.

"I'm not embarrassed because I'm not rubbing one out, and if I were, I'd not be coy about it," said Aster. She'd have fingered herself right there, in front of everybody, without shame, just to shock them, to prove Flick's point about *should*. "If you're trying to rile me, which I suspect that you are, you'll have to do better than accusing me of something as banal as self-stimulation."

Vivian came and lay on Aster's bunk, rested her forearms on the thin mattress. "It certainly smells like you're in here doing something as banal as self-stimulation."

Giselle laughed, much too enthusiastically given the hour, and Aster could tell she was still upset by her actions. Killing her fire. Calling her delusional. The greatest of sins in Giselle's book.

"What're you fantasizing about, Aster? Your precious botanarium?" Giselle asked. "Oh! Oh! Pipets! Test tubes! Vials! Selidium hyproxate! Plants!" She devolved into a series of pants and moans, a grand performance for Vivian's amusement and Aster's discomfort. "Oh, petri dish, more!"

Not to be outdone by her mentor, Vivian joined in: "Oh, metric scale, right there! So close, just switch from ounces to grams, and, ah, ah, ah!" She threw her head back, closed her eyes.

"If those are the vocalizations you two make while having sex, your partners must be very displeased and highly disturbed," Aster said, dipping her finger back into the jar of salve.

"Already ready for another go?" asked Vivian. "You're insatiable."

"Leave her be," Mabel said. "It's always the same two or three jokes with you. You're dull." Her voice was rough from coughing fits.

"Dull and crass," Pippi added, less concerned for Aster's welfare than she was with the unseemliness of it all.

Aster pulled on boots over three layers of socks, wrapped her medicine belt around her waist. She sat at the edge of her bed in wait of morning cabin check. She had a new routine since learning to read her mother's journals correctly: head-count, breakfast, study, work shift, study, curfew, study.

After the guard released them following morning cabin check and headcount, she headed to the Quarry Wing kitchen. Pippi nodded at her, then poured yellow cornmeal into a pot of simmering broth, the scent of pork belly, onions, scallions, and gingerroot filling Aster's nose. Bowls of savory porridge were one of many things that would sustain them throughout the morning, and women hustled to prepare the day's meals.

Aster's Aint Melusine stood at the center of it all. She scooped spiced brisket into little circular crusts, orange from turmeric and crushed chili peppers. Once folded over into half-moons, they'd go in the fryer, get packed up with cheese and sections of stone fruit. A late-day supper made the afternoons easier to bear when working twelve-hour shifts in the Field Decks.

"Pippi, the potatoes are done. Safiya, please, child, don't overwork the dough." The air of regal grace about Melusine inspired everyone in proximity to comply. Woman One and Woman Two and Woman Three and so on. Aster's head was too bloated with new findings to sort faces to names. "You, girl, finish these," Aint Melusine said, pointing to the meat patties she'd been stuffing. "Aster, I need to speak with you."

Aster grabbed a jar of buttermilk and a plate of griddle cakes fresh out of the frying grease. The cakes were soft, crispy, and hot as she cut in; they smelled of cornmeal and maple. "Do you mind?" someone asked, bumping into her. "Wait for breakfast time like the rest of us," she said, then snatched the plate away. A little girl ran past Aster with a pan of something hot, steam coming off of it, and nearly dropped it when a woman snapped at her for running.

Aint Melusine pointed to the pantry. Aster nodded but snuck the jar of buttermilk with her. Once inside the pantry she removed the lid, took several sips of the thick liquid.

Without honey or pureed peaches to sweeten it, the milk was sour, but it filled her belly fine. Ravenous, she gulped up the whole jar, set it empty on a shelf next to a bag of millet.

The lightbulb up above shined brightly, and Aster moved to slide her goggles from her forehead to her eyes.

Melusine tugged the metal pull, and now the only light was what came through the crack under the door. It was just enough to illuminate Ainy's face. The wrinkles drew her skin into the loveliest, sharpest angles.

"You don't come swooping in here to peck at whatever grabs your fancy. What's that matter with you?" Melusine asked, closing the doors of the pantry behind them.

"Apologies," Aster said. Admittedly, she'd been distracted this last week. She ran her fingers along sacks of food: yucca, oats, black-speckled peas, red onions.

"What's gotten into you? I heard you stopped seeing patients?" Aint Melusine asked. Aster scratched behind her ear, picking an old scab. "Pippi told me about you and that guard."

"What guard?"

"You know what guard," said Ainy.

Aster didn't know. She checked the time on her pocket watch. It was four thirty. At five thirty they began lining up for shifts. It'd be a waste of time to go to her botanarium this morning, and she'd finish her reading in her cabin today despite the bustle of her bunkmates readying themselves.

"Look at me, child," Melusine said.

"I'm not a child."

"You're a child of the Heavens. You're *my* child."

Aster resisted the impulse to say, *I'm not* your *child*, because she didn't mean it, because it wasn't worth the hurt, however mild and brief, it would cause.

"Pippi told me you told off a guard the other night. That you struck him. That sounds like a pretty childish thing to do."

That was days ago. Aster had already cast it from her mind. "He beat Pippi and Mabel," she said.

"Then he beat them. That's how it goes. Unless you want to get your ownself hurt ten times that, it'd behoove you to learn it. Pippi said he saw your face."

Aster let her head drop forward knowing Ainy wouldn't like her reply. "He did. Saw my face, heard my voice, read my name."

"Stupid," said Aint Melusine. "What possessed you to do such a thing?"

"My mother, I think." Aster recalled how she'd felt that night, her emotions charged.

Ainy's brow pulled tight and she sat her hands on her hips. "You can't let this cold get to you. You can't let these blackouts make you uneasy and go and do something to get yourself kilt. Your life is worth more than the careless mistakes you're making."

Someone knocked on the pantry door and Aint Melusine shooed them away.

"You always said to heed what spirits are telling me," said Aster.

"What spirit told you to get into it with that guard? Certainly not a spirit to be trusted if they didn't also tell you to finish it."

"Finish it?" said Aster.

"Finish him. Death ends a issue. A fight makes it fester on and on. I taught you better than to open doors you can't close." She'd heard those words from her Aint Melusine before, but in a story. Perhaps a history lesson. She frequently lost track of fable and memory when it came to Ainy's tellings.

She vaguely recalled a tale that took place decades before Aster came to be Aster, in a decade known as the Wishing Time—a great flood had washed X deck away. Aint Melusine had called it the Baptism, flipped through the tissue-thin pages of her brown scrapbook, and pointed to a photograph. Despite monochromatic coloring—dull grays, whites, and blacks instead of rich browns, vibrant maroons, peachy pinks—the photo revealed the world to a level of detail Aster had never before seen in paper form, light doing what a painter's brush could not. Six women wearing hooded fur coats kneeled in the snow before an endless stream of water, stretching either way outside the bounds of the photograph. *This is a picture of the world that existed before this world,* Ainy had said. *Like X deck, something came and took it 'way. But we remember. We remember. We must try to remember even that which has been forgotten.*

Aster had been seven when Melusine explained X deck and the world of the photograph, her gaunt, charcoal hands twisted by arthritis. Aster sat in a tub of warm water and listened to her caretaker speak. She drew her finger along the surface of the soapy liquid and made designs. *Pay attention.* Melusine popped Aster's hand two times hard, and water splashed. *This is an obscura,* Ainy had said. Fascinated by the little black box Ainy held, Aster had forgotten her stinging fingers.

The obscura made pictures like the ones in Aint Melusine's book. Ainy's meema gave it to her, and her meema gave it to her, and her meema gave it to her, and so on, all the way back to the Great Lifehouse. One picture per generation, that was the rule, no more, because the device only had so much juju. *You got to document. That's what our work is, as womenfolk, memorating any way we can. Do you count yourself among us?*

Aster batted the water in the tub violently, her way of saying yes. *That's what I thought,* said Ainy. *You never know when a memory's gonna save your life.*

Late to learn to speak, Aster didn't yet have words, and she had grunted so her Ainy would continue. *See, look at X deck, here.* Ainy had pointed to another black-and-white photo in her book. It depicted a long, empty corridor, filled with standing water. *I took this myself.*

Finding this photograph less interesting than the one on the Great Lifehouse, Aster had glanced at it no more than a second before returning to play with the soap bubbles in the tub. *Not everything that's important looks important, child,* said Ainy, smacking Aster once more. *You got to document.*

One day Aster stole the obscura from Melusine's trunk, examining its cube body, looking through the tiny hole. On accident, she snapped a picture, a photo appearing immediately, nothing at first, then metamorphosing into an image of Aster's foot. A document of her foot. For symmetry's sake she took a photo of her other foot, then her knees, Ainy's jar of cocoa butter, a comb made of bone, a dent in the bedpost. She had taken forty-one pictures until it refused to take any more, the juju gone. Clicking and clicking and clicking, but nothing happening, Aster slammed the obscura into the wall.

When Melusine returned, saw the broken machine and the photos surrounding Aster, she said, *Child, you been in my trunk! Aster shook* her head no. *Little girl, I'll ask you one more time. You been in my trunk?* Again, Aster shook her head, this time more aggressively. Ainy Melusine pointed to her open trunk, the things inside messy and out of place. *I mighta not noticed for ages if you'da just closed it. Shut the shit you pry open, girl.* She walked away, slammed the hatch, and did not speak or look at Aster for weeks.

"I just want you to be careful. Don't think they won't kill you. All that cheek you got, it's only a matter of time," said Aint Melusine now, opening then shutting the pantry door behind her.

Thousands ascended the central stairs in order of wing and deck—two out of five of the Tarland decks as well as W and O decks. Aster estimated eight thousand workers in total, perhaps fewer. Aint Melusine lived in Q but didn't work the fields. Too old, too arthritic.

Giselle turned to give Aster a sharp look. "Watch where you're going," she said, Aster having stepped on her heel.

Lost in thoughts of her mother, Aster had blanked out the better part of the walk and had missed their arrival to the center gates of the Field Decks. "Pardon me," she said, yawning. She hadn't gotten more than two hours of sleep per night the last week. Her free time belonged to Lune now.

"Have you got tiny spikes fixed to the bottom of your boots or something?" asked Giselle, her arms crossed over her chest. "That's a decent idea, actually." She bent down in the crowd of Q-deckers to rub her chafed heel.

"Don't blame Aster. That's why you supposed to wear shoes," said Pippi, tucking a loose piece of her white head scarf under a fold. She was perpetually midpreen.

"Shoes is blister machines," said Giselle. Upon standing, she unfastened the top button of her dress, sweaty despite the cold. The eleven-flight climb to the Field Decks had warmed them near as good as a heater.

"I'll give you that," Mabel said, wheezing, lungs still recovering from the journey. When she stayed on oxygen all night, she tolerated her day's work with little flare-up, but the stairs tested her lungs' limits.

Aster could tell Pippi wanted to wrap an arm around Mabel's waist, but they were near the front of the crowd today. The guard up front might see.

"You got to put in for reassignment," Pippi said.

Mabel shook her head as she caught her breath. "I'm not spending my days away from you," she said, her whisper-tone unnecessary. Except for a word here and there, guards didn't know the languages specific to a deck. The recent intrusion of the guard must've been fresh in Mabel's memory.

"First group, it's time!" the guard escorting them shouted.

He beat his baton against the wall, herding the fifty women assigned to cut sugarcane into a short, wide corridor. There were few enough of them that they could line up inside all orderly. They fixed themselves into five rows of ten, and once all of them were inside, the guard checked his watch and closed the hatch behind them.

Two minutes later, he reopened the hatch, the corridor now empty, the women gone. "Second group, come on!" he barked. Aster hurried with her bunkmates into the corridor. They numbered one hundred in all and could not form neat lines.

The guard shut the hatch behind them, and for one minute they were trapped. Giselle grabbed Aster's hand hard until the hatch on the opposite end opened. "Quick now, quick," said their overseer, ushering them into the field from atop his horse. They didn't need instruction to move hastily. They all but ran out of the portal toward the heat.

"Hut, hut, get on now!" the overseer called. The whiteness of his skin and of his horse's fur made him easy to spot despite the dark.

The last few women stepped out and everyone held still, the deck shuddering into motion. As it rotated clockwise to make room for the next deck at the entry point, Aster clung tight to the trunk-like stalk of a banana tree. Giselle grabbed Aster's suspenders for support.

"My stomach," Giselle groaned.

Aster knew the feeling intimately. It wasn't the turn of the decks, but the reorienting. Their eyes and minds learned as children, as babies even, to adjust to abrupt shifts in what was up and what was down, but it took their guts a few moments longer. Relative to where they stood on the steps and in the corridor one minute ago, the ground, the sky, their entire surroundings, had shifted thirty or forty degrees down.

Two decks rotated above them, one moving right and the

other left, forming a narrow gap. Light spilled through the sliver. Baby Sun still mostly blocked, it wasn't bright enough to be day yet, but Aster began to make out the individual forms of trees in the banana forest if not the shape of the banana bunches themselves. In half an hour, after the completion of the morning rotation, the sky would be white and the temperature fifty degrees Celsius.

Aster glanced up toward the band of light, newly appreciative of the mechanics of the Field Decks, aptly called the Sphyrum by guards.

"Steady now, steady," said the overseer to his horse, or maybe to one of the women.

Aster braced herself against the banana plant more firmly as the field turned.

The Field Decks formed a massive sphere. Planks of varying size, each of them a different field, forest, or orchard, came together to form spherical layers, one inside of another inside of another inside of another.

A woman fell and cried out.

"I said steady!" the overseer yelled.

Aster didn't know how many levels or strata there were, but planks rotated sideways, upward, downward, backward, forward to accommodate diverse plant needs, Baby at the very center. She'd always had a basic idea about the design of the apparatus, but she hadn't understood it truly until spending time this week with Lune's renderings, the Sphyrum's blueprint disguised as an elaborate sigil.

It had never occurred to Aster that when she worked one field, she stood upside down in reference point to a woman working a field on the other side of Baby. Or that when she stared up at the bright sky, Baby Sun a faraway orb of bubbling white, there were layers and layers of decks in front of her. She couldn't see them because they were rotated out of sight to let Baby's light through.

Aster bent her knees, widened her stance in preparation for the remainder of the twenty-minute rotation, but the field juddered to a stop. Her hands slipped against the stalk of the banana plant and she lost purchase. Giselle toppled sideways then down, bringing Aster with her. It was another blackout. The electrical outage forced the Field Decks into complete stillness.

Women screamed as they too fell, the force of the sudden stop slinging them about like rag dolls. The overseer's horse bucked and neighed and threw him to the ground. A loud crack snapped through the field as his body made contact with the earth, but there was no accompanying scream.

Aster yelped. At first she thought it was Giselle's nails she felt, digging into her shoulder to keep steady, until she looked up to see Giselle's horrified face now several feet in front of her.

"It flew," said Giselle.

A hoe had lodged itself deep into Aster's shoulder blade. Pain spun through her, tears sculpting salt trails down her face. The white streaks would be visible in several hours once the water evaporated, easy to spot against her dark skin. She gasped with each intake of breath.

Giselle crawled toward her and, before Aster could stop her, ripped the blade of the hoe from her shoulder. Aster felt blood gush.

"Aster? Aster?" someone called. Pippi or Mabel. "You all right?" Aster didn't think she was. "Let me get you something for the pain," said Pippi, running through the semidark, presumably toward one of the women who kept poppyserum in their medicine belts. Aster didn't. Too much risk of confiscation by a guard.

Aster looked around. She wasn't the only one who'd gotten hit. Someone had left the toolshed door unlatched at the end of yesterday's shift, and it had fallen open during the hard stop. One rake had made its way into a woman's ankle, another into a woman's chest. That wound might be fatal.

The overseer's mare continued to buck while three women tried to wrangle her. One fashioned a lasso out of tied-together head scarves. Aster crawled to a sitting position, then pulled up against the banana plant stalk with her uninjured side to stand.

"Aster, here," said Pippi, traipsing through the densely planted trees. "Could only get a little. Heavens, sit down. Your skin looks clammy. Aster?"

Aster scanned the field for the overseer, smiling widely when she didn't see him.

"She's in shock," said Mabel, panting. "Give her the poppyserum."

"I can't see nothing. It's too dark," Pippi said.

Aster grabbed the dislodged bloody hoe and stumbled forward through the banana trees, using their stalks as support. "Aster!" her bunkmates called after her. She didn't let herself feel the gaping wound in her back, instead choosing to see this blackout for what it was: a blessing. She stepped over leaves, weeds, and moaning bodies until she made it to the field's end. A loose net was wrapped around the edge.

Aster used the hoe to cut through the rope to create both an opening and a bridge. She crawled through the hole and tossed the rope forward, hoping someone in the next deck over would grab it. "Catch!" she shouted, not knowing if anyone would hear her over the sounds of crying and yelling. Another deck sat directly on top, leaving the field sheathed in blackness.

Aster felt a pull. "Tie it off!" she yelled, then tugged the rope taut. It felt secure, and she tied her ends off against a piece of uncut net. No time for a prayer, she crawled the fifteen feet across, each hand on the rail formed by the rope.

She was now in the outermost shell of the Sphyrum. Below her was only metal wall. It was too dark to see how long the drop was.

"Are you mad?" said a Quake Wing woman on the next field. Aster ran past her, squinting to see in the dark. If her timing was right, she was in one of *Matilda*'s rice fields. Her boots squished in the soggy wet soil.

She made it to the short, wide corridor adjoining the Sphyrum to the central stair and ran through it, but the hatch on the other side was closed. Aster banged against it, desperate.

"Who's there?" a voice called. It was the guard who'd herded the Q deck women today.

Aster kept banging. When the handwheel began to spin, she got in position to sprint. She jolted forward as soon as it opened, knocking the guard over, tripping over the women still awaiting their turn to enter the Field Decks.

"Do you have a match?" Aster asked people she passed, having forgotten her lighter. She didn't have time for niceties. The blackouts usually lasted no more than an hour.

"Here, Aster," someone said.

She startled upon hearing her name. Aster didn't think anyone could see her in the dark.

"Only you could act such a fool." Aster thought the voice belonged to a Quince Wing woman who often worked the melon patches. Maybe she was a patient.

The woman pressed a whole book of matches into her hand. "My sincerest gratitude," Aster said, and continued to run down the steps through the women waiting to board the Sphyrum. At O deck, she left the stairs and dashed into the corridor, took off her button-up. She had an undershirt beneath it.

Guards had abandoned the deck to go who-knows-where. Aster paused and leaned against the wall, letting her eyes adjust further to the lack of light. Once her heart settled, she wrapped her button-up around the blade of the hoe, rubbed salve from her medicine belt onto the fabric. The coconut oil base of the salve would help a torch burn longer.

Aster flicked through four matches before getting one to light. Her shirt caught fire, and the corridor lit up. "You!" called a guard. Aster ran portside away from him as fast as she could, but the gash in her back slowed her down considerably. It was getting harder to deny its existence.

According to Lune's maps, there was an access tunnel on the other side of the ship that led straight through the shells of the Field Decks to Baby. If she wanted to learn more about her mother, she had to go where she'd worked.

"No time, no time, no time," she said aloud to herself, her pace slowing from a run to a jog then all the way down to a walk. She would pass out before she made it to the access tunnel. She might pass out right here. Aster visualized her mother's map. Forty-five minutes to the tunnel, fifty-five maybe. She'd pass so many guards on the way.

Aster shifted course. It wouldn't take but fifteen minutes to get to the Surgeon's updeck clinic from where she was if the portside stairs were empty. At this hour, they should be. Her feet had been carrying her there all along.

Emergency dimmers lit Granite Wing, but what for? Upper-deckers didn't wake this early.

Aster ditched her torch in the stairwell and struggled up the remaining steps to the Surgeon's clinic. If he was caring for Sovereign Nicolaeus, he might not be there. She banged the knocker at the top center of the hatch to the rhythm of a lullaby her Aint Melusine sang.

"Aster?" Theo asked, recognizing the unique knocking pattern. She heard him limp to the door and turn the hand-wheel, but the sounds were muffled. She was beginning to lose her hold on consciousness. As the hatch opened, Aster fell forward into Theo's arms.

"God," he said, steadying her.

Aster staggered out of his grasp and supported herself against the wall. Her hand slipped against a placard on the wall before she managed to right herself completely.

"What are you doing here? What's happened to you?" Theo guided her toward the front office of his clinic and shut the hatch. "Did anyone see you?"

"I need you to write me a pass to Baby," she said, then slid down the wall to the floor. She knew the liquid sticking her undershirt to her back was blood, not sweat. There wasn't time to go to Baby now, but if Theo wrote her a pass, she could return to the Field Decks before the end of the blackout and visit Baby after work shift.

"I can't," he said. By the look of him, he'd not yet been to bed.

Aster rubbed the back of her neck, the stretch of her arm pulling the wound on her shoulder blade. She winced. "When you came to me last week, you called our relationship an acquaintance. Do you stand by that?" She fought to keep her breath steady as she spoke.

"I—"

"I was too baffled to say anything then, but I've had time to process," she said, aware this was not the ideal moment for such a discussion. Words flowed as freely from her as the blood from her back. Unable to form a coherent thought, she let her animal self take over, mouth moving on instinct. "If we're acquaintances, then I can't make you your medicine anymore. It takes days to formulate . . . Did you know that? Too much time to devote to an acquaintance. For a friend, on the other hand? That's no time at all. For a friend, it's not work to make it, but a pleasure and an honor . . . Are we friends or are we not? If we are, it should be no trouble to write the pass. If we aren't, then I'll leave now."

She thought of Giselle and Aint Melusine, of Mabel and

Pippi. Even Flick and their great-grandmeema. So many people's well-being weighed on her mind.

"I don't have time to nurse an acquaintance," she continued, "especially not one as old as ours. An acquaintance this
old that has never bloomed into friendship never will, and it's
hardly worth the upkeep and maintenance required."

She peered up from where she sat against the wall, Theo
tall above her. He was holding out a small card. "I don't know
how well this will work," he said. "My power doesn't have
the reach it once did." Aster's shoulder hurt too much to grab
the pass with her right arm, so she switched to using her left.
"Did someone—"

"The decks were midrotation when the power cut. It was
an accident," Aster interrupted. She felt too woozy to read
the pass, the fine inked lettering nothing more than randomly
assorted lines to her mind in its current state. Strange, strange
geometry. In minutes she'd pass out, surely she would. The
flame in Theo's oil lantern whipped about its glass confine-
ment. His office had the look of a dollhouse. Everything perfectly placed. A book open on the desk. Steam rose from a
mug of chicory coffee.

A prickling sensation spiraled from the gouge in Aster's
back to her chest, stomach, pelvis, thighs. It wove its way up
her spine, settled into the fleshy matter of her brain. "Am I
your best friend?" she asked. Then her voice went, and she
couldn't even remember the question she'd just posed.

"I'm going to turn you around now. Is that all right,
Aster?"

She'd learned that habit from him. Narrating every action you planned to perform on a patient. Always waiting for
a clear yes or no before proceeding, no matter how much it
slowed the process.

"Careful," she said as she turned her back away from the
wall.

Theo crouched down to her level, slipped a suspender off her shoulder, and removed the scissors from her medicine belt, using them to cut through her undershirt. Aster closed her eyes when she heard his sharp intake of breath. She didn't need to be reminded of how bad it was.

"I have to repair this now," said Theo.

Aster supposed that was the real reason she'd come here. Nothing to do with Baby. Nothing to do with a pass. "Is there tendon damage?"

"Yes."

"Arterial damage?"

"Yes."

His steadiness calmed her. He rubbed his hand against her uninjured shoulder, touching his thumb over one of her more prominent scars.

Their partnership revolved around sewing up each other's various wounds. They'd become intimately familiar with each other's frailties. Theo knew her every brittle bit.

"Have to make it back to the Field Decks before the end of the blackout," Aster said, using the last threads of her lucidity to communicate.

Theo rubbed his eyes and shook his head. "No. No, you have to stay here. I can't let you leave."

"As soon as the power returns, my overseer will know I'm gone," she said, but she wasn't sure that was true. More likely, he was dead. She prayed they'd forgotten about her in the chaos of bodies and wounds and darkness.

"You've lost several pints of blood," Theo said, still crouched behind her. She could feel his eyes examining the wound, deciding where he'd need to sew, which tools he'd need to use.

"And Nicolaeus? Don't you have to see to him?"

"I've been instructed to assure his comfort and nothing more." Theo stood up and went back through the front office to the clinic, returning a moment later with several bottles of blood. He was going to do a transfusion.

"You're operating on me here?" she asked.

"We can't afford to move you." Worry creased his eyes. He positioned her onto her stomach and anesthetized her as he had during her hysterectomy, her double mastectomy, various reconstructions after tussles and altercations. "It's good to see you," Theo said. "Our last meeting didn't go as I'd hoped. I haven't thought of much else but you since."

Aster grunted, half asleep, lulled by the gentleness of his voice and the pain relief of the anesthetic.

"Why do you need to go to Baby?" asked Theo, but Aster was already well into a dream, images divided between memories of the past day and the world of her mind's own making.

The overseer's mare was standing on her hind legs. Lune's notebooks. Maps made of gospel, seals, devil summons. Mangled memories. Giselle's curious ravings. The horse trotted off and Aster followed after until she was tracking the ghosts of X deck with her mother's radiolabe. It ticked and ticked and ticked, but whenever she turned, there was only absence and cold. She hid in a cavern on a moon made of ice in the cloak the old woman gave her, rabbits all around. They were rotting away and Aster had to amputate their feet. Their severed paws made a path in the snow leading out to the horizon. Snow fell, covering them so Aster could not see, but she knew the way forward was straight ahead. It always was.

"I'm chasing my mother's ghost," Aster whispered out loud, suddenly conscious. Theo instructed her to count down in her head from one hundred. She made it to ninety-four before fading back into unconsciousness.

Aster didn't stir for two and a half days. Upon waking, she would remember why she didn't like to sleep in long bouts. Memories couldn't be intimidated into retreat while asleep.

It was Theo's lips pressed against the skin of her hand that first woke her. She was in the Q deck infirmary. He used a medicine dropper to feed her water. "I'm glad you're awake," he said. "There's much to tell you."

Giselle had disappeared.

VI

On Q deck, a child's schooling began in infancy. A mother wore her babies and toddlers on her back or hip as she talked to them through her work preparing soil or harvesting cassava. She counted rows of crops out loud with silly rhymes, recited poems, and by three or four, most children knew their numbers to one hundred, how to do sums and differences, and how to make bearing a load easier with a pulley or lever.

At five and six, a child began work proper, helping her meema divide harvests by weight in barrels to send off for processing. A girl of ten knew addition, subtraction, multiplication, division, fractions, percentages, basic probability, and how to make equations even on both sides. She knew the life cycle of a plant. She knew how gears rotated the Field Decks beneath Baby.

She knew basic medicine craft: how to suture a wound, set a bone, prevent infection with special creams. She knew which medicines she had to steal from upperdeck dispensaries for which ailments, how to make medicine from crops grown in the Field Decks, and how to grow medicinal plants in vents and ducts where guards couldn't see.

Certainly, Aster's education in medical botany began in the Field Decks with the guidance of various Quarry Wing caretakers and elders, but it was only more advanced study that allowed her to craft medicines as expertly as she did now. She cobbled together a curriculum from healers, from discarded books, from medical journals on genetics and biochemistry. In the early days, Aint Melusine stole them for her. Working the upperdecks as a nanny meant she could sneak her way to the Archives. Later, the Surgeon wrote Aster passes to go to the Archives herself.

Aster experimented, learned what she could from experts on plants, many who lived on Q deck and hybridized new, wondrous species in their wing's kitchens or air ducts, often under an overseer's nose on the Field Decks themselves. In addition to quarters, U deck and V deck held *Matilda*'s manufacturing plants. There, lowdeck workers synthesized chemical materials for the ship during their shifts. Expert chemists, they funneled all of *Matilda*'s waste down into the Bowels and processed it into mineral blocks that could be used to make everything from sodium hypochlorite to the peroxide from which the Tide Wingers made their starjars.

Lune must've sought an extended education for herself too, one like Aster's. Full of stolen books, journals, and workbooks. Tutorials with experts in the craft. Aster couldn't fathom how else Lune came to know so much. More than Aster. More than Theo. More than anyone on *Matilda*, Aster reckoned.

These are things I like to tell my mother, Lune wrote in her coded journals. That phrase indicated that the passage was highly secret. It took Aster a bit of time to get that, but she knew on Y deck, the affectionate word for *mother* wasn't *meema* or *meem*, but *mumma* or *mum*. Next, Aster needed only to recall what her language teacher Ms. Beeker used to say when telling her to keep quiet about their secret lessons: *Mum's the word.*

When Aster put the two memories together, she knew that *things I like to tell my mother* was code for a secret. Lune had many secrets, most of them about Baby. Aster was headed to the Nexus now, where hopefully she could uncover some of them. Lune had worked there near every day of her life, monitoring Baby's function, directing her electrical output.

Aster presented her pass from the Surgeon to the three guards on patrol outside Baby's access tunnel, keeping her head down. Pain medicine unsteadied her. She'd given the last of the nondrowsy variety to Theo for his leg and needed to make more.

"Go ahead," said one of the guards. Aster pressed forward but then stopped when he called her back. "What do you say to me?"

"Thank you, sir."

"Look at me when you speak."

In precisely measured steps, Aster turned toward him, then lifted her gaze to his. "Thank you for letting me through, sir," she said, wondering if she'd accidentally slighted one of Lieutenant's watchmen. She'd been feeling his presence more heavily lately but knew it was just her imagination. From the moment Theo first informed her that his uncle was slated to replace Nicolaeus, Lieutenant had been a constant anxiety.

"That's better," the guard said. Aster waited for an explicit dismissal before carrying on. The guard waited several seconds before gesturing her forward.

She was glad the poppyserum she'd taken for her shoulder had a sedating effect, lest her insolent nature get the better of her. Now was not the time for an altercation. If she was taken into custody, she wouldn't be able to keep searching for Giselle.

Aster peered through the glass hatch at the end of the access tunnel onto what resembled the inner workings of a complex radio. Spools of copper wire transformed electrical signals across an expansive network of circuits while small red lights flashed on lacquered wooden control boards. Machines that looked to Aster like some sort of typewriter-telegraph hybrid spat out reams of hole-punched cardstock. Aster didn't know what the pattern of dots meant, but she assumed they were a record of the Nexus' informational output.

Women operated massive switchboards, running to and fro between panels lined with neat rows of rotors and cogs, buttons and knobs. From the Field Decks, Baby appeared self-sustaining. She hovered in the sky, a great sphere of indomitable light. From here, Aster could see her strings. Her puppeteers.

The Nexus, a large glass ring surrounding Baby, wasn't much like what Aster's mother had described in the journals. Her code hadn't allowed for precise depictions. Lune's goal hadn't been quantitative accuracy. She'd meant her notes to be references for herself. No need to paint a picture of what she knew by heart.

A woman on the other side of the hatch waved her forward, shouting several commands, but Aster couldn't hear her through the soundproof barrier. Realizing her error, the woman opened the hatch and poked her head through. "We don't got all day. We been expecting you."

Aster hadn't heard Y deck spoken out loud in years, and she had to translate word by word in her head. Different sentence order.

"Put one of those on," said the woman, pointing to a wardrobe. Several sets of protective gear hung from the brass hooks, each containing a jumpsuit, a pair of goggles, and over-the-ear headphones. "My name's Jo. You're Ms. Aster, right? Surgeon said you'd be doing our radiation tests this month in place of him. You're a few days late."

"My sincere apologies," said Aster. This was the first opportunity she'd had, too distracted by Giselle's recent disappearance.

"Just get to it now that you're here," said Jo.

Aster nodded as she pulled the jumpsuit over her clothing, exploring the fabric with the pads of her fingers. It was made of thick linen, and a small hole in one of the seams revealed an inner layer of something metallic and woven, unfamiliar to Aster. The inside lining was soft, stretchy, and absorbent. A knit jersey, maybe. It felt wonderful, and she loved buttoning herself up into this protective cocoon. It was heavy and present, putting deep pressure on her joints and limbs. She'd have to see about getting some of these coveralls for herself, though they'd be too hot to wear in most Field Decks.

Once inside, Aster rushed to pull on her goggles, hoping she'd done it quickly enough to save herself from blindness. She'd never seen anything so bright before. The glass on the hatch must've been strongly tinted.

"Maud will show you where to set up," said Jo, then ran off to attend her console. Aster didn't know who Maud was, and Jo made no move to inform her.

Aster took the opportunity to observe Baby, awed by her clockwork.

"Pretty, ain't she?" said one of the workers, arms crossed over her chest as she stared at the fusion reactor beyond the wall of glass. "I'm Maud."

"Aster."

"What?" Maud tapped on her earphones.

"I said I'm Aster."

Maud tapped on her earphones again. "What?"

"Aster!"

Maud smiled with a nod. "Good to meet you, Nestor. I'm gonna set you up in the break area. You about ready to get started?"

Aster shook her head, hands stuffed into the pockets of the jumpsuit, and made sure to speak as loudly as possible. "I'm not ready at all. I am transfixed. I want never to move from this spot again."

Maud laughed and put her foot up on one of the chairs in front of a console.

"Is this what a star looks like, then?" Aster asked. Ainy's

stories hadn't done the night sky justice if there were billions of Babies studded into its black fabric.

"I like to think she's even prettier," said Maud, gazing proudly upon the sphere of bubbling light, like she was its mother and had designed it herself. "Of course, I can't say for sure."

Squinting, Aster tried to make sense of Baby's parts, but physics wasn't her area. She couldn't tell the difference between this and conjure. Finally seeing it this close up, she half-believed Baby was the work of a coven of lowdeck soothsayers.

Maud punched several red keys on one of the panels, and Aster wished she had a notebook to write in. She wanted to look busy, important, at work, like the rest of the women in the Nexus. This was where she was meant to be. Not a Q deck fieldworker, but a Y-decker tending to the sun.

Maud pointed at Baby, then made a wide sweeping gesture with the same arm. "At the very core you got a supercharged electromagnet. That's what creates what I like to think of as fertile soil. It makes the right environment for the reactions to happen. The magnetic field confines the hydrogens and gets them hot enough to collide. You can't see it, but there's a small pipe that feeds her deuterium. When their nuclei fuse, some of the mass turns into energy."

Aster understood the basic principle, if not the *fertile soil* analogy.

"See that glass sphere around her?" said Maud. "She holds the water. The excess energy from the hydrogens combining to heat her up."

Aster knew the rest. High pressures in the glass sphere kept the water from turning to steam. That water went on to heat yet another body of water, which then did turn to steam. The steam spun the turbines, which generated *Matilda*'s electricity. The reason for the two bodies of water: to protect the ship from the irradiated water right next to the fusing deuterium.

"Aren't you worried the glass will break?" asked Aster, curious about how it all stayed together, and Maud laughed so hard that several women in the Nexus turned to stare. Aster felt mortified for having shown her ignorance to the women who would've been Lune's peers. She respected and admired them; she wanted them to respect and admire her in turn. "I can leave, if that's best," she said. It was rare for her to meet people so far above her own capabilities. This was what people meant when they said she intimidated them, and here it was, turned back on her.

"I'm so sorry, love," said Maud. She threw her arm around Aster and pulled her in close. "I thought you were joking. It's not like the glass from a cup of water, is it? Think of the hardest glass you can, and this is harder. I suppose it's not even glass at all. Just what we call it because of how it looks. Don't you worry, Nestor. If it fell thousands of feet, that glass would stay solid."

It all sounded quite suspect to Aster, but she wasn't a materials engineer. She had to trust Maud's analysis.

"Come on. I'll show you where you're going to set up." Maud led her through the Nexus, explaining different areas every few feet, showing Aster the additional magnets on the outer layer of Baby. "Those provide the torsional vibrations needed to properly confine the hydrogen into a sphere. That way it doesn't touch the glass. Well, the not-glass," Maud said, smiling. "Through here, love." She spun the wheel to open a hatch, revealing a small room with folding tables. "We take our meals here. The girls know the routine so should you have any questions, you just ask one of them. You can take off your goggles and headphones, but best to leave on the overalls. I'll be out there if you need me. And I'll be seeing you soon enough when it's time for my break."

The sounds of the break room bowled Aster over when she removed the earphones, as what was usually a quiet hum roared in her ears. The women all had radiolabes, each of them ticking and tocking a steady pulse. Aster's, of course, remained silent. Broken. Dead as Lune.

"Don't look so flummoxed, girl," said one of the workers on break. "You only got to be concerned when they really get going fast. There's always gonna be a little bit of the harmful stuff getting through. We're in the hot zone."

Aster thought of that aphorism Aint Melusine always said, something about heat and getting out of the kitchen. She began to set up her station the way the Surgeon had instructed. She was here under the guise of collecting blood samples for traces of radiation damage. These examinations were done monthly, usually by Theo himself, but this was the only way he could think to get her a pass into the Nexus.

"I'd like to go first," said a young woman—girl, really—with fairish brown skin and a mess of freckles, head shaved almost bald. Square jaw, square shoulders, square hips. Her lips, though, those were round as apples. Plump too. She was pretty, and something about her reminded Aster of Theo. Harsh and neat. Eyes like wilderness. More superficially, it was her light skin mixed with features Aster usually associated with dark skin.

Aster waved the girl over and found her name on Theo's charts. *Jay Lucas, sixteen years old, Yarrow Wing.* The box marked *High Risk* was ticked. Aster guessed it was something to do with her pale skin. She had several visible brown blotches that looked potentially cancerous and a few scars where moles had already been removed. There was a note next to her record in Theo's fine cursive: *Achromatosis.* Albinism.

"I've got difficult veins. You'll have to go for my hand," said Jay, dark eyes fixed on Aster.

Aster wrapped a rubber cord around her wrist and instructed her to squeeze and unsqueeze her fist. Aster saw a good vein right across the center, and she rubbed the spot where she'd poke the needle for the blood draw. "This will—"

"Pinch. I know."

"You remind me of the Surgeon," Aster said as blood filled the first tube.

Jay smiled, and Aster felt proud that she was the one to bring it on. Jay didn't seem the sort to smile much. "I was going to say the same about you. You act just like him. All business. Proper and funny-talking. But he's nice."

Aster nodded. "He is. And he's good."

Aster wanted to say, *He is my friend*, but she wasn't here to chat about Theo, much as he was on her mind these days. It felt good to be seeing him again. It felt good to know that if she'd radio him, he would answer and be by her side.

"You're smiling and biting your lip," said Jay, grin wider now, seeming so much younger than she had half a minute ago. Like a proper sixteen-year-old. Ready for gossip. Ready to talk about who liked whom. There was nothing harsh in that happy face. She was just a little girl, and in this moment it was impossible to believe she would die from cancer in a few years.

"I am neither smiling nor biting my lip," Aster replied, but she was, goodness, she was. Everything was wrong, but she was giddy. So close to her mother here. In Lune's cathedral made of artificially generated light and heat. And the poppy-serum. And Theo. "We are all done here," she said, and Jay nodded and went to have her lunch at one of the other tables. Aster could hear her giggling with some of the other women, but unlike with Maud earlier, she felt in on the joke.

Aster had intended to use this time to ask questions, but she was too taken to speak on anything significant until Maud herself came to have her blood drawn. "Thank you for showing me Baby," Aster said.

"It's my pleasure. She is my pride and joy, after all."

"It's a shame that something so beautiful is dying." Aster cleared her throat. She didn't know how to be subtle with these things. The words sounded false and put-upon. She hated it and longed to say what she came here to say.

"Don't you worry about Baby. She's doing just fine," said Maud.

"People say she's ill. What else could explain the blackouts?" Aster asked, though she could think of a number of things. Poor wiring, for one.

"You sound like the Sovereignty, always on our asses, demanding answers. All we know is, Baby is acting just how she's supposed to act. We've kept her fueling consistent. The quality of the deuterium has not deteriorated. She continues to put out the same energy per day as she has for hundreds of years," Maud explained, her initial warmth and friendliness turning suspicious, wary.

"I'm of the opinion someone's using electricity who's not supposed to," said a young woman—almost all of them were young. Y deck women who worked the Nexus didn't tend to live much past forty. Maud and Jo were the oldest at thirty-nine and forty-four, respectively, according to Theo's charts.

"Mhmm," said someone else. "I heard they're putting an ice rink in the upperdecks. That would certainly explain it."

"I don't think so," said Aster, and all the women turned to face her. She didn't see any chastisement in their expressions, so she continued: "The upperdecks have had an ice rink for many years. It certainly draws a lot of power, but it's nothing new and therefore wouldn't be responsible."

"Oh, and how do you know that? You go ice-skating there on the weekends?" said Maud.

Aster knew from a story Theo had told her. As a child, he'd begged his mother for ice-skating lessons not long after he'd begun recovery from his polio. He told her he wanted to feel graceful again, and with one leg half gone, the ice was one of the few ways that was still possible. He'd used the words *the only way to glide*. His mother had relented, but when his father found out, he'd beaten Theo with one of his skates.

"The Surgeon informed me," Aster said.

"I still say an EMP is the best guess for these kind of read-outs," said Jay, scratching her shaved head. "What else could wipe power like that?"

"What, somebody's hiding electromagnets in their pockets? Under their bunk? Even if they were, to be big enough to suck that much power, they'd have to be Baby's," said Maud. "And, uh, we'd know if they was acting up, even if only for a split second 'fore we all blew up."

Aster wrapped gauze around the sore area on Maud's bicep, taping the end to hold it secure. "Magnets?"

"Mmmm," said Maud. "Don't get me wrong. Magnets is a good idea except for the part where there aren't any magnets big enough to do what Jay's talking about."

"I don't understand what magnets could have to do with it at all," Aster said, feeling out of her depth again.

"You need a really strong electrical current to generate some magnetic fields," said Jay, wiping a crumb from her lip with her thumb. "Something could've used *Matilda*'s current to power their magnet. That's the only thing I can think of big enough to suck up so much electricity. You understand?"

Aster recalled the last blackout, the sudden, jerking stop of the deck. She'd attributed the blade flying into her back to that, but—

The speed required to generate that much force couldn't have come from decks jolting. The farming tool had broken bone, severed tendons and arteries. A blade affected by a powerful magnet could've done that easily.

She knew that it was true, even without much evidence.

Clues from her mother's journals were coming together. Lune had discovered the cause of the blackouts: a magnet. Aster didn't know what it meant, but she would. Lune had had this same realization some twenty-six years ago. She hadn't known what she'd find on the other side of the mystery, but she'd risked everything seeking it out anyway.

Aster wished Giselle was here. She'd shout, *Another clue! Another clue!* Giselle would yawn and explain that she'd figured it out ages ago, but she was glad Aster had finally caught on.

Aster reached for her radio, so tempted to contact Giselle. Three days and not a word. Three days of not knowing if Giselle was alive or dead. She liked to disappear, but the ease and frequency with which she did it made it harder, not easier, to bear.

Once when Giselle had run off like this, Aster had reached out over the radio right away. Giselle had left hers on while in the custody of a guard, however, and he'd found it in one of the hidden pockets of her linen dress skirts. He'd punished her for the contraband quite forcefully and confiscated the radio. Aster was reluctant to reach out to Giselle in that way ever again, even after finding her a new radio.

Aster stayed long after she'd drawn the last woman's blood, the tubes safely tucked in their slots in the cooler, but the time eventually came for her to leave. This pass had a time stamp.

"Send the Surgeon my regards," said Jay, that wide grin back on her pale face. Aster prayed the girl would live forever, but of course it couldn't be so.

On her way out, she took the chance to admire Baby close-up one last time. It was likely she would never return to the Nexus again. Someone had tacked a large sheet of paper on the glass, obscuring the view from where Aster stood.

She recognized it immediately as a map of the grid, like the one Lune had in her notes. The fish dissection that wasn't a fish dissection. Aster walked up closer to it, squinted her eyes. It was hard to make out all the lines with the murkiness of the protective goggles, but she knew their map had something missing.

Lune's map showed circuitry pathways nonexistent on this rendering. She'd discovered the impossible magnet, had plotted and charted how it drew power. She'd gone looking for something that didn't exist and found it.

PART II

METALLURGY

VII

I was always a rather small, trifling thing. My nanny would pick me up and fly me through the air as she called me Bird Bones, which she first abridged to simply Bird, and then later amended to Birdy.

For that, she got a slap from my father, who thought Birdy too feminine a nickname. I was already prone to an unnatural girlishness, and, *Heavens, don't encourage the boy, Ms. Melusine.*

My sissyness and my sickliness were two sides of the same coin to my father. I was weak and didn't belong. The feared scandal of my birth—bastard child of a black woman—had already forced his resignation as sovereign. The least I could do was be a good and strapping lad. I suppose he thought he had a chance after all, when I turned out so pale. Though he was unable to impregnate his wife, the Heavens were giving him another chance at a son. Pity for him how it all turned out.

Sometimes I smile as I imagine his disappointment, and I do so now as I gather up myself to go. What would Father think of my closely shaven face? My peculiar wardrobe? He would disown me, and that heartens me. I have done at least one good thing: become a person my father would hate.

I glance at my wristwatch and note I'm going to be late for my meeting with Aster, but Uncle has called for me. When he bids, it's best to come. I should radio Aster, let her know of the change in schedule, but it's too much of a risk for her. In the fields, an overseer might see.

"Theo, lad, sit down," Uncle says when I reach his chambers, greeting me with a firm handshake. He's smiling and his voice is warm. The Sovereign's illness has him in good spirits.

"I hate it when you call me *lad*," I say.

He laughs deeply and gruffly. "I do suppose you're a man now."

No, not quite. Not at all. That is the exact opposite reason why it upsets me when he calls me things that mean boy.

"I get taken by how youthful you look at times," he says. "Sometimes it feels you are getting younger, not older."

It's the medication I take, an expected but welcome side effect of the special serum Aster makes me for my postpoliomyelitis syndrome. It's a testosterone antagonist. I don't think she knows.

"There was always a way about you," says Uncle. "Suffice it to say, you are angelic. There can be no other explanation for the medical miracles you perform and your childish smoothness."

Though more forgiving of my sissyness than my father, it comes out sometimes. His—not quite disdain, not quite repulsion   would it make sense if I called it *attraction*? I fascinate and excite him in a way I do not think is entirely wholesome, and it's been that way since I was very young.

I don't know if he's ever hurt me in that way adults can hurt children. I certainly have no memory of it. But then, I have no memory of most of my childhood. Aster tells me she thinks I was hurt so badly that the only way I could go on was to pretend so hard that it didn't exist until it was true, but what happened still lives in my body, like a witch's curse. It is neither here nor there.

Uncle's had his maid set up a coffee service in the smoking room, and I sit as far away from him as I can in one of the chairs, purposefully avoiding the sofa. If I sat there, he'd certainly sit next to me, too close.

"I trust you're well," I say, and help myself to coffee. I

typically take it black, but adding cream and sugar gives me more to do with my hands.

"As well as can be expected. I am saddened by the state of Sovereign Nicolaeus's health, but the Heavens takes us when it does, and as it is its will, it is to be praised. To God we must surrender."

"And is it the Heavens' will that you replace him when his time finally does come?" I ask.

"You know better than I, Heavens' Hands Made Flesh," Uncle says, and he believes it. He's always believed in me.

"On this matter, I don't know what the Heavens would have, but I do know most certainly that you will take Nicolaeus's place, as that is what the Sovereignty wants."

"Does the Sovereignty not follow the Will of the Heavens?"

"They follow something," I say.

Uncle nods. "Indeed. You too believe they've lost their way."

I believe their way has always been one of godlessness.

After the requisite small talk, we move on to the matter he really wants to discuss: Aster.

I do not tell him that I'm on my way to meet her. I doubt it'd go over well. He says that I am too lenient with her and others of *her ilk*.

"I know that it's in your nature to be kind to the down-trodden, but she's not good for you. She's dangerous."

He thinks she's dangerous because she has an influence on me, and anyone influencing me means that he cannot exert perfect control over me. "She's harmless, Lieutenant."

"None of them are harmless, Theo. They are animals, and if it weren't for us bending them into some kind of shape, they'd live in complete chaos and sin."

I wonder what he'd say if I confessed the depth of my feelings for Aster right now. The regard I have for her is not parallel to anything I've felt toward another. Heavens forgive me, but despite vows promising the opposite, I've imagined what it would be like to be entwined with Aster, to touch her, to let all my secrets trickle out of me and into her, to take hold of her burdens.

"I'm very tired," I say.

"Of course. I don't mean to keep you."

And yet he has. I hope that Aster understands. She's keen on schedules and keen on people sticking to them. We're similar in that way.

I like cycles and repetition. I like a good sense of rigor in my day. It helps me mark the passing of time. It helps me honor each moment. I have no personal sense of time, no real feel for what it means when sand passes through an hourglass. Sometimes it takes an hour. More frequently, it's an instant, days, universes.

"Goodbye, Uncle," I say, and hurry as much as I can, which isn't much. My leg is always in some kind of pain.

When I reach the Sphyrum, a guard salutes me. He abandons his post to walk me through the corridor adjoining *Matilda*'s main staircase to the Field Decks. If I've timed it right, I can enter the Maple Wood on its way to Baby. It will pass the wheat field where I agreed to meet Aster, and at precisely 18:39 there will be a gantry connecting the two decks.

I consult my map of the Sphyrum as well as my wristwatch and walk past the guard. "An honor to serve you, Surgeon, sir," he says.

There's a metal-grated portway at the edge of the field that will lock in place with the gantry, and I stand there alone as the deck lurches into motion toward the sun. I almost tip right over.

There are thoughts of jumping, I admit, but these are not fully realized impulses. Vague what-ifs. Nothing more.

My father raised blue field spaniels, hardy, spry hunting

dogs. I learned from him that sadness is the hardest thing to breed out of a bloodline. A hound with no prey drive was no hound at all and should be killed. I saw him drown a whole litter once, and I think he meant to drown me too. *Conform or die.* That was his motto. I am oddly doing bits of both, each half-assedly.

The deck slows to a stop and docks into place with the gantry, and I have one minute to walk across. As soon as I do, I spot Aster.

Her shift is over, and except for a few stragglers, the others have left for their home decks. It's hot, so she's torn off the sleeves from her shirt, rolled up her trousers to the knee. One of her kneesocks stops midshin and the other ruffles down at her ankle, just an inch of blue fabric peeking out of her black boots.

It's been four days since Aster staggered into my clinic bleeding, dazed, split open. I hasten my mind away from images of her torn body that morning, but now, as I watch her, I am reminded of the twenty-two-centimeter gash.

I reknitted her shattered scapula together with the help of an injectable osseous tissue, sutured the slit in her subclavian artery, and grafted blastema-mimic onto her injured tissue, but healing is not a perfect science.

"You came," Aster says when she hears my approach. Eyes closed, she brushes her hand over stalks of wheat, head tilted up to Baby Sun. Its light wanes now that day shift has ended. Decks overhead creak toward each other, ushering in night.

Like a child, I marvel at the moving parts. A little girl dissecting her first radio.

It was Aster who informed me that *Matilda*'s architects designed the Sphyrum as an homage to the Celestial Sphere, a theoretical model of the Great Lifehouse and its surrounding astronomy. I don't believe there's a book, brochure, or pamphlet in the Archives that Aster hasn't read. She picked up the tidbit about the Sphyrum's design from an old preship newspaper article.

In the model, the Great Lifehouse rests at the center of an imaginary sphere, stars revolving around it along various axes. If I understand it correctly (and I very well may not; astromatics never much enthralled me), the Celestial Sphere was distinct from the worldview pretelescope scientists held that the universe revolved around a single, insignificantly sized planet. Rather, the Celestial Sphere provided a way of understanding relationships in the horizon, the poles, and the night sky to determine the location of stars relative to one's location on the Great Lifehouse at a given time.

In the Sphyrum, the sun is at the center and the land revolves around it. It is, in fact, the very opposite of the Celestial Sphere, but then tributes shouldn't be perfect imitations.

"I wasn't sure you'd be able to make it," she says.

Her invitation had been quite terse. More of a demand. She'd contacted me on my radio and said to come to the wheat fields for prayers. *Not to the banana fields?* I'd asked, which was where I thought she'd been assigned. *No,* she informed me, her sharp tone cutting through the crackle of the radio static, *Wheat and banana share no sonic similarities. You should have your hearing checked,* she told me. I can't say for sure whether she meant it in earnest, but given the overannunciation of her remaining instructions, there's a reasonable chance she did.

"At any rate, I appreciate you made it at all," she says, tipping the straw hat she's got on, seemingly not upset by my tardiness. "I found a larval specimen of Lepidoptera. Look. Isn't it beautiful?" Aster holds up the yellow-spotted caterpillar resting on her middle finger.

"These are a danger to the wheat crop, no?" I ask.

She helps the caterpillar onto my hand. Her fingers are calloused and dry, and when they scrape against mine, they're coarse enough that I briefly confuse the contact for static shock.

"This strain of wheat produces a toxin that the larvae find malodorous, so it's not of particular concern. Mostly they eat the nasturtium."

Then she kisses the caterpillar as it sits in my palm. She does that. Kisses bugs. Leaves of plants. Microscopes. Paper. The muzzles of the draft horses.

"Here, I would like it back now," she says, and plucks it from my hand, bending down to set it onto the petals of a red flower. Then she lies down on her back. It is clear that this is where she's most at home, even more so than in her botanarium.

"You're moving stiffly," I say.

"It was, as my Ainy would say, a very long day."

I'm surprised by how closely my disapproving groan resembles a growl. I'm always surprised by my body. The way it moves and occupies space. Its height. Its presence. "You're supposed to be in recovery," I say.

She shrugs.

"And your shoulder? How's it doing?"

She shrugs again. "Hopefully I'll get some rest tonight. The cold and the pain have made sound sleep quite impossible the last several nights, but I have work to do in the fields," she says, stretching her shoulder. "I might get permission from the overseer to stay the night. The heat should help soften the joints. I am surprised more women have not had similar ideas, but I speculate they prefer the relative safety of their quarters to the openness of the Field Decks."

Relative safety. That's the most any of them can hope for. Aster's sickle sits next to her on the ground; it's the one she's been using to harvest grasses of wheat despite the severity of her injury. I don't know what it is that keeps me from picking it up and slicing it through—everyone. My uncle. The overseer I see in the distance. The guards. Sovereign Nicolaeus.

"Come with me. I have something to show you," says Aster, standing up slowly.

An overseer watches me follow after her, smiling. I cringe because I know what he's thinking. I know what he's got on his mind about what we're about to do.

I am not that sort of man. The sort to follow a woman into the brush and do with her whatever pleases him. I don't think I'm a man at all.

When I make eye contact with the overseer, I do not smile. I stare at his face hard and do not blink, though the pollens in the air make my eyes want to twitch. His gaze runs from mine, and this is good. People do not know what to make of me, and this pleases me. I don't want to be scrutable.

Aster brings me to Moon. She's the she-dog, half wolf, that lives in the barn where the wheat grinder is. The structure is made of wood, the white paint chipped. Though I have never been "outside," of course, it is here that I can begin to imagine what it's like.

Moon is huge. A beast, truly, but sweet as a pup. She doesn't like to leave the barn, and she survives on the scraps people bring her. Aster pats the dog on the head, rubs her cheek against her jowls as they're nuzzling.

I let Moon smell my fingers. She licks them, then settles onto her rug to have her belly petted. "Later, Moon," says Aster, and heads to the back of the barn. She's almost limping, and I think to invite her to my cabin where there is a bath with running hot water. No pass I could write would allow her that high, and it would be bad-mannered to invite a young woman into my home, but I wish it could be so.

"Look," she says, and she smiles at me, something she doesn't do frequently. She points to a little nook in the back corner of the barn. There's a wood bench, and on top of it is a jar filled with water, candles, and an idol of the Mother, she who carried God in her womb and birthed him, the universe itself, the Heavens. "Do you like it?"

"It is an altar," I say. There is a pillow in front of the

bench for kneeling. Photographs, grayed, of people no one knows, are tacked up against the wood of the barn wall. "What for?"

"For you. To let you know that I appreciate what you do for me. To cement our . . ." she pauses for a single second, "to cement our friendship. I regret how harsh I was with you. This is an apology for my severity and a thank you for fixing my shoulder. I know you like to pray in the Field Decks. I thought you might like to have a special place. It is not the same as being out there, I know, but—"

"Thank you," I say, and kneel on the provided cushion, touch the idol. Flecks of powdered sawdust rub off onto my fingers, and the smell of sweet maplewood is heady and strong.

"I made that myself," says Aster. "And can you tell that I dressed up for this occasion?" Her hands are in the pockets of her rolled-up trousers. I see now how good the material is, no signs of dirt or holes. Her shirt is soaked through with sweat, but I imagine at one point today it was crisply ironed. "Do you like it?"

"I always like the way you look," I tell her, then turn away. "Would you like to pray with me?"

"No, but I will join you to make you happy. I like to make you happy." She's never said anything like that before.

Aster kneels next to me, and I scoot over so that her knees will be cushioned by the pillow. Her bare arm touches mine, and I wish I wasn't still in my white coat. I think of taking it off. Rolling up the sleeves of my shirt. Instead, I light a candle. She lights one too.

"If it is not considered too blasphemous, I will do my anatomical recitations," she says. "I have to keep my memory sharp."

"The body is part of God's creation, isn't it?"

"That's a rhetorical question, which is meant to assure me

that it would not be blasphemous for me to do my anatomical recitations, correct?"

"Correct," I tell her, nodding.

I hear her say, "Deoxyribonucleic acid, endometrium, endosteum, endothelium, enteroendocrine, inguinal falx," and I begin the Evening-Hour Litany, words describing devotion to things I have never seen: oceans, mountains, deserts. I long to see them, though I know I never will.

I think it was my nanny Melusine who made me the way I am. A queer. Not a man or how a man's supposed to be. Bent. On Q deck, all children are referred to as girls. All people—all Q-deckers at least—are assumed women unless there's a statement or obvious sign otherwise, such as the fashions they wear or the trade they choose.

The more bold among the Guard call me *faggot* when they are drunk, or whispering. Because I refuse to keep my beard. My earrings, though religious in nature, are a practice most other highdeck men have long ago abandoned. I have three black dots under each of my eyes, drawn there with a coal pencil. It is religious, but still they know that I am off. Because I am an anomaly, because they see me as someone holy, they can tolerate my differences.

Aster is still reciting next to me, even though I've stopped, and I don't interrupt her. I blow out my candle. I look up and imagine this barn as a temple. I imagine God filling the walls.

"Let us stay in here until Baby Sun is fully set," says Aster.

"I cannot."

We both hear someone approach, a stranger crunching in the dirt beyond the door. As silently as I can, I stand, putting proper distance between Aster and myself. The door comes open and a guard enters.

"Surgeon," he says, surprised to see me.

"Yes," I say, and do not bother to use his rank. I fully admit I am petty and disdainful. It is my pride, my greatest sin after fear.

"An overseer told me he saw someone take a worker in here. Didn't know he meant you."

It was no doubt the same guard who'd insinuated with his smile that my intentions toward Aster were untoward, and he'd taken issue with my response to him. He likely hadn't known who I am.

"Aster and I are discussing work," I say.

"Right. Right, sir, of course. My utmost apologies for interrupting."

"Sir?" Aster says.

"What?" the man replies.

"I have work to do tonight. May I sleep here and work through the evening?"

"You plan on stealing some crop?" he asks.

"No sir, of course not, sir."

"You can stay so long as you behave," he says. "I'll let your wing guards know so you'll be excused from curfew, but you still got to be there for morning headcount."

"Yes sir."

He tips his hat to me then departs the barn. Soon it is dark, Baby Sun shaded for the night.

"We can sleep here," says Aster, pointing to a bundle of straw.

"I am not sleeping here," I tell her, though I want to, I do.

"Then I will sleep here and you can go off and be important. Stay and have supper with me at least."

She unpacks a satchel containing tins of food. One is filled with red soup. It looks spicy and rich. Oxtails and beef knuckles and marrow bones rubbed in a paste made of red pepper seeds, then left to roast in an iron pot over the fire all night. Served with cornmeal dumplings. Ms. Melusine used to make me this dish when I was young, when she was my nanny.

I no longer eat animal flesh, but Aster has brought me twice-fried plantains and a salad of cold lentils, chopped red onion, cilantro. Sautéed dandelion and mustard greens, squash blossoms. It is all Ms. Melusine's cooking but I appreciate that Aster thought of me, that she planned this, a gift and a supper.

"Theo?"

"Yes?"

"I have been thinking lately about the dead. Lieutenant has made it so cold that the hairs on my neck stand up and the skin on my arms turns to gooseflesh. I think it's my mother's hand stroking me sometimes, before I return to my senses." Aster pulls her knees into her chest and rests her cheek against my shoulder. I want to kiss the top of her head.

"I must go," I say before hurrying through the rest of my supper.

I go out into the fields, then into the corridor, and then updeck. I make sure my radio is on but thankfully no one calls for me. Once in my cabin I pray again, this time to be rid of impure thoughts. I pray for deliverance for Aster and Ms. Melusine and Giselle, and, selfishly, for myself. I undress. I beat my back with the five-tailed whip, then lie in a salt bath until I pass out.

Later, I barely hear my radio calling out to me. The water is cold and has wrinkled my skin. Draping the towel around myself, I move toward the handheld transceiver.

"The Surgeon, copy," I say.

It is Uncle and he has news.

VIII

Aster's radio buzzed to life with a staticky moan.

"Aster, do you read?" asked the Surgeon.

Sun shined dimly upon the Field Decks. Wind from the air filtration system rocked flowers into a waltz. It felt good to be away from the chill of Q deck and the hoarfrost of the Ancestors' whispers. Staying the night had been wise.

"Aster?"

"I read," she said, bringing the two-way to her lips. Dandelion blossoms floated upward and away into the not-sky. She caught one, mashed the tufts of white between her fingers.

"Are you all right?"

Aster knelt, knees to dirt. "I am as you left me yesterday evening," she said, though technically she'd relocated. Upon waking, she had left the wheat fields, chasing Baby's light from deck to deck, settling in the field of wildflowers.

"Sovereign Nicolaeus is dead," Theo said, pausing for what seemed an inappropriate length of time before Aster realized he was giving her space to have a reaction.

"All right."

"I wanted to speak with you before the general announcement. Are you sure everything is fine?"

She dug her trowel into the muddy soil.

"Aster?"

"I don't hold Sovereign Nicolaeus in particularly high esteem. Why would I wish to know of his demise before the general announcement? He was ill, was he not? This is expected."

"I'm contacting you to ask if there's something you know that I don't."

Aster thought of her mother's journals, the jagged irises she shared in common with Nicolaeus. "There's much I know that you don't." She managed, just barely, to keep herself from laughing at the sound of Theo's indignant sigh.

"You're taking the piss."

"I am."

"All I need to know is if it was you."

"Was *what* me?" she asked in return, lips right up against the radio. Aster recognized the gargled sound Theo made as an expression of incredulity, but truly, she didn't know what he was talking about.

"Tell me and I'll take care of it, but I can't do that unless you're up front, unless I know where your tracks are so that I can cover them. Now's not the time to play ignorant."

"Then don't speak so vaguely. Too much of my day is spent decoding euphemisms, then dealing with the aftermath when I decode them wrong." She slipped her pocket watch from her trousers and gave it a look: 04:05. She needed to get a move on if she wished to visit her botanarium before returning to her quarters for headcount.

"I'm asking if you're the reason the Sovereign's dead."

Aster's brow crinkled into tense knots. "Why?" she asked. Days ago, Theo had come to her for help keeping Sovereign Nicolaeus alive, and now he accused her of having a hand in his death. "Giselle's missing, my shoulder hurts, and my mother's autobiography is written in incomprehensible riddles," she said, speaking boldly despite the public location because she knew she was alone. "As much as I'd like to have had time to kill Nicolaeus, I've been quite occupied."

"Just—will you meet me in the morgue as soon as you're able?"

"Aye," said Aster, taking pity.

"Be careful traveling the corridors. Guards will want nothing more than to exploit the break in order."

"Though *Careful* is not my middle name, I will endeavor to behave as though it is," she said, then went silent as she heard twigs crack in the distance. She cut off the transmission and slid the clip of her radio onto her belt, taking care to avoid bumping it against her radiolabe.

She ducked beneath a canopy of flowers, gripped her trowel. The blade had a satisfyingly sharp point. If called upon to do so, it would break skin.

Next to her, on top of her logbook, lay the olive cardigan Theo had knit for her. She wondered if she had time to button it on. Were she to wear it, the approaching stranger might take her for a finer lady than she was, and spare her whatever violence they intended.

"Hello?" someone called, high-pitched. "Is someone there?"

Aster let the trowel go slack in her hand. It wasn't a guard who approached after all, but, judging by the shy, questioning tone, a civilian.

"Are you there?" the voice continued to call out. "I know I heard someone. Please answer."

She pronounced each word with curious fullness, drawing the sounds out, her greeting a bit like *heh-low*, rather than the *uh-lo* or even *ah-yo* to which Aster was accustomed. An upperdecker, then.

"Is anyone there?" the woman asked again, emerging through the fat stems of the dandelions. She wore a light-brown frock, buttoned chin to waist, the skirt flaring modestly outward. Blue veins showed through the white skin over her temples, and pearl earrings dotted each ear. "There you are. I knew I'd heard someone. These weeds are immense, and I seem to have lost my way. Would you mind terribly escorting me back to the path? My name's Samantha. You can call me Mrs. Sammy, if you'd like." She twisted her index finger into the strands of baby hair crowned about her forehead.

Aster's hair, rough as cornbread, protruded in similar fashion, too short at the edges to fit into the ribbon tying her bun. Drawing a hand across her face, Aster wiped away the strands that had become stuck to her forehead. The wide-brimmed hat she wore disguised most of the uncooperative coils.

Samantha (Aster flatly refused to think of her as *Mrs. Sammy*) was not wearing a hat. She did, however, carry an ivory parasol edged with lace, a prudent accessory. Though they had ample recreational space, upperdeckers enjoyed strolling the more comely of the Field Decks before the morning shift workers came, even though Baby leeched radiation.

"Aren't you listening?" Samantha said, twirling her umbrella lazily. "Are you ignoring me?"

Yes, she was.

"A woman comes to you in need of help, it's only right to offer your hand," said Samantha. "Or are you deaf? Dumb?"

Aster stabbed her trowel in the soil, glanced up. "If I said, *Aye, yes, I am, in fact, deaf, dumb,* am I to believe you'd leave me to my work and be on your way?" she asked, and it was a genuine question. If she could avoid conversations in the future by admitting to infirmities, she'd do so.

"Excuse me, but—"

"You are excused," Aster cut in. "And to clarify, by ignoring you, I'd wished to convey I had no desire to speak with you, an overture my compatriots would've universally understood. In your language, a gesture of prolonged silence obviously means something else. However, now that I've elucidated, there's no further room for misunderstanding," she finished, eyes on the woman's shiny white patent-leather boots, chunky heels in the soil.

Aster had stated her piece as eloquently as she could and

would pay the woman no further mind from here on out. Back to root-picking. Eight women in Swan Wing had taken ill with the blood sickness, leucocytes accreting in greater numbers than was healthy. A precise solution of taraxacum root, accebum blossom, livilia sap, spiny alva alkaloids, and enzyme inhibitors Aster synthesized in her botanarium would target and destroy the wayward cells, slowing if not stopping their progress altogether. She didn't have time for the ship's Samanthas—not yesterday, not today, and very likely not tomorrow.

Aster sunk her fingers into the luscious soil, its texture neither wet nor dry. She didn't have time to waste, but she wasted some anyway, luxuriating in the feel of granules against her skin, nesting into her fingernails. Thank Heavens for this moment. This chance to catch her breath. She would find Giselle. She would trace her mother's tracks. She'd meet Theo. But for now, at this very second, she would dig.

As Aster made her way back to the path, she saw Samantha standing next to a guard at Heavens' Gates, the massive double-paneled iron hatch dividing the field and the corridor, tall as two Asters, an oval at the top. Samantha made exasperated hand movements. The guard nodded his head. Aster walked toward them as slowly as she could.

The guard had peachy-white skin, red sunburns on his nose, peeling. Curls of blond hair stuck out from his burgundy wool cap. He examined Aster with alert blue eyes as she got close enough to hear their exchange, and she recognized his face.

It was the guard who'd barged in on her cabin less than a fortnight ago, inebriated, the one who'd beaten Mabel and Pippi with the belt after seeing them in bed together. He cleaned up into something much less soft. That night, he'd been easy to overcome. Aster didn't think the task would be so easy today.

"Come here, girl," the guard said, and Aster knew better than to disobey. At least he didn't appear to recognize her. "This woman says you've been giving her trouble."

Aster looked at Samantha, then back at the guard, and answered honestly: "She interrupted my work."

"It wouldn't have taken you but a moment to show me the way," said Samantha. Aster ventured a glance toward her pocket watch. "My apologies, am I delaying you by holding you accountable for your disrespectful attitude?"

"I can take her into custody if you'd like," said the guard, fixing his gaze on Aster. It wasn't recognition in his eyes, but something close, and she bowed her head down.

"That's really not necessary."

"Would you feel better if I got her to apologize, then?" he asked.

Samantha flicked errant strands of hair behind her ear. "This isn't about how I feel, officer, and this isn't a personal matter. It's a Matildan matter. Our social order depends on our ethical order, and our ethical order depends on acknowledging and rectifying moral wrongs. So yes, an apology would be appreciated, but not for my benefit, but the benefit of the society in which we all live." Aster had not met an upperdeck woman quite so showy before, and she seemed to be playing a part. It reminded Aster of Giselle, when they played house as children, and Giselle's exaggerated upperdeck accent.

The guard nodded perfunctorily at Samantha's speech, then turned to Aster. "How about it, Aster Grey, assistant to the Surgeon? Would you like to apologize?"

Aster licked her dry and cracked bottom lip, the iron tang of blood spreading from the tip of her tongue to the whole of her mouth. "No," she said, though she'd quite meant to say yes. Theo had called for her. Sovereign Nicolaeus was dead. She had a list of fourteen things she needed to do today. She had every reason to seek the easy way out via feigned contrition.

"I never!" gasped Samantha. If she'd had pearls, she'd be clutching them.

"I can sort her out," said the guard with the hint of a smile.

Samantha closed her eyes and left them shut for several seconds. "Fine," she said, then pressed the large amber button to open the hatch.

"Wait," Aster called out, jogging after her, putting as much distance between her and the guard as she could. "Let me walk you back to your cabin."

Samantha gave Aster a bewildered look, taken aback by the sudden reversal in attitude.

"I'm certain that's not necessary. Mrs. Samantha is perfectly competent," said the guard. "Besides, you're not allowed to her parts at this hour, Surgeon's pass or not."

Samantha glanced between Aster and the guard, then stepped in front of Aster, seemingly happy to play savior. "I would appreciate her taking me back to my quarters. Come on. Let's go."

Aster nodded, a sack of dandelions slung over her back.

Samantha reached out an arm and wrapped it around Aster's waist, pulling her near.

"I'm afraid I can't allow that," said the guard. He brushed his thumb over the glossy wooden tip of the baton strapped to his belt.

"Surely you'll let the rules slide just this once so she might take me home," Samantha said. The quality of her voice had changed, more strained now.

"Rules is rules," the guard said. In a lazy, mocking tone, he added, "After all, our social order depends on our ethical order, and our ethical order depends on acknowledging and rectifying moral wrongs, doesn't it, Samantha?" Now he appraised Aster. "Most people don't count on my memory being what it is."

Samantha turned to Aster, squeezed her tightly, then let

go. "My apologies," she said. "You'll be all right, won't you?" She stroked a palm across Aster's cheek, her fingers cold and clammy.

"You need to leave," the guard said, "or I can write you up too."

Samantha hesitated a moment and then ascended the maroon-carpeted staircase back toward her upperdeck oasis, the skirts of her dress gathered in her hands.

Aster let out a quiet, undignified squeal as Samantha disappeared up the steps. She needed to radio Giselle. She hadn't wished to put her in danger, but she had no choice now. She just hoped there was time. Hoped Giselle was close by, safe, not in custody. She switched her two-way to Giselle's frequency. She couldn't talk, of course, but she could tap. She beat her finger over the radio's microphone to relay a distress message. *Mayday. Wildflower Wing.* She repeated it three times, then cut off the signal.

"Follow me," the guard said. He grabbed Aster by the shoulder, her dandelion roots tumbling to the grated floor, and guided her along.

Aster looked up when the guard jerked her to a stop. She realized now that he'd said something. "What was that?" she asked. His lips moved, but Aster couldn't make sense of the sounds issuing therefrom. The Silence had come, and like always, at the worst possible moment. It was a temporary deafness that reminded her of her youth. The stress of it aggravated the condition, and though she wanted to sputter out, *Please slow down while I gather my wits,* her tongue would not cooperate. She hated the way her mind seized into itself sometimes.

"Aster," she heard the guard say. She didn't know what else he said precisely, but years of similar run-ins told her that it was, no doubt, some variation of the usual: how he was going to whip her good for sassing him; or how she looked ugly, like a horse, with her black skin and moon-fat eyes and flaring nose, and because of this, he was going to have her; or how she looked beautiful, like a horse, and because of this, he was going to have her; or how he liked the way she made her corn grits, with the maple syrup and the cinnamon and the cardamom, and could she teach his woman how to make them like that?; or how she smelled so good, like chicory, or how she smelled so good, like tea, or how she smelled so good, like the ocean, even though nobody on this ship had ever smelled the ocean, because there were no oceans in space.

She didn't bother sussing out the specifics.

"Are you listening?" he asked.

This, Aster did understand, and she closed her eyes, concentrating deeply, so that her words might return to her. "No," she finally said, "I'm not listening to you."

"You cow."

"You cow," Aster said back, knowing she wasn't supposed to. Mimicry reminded her how to use words.

"You want me to teach you a lesson?" he asked, closer now. His breath barbed her neck, chin, lips.

"All I want is to be on my way." She slid her hands into a pocket of her medicine belt, felt around for the syringe third to the right. He laughed, a bloated sound rooted to his chest that barely made it past his lips. He stood closer, and she felt his heat.

"I've killed men before," Aster said, a lie. "If pressed, I'd do it again." She saw the faintest tremor in his otherwise steady pulse, his neck hiccupping then going still.

His eyes turned to sickles as he examined her. "Look at me," he snapped, but Aster's eyes moved sideways and downward, to the grate beneath her feet. The guard's boots were scuffed, needed shining, nothing like Samantha's had been.

Aster didn't know what made her squat down, lick her thumb, rub it over the fading black of his shoes. A small peace settled over her as her fingers moved methodically over the leather, making it glisten. The rhythm of the movement allowed her to think.

The needle in the syringe was a tiny one, meant only for small shots of anesthetic, but Aster thought in a pinch—and it was a pinch—it'd do. As his fingers seized a wad of her hair, yanked her up, she uncapped the syringe and lifted it bit by bit from her pocket.

Aster stabbed the guard in the hip with the needle. He groaned, then made like he was going to backhand her, but she ducked. Fifty meters to the stairway, she could make that easy, and if the needle slowed him down at all, she had a shot. "Little devil," the guard said, and grabbed her by her suspenders. She wiggled, bending herself out of his grip. His hand moved to the waistband of her trousers, nearly pulling them off as he yanked her backward.

A loud pop rang through the corridor, and Aster fell forward, freed from the guard's grasp. The insides of her ears pounded, and she covered them with her palms.

"Aster? Aster? You all right?" Giselle had come. Her hand jostled Aster's shoulder roughly, aggravating her wound. "You didn't get nipped by the ball thing, did you?" She came around in front of Aster, squatted, her short dress riding up, revealing brown thighs, a silver and brown machine—a rifle—slung over her shoulder with a leather strap. Blood pooled on the floor. "Aster?"

She shrugged out of Giselle's hands, stood up. The guard lay still on the floor, opened up and spilling out. The healer in Aster wanted to sew him together.

"Night Empress," Aster said, despite knowing this was make-believe. Giselle so looked the part, with her device just like the comic book heroine, launching magic pellets. "You got blood and viscera on me," she added, though it was only a small amount.

Giselle checked the gold watch on the dead guard's wrist. "We need to get on before curfew," she said, and gestured right, toward the corridor. She ran off, gun bouncing against her back and hips.

Aster unbuttoned the guard's shirt, spotted with pink, pulling it off his arms then dragging it from beneath his body. The blood would wash out with a little scrubbing. His trousers, maroon, were soft and thick, lovely against her fingers, not scratchy at all. They'd trade well. Aster yanked them off, then his boots, bundled the clothing into her arms.

With the heap of thieved clothing in her arms, Aster followed after Giselle. The sound of the gunshot had attracted other guards. They'd reached as far down as the bottom of the Field Decks, skipping overs stairs, jumping down whole flights. "Oy!" Aster heard through the grate of the deck above her, boots stomping.

"Follow me," she said. There was a way to get into the air ducts from the furnace cabin, present on each deck, and she made her way portside to get to it.

"How do we get inside?" asked Giselle, glancing back over her shoulder to see if anyone was approaching.

Aster took out her key, slid it into the scanner. "Like so," she said when the door to the Heat Bay opened. It was too warm and low on oxygen to hide there for any significant amount of time, but Aster crawled up the pipe to reach the ceiling, and used her shoulder to bang in an opening to the ducts. Voices came from outside. "In there, we're coming in," they said, but Aster knew she had a minute. Officers didn't carry keys like the one she had—a copy of the Surgeon's. She hoisted herself into the space she'd made in the ceiling, then reached her hand down to help Giselle climb up.

Both their palms were sweaty, and Giselle slipped. Aster heard the lock click open, and she tried one more time to pull Giselle up. "Grab my shirt," she said. Giselle clawed Aster's cuffs, nails digging into her wrists. Aster edged her body backward so she could pull her up.

There was no covering the hole she'd made in the false plaster ceiling to reach the duct, so they needed to move quickly. Sweat and grime clung to Aster's skin as she shimmied through the duct. Her bones moved reluctantly, hinged too tight. Salt made her eyes burn. The feel of the guard's hand still buzzed against her cheek.

The pipe smelled of mold and spores. Aster wanted to bottle them up and examine them under the lens of a microscope. They were the Gods and the Heavens. Bacteria sprung into existence first, before bug-eyed fish, before serpents, before thick-legged women with shoulders and backs so strong they could carry their whole families on them. Before they built a ship to fly to touch Gods.

"Would you stop that?" Giselle said.

"Stop what?"

"That hollering with your hand."

Aster hadn't realized she'd been smacking her hand against the metal piping as she crawled. "It helps me think," she said. Giselle was in front, her ass in Aster's face, her bare feet scarred on the bottoms. "Where have you been?"

"With your mother," Giselle said.

"What?"

Giselle shrugged from in front of Aster, her knobby shoulders rising. "I got to go," she said, spying a vent large enough that she could crawl through. "You know where to find me. I'll explain everything when I can."

Before Aster figured out her words, Giselle was gone, and she had no idea at all where to find her. Like that, Giselle had disappeared again.

IX

Official news of the Sovereign's death came at 05:03, Sergeant Thompson waking the women of the cabin via loudspeaker shortly after morning bell. Aster had just settled into her mattress for a quick refresher before her meeting with the Surgeon when Thompson's voice came on.

The bell struck three times, followed by: *"Rouse yourselves! The Heavens are high, and humankind is low, and daily we must strive to attain that highness to which we are destined. Wakeful minds and wakeful hearts. You'll be allowed five minutes for mindful prayer before I continue with today's announcements."*

Mabel, Pippi, and Vivian yawned awake at Thompson's address, rubbed their sleep-swollen eyes. Aster felt herself calm as they stirred, soothed by the familiar cadence of blankets shuffling, snores easing into soft wheezes.

"Nice of you to join us," said Vivian. "Thought for a moment you'd gone the way of Giselle. You heard from her at all?"

"Yes," said Aster, refusing to elaborate.

Vivian, Mabel, and Pippi had slept on a floor pallet to share body heat. Aster had wished to join them when she returned from the Field Decks, but she didn't want to impose on their carefully constructed knot. Instead, she'd laid alone on her cot, freezing, wishing Giselle was there. It wasn't but a few days ago that they had been the ones on a floor pallet, warmed by each other's bodies as they studied Lune's journals.

Aster shivered at the thought that she might not see her bunkmate again. With Nicolaeus dead and Lieutenant in the wings, the possibility seemed more likely than ever. That rifle-machine had only so many bullets. Giselle couldn't fight off the whole Guard, and Aster doubted she could fight off even one Lieutenant.

She sat up and pulled her knees into her chest, eyes closed. She didn't like to be agitated but she was. Her equilibrium had taken a more than sizable decline. Seeing Giselle and then losing her again, the murder of the guard—she hadn't even had breakfast yet.

"Someone light a lamp or candle, something," Vivian said. "It's dark, and it stinks. I feel like I woke up inside somebody's nethers." She emerged from the mass of rugs, quilts, afghans, and floral-print sheets.

"You are so foul," said Pippi, looking prim despite the ragged state of her nightclothes. She stood up and flipped on an oil lamp to its lowest setting. Flickering, dim light illuminated the tiny cabin.

"Turn it higher," said Vivian, throwing a shabby pillow at Pippi. Pippi turned the dial up one click, and the lamp shined two shades brighter.

Pippi and Mabel moved off the floor to sit next to each other on their cot, their legs overlapping. Rusted bronze walls cast the room in stubborn darkness, no matter how many lanterns were lit. Mabel and Pippi were always touching in some kind of way to ward off the gloom of it, and that was to say nothing of the cold.

Vivian went to turn up the receiver of the loudspeaker, a blanket draped around her shoulders like a cape. "Quiet, it's starting," she said.

Again, the bell clanged three times through the loudspeaker before the message: "*Now that your hearts have been tempered by prayer, you are ready to hear the Word. It is with a grieving heart that I must inform you that Sovereign Ernest Nicolaeus's spirit joined the Heavens during the night. Work shifts will continue as scheduled. Labor* will be a great balm to you as you mourn. We must not let our sorrow impede Matilda's journey forward to the Promised Land. The cosmos is large, but our spirits are formidable."

"The Sovereign's dead; long live the Sovereign, I suppose," said Pippi, stretching and yawning. She removed her scarf and undid the plaits, brushing each one out before putting the smoothed strands into a high bun.

"Long may he reign and all that," Vivian said, rolling her eyes. She threw on a thick brown flannel shirt over her night-gown and pulled some work boots over her wool tights. That was the extent of her get-ready routine.

"I can't believe how blasé you all are acting," Mabel said, coughing. She patted her chest and wiped her watering eyes. "Pippi, my spectacles."

Pippi was already on it. She handed Mabel her glasses and ointment for her chest. She also picked out Mabel's clothes from the trunk, all garments she had procured herself in an at-tempt to improve Mabel's poor fashion sense. Pippi always had Mabel looking quite smart in a long skirt, blouse, and blazer. The ensemble suited Mabel's dowdy and academic ways. It was just the sort of outfit a middeck journalist would wear.

"Have you got anything to say about this?" asked Mabel, the question directed toward Aster. She was doing her cultural anthropologist act, acquiring the facts, investigating, collect-ing data. Aint Melusine would be proud.

"You *were* gone last night," said Vivian, her hands on her skinny, practically nonexistent hips. She wasn't quite a per-fect rectangle, but almost. She was what an upperdecker might call *boyishly built.*

"I had nothing to do with his passing. He'd been ill," As-ter responded before realizing that this incriminated rather than exonerated her. Sovereign Nicolaeus's poor health had been secret. She only knew because Theo had broken protocol by telling her.

"Aster!" cried Mabel, working herself into the outfit Pippi had picked out. "How long have you known?"

"She's probably the one who made him sick," said Vivian, but who knew if she really believed it? Her personality revolved around being the rude one, and she kept up the act to maintain her identity. In the process she'd become a caricature of herself.

It made Aster miss Giselle more. Her meanness was pure, forged from pain. It was a cruelty Aster could understand if not always tolerate. She would always forgive a bitter, scarred thing lashing out.

"Ill from what, Aster?" asked Mabel. Pippi passed her a belt for her skirt.

"I'm not sure, precisely," Aster said, getting her own self ready to meet Theo. She went to the leather trunk to retrieve some clean clothes, her bloody ones from earlier already discarded. She decided on a pair of gray trousers, a dull brown shirt. She buttoned her suspenders to her slacks, then pulled the elastic over her shoulders. It wasn't a particularly warm outfit, but it didn't need to be. The middecks weren't subject to the energy rations.

"I wondered why he stopped doing the announcements," Mabel said, invigorated by the prospect of a scandal, "but I figured it was something to do with the blackouts. Like he'd gotten hurt, or they needed to keep him sequestered somewhere for his own protection while they figured it out." She walked toward her busted radio, turning the knob, searching for the right station.

"Baby, he only just died. There's not going to be any news for a while, so why don't you stop worrying?" said Pippi, squeezing Mabel's shoulder.

But Mabel's idea was a good one. Underground reporters in the lowdecks might have knowledge Aster didn't and would be broadcasting shortly.

"I can't believe he's dead, *really* dead. He's been sovereign since before I was born, and now he's just—not. This is . . . I don't know. I need to get writing." Mabel sat near the radio, ear pressed to the output.

"I'm meeting the Surgeon now to discuss it," Aster said. "I will relay any discoveries about Sovereign Nicolaeus's demise to you when I return."

Mabel smiled but was too distracted to bombard Aster with a list of questions to ask Theo, as she usually might. Aster's intel made Mabel's underground news bulletin one of the more popular on Q. She thought of telling her how the guard who'd barged in on them and beaten her last week was now dead, but that was a dangerous piece of knowledge. She could come under scrutiny if the wrong person found out she knew.

"Will you be at shift today?" asked Pippi.

"I suspect so. We should be finished by then." Aster strapped on her medicine belt, looping the leather through a brass buckle. Next, she clipped on her radiolabe. Once it was secure, she pulled out the goggles she kept in the left pouch of her bag and slid them over her face.

"Don't pretend like your little Surgeon can't just write you a pass whenever you want," said Vivian. She now wore a hat pulled over her ears and a scarf.

"He can't," Aster replied. It was one thing to write passes for free movement and quite another to write one excusing her from shifts. Work was the backbone of morality, and so on and so forth. The Sovereignty's Guard wouldn't have it.

J deck's corridors crisscrossed according to little discernible pattern, but Aster knew the passageways well. Bare bulbs cast a dim yellow glow every few meters, hanging like halos. Aster tapped the side of her fist against every third hatch, bumped her hip into every fifth handwheel. It was a game she played, to focus. The beats her body made, counter to the beats her surroundings made, amplified the hidden sounds: the hiss of steam behind the walls, the creaking of *Matilda*'s rusty joints. Should footsteps approach from behind, she'd hear them and be ready.

Aster turned a corner and saw Officer Frederick making his rounds. "Ayo," he said in greeting. He stood at the intersection of Juniper and Jasper, dark hair pasted wetly to his forehead. Of all the guards who worked the lowdecks, he offended Aster least, though she hadn't forgotten this morning's altercation.

"Good morning," Aster said, forcing herself to meet his eyes. Blisters on Frederick's nose and ears, courtesy of Baby, meant he'd just gotten off a long watching shift in the Field Decks, and she wondered if he'd been one of the men chasing her and Giselle. "You don't usually work this junction."

"I'm sure you've heard the news by now. Got reassigned to J deck to help manage any wanderers from Jutting Cliff Wing. Sovereign Nicolaeus's death has everyone out of sorts."

"Wanderers?"

"You and the Surgeon are going to have a whole lot of company today."

Aster fished into one of the pockets of her belt. "For your burns," she said, and handed him a small vial, mostly because the sight of his flaking nose was an eyesore from which she wished to be spared. Besides, small favors such as this kept him on her side. She might need a favor from him one day.

He smiled widely, revealing gapped but straight teeth. "Thank you, love."

"You're rather joyful despite the news," said Aster.

Frederick straightened his face, his manner stiffening. "It's my way," he said, "but you're right, it's not appropriate. I've got to work on my mourning face. It's not that I'm not sad. I just . . . I didn't know him, you know?"

He was so different from the guard this morning. Not better, not worse. More confounding, perhaps. Aster didn't know what to do with his genuinely friendly manner. She didn't know how many lowdeckers he'd beaten—if any—or how many times he'd stood by watching one of his fellows do similar.

She did know some of his life story. He'd shared it multiple times. He was an upperdecker, one of the few low-tier guards spawned from Matildan elites. He was the fourth child of five boys and, Aster suspected, the family disappointment. He wasn't handsome. She doubted him much good at school.

"And the man was old, yeah? Seventy-fucking-four. 'Sides, he's been sick for weeks. Who didn't see it coming? Took ill same day the blackouts started. Guess his heart couldn't take his ship falling apart."

Aster had known the timing between the first blackout and the beginning of Nicolaeus's health coincided, but she didn't realize the two events had begun the exact same day.

"Tell me, are there other guards I should be wary of? Off-schedule?" Aster asked.

Frederick applied Aster's burn ointment, slapping generous glops over his face. "Bayard and Timothy have been sent to guard the morgue, so things should be quiet until you get there. Holler if you need me."

Aster nodded her head, as was expected of her, but she would never holler for him, nor any guard. The remainder of her travels went without incident, and when Frederick had said the Surgeon and she wouldn't be alone, he meant it. Jutting Cliff Wing was filled with rosy-cheeked, rosy-lipped, rosy-gummed upperdeckers. In the nebula of pink, Aster stood out. Brown. All brown.

Bits and pieces of overheard conversation indicated there'd been an information leak. A woman with long hair braided down her back said that the location of the body was supposed to remain a secret. Everyone assumed he'd been taken to the B deck processing morgue, given his status. "Thank Heavens for loose-lipped servants," the woman said to whomever stood beside her.

"I still don't understand," her companion said. "Why go through the trouble of transporting the body down here?"

B deck's morgue lacked the broad range of surgical supplies of J's. They weren't necessary there. In the upperdecks, you lived, you died, you were processed back into *Matilda*, no questions. If they brought the body to the Surgeon, the Sovereignty wanted an autopsy.

"Oy, you, want to make a quick piece?" a boy asked, seventeen or eighteen, his face scratched with red blotches from unhealed acne scars. "I'll give you a silver piece to help me lug this." He pushed a handheld phonograph toward Aster.

"No," she said, then slipped by him. Coins, though not quite worthless, were of little use to her. A bit of silver held value on the upperdecks, maybe, but below L deck, only tradable goods mattered. He might've had himself a deal had he offered her a pair of new knickers.

A gray-haired man, fat, stood interviewing an inspector. He wore dark slacks that were too small, the hemline falling above his *medial malleolus*. Ill-fitting trousers aside, there was an elegance to his appearance. The spectacles about his face smartened him up. A perfectly trimmed mustache projected gentility. Aster stopped a few feet away to eavesdrop on his conversation.

"Inspector, sir," he said, "the announcement specified the suspected cause of death was a heart attack. Can you confirm that?" He wrote in a notebook, graphing ink onto ivory pages.

"At the moment, no, I can't," answered the inspector. "All I can do is reiterate what Sergeant Barrett already spoke earlier, that Sovereign Nicolaeus was found by one of his nursemaids this morning in bed, and preliminary reports say his heart gave out."

Aster smiled at their ignorance, haughty that she knew something no one else did.

She was working her way through the crowd when a man grabbed her from behind, grip tight on her elbow, pulling her whole right arm behind her back, jerking the shoulder. She could tell by the feel of his jacket that he was a member of the Guard. One of his medals pressed coldly against her neck.

All attention shifted to Aster, and many of the upperdeckers began to chatter in chorus, louder than they'd been before.

"Order!" a guard called out.

Aster's goggles filtered out the worst of it, dulled the lights and muted the colors. Still, vents hummed fussily. Up above, copper pipes shook. *Matilda* had a way of pricking the senses. That was to say nothing of the onlooking mob.

"My pass," she stuttered out. "In my trousers."

The guard slipped his hand into her back pocket and grabbed the pass. News reporters scribbled stories into their writing pads. Those here for no reason other than curiosity gossiped anxiously, their eyes set on Aster as they conversed back and forth.

"Does it check out?" asked another guard as he walked up, pressing himself between two onlookers who wordlessly observed everything unfolding.

"You work for the Surgeon?" an inspector asked.

Aster nodded. "Aye, his assistant," she answered, though she'd characterize it as working *with*.

The inspector led Aster through the wing's visitors, most of whom stood back as she neared. Once they arrived at the end of the corridor, a guard reached to pull the ringer. Aster said, "No need," waving away his arm. She inserted her key—a metal hole-punched card—into the lock slot. The hatch clicked open, and she entered cabin J-00.

X

The Surgeon smelled of witch hazel, menthol, and pine. A bar of soap, ivory and withered, sat squatly in a porcelain dish near the morgue wash station. The creamy lather that ran off the sides suggested he'd used it to freshen himself not long before Aster's arrival. He required of himself impeccable cleanliness, purity, perfection.

Aster had walked in on Theo once before, his shirt hung over a chair while he scoured his pale skin till it turned pink then red. Water, still wafting steam, splashed as he dipped a rag into a pail. She'd left, slipping out as easily as she'd slipped in, before he'd privied to her presence.

When first she met him, Aster thought Theo's obsessive hygiene a function of his devotion. Ritual cleaning was a standard part of many religious practices, and though Theo seemed to perform these acts more often than what was typical, his dedication seemed within the realm of reason. But in time, Aster saw his piousness as something more.

Belief played a part in it, but so did compulsion. He may have prayed five times daily because the scriptures demanded it, but there was no denying that independent of God or religion, his mind demanded it too. Pathologically inclined to blame himself for every wrong thing about the world, he thought that if he just fasted for the right number of days, recited his verses at the right times, he might be able to stop some of the bad.

Theo was not his first given name. Thirty years ago, his father looked upon him and wished to name him Sedvar, after himself, a dreadfully old-fashioned name with a meaning very unsuited to Theo: *merciless in battle*. "Merciless in *spiritual* battle might be accurate enough," he'd said once, attempting a joke. Aster and he had apparently reached that point in their association where it was acceptable to divulge irrelevant personal details.

"Your father was Sedvar Smith?" Aster had asked, recognizing the name of the sovereign who preceded Nicolaeus. They were dining in Theo's office, she sitting on papers stacked atop his desk, he in the dark-green leather chair with four scratched wooden feet, legs crossed.

"Yes, Sedvar Smith," said Theo. Aster had shifted her focus from the swirl of dark gray on his tie back to his face—which she'd recently learned he took the time to shave in the afternoon, in addition to in the morning.

She'd only known him for two years at that time, and there was never trusting a man who was son of a sovereign, nor was there trusting any man at all, or any woman, or anyone. Aster had softened to him more after piecing together the details of his life. He was the Sovereign's bastard child by a lowdeck woman, and he hated the Sovereignty even more than she did.

"Would you like to hear how I chose my name?" Theo had asked.

Aster took a bite of maize flatbread and dipped it into her tin of stew. "I am indifferent."

"Theo Thackeray was the protagonist in a series of stories my nanny told me as a child, revolving around the adventures of a farmer girl who solved mysteries—like, who stole the great harvest pumpkin, or where did all the draft horses go? So I declared to my father at eight years old that he was to never call me Sedvar again. I was Theo now, after Theo Thackeray."

Aster had known it was a lie, one of those convenient tales that was too spot-on, too cute, too thick with meaning to be

true. The real reason he chose *Theo*, Aster suspected, was because it was a name that expressed his obsessive devotion
to God. The Surgeon's love for the Creator and the Heavens
whistled from him like a birdsong: so much a part of him as
to be quotidian.

Now Aster washed her hands after stepping into the
morgue in preparation for examining Sovereign Nicolaeus's
body.

"I trust you made it here without incident?" Theo said,
not looking toward her.

"Define the parameters of *incident*," she responded.

Theo set his pen upon his pad, turned to observe her. His
eyes roved up, down. "You are uninjured?"

"Yes, though there was what you might term a close call.
I am recovered now, however." She wondered how much he
knew about the murdered guard, and if he believed she had
a part in it.

"I would've come for you, or at the very least sent an escort," he said. "You shouldn't be in the corridors alone right
now. It's a dangerous time."

"And you'd be wise not to concern yourself with what I
should and shouldn't do, as you aren't me, and therefore ar-
en't qualified to make such judgments."

"You can't dictate what concerns me," he said.

Aster found a smock to put on over her clothing, pushed
her goggles up to her forehead. "I am tired of being told what
I *should* do and what I *should* be wary of. Do you want my assistance with the body or not?"

Sovereign Nicolaeus lay split open on the table several
feet in front of her like the bitterest of grapefruits, organs
half-removed. Clearly, Theo had already completed the better
part of his investigation, and had only invited Aster here in
order to: a) confirm his findings; or, b) provide her with an
impromptu practicum.

"Has he been dead for very long?" she asked, letting the latex gloves snap against her skin as she pulled them on. The elastic hugged her bones pleasingly.

"A few hours, I estimate." Theo stood at the counter on the opposite side of the room, his back to her, and he barely cast a glance in her direction to say, "Come now, get started."

No stranger to the inside of the body, Aster stood loosely as she put on her face mask and waited to approach Nicolaeus's stiff, unmoving cadaver. Her muscles relaxed even more when she was forced to consider the problem before her. "Should I look for anything in particular? When you came to me before, you seemed pretty certain it was poison. Do you stand by that?"

He moved toward her, removing his gloves, their sweet, powdery smell filling the room. He had delicate, spindly fingers, made for gentle, fine tasks like crocheting lace and sorting beads and incising cadavers. Their skeletal, smooth structure stood in stark contrast to Aster's: stubby, calloused, and dark.

"If you plan to stand there and stare for much longer, let me know so that I can fetch myself breakfast in the meantime."

"Aren't you fasting?" she asked, though she had no reason to believe that he was except that he seemed always to be fasting.

"Pay attention to the matter at hand. You're stalling," said Theo. She noticed that he didn't deny that he was midfast.

Aster had accompanied him during autopsies before, but to observe, not perform. "I am incapable of a touch as light as yours. I will unintentionally crush him with my grip, and there will be no body left to examine." The excuse, though rooted in genuine self-consciousness, obscured the actual source of her reticence, and she could tell from the way Theo's eyes flashed to and then away from her that he was skeptical of her explanation.

"You're capable of far more than you give yourself credit for. An autopsy is no different than the numerous other procedures you've performed under my tutelage. You are more accomplished and diverse in skill than any of my colleagues. Go."

"Am I? Do you consider me your intellectual equal, then?" Aster asked, flattered by his praise.

"I do not," said Theo.

Aster was glad that Theo's eyes were not on her but on Nicolaeus. She didn't wish him to know the expression her face had taken on in response to his abrupt denial. She shouldn't be offended. For all his kindness, the Surgeon was a strict and precise man. Rules and rules and more rules and ever distant. It would be out of character for him to lie to protect her ego.

"Aster, you're not my intellectual equal. You're my intellectual superior," said Theo, biting his lip. "As far as one accepts intellect as a valid category by which to organize people—and I'm not sure that I do. But the raw data suggests you know more than me about a wider range of topics, and your ability to reason through complex problems surpasses my own. Which is why I don't understand your hesitation to proceed with this autopsy."

He scratched the bumpy skin along his jawline, red from razor burn. It was a rare sight given how meticulous he was with the blade. He was as distracted by the recent goings-on aboard *Matilda* as Aster was.

"It's now clear that your hand is not in this as I previously thought, or you wouldn't be . . . standing all the way over there." He waved his hand dismissively in her direction. "So, I must ask, why is my bold, brazen, blunt Aster suddenly so shy to examine a body? Once upon a time it was one of your favorite things."

Because Nicolaeus and my mother are inextricably linked, she wanted to say, *perhaps by more than their mangled irises.* Aster feared what answers she'd find inside the Sovereign's cadaver. Worse yet, she worried there were no answers to find at all. She had happened upon an erased chalkboard, and though she could see the unsettled dust of calcium carbonate, there was no putting together what had been written there before. Everything left a trace, but sometimes a trace was not enough.

"I feel like I am chasing a figment of someone else's imagination," Aster said, and instead of waiting for what would no doubt be Theo's perplexed reaction, she approached Sovereign Nicolaeus's body, ready to face whatever was there or not there.

Though upon reflection, *ready to face whatever* was not accurate at all, given what happened when she reached the cadaver. For the first time in twenty-five years, and for the first time since Aster was born and Lune had died, her radiolabe beeped. It beeped. And it beeped. And it beeped and it beeped and it beeped.

Though when she considered it more fully, Aster supposed it rather more clicked. The sound of Giselle's magic machine came to mind, which she'd seen described in *Night Empress* time and again, but could've never properly imagined. Aster had easily heard it over the noise of her world ending. Not the crack of the gun blast but quite before that. The bolt of the barrel unlocking, the firing pin cocking. The joyous, wondrous, satisfying *tick-tick* of parts working together in harmony.

"Excuse me, Theo. I'm in the midst of an auditory hallucination. Perhaps it's best I sit down." Disoriented, she braced herself on the metal slab where Nicolaeus lay.

"It's there, Aster. It's there." Theo grabbed her from behind by both shoulders and squeezed hard. "It's there, and I'm here, and we are both hearing this together."

She let herself slump into his arms, but only for a second.

She righted herself and unclipped the device from her medicine belt. The radiolabe that didn't work worked. "Mother, oh Mother, oh Mother," she said. Oh, how it ticked! Aster so loved the sound.

"Try moving from him," Theo said, and gestured to Sovereign Nicolaeus.

She did, and once two feet away, the radiolabe became silent. Close, it ticked. Far, it didn't.

"But radiation poisoning doesn't make any sense," said Theo, perplexed as Aster but clearly less affected on a personal level. She saw him eye the storage closet where the protective clothing was, similar to the suits she'd worn when visiting Baby.

"Maybe it's not meant to detect radiation. Or at least not the typical sort," said Aster, reminded of her days chasing ghosts in X deck, the radiolabe out in front of her. She had been so desperate to find a piece of her mother in those days, and now here she was, everywhere. Had been all along.

"Scan it over him," said Theo, and Aster nodded. The beeping continued as she did so.

She had difficulty accepting that the man before her had ruled Matilda for the last thirty years, and was now reduced to a heap of material pieces that in a few years' time would turn to dusty bone if left to their own devices. She removed her mask, as it scratched her face and pricked her skin and made it difficult to breathe.

"I've told you many times that we're to wear our masks always," said Theo. He had, but she made no move to put it back on.

The tick of the radiolabe persisted in the background, and made it difficult to focus on the body gray and decaying before her. Not that she wanted the noise of it to stop. She never wanted it to stop. She'd take to sleeping next to Nicolaeus's corpse if it meant hearing those sensors indefinitely.

"I might have an idea," said Theo, hand on his cocked-out hip. It wasn't a gesture he'd perform in public, and it was good to see him behave so unconsciously, letting his body move in the ways that came naturally to him. "Before, I assumed a botanical poison because—"

"Because you thought that I killed him."

Theo nodded. "Right. And my autopsy earlier confirmed my findings. That's why I contacted you. I think I was onto something, just a little bit off. Have a look at him, and tell me what you think."

Aster began with the external examination, checking the tips of his fingers and toes for needle marks, paying special attention to the undersides of things. Knowing Theo would've already run tests for the most common narcotics, Aster only did this as an extra precaution.

When she went to examine the lids of his eyes for swelling and popped vessels, she smelled an odd but familiar scent near his lips, like lavender but more bitter, with a streak of something quite musky. She could see why Theo would've suspected poison. Distinctive smells often suggested as much.

"The toxicity screen didn't reveal any of the typical culprits. Another reason I suspected your hand," said Theo.

"The irises really are quite remarkable." Aster had never seen such a thing in her life. "They look like broken gears. Believe me, if I could make a poison that did this, you better believe I'd give it to every upperdecker on this ship. Excluding you, of course. You were right to suspect me."

Aster continued her examination, noting the general wear of tissues. The same smell she'd noticed on his lips was in his gut as well. The lining of his mouth and throat were inflamed. His kidneys showed early signs of necrosis. His stomach was discolored and swollen. Aster wasn't a toxicologist, and she tended to work with bodies when they were alive, but she knew what the effects of long-term exposure to toxins looked like.

"Heavy metal poisoning," she said.

Theo smiled so wide it verged on laughter. "Exactly," he said. Aster smiled too.

Heavy metal poisoning explained why Lune's radiolabe might've gone off for Nicolaeus and only Nicolaeus. She could've calibrated the device to respond to a specific form of radioactive metal.

"May we use the centrifuge?" Aster asked, clapping her hands together and interlacing her fingers. She often begged to use it but there was rarely justification. She'd built one herself from repurposed materials for use in her botanarium, but it was hand-cranked and didn't have the panache of the one in the morgue.

"We may," said Theo, walking over to the counter to set it up. He poured Nicolaeus's blood into two test tubes and mucus from his stomach into another and told Aster to have at it. She clicked it on and watched it whir, the materials de-homogenizing beneath a shield of metal cartridges. Soon, the parts of the mixture would be separated into layers by type, the heaviest of them at the bottom, the less dense ones near the top.

After three minutes, the machine stopped.

"That was quick," said Theo.

Aster smacked the centrifuge with her hand. "It's broken. It still had several minutes left." She pressed the start button again, but nothing, and she checked to see that it was still plugged into the electrical outlet.

"See if it's done," Theo told her.

Aster removed the test tubes by hand, ignoring the tongs he would've likely used.

"Lord above," said Theo, voice soft and reverent.

The materials had separated, but not as expected. Floating

at the top of each of the five test tubes was a silvery, viscous layer, lighter than any of the other substances. Aster didn't know what metal in existence behaved that way. Lighter than water. Liquid at room temperature. She'd have expected it to gather as sediment at the bottom of the tube.

There it was, the poison that killed Nicolaeus. Maybe Lune too.

"Careful," said Theo.

Aster pulled her face mask back on as she extracted the substance from the tube and placed it onto a slide to view beneath the microscope. Her breath caught.

"What is it?" asked Theo.

Aster could see nothing of the substance's structure. It appeared the same through the microscope lens as it did to the naked eye. Whatever this stuff was, it was made up of something too small for the microscope to capture and magnify. "Look," she said, and Theo looked.

"Come." He slipped off his lab coat and face mask, grabbed the slide, and walked briskly toward the door, brown eyes alert. Aster followed him, having no idea what else to do. It was hard to turn away from his religious fervor, his dynamism.

The crowd parted for Theo as he whipped through the corridor, and Aster stayed close on his trail lest she be subsumed by the mass of zealous reporters. She lost track of where they were going except for a vague directional sense that they were traveling down. Soon they were in the lowdecks, but not the portion of the ship allotted to residences. They were in one of the industrial wings. "Why?" asked Aster, but as soon as she asked it she knew what Theo had in mind. The laboratory in the chemical-manufacturing plant housed *Matilda*'s only electron microscope. It surely would discern what the optical microscope missed and reveal some aspects of the silver substance's structure.

"Sergeant Hamilton," said Theo. Hamilton was hunched over a desk, scribbling figures onto a pad. Workers in the laboratory glanced up from their tasks.

"Surgeon, sir," Hamilton said, standing and giving a salute. He was a small, wrinkled man with graying hair. "I must've forgotten we had an appointment."

"You've forgotten nothing. My colleague and I require immediate use of your electron microscope."

Hamilton nodded and snapped his fingers. "Indrit, Jai, you'll have to finish what you're doing right now." The chemist in Aster wondered just what that was. Perhaps they were measuring the bond lengths of nanoengineered oranium or observing the form of hypercharged synthetic proteins—things Aster had only ever heard of by way of eavesdropping.

The microscope was taller than her, and she had to get on a step stool to reach the eyepiece. She inhaled, closed one eye, and looked.

"Holy, holy, holy," she whispered under her breath. She couldn't stop. "Holy, holy, holy, holy." She felt her body rock. Had it not been for Theo's hand at the base of her back, she'd have toppled off the step stool. The electron microscope was just as ineffective as rendering an image of the silver substance's macrostructure as the optical microscope.

It wasn't a logical thought, but she thought it anyway: *This is the stuff ghosts is made of.* She heard it in her head in Aint Melusine's voice. Aster thought to call it *eidolon*, after the wraiths of the ancient world.

It was no wonder why such a substance, whatever it was, interested a particle physicist like Lune. Wherever her studies of the electricity spikes had taken her—that was where the eidolon was. She'd found out one of *Matilda*'s secrets, and if anyone was *Matilda*'s secret-keeper, was it not the Sovereign himself? Aster needed to go where her mother had gone. There, she would find out the extent of their connection.

"Giselle," she said.

"What?" asked the Surgeon.

Aster shook her head and waved him off. She knew where Giselle was hiding.

XI

Aster ran to her botanarium straight after shift, barreling down and down and farther down. Running had become her favorite mode of transport. She lived for that brief snap of true flight, both feet in the air at once. Jumping down a half-flight of stairs then catapulting down another. Aerial Aster. Sky Master Aster! Barely Avoiding Disaster Aster! There was less time lost in transport when she ran as fast as she could, no care for her own safety.

She didn't know how long she had before her mother's trail disappeared. The blackouts wouldn't last forever, and after sham deliberations, the Sovereignty's Council would appoint Lieutenant *Matilda*'s new head. A calamity, to be sure.

Aster prayed in her lazy way, neither believing nor disbelieving, that the Council would give themselves fully to the show of it all. Righteous hemming and hawing over potential candidates. A vetting process. Debates about who was most worthy. It could take up to a month for them to decide that as sibling to a previous sovereign and as uncle to Heavens' Hands Made Flesh, Lieutenant belonged on the throne.

Aster tore off some bread from the stale wheat loaf in her cupboard, slicing off the moldy areas and adding generous portions of butter and purple honey. It wasn't much, but once—if—she located Giselle, she'd have time for a proper meal.

She rifled through Lune's notes and folders until she found the page labeled, *Fish Dissection*. She studied the circulatory system as she had before, paying special attention to those areas not shown on the electrical grid map in the Nexus. Aster could see a number of capillaries and routes that went to the fish's brain, what she'd been thinking of as the Eidolon Hub since this morning's discoveries, but she couldn't figure out how to get there herself. Shame, because that was where Giselle was hiding. Where Lune herself had gone in her investigations of the blackouts. The source of the power sink, of the eidolon.

Frustrated, Aster threw her radiolabe down on the countertop before picking it back up and clutching it to her chest. She wished to scan it over Lune's notes. She wished it would tick over the solutions. She wished and she wished, and though what she wished for didn't come, the act of holding the radiolabe reminded her of something. Ghost-hunting through *Matilda*'s corridors in X deck but also Y, where Lune had lived.

The end of the hidden Y deck shaft, of course. She had discovered it when taking language lessons with Ms. Bleeker, experimenting with her radiolabe. Aster had never been to its other side: a tunnel to the top of *Matilda*.

There was an old dumbwaiter line that went from Y up to Heavens knew where, no stops, out of service behind a wall no one questioned. To get there, you had to make your way down to Yak Wing, pry open the elevator doors, then climb the ladder in the shaft. Aster had discovered it when she was nine, after having language lessons in Yellow Warbler Wing. She'd wandered into Yak and found the strange metal hatch labeled, SERVICE LIFT. At the time, the letters had been unfamiliar, and Aster had to later ask the Surgeon what they meant. Eventually, she'd figured it out, used a crowbar with Giselle's help to pry it ajar.

They used to talk about making it to the very top one day and hiding out there. They imagined a hidden deck only they'd know about. Grander than the upperdecks. Full of swimming pools and gardens and spice cakes. Home of the angels transporting *Matilda*.

One night they tried it, loaded up backpacks and climbed. They made it a few hundred feet before having a sit on a wide service ledge. Stayed there until morning. The next day they climbed fifty more feet, sitting again at the next ledge, their little legs so tired and requiring a full day of rest. They did this for three days, surviving on canned peaches, having no way to cook the dried beans, rice, and oats they'd brought with them.

When they'd returned downward to gather more food-stuffs, they'd been caught, and punished *appropriately*, which, in the eyes of the guard who'd found them out past curfew in Yipping Wolf Wing, was a public whipping. For missing headcount three days in a row, they'd been locked in the brig-box without food or any human contact for a period of eight days. They'd abandoned plans of running away and dreams about the hidden deck.

That was over fifteen years ago. Surely she could climb it in one go now.

What she found was grander than the Field Decks even, a glass dome hundreds of meters high. Aster's neck strained as she peered up. It truly appeared to be a passageway to the Heavens. Maybe her childhood self had it right all along. Stars, them was stars she was seeing. Shining silver specks burning holes in the sky. Light-years and light-years of them. Too many to count.

She'd seen pictures before, mostly in *Night Empress* comics, but she'd always assumed the artist had taken some liberties. Surely, megaspheres of fusing hydrogen shined a bit brighter than what she saw in those drawings. Shouldn't it look like bombs going off in the sky everywhere above her?

She knew it was their distance that made them seem

small. How far away they must be to be reduced to dots. How astonishing to learn how colossal the Heavens were. Aster finally understood Theo's devotion. The spectacle before her deserved all of her praises.

Small shuttles were lined up in neat rows, some worn, some pristine and untouched. Giselle sat among a slew of papers in an area that Aster guessed was a runway or repair area, open and spacious.

"Quite the climb, yeah?" said Giselle.

"Yes." Aster felt blisters splitting the skin over her heels, arches, and left instep. She couldn't feel her legs at the moment, but she suspected when she did, they would hurt more than they ever had before, excepting instances of corporal punishment.

"Took you long enough," Giselle said, her tone equal parts playful and accusatory.

"I can't run away at a whim to chase after you."

"You could if you had your priorities straight. After all this time, how can you still be so caught up in their rules?"

But it wasn't the rules of the Sovereignty that hindered Aster. Her own rules did. Responsibility to Theo and Aint Melusine and her bunkmates. Most of all, it was her need to solve this mystery on her own terms in her own time.

Lune was her mother. Aster had lived inside of her. She wanted the same things Giselle wanted, but it was personal. It was her very own history come to life, breathing hot dragon breath all around her, begging her down its scorched throat.

A scientist, Aster had learned something Giselle had not: decoding the past was like decoding the physical world. The best that could be hoped for was a working model. A reasonable approximation. That was to say, no matter what Aster learned of Lune, there was no piecing together the full mystery of her life. There was no hearing her laugh or feeling her embrace. A ghost is not a person.

Giselle gestured for Aster to come closer. Nicolaeus's rifle was slung over her back, blood marred her clothes, and she looked beautifully demonic. "Check this out," said Giselle, holding up a sheet of paper. She must have taken some of Lune's notebooks and folders from the botanarium and brought them here.

"Giselle—"

"Don't worry. I didn't get smudges on them or bend them or whatever you're afraid of. I was careful. Now look. I noticed something."

Aster sighed and took a seat next to her, stacking the scattered pages back in order.

"All right, now first you got to look up." Giselle pointed to the domed glass ceiling, then stood and ran to a light switch, flipping it so the room was dark. With the lights off, Aster could see the stars outside so clearly. She estimated thousands in her visual range. "Does anything stand out?" Giselle asked.

Aster searched the Heavens, trying to identify a pattern, a bright spot. "I see stars."

Giselle ran back from the light switch to join her, this time holding a little lantern in the dark over the page she held. "Now look at this."

"Molecule models," Aster said, brow scrunched, though she knew it was another of her mother's tricks. The drawings of cellulose polymer, sucrose, cysteine amino acid could've been a biscuit recipe for all Lune's obfuscating.

"That's what I thought at first too. Or at least something to do with alchematics. But they're constellations, Aster. Look again, up at the sky, then at the page."

Aster set her gaze to the stars, searching for the same dots and lines in her mother's drawings, but saw nothing.

"*Look*, Aster."

"I am looking."

There was such a mass of them, bright and white, that she

couldn't sort them, or tell one from another, and they blurred together into a great heavenly array of sparks—until she saw it. The propane molecule. Three stars in a wide, obtuse triangle. Three carbons. Three stars.

"You see it, don't you? Don't you?"

"I see it," said Aster, feeling herself smile, though she didn't know what any of it meant.

"Your meema drew a star map."

Aster took the paper from Giselle's hand, traced her finger over the molecules disguising aphorisms, and kissed each atom, each star. She imagined the movement of her mother's hand as she drew the figures, fingers clasped around a pen. Were her fingers thin, delicate? Or stubby and meaty like Aster's?

"The only thing I can't figure out is this, here in the middle," said Giselle, pointing to a molecule of H_2O, drawn larger than everything else, the atom of oxygen directly in the center. Aster compared the star map to the night sky, and saw only a smattering of small stars in the place that the H_2O indicated there was something more significant.

"I am curious how my mother would have gotten up here. Certainly not through the dumbwaiter shaft," said Aster.

"Here." Giselle hopped up, flipped the lights back on, and led Aster up to another room. It looked to be a control center, sharing much in common with the Nexus. Consoles, switchboards, transmitters, receivers, stations with dials and buttons. There were papers strewn everywhere—all over the floor, taped to the walls, to the glass separating the room from the shuttle area. All of it, Lune's handwriting.

"You'll be pleased to know none of it's in code," said Giselle, "which is probably why I don't understand none of it." Lune wouldn't have had to disguise the notes she kept up here. The journals she kept in code were in case a guard confiscated them. Aster scanned the various papers. Ninety percent of it was mathematics so far beyond her that her eyes strained to make basic sense of it. Diagrams. Models.

"Back to how your meema got up here. I got the idea when I saved your ass from that guard, when we were running away and you lifted me up through that vent in the ceiling. See?" Giselle peered up at a metal plate in the ceiling of the control center, screwed in place. "What if she got in through there?"

Aster often thought of her mother, of the young woman named Lune Grey and her strange experiments, her Y deck life, her research, her suicide. She wondered how she looked. What clothes she preferred. How she felt about the Sovereignty. Never once, however, had she imagined her mother crawling through the ship's ducts like Aster so often did. It was hard to imagine the dead having adventures. It was hard to imagine her as a person at all.

Aster stood on top of the control board, boots pressing into dead keys, took the knife out of her boot sheath, and used the pointed tip to undo the screws. They were tight in there, and it took her several seconds to make the first bit of metal budge. She was up there for ten minutes loosening all four. Aster lay the thin metal plate onto the floor, then hoisted herself inside, struggling because there was nothing to get leverage on.

"See anything?" called Giselle from down below.

"Black," replied Aster, breathless. She crawled through the airway for several meters until she saw another vent plate, this one leading down into a staircase. She couldn't reach the screwheads from this side and used her knife to saw open the sides.

"Aster?"

"Get me the axe in the firebox," she yelled, then crawled back and reached her arm down. Giselle placed the wooden handle of the axe into her hand.

"Find something?"

"Perhaps," said Aster. She went back to the other vent and rammed the head of the axe into it until it began to split open. The toothed metal cut against her torso as she lowered herself into the staircase. She was at the top of the main staircase that went from the middecks all the way up to A and one level above, dead-ending into a wall. Aster pushed her hand against the wall, felt the plaster, the wood. Not quite a false wall, but not as sturdy as the walls that lined the rest of the stairwell. Someone had built it years ago to obscure entry into the Shuttle Bay.

Aster had a good idea when it was built. The disaster referenced in the recordings Theo'd let her listen to: 255 years ago.

Back in the Shuttle Bay, she watched Giselle, who looked more glorious than Aster had ever seen her, shining triumphantly with madness. A sky that was an actual real sky above her through the glass. The blaze of stars. There was an excitement coming from Giselle. She was standing on the edge of a new world and so ready to jump. How Lucifer felt upon leaving the Heavens. He didn't fall. He dove.

"I think your meema found a way out, Aster. That's what that thing in the center of the star map is. Maybe it's the Promised Land. Or something else. She knew how to get there."

"Then why would my mother kill herself?" Aster tapped the thick glass of one of the shuttles, the sound of it so dead she knew there'd be no breaking through. She reckoned it was the same glass that made the dome.

"I read that note, Aster. All it said was that she had to leave you. What if she didn't kill herself like you always thought? What if she was planning escape? Something bigger than you or me or *Matilda*." Giselle put her palm out, predicting Aster's protest. "We've all spent our whole lives believing this ship is it. If you knew it wasn't, wouldn't you give up everything too? I would cut out my own heart and throw it into the beyond for the split second it would beat somewhere other than this cursed fucking cage." She did not unravel in her rage, but became tighter: lips pursing, neck muscles stiffening.

"Why do you think I risked going to the Sovereign? For an adventure? Because I was bored and I found working shifts too dreadfully dull? It was because I knew he was part of Lune's secret, and Lune's secret is the way out. I have to get out. I have to burn this metal world of torture and despair." Giselle lifted herself onto the wing of a shuttle called *Lioness*. "I killed him, you know."

Aster exhaled a tremulous breath. She closed her hands into fists, widened her stance.

"I just thought it, and it happened," said Giselle. "It was so easy too, Aster, you have no idea how easy. First time I went to him was during the blackout. I gave the nurse 125 grams of poppyserum to take her place. She said yes. So I dressed up like her. Even in the light of day, the guards couldn't tell the difference. And he saw me. He said, moaning and writhing and coughing, *Who are you?* And I said, *Hello, Sovereign, my name is Giselle. I am your nurse today and here forward.* He said, *Aren't you pretty?* Then passed out. And every day I tended to him. And I searched and searched his room. You know what I found, Aster?"

Aster needed to know if it was the eidolon. She needed to know how her mother and Sovereign Nicolaeus were connected.

"Nothing. I found nothing. Until I put aside his trunk and moved the little rug he had underneath. It was such a beautiful rug. Dark red and this lovely arabesque. A magic carpet from a story. And under the rug was some hinges and a latch. And so I opened it. And there was stairs. And I walked down those stairs. And I saw it. The most beautiful thing I ever seent. It was this." Giselle pointed to the sky. "I saw the stars. He had his own view of the whole world that he could see anytime. There was a couch and a table. A cabinet of spirits."

That meant the sickness came through the glass. Lune had gotten it in the Shuttle Bay and control room. Nicolaeus had gotten it from his private quarters. The only two parts of the ship with windows, unprotected by the metal hull. Aster guessed it was a combination of exposure to eidolon and radiation from the outside of the ship.

"This morning, I was pacing about, wondering what I was going to do. And he said, *Don't you worry about me.* And I said I wasn't worrying about him. I was worrying about myself. And he asked me to come closer, and I came closer, and he was sick and lying back on his pillows, and he reached up and touched my lips, and I closed my eyes and wished he was dead. And he died, like that, on my command." She hugged herself tightly. "I haven't even cried thinking about what I done," Giselle said, but tears mixed with intraocular fluid in her eyes, glazing the whites surrounding her irises. Giselle, like Melusine, like Aster, was not prone to breakdowns, but sometimes the sorrow seized you. She appeared on the verge of collapse, her taut lines growing so rigid they'd soon snap.

"For so many years I believed my mother slit her own throat," Aster said. "Crawled into some forgotten crevice of *Matilda* to die alone because what is a life of only suffering?" She thought it might be right, good, nice, to reach out and lay her hand on Giselle's knee, that doing so might translate her garbled thoughts into a language Giselle could understand.

Instead, Aster tinkered with the pieces and parts of a shuttle called the *Fleeting,* until she found a knob. She pressed it—nothing. Turned it—nothing. Only when she twisted the tiny metal button counterclockwise did something happen, the faint sound of clicking, and then a keypad appeared. When she rolled the knob in the reverse direction, the keypad flipped and disappeared back into the door, no visible cracks or seams.

"I was never angry with her for committing suicide. I felt

only thankful that she had sacrificed her own well-being for so long in order to bring me into this world." She watched Giselle for a reaction. "They can beat me and beat me and beat me until every bone in my frail little body breaks, but until they kill me, I am glad. I am so glad." Aster didn't know why she was confessing this. The moment seemed right, she supposed. "But what if my mother really found a better world? What if they could never lay a hand on us again?"

It sounded like a dream, but Aster believed.

XII

V deck felt colder than Q and it hurt to breathe. The bundles of chickadee flowers burned by a young woman named Haneefa did not help matters. Vents absorbed and filtered most of the smoke, but the air of the cabin nonetheless thickened. Naveed's sallow face, usually a vibrant, olive-tinged gold, sucked in, creating cavernous hollows under her cheekbones. Aster could barely make out her wan figure through the gaseous particles of gray.

Naveed was with child, and ill. The other inhabitants of V-01003 had abandoned the quarters to give Naveed space and quiet. Only Haneefa, Naveed's older sister, remained. "A bunkmate is heating a tub of water in the head. They'll be back soon," she said.

Aster placed her hand over Naveed's forehead. "Her body temperature has already surpassed acceptable levels. Whatever the ailment be, I do not believe a fever will effectively treat it. The time for sweating it out has passed. Do not bring warm water."

Haneefa placed a small sheet of folded paper atop burning greenery, watched it turn to ash, then squashed the tiny flames with her hand in prayer.

Aster lifted Naveed from the floor pallet to the table and laid her on her back, careful to set her head down gently, like an egg into a nest. Naveed was nineteen years old, but slender and not particularly heavy.

"You're an ox," Haneefa said, fetching a pillow. "The way you carry her around like that."

Strands of Naveed's hair weaved through Aster's fingers. Naveed moaned weakly, the little black mustache over her lips wet with sweat. Aster fixated on every detail, trying to distract her mind from what she'd found in the Shuttle Bay.

She was jittery from anticipation, from cold, from anxiety. Restless energy made her heart thump in a steady hum. It hadn't taken very long in the control room to piece together more of her mother's story. The papers that weren't Lune's handwritten notes were readouts from the various consoles and stations. They recorded the entire history of Matilda's flight. Aster couldn't understand the logs, but she understood Lune's summary of the logs. Of particular interest to Aster:

> It comes as no particular surprise that this was the section of the ship to malfunction so catastrophically; it was the only section of the ship managed by the Sovereignty. Thank Heavens for their misplaced belief that only the most holy should be in charge of the direction of Matilda's journey, as that belief led to a good many of them dying.

> Measure twice. Cut once. It's not difficult. If you're going to rely on a computing console for your numbers, by Heavens, account for the mass of your own goddamn ship when inputting your data for the navigation projections! It's basic astromatics when a spatial condenser is in play.

> It was bold to plot a course through an asteroid field and a clever tactic to simulate the course of the asteroids to predict the best path. But for an accurate simulation, you've got to consider the mass of the ship and it's resulting gravity—not typically relevant in such matters, but certainly relevant when you've got a thousand tons of siluminium pumping around you, creating a distortion balloon.

Perhaps they hadn't needed such precision when navigating through empty space, or even when avoiding larger planetary objects, but it's definitely an issue when approaching a storm of gigantic rocks.

Aster loved to read Lune's true voice rather than the deliberately obscure personality she'd come to know in the other journals. For once, the answers were being handed to her. She'd learned eidolon's true name: *siluminium*. A rare metal that allowed *Matilda* to travel at velocities approaching light-speed by compressing space.

Lune's poor opinion of the Sovereignty was a joy to witness, as was her intellectual indignation at what turned out to be a significant calculation error:

An asteroid had grazed *Matilda*. The impact didn't break the hull, but it did dent the control area of the ship, metal pressing into the pipes that cycled the siluminium. The liquid leaked through, a large portion of *Matilda*'s uppercrest dying from metal poisoning days later.

Thank Heavens someone had the good sense to switch the navigation system to automatic. I feel we are safer in the hands of a machine than we ever were with those lot.

Aster was slightly more forgiving of the navigators than Lune was. At least the asteroid hadn't hit the glass section of the hull that made up the observatory dome of the Shuttle Bay. That would've caused a breach in the air supply, destroying the ship immediately. It didn't matter if the material was the same superglass that contained Baby.

"Do you need anything?" Haneefa asked, her hand on Aster's shoulder.

Aster wished she didn't have to concentrate so much right now. She wanted to think about Lune, eidolon, *Matilda*, the

Shuttle Bay. "I am going to lift your dress and reveal your nethers. Is that acceptable?"

"I'm not shy," said Naveed.

Aster placed her hand on the young woman's belly, which barely protruded at all. She pressed, imagined the fetus's tiny elfin shape. Barely the size of a nut.

"Did you take something?" Aster asked. "To extract it?" The symptoms were too pronounced to be anything like influenza. Red dotting in the whites of her eyes concerned Aster, and the blood vessels surrounding them were discolored and engorged. It was unlikely to be a sickness if no one else had gotten it. "It's fine if you did, but I need to know."

Naveed's eyes scooted toward her sister's, then she closed them, her whole face squeezing into a little knot. "Navi, what did you do?" Haneefa asked. She made the sign of the star over each of her cheeks.

Aster fixed up a dose of activated charcoal and castor oil and held the spoon to Naveed's lips. "Drink. This will help."

Naveed took a sip, coughing roughly, spit spraying on Aster's hands.

"More," said Aster.

Nodding, Naveed took another spoonful, then another, her face contorting.

Next, Aster removed the appropriate tools from her belt: a jar, some tubing, a large syringe for suction.

"What's that for?" asked Haneefa.

"To terminate," Aster said. "The fetus. Not Naveed. That is what you would like me to do, correct, Naveed?"

"Aye, please. Please. I'd have come to you first but I needed it right away and knew you were busy. It's just a small thing inside me and people are dying."

"Navi, you can't do this," Haneefa said. She wiped a wet washcloth over her sister's neck. She turned to Aster, her eyes widening. "They'll flog her for it, send her to the brigbox. I've heard of even worse happening. Night cabin checks are soon. A guard will see."

"No one will see. I move quickly and efficiently," said Aster. She rubbed petroleum jelly between her hands to warm it, then slid her palms over the ends of the speculum until the metal wasn't so cold to the touch. "She will not feel safe until it is out of her, and she will not begin to recover from what she took until she feels safer, calm. I will take care of the poison once the fetus is removed. Naveed, what did you take?" Aster spread her open. "Is this position comfortable?"

"I wouldn't call it comfortable."

"Acceptable?"

"Yes."

Naveed's belly heaved in and out several times, and she thrust her head to the left, spitting up a small amount of bile onto her sister's chest. When she calmed, she wiped her mouth, said, "I don't know what I took. Bought it off Jane from Quince Wing. She said it'd work."

Aster forced another dosage of charcoal into her.

Haneefa swore, grabbing a towel to clean the bile off herself. "That greedy cow would sell a ball of lint and call it a cure for cancer. For all you know, you swallowed a vial of arsenic, stupid, stupid girl."

Jane was the queen of snake oil and an embarrassment to the science of alchematics. Aster didn't understand why people continued to seek out her half-cocked serums. "What did it taste like?" she asked.

"Shit," said Naveed. "Deathly bitter, and sulfurous. I don't even remember what color it was."

The swelling in the eyes suggested something in the Evening Vein family, but there was none of the characteristic paralysis of the extremities.

"Tell me my stupid, stupid sister will be okay," Haneefa said.

Aster nodded, removed a cloth pouch, and sprinkled herbs onto Naveed's graying tongue. The abortion proceeded painlessly—a brief suction, then nothing.

"Do you know what it was?" Naveed asked, scrambling to get a look at the jar. Aster had already emptied the contents into a pail. "Girl? Boy?"

"I don't understand such things. I have to go." Aster took off her gloves, rubbed witch hazel tonic onto her hands. It was twenty till, and she could make it back to Q deck easily if she left now. "I will be back to check on you at my earliest convenience. The activated charcoal should be sufficient, however."

"Can you forge a pass from the Surgeon to get her out of shift tomorrow?" asked Haneefa. "She needs rest."

"I cannot."

"Please?"

"I cannot." She wished she could but she wasn't brave enough to do so. She was so close to finding out what happened to Lune. To finish what she started, she needed freedom. Getting in trouble would compromise her ability to roam the ship with few restrictions. Aster also had Lieutenant to think about. He might recognize a pass she forged. He was a careful and diligent despot.

"Sleep until morning bell, if you can. You do not look well. It is likely your deck overseer will allow you to miss without a doctor's pass."

She left the clotted tissues from Naveed's uterus in the jar. She would burn them when she got the chance, but for now they remained tightly sealed inside.

Vacuum fetal extraction had been the first thing the Surgeon taught her, and all these years later, she still did not like it. It made her remember she was an orphan.

Ainy used to tell a story about a woman who had thirteen sons, and each one was a god, born from the spirit of night.

Each son had a power: One to heal. Another to inspire nations to war. Another who could capture the essence of things such as flight in birds and transfer it to another (so the fish might soar, the blackbird might plunge to the depths of the sea). And so on. They started out well enough, raised up good by their dear meema. But after a time the world turned them into cruel gods and they made it nastier still.

This, as a child, had been the part where Aster grew interested. Magical godbeings were par for the course in Ainy's stories, and didn't necessarily lead to much excitement, but angry mothers meant bloodshed and trauma. Ainy herself was an angry mother, probably. She had no children by birth, but plenty by spirit. She was surely as disappointed in Aster as the godbearer was with her thirteen sons. That was the state of things, everyone disappointed because they all had too many needs, and no one could ever satisfy them.

In the story, the sons argue over who will inherit the mother's land, and instead of writing it out in her will and risking one getting angry, she puts on a fight to the death, the whole world their arena. She referees in the sky, and watches as they tear the planet to pieces, peers down upon them with great sadness. Then she leaves to wander the stars and the Perpetual Night.

It was not a satisfying ending, but Aster took it to mean: don't have children.

That was part of the reason she'd had Theo remove her uterus. It was a rejection of motherhood in general, and tangentially, a rejection of her own mother.

Aster gathered her tools, nodded a farewell to Naveed and Haneefa, and headed back home. *Home.* She bowed at the statue in front of the Valley Wing Temple, as was the custom here. Metal arms opened widely, suggesting embrace, but the face showed signs of world-weariness, cautioning passersby not to rely on her too heavily.

Aster loved that statue, and Quarry Temple had nothing like it. She went there now and saw the burned-out candles and torn books of scripture in languages no one could read. Women came there to pray sometimes, but Melusine had effectively turned it into a sick room for Aster. Q-deckers from many different wings lay on the wooden slats moaning, waiting to be fixed or to die.

Aint Melusine lay there on a cot now, preferring it to the claustrophobic den of proper quarters. "Excuse my lateness," said Aster, sitting down on a stool in front of her Ainy.

"You don't need to excuse yourself," said Melusine. "I know you got more important patients to see. I can deal with a little pain. That girl all right? Naveed?"

Nodding, Aster removed vials of steroid from her medicine bag and needles from her medicine belt. "I've found Giselle."

Queen of manufactured distance, Aint Melusine did not react at first. She hiked up her skirt so Aster could get at her knees. "She well?"

"No. She hasn't eaten since she left during the last blackout. I told her I'd have some food for her in the cabin if she comes back tonight."

"She won't come," said Ainy, shaking her head. She began to pull down her stockings. "Too afraid of the consequences of coming back. I can't blame her for not wanting to get beat. She's not a hardy thing."

"I thought if she came in the middle of the night, after cabin check, she could leave before morning curfew. It's risky, but Giselle has done riskier things," said Aster, remembering this morning.

"Where is she?"

Aster poked the syringe into the vial and filled it. "Do you know what a distortion balloon is?" The answer would likely be no, but Aint Melusine had been around a long time. Perhaps it had come up during the blackouts twenty-five years ago.

"I don't," said Melusine, sounding so serious. She always was. Not stern, just focused, solemn. She had the demeanor of a recluse forced into a town's mundane social goings-on.

"Do you know why a ship might draw from an internal power source some of the time, but not most of the time?"

Aint Melusine thought on that one. "Say there was a ship called *Danilda*. Say it was floating in the Heavens. Say an object in motion stays in motion because I heard that once. Like a marble on a wood floor will roll damn near forever if it don't have nothing to get in front of it. But say you want to change its direction. You got to give it a little flick with your finger. It only needs a flick every now and again. Aye?"

"Aye," said Aster. "Of course." *Matilda* used the magnets when she needed to change direction, drawing on the ship's internal power to activate them. That was what caused the blackouts. The automatic navigation systems detected another asteroid field, perhaps some planetoids. Aster made a note to look through Lune's journals to get a sense of what it might have been that caused the ship to change course twenty-five years ago and produce the wave of blackouts.

"I had a sister named Inertia," said Melusine. "Died. Ill from the day she was born. Mother thought if she named her that it would keep her alive. Keep her in motion." Her bare legs shivered, thick hairs doing nothing to insulate her from the cold. "Get on with it then."

Aster hated to do these injections, but the steroids were the only thing that kept Ainy's arthritis aches something close to manageable.

"Do it," said Melusine, her body tense as she awaited the painful injection.

Aster pressed the needle into her left knee, and Ainy

winced. Tears ran down her face, and it was the second time today Aster had to see a woman she loved cry. They were all such weak, soft things. Chalk.

XIII

Aster loved the hermit women in her Aint Melusine's stories. As a child, she fell asleep to the images Ainy's descriptions conjured. Wooden cottages and herds of goats. Porridge and gnarled walking sticks. These feral witches always had on them a pipe and a cough and a curse.

Ainy's stories of the Great Lifehouse made solitude seem attractive, and Aster wanted to be one of those women who could bear lonesomeness well. Ornery as she was, Aster knew much of being by herself, but as she lay in her cot shivering, she couldn't help but wish for a bed partner. The one she wanted couldn't or wouldn't come. There were some rules Theo risked breaking, but Aster doubted sharing a bed with her was one of them.

She hated her newfound neediness. For years, the only connection she required was to the toys she'd been given, a cigar box of ivory idols wrapped in a browning handkerchief. One stood the size of a middle finger, faceless, in robes, its arms crossed over its chest and its head tipped up. The other was more intricate, a woman aiming her spear into nothingness, a battle-axe on her hip, a bow on her back. It wasn't until she met Ainy that she was told the proper story.

Brer Boar gobbled up all the worlds before all the worlds could gobble up him. Then came Huntress. She chased him for millennia, his tusks ripping gaps through time, slipping out of her grasp always. Spent, Huntress decided to make a new world, shaped starfuel into a gas globe full of all manner of creatures. She hovered over it, watchful, until Brer Boar came to gobble it up too. As he charged forward, consumed with hunger from so many years of running, she slung her spear into his temple. She lay him into her lap, overwhelmed with such sadness that she wept, her tears freezing in the great coldness of the cosmos and making a magnificent frost bridge. She walked across it, carrying Brer Boar in her arms, and once at home she sliced his tummy open until all the worlds emerged again. She missed Brer Boar more than she'd missed the worlds.

Aster had hugged the hard, angry pieces to her chest. Passed around from one hot body to the next, the rigid lines of the statues were a lovingly harsh constant, till at three years old she found herself in Aint Melusine's arms. Ainy kissed the bone-wrought idols and said, *These are symbols of the people who came before us, whose lives were so great they became gods. They exist inside you because we all have a common Ancestor. Understand, babwa? They are far away from us now.*

Aster pulled blankets over her head, used the heat of her breath to warm the self-made tent. "If you can hear me, come. Please," Aster said into her radio, not expecting Giselle to reply. She felt guilty that she was calling on her to abate loneliness more than anything else, even guiltier that Giselle was not the first person she thought to call on.

"It's not safe," Aster finally heard through the radio, "and you can't make me come." Giselle's voice sounded hoarse, like she'd been screaming. Probably had. Shrieking at the glass dome of the Shuttle Bay in an attempt to crack the glass.

"Many of the guards have been stationed to watch the J deck morgue," said Aster. "The corridors are relatively clear. You need food. You need water."

"I'm not hungry. I'm not thirsty. I had some apple today 'fore I came back to the Shuttle Bay this morn'," she said, but Aster detected the breathy undertone that meant Giselle was fibbing.

"I saved some supper for you. Made it into sandwiches so you can travel with them easily. Buttermilk plantain biscuits and braised goat curry," said Aster, trying to make it sound enticing. Earlier, she'd wrapped each one in brown paper, tied them with twine. Giselle would love the pretty packaging. "And some vacuum flasks filled with fresh-squeezed juice. It'll stay nice and cold how you like it."

"Orange?"

Aster nodded as she spoke. "Mhm."

"How do I know it's not poison?"

"I tested it for you. I tested it in the botanarium," said Aster, and she had. Giselle would've known she was lying otherwise. "And I tasted it, and here I am, talking to you, not dead, not poisoned."

"They make a poison that just targets me. My cells. My DNA."

"That's why I also made sure to look at the food more closely in my lab." Aster couldn't test for everything, and she certainly couldn't test for a type of poison that existed only in Giselle's head, but she hoped the detection kits she had for arsenic, formaldehyde, cyanide, and heavy metals would suffice.

"It taste good?" Giselle asked.

"Ainy made it."

"Is there black-eyed peas in the goat curry?"

"I picked them all out for you. It sounds good, doesn't it? So why don't you come? You don't have to stay very long. I've packed it all up in a bag for you."

"It's cold down there," said Giselle.

"Then we can lie together under the covers."

"All night?"

"All night."

"I'll think about it," said Giselle, then cut off the transmission.

Aster waited, her radio on should Giselle reach back out, but it seemed increasingly unlikely she would show. One hour passed, then two, then three. What if she had started to come but was caught on her way?

Unable to sleep, she distracted herself with one of Lune's notebooks. She scanned over the passages, searching for hints.

After using the lavatory, I see the H deck guard in front of me. I stare into his dark pupils, unafraid. I will not run from him, nor will I indulge his protective instincts by seeking to move past him. So what if he apprehends me? Pushes me backward? All he has done is saved me a bit of time on my journey, so I might be returned to my quarters more quickly.

Aster knew it referred to the obstruction that caused *Matilda*'s piloting systems to redirect, because H *deck* was her code word for the *Heavens*, but she didn't know what else her mother was talking about. Frustrated, she tossed the notebook to the floor and switched to *A Concise Grammar of the Ancient Tongues*, focusing so that only Marcus Leavitt's prose filled her mind.

Aster scribbled notes onto a slate by candlelight. It was rare she needed to write things so as not to forget, but such was the depth of detail of the Ancient Tongues. Other books required she consult additional books at the end of each paragraph, and then additional books after that, ad infinitum. ("*Speakers of the common tongue become most familiar with old tongues through specific stock phrases, 'carpe diem,'[6] 'ad infinitum,'[7] 'in cognito,'[8] . . . et cetera.[9] But these languages are about much more than adding '-us' or '-em' to the end of a word. The Ancient Tongues are orderly, systematic yet vibrant dialects suited for taxonomy and the sciences or poetry and the arts. To know the Old Tongue is to know one of Common's greatest ancestors, and to know the ancestors is to know yourself [Leavitt iv].*")

Aster loved the way the pages felt, their heftiness, their texture. The paper hummed. Chalked with charts, diagrams, and tables, the book contained what a person could not—an order, a system, a rubric. Grammar textbooks reduced a language to something graphic and chartable, subject to scrutiny.

Aster welcomed these straightforward, detailed explanations after dealing so long with Lune. She craved clarity, transparency, and answers. She was tired of wondering. She wanted to get to the knowing part.

Aster felt water sprinkle onto her face and sprung up in her cot. She'd fallen asleep.

"Hush," Giselle said, "or you'll wake all the others."

Aster shuffled backward in bed when she saw Giselle still had the rifle.

"Don't worry. There's no juju in it."

Aster couldn't believe she'd risked carrying it through the corridors when there was always a chance of guards about, especially when it wasn't even working. "You need to give that here," she said, grabbing the gun. She needed to find a safe place for it where no one from the Sovereignty could see.

"Aster!" Giselle rasped, loud enough that the other women began to awake.

"What's going on?" Mabel asked, voice strained and whispery. She fumbled around for her glasses and took a long drink of water to soothe her throat.

"Aster stole something of mine," said Giselle.

Pippi rubbed her eyes and straightened her night scarf, pink rollers poking out from underneath. Vivian hopped down from her bunk and went to the sink to splash water on her face. "Is it morning already?" she asked. It nearly was. Giselle had waited almost the whole night to come.

"Give it back," said Giselle, and lunged at Aster to pull it away.

"Ladies, stop it," called Pippi.

Aster held the rifle as tight as she could, her grip weaker than she'd like because of her injured shoulder. Bruising pain swept across her back and through to her chest, punching the air straight out of her lungs.

Then there it was again, the explosive boom Aster had heard for the first time yesterday morning, louder now, this time making her ears whistle sharply. Around the cabin, the other women seemed to be experiencing the same, their palms pressed to their ears.

The rifle had gone off, the bullet impaling the metal wall. So much for no juju.

Undeterred, Giselle straddled her arms on either side of Aster's head. She was so close that her short hair fell into Aster's mouth, making her cough. At that, Giselle placed her palm over Aster's lips and pushed down hard, thumb blocking her nose so Aster could not inhale. Giselle's forearm pressed into Aster's chest, right over her sternum. "Give it back," she said. "It's mine."

Aster did not struggle, her body limp but for her arms wrapped around the rifle.

"Leave her alone," someone said.

"Giselle, you're really hurting her," said Pippi. She was crying.

"Mind your business," Giselle shot back, then increased the pressure on Aster's jaw, covering her lips and nose.

Someone began to light candles and oil lanterns, glints of mournful light shooting everywhere.

Do you know the story of how the lightning bug came to be? Melusine had one day asked. Aster knew the story, yes. An arrogant young god was the ruler of Light, and because Light brought him so much joy, he hoarded it close so that the whole universe was blacker than the blackest black, blacker than asleep, blacker than dead. But some of the Light was rebellious and escaped. God froze them with the might of his words to punish them, and those became the stars. But some Light made itself so small in order that God would not see, and flitted and flew around at will, prodigal luminescence.

Aster weighed too many pounds to flit away, and so

she began to writhe until Giselle loosened her grip. She bit Giselle's fingers hard, drawing blood. Giselle screamed and jerked back, clutching her hand to her chest. Aster gasped oxygen, dots in her eyes.

"I hate you. I wish I'd never come," said Giselle, and dashed out the cabin. The bag of food and necessities Aster had packed her sat by the hatch.

"You've got to go after her," cried Pippi.

Aster was already on her way. "Hide that for me," she said, pointing to the rifle, then grabbed the satchel by the door.

She ran after Giselle, and it didn't take long to catch up. Giselle was too weak to move very fast. "Leave me be!" she yelled.

"I will, but promise me you'll be quiet, that you won't draw attention to yourself," said Aster. "And take this."

Giselle took the bag and threw it on the ground, the carefully wrapped sandwiches spilling out. "You can't make me eat your poison."

"Please," said Aster.

"Oy! You two!"

Aster glanced behind her to see the guard approaching, Lemuel. She knew his name because he could often be found sneaking about with one of the women from an upperdeck, his fingers tangled in her not-blond-but-but-not-brown-either hair as she pushed him off, laughing, to say something like: *Lemuel, it's filthy down here. Is there nowhere else we can go?*

"We were just going to the bathroom, sir," Aster said. "We thought it'd be no harm since it's almost headcount anyway."

"Up against the wall, the both of you," he ordered.

"This is your fault. This is your fault. This is your fault," Giselle whimpered under her breath.

Another guard came from around the corner, this one older, his uniform more decorated. "What's this?" he asked. Lemuel straightened his posture, but this did nothing to fix his unbuttoned shirt, his ruffled hair, his loose belt buckle.

"I caught these two trying to sneak out, sergeant," he said. The sergeant regarded Aster and Giselle boredly and told Lemuel to handcuff them.

They both got the cane, six lashes against the bum, four across the back. "Strip," Sergeant Warner said.

Giselle and Aster both cried, the level of discomfort such that tears could not be unwilled to fall. It happened, like breathing, through no say of their own. Aster, sometimes, liked to count the droplets.

"Put them in the brigbox until shift," Sergeant Warner said. "Today's too big a day to deal with them properly, but that should get the message through."

A guard grabbed Aster by the elbow and dragged her to the hatch. She couldn't walk properly, sore as she was. Giselle got up to follow, limping, but Warner grasped the waistband of her knickers and pulled. "On second thought, not you," he said, releasing his grip so that she crashed to the floor. "According to reports, you haven't reported for evening or morning headcounts for some time."

Giselle balled into herself on the hard metal ground, but the guard pulled Aster along and closed the hatch so she could no longer see. The brig was a tiny cell the height of a cornstalk, the width and depth of a newborn colt. She could not stand or lie, only sit with her knees pulled into her chest, her bottom and back and everything aching like whooping cough.

Aster didn't realize she'd passed out until voices awoke her. She wasn't sure how long she'd been sleeping, several hours or several minutes. With her eyes still closed, she tried to stretch, but remembered she was locked inside a brigbox.

"Maybe things'll calm down around here then," one of the guards said from the outside. They spoke in a strange accent, but she understood, if with difficulty.

"Where do they do it? I've never been to one before," another asked.

"E deck."

Aster shifted as much as she could in the tight space and pressed her ear against the metal wall.

"I don't understand why they're doing it so quickly."

"My guess is to restore order. That guard went and got his head blown off and people've lost faith in the Sovereignty's ability to govern, what with the blackouts and all. This should get things moving back in the right direction."

Aster coughed loudly to let them know she was awake. "Water," she said. "Water, please, sirs."

Keys clanked, then the tiny door was open. "Out," one said, pulling her. It hurt to stand, even more than it did when they first threw her in.

"Drink," said the other, handing her a metal bowl. Aster grabbed it ravenously and started to sip, then stopped suddenly. She scrunched her face and twisted her tongue. It was piss. The two of them laughed riotously.

How pathetic that this was a source of humor for them, tricking someone into drinking waste. Aster swallowed, put her lips to the bowl, closed her eyes, and drank the remainder of the urine without stopping for air. She handed the empty bowl to one of the guards. "Thank you, sir," she said, then licked her lips and tried not to gag. "That was delightful. I love urine."

The guard grabbed her by the back of the neck and pushed her toward a metal box, not her previous enclosure but another in the room. "Just for being smart," the man said, "you're going back in." He unhinged the lock and swung open the door. Giselle sat crouched inside, her body a mess of flowering bruises: irises, peonies, pharynxia, sheep's tongue blossoms, violets—rhododendron in some places. Beneath skin, blood seeped from inflamed vessels. Giselle's head drooped to her chest. She wheezed, and her eyes were closed.

The guard shoved Aster inside so that she barreled into Giselle's body. When he snapped the door shut, she and Giselle were forced to embrace, their limbs twisting and joining like the molecule models Lune drew.

The men continued to talk for a few minutes more, until they quieted and left the cabin altogether. Aster tried to reposition, but it was impossible.

"You stink worse than death," Giselle said, the words coming out in strangled pants. Aster could feel her warm breath. It tickled her elbow and made her shiver.

"You're awake," said Aster.

"Been awake."

"I thought they knocked you out."

"They didn't." Giselle's voice shook, couldn't seem to find its footing.

"Are you all right?" Aster asked stupidly. She wished she hadn't.

Giselle released a loud, labored breath. "It was fine. I liked what they done to me."

There was so much to which the body could become accustomed. Aster used to think, *Never again—never again* or *I will would surely die*, but she never did. "I regret that this happened to you," she said, though she didn't know exactly what had. She could guess. The cruelty of the guards only took a few forms. They were predictable in their violence. "Do you wish me to—"

"Do you know what those men were saying?" Giselle asked. "I only understood here and there. What's a coronation?"

Aster had caught most of what the guards said, but had come in too late to understand the context. Giselle had provided the missing conversational link. "That means they're appointing the new sovereign."

Both of their breathing had calmed, reduced from heaves to occasional whimpering.

"Already? God above, I thought we had more time." Aster did too. "It's gonna be that man you used to always talk about it, isn't it? Lieutenant. Like the Surgeon said: You got to do something. You got to stop it." Though Giselle had never met him, Aster's stories had apparently been vivid enough to convey his darkness.

"Yes. I will march right up to E deck and tell them not to do it," said Aster.

"You could try. They might not listen to you . . . But what about the Surgeon?"

Before Aster could respond, a guard opened the door. "Back home with you," he announced, then led them limping down the narrow passageways to Q deck. This early, everything felt void, no smells of cooking, no wandering children crying for their meemas.

"Can I piggyback?" Giselle asked. Her voice came from behind Aster, who glanced back to find Giselle leaning up against the wall. Aster hoisted her onto her back, her forearms beneath the underside of Giselle's knees, which were sticky.

Except for a few straggling women, Quarry Wing was empty when they returned. None asked what had happened. Everyone else was already off to their chores, gathering eggs and heating baths. Aster eased Giselle down into the cot. "Do you want a bath?"

She shrugged, so Aster went to the sink and filled small pail halfway up with water, heated it on the kitchen stove. After it reached a boil, she filled the remainder with cool water and tested the temperature with her fingers.

Aster reached up to her bedpost and grabbed her medicine belt, took out a small pouch of dried calendula and a little vessel of silba oil, mixing them into the water along with a light squeeze of soap. Using a small flannel cloth, she began to wash Giselle, careful of the wounds. "Too hot?" she asked.

Giselle shrugged again. She barely flinched when Aster rubbed over the bruises with soapy water. When it came time to clean the in-betweens of her legs, Aster first squeezed water from the rag over the hair and skin, then sponged the area quickly in two swipes, stopping when Giselle stiffened and forced her eyes shut.

"Aster?"

"Yes?"

"Are you going to do something or not?"

Aster dipped the washcloth into the bucket, swirled, then wrung it out. "Flip over," she said, then finished with Giselle's chest, stomach, and thighs. Giselle turned slowly, and Aster draped the sheet over her lower half and got to work on her back.

Giselle grabbed Aster's wrist. "If you're going to do something, you do it big," she said. "Burn the house down."

"What can I possibly do? I am as helpless as you."

"Just something! Anything!" Giselle shoved Aster away, spilling the pail of water sitting on the stool and knocking Aster to the floor, her shoulder and back making painful contact. "I'm clean. Go. Go!" Giselle lowered her hand down and reached for the fallen bucket, only to bash it away.

Aster grabbed the chair and slowly pulled herself up into a standing position, using her boots for traction. She patted Giselle's back dry with a small towel, then brought the sheet up to cover her fully.

"Wiping me clean won't help. Neither will patting me dry. Neither will feeding me or giving me water," said Giselle.

Aster understood. Those were all such small things in comparison to the disaster of Lieutenant at *Matilda*'s helm. Drops of goodness in a pool of fresh blood.

XIV

The year Aster met Lieutenant, a decade ago now, she and Giselle still played house.

Aster smeared wood ash against her cheeks to make it look like she had a beard, then said in her most husbandly voice, "Bring me my pipe, stupid woman. I wish to read the newspaper and cannot do so without first having a smoke."

A girl a few years Aster's senior—seventeen?—poked her head in through the hatch, belly fat with child. "Ey, witch-freak, toss me my stockings," she said, nodding toward the bundle of soiled laundry beneath Aster's feet: her tuffet.

"Don't you know he's the man of the house?" said Giselle, playing Wife to Aster's Husband. "You better give him the respect he deserves."

The girl in the corridor crossed her arms and leaned into the hatch frame. "Fine, then. Witch-freak, could you please toss me my stockings, if it pleases you? *Sir*?"

"I am not a witch," said Aster. "I am a scientist." The *freak* part she could not contest and let stand. She tore through the pile of laundry till she found the girl's thick, off-white hose, one knee darned with red thread, the other patched with brown corduroy. "These?"

"Yeah, give them here."

Aster tossed them to her and cleared her throat to get back in character. "Damnit, Wife, I said get me my pipe."

"All right, all right," Giselle said. She tied the sleeves of her pullover about her neck, a makeshift apron, then dusted talcum powder here and there over the burgundy-colored wool. The idea was she'd been making butternut fry cakes and flour had spilled upon her. Aster appreciated Giselle's commitment to visual realism, and nodded her head in salute before unfolding an old star map to pretend it was the *Matilda Morning Herald.* "Food shortages continue as a result of the blight," Aster fake-read. The two remained for a good while in companionable, married silence, Giselle dusting, Aster reading.

It was a long time ago now, but Aster still remembered the way she counted down the minutes in her head, waiting to say: "Wife, I require supper. I am hungry, as the mental effort required to digest politics is quite taxing. You would not understand." She copied, perhaps exaggeratedly, those things she'd overheard when she worked the very occasional shift in the upperdecks, polishing brass mantelpieces as Mr. Jacobs or Mr. Callahan or Mr. Brown scolded their wives. These men had white skin and perfect clothes. "I said, make me supper!"

Giselle whipped her head toward Aster, swept the "silver" she'd been polishing (tin mugs) to the rusted iron floor. "Cook your own goddamn supper, fool, if you so hungry." She stomped forward wearing heels one size too large, crossed her arms over her chest. "Why don't you ask that slut secretary of yours to make you supper? Huh? Huh? You saw her again, didn't you?"

Aster slid her hands into her trouser pockets, and this time when she spoke, she used her own voice and not Husband's, the curtness giving way, the vowels rounding out. "This is the part where Husband would typically hit Wife as a punitive measure against her back-talking, but I do not want to hurt you." She spoke the words resolutely, prepared for Giselle to condemn her peculiar speech mannerisms.

Giselle had become invested in her role, however, and said only, "Hit me. I don't mind."

"Is this what you call a dare?" Aster asked. "Or are you

testing me? Is this one of your tests of my loyalty? I have told you before, I find those upsetting and an inaccurate measure of my regard for you."

"It's the rules is all. You're the man, and I'm the woman. When I get out of line, you got to pop me, so pop me."

Aster put down her fake pipe, stood. "Fine. I'll strike you so that we may preserve the integrity of the game, but I will do so gently, to minimize your physical discomfort."

"Do it hard," said Giselle, putting on her Woman voice, which sounded very similar to her fourteen-year-old voice, a notch more rasp to it. "Just don't do it so much that I start crying and carrying on. I don't want my makeup running."

So Husband smacked Wife and Wife fell back onto the cot. Aster climbed on top of her, Husband's knees straddling Wife's thighs, forearms on either side of her head. A small trickle of blood dampened the old bandage over Giselle's jaw.

Aster reached a finger down, drew it across the strip of fabric. "I seem to have opened up your cut."

Giselle's chest heaved. "It doesn't hurt," she said, but Aster was already sliding off the cot. Her med-kit was near the rest of her possessions, under her bunk. She removed a fresh cloth, adhesive tape, and cream she'd made a fortnight ago, using ingredients from her botanarium.

"Your face is your greatest advantage," Aster told her, quoting something her Aint Melusine oft said. "It is pretty, and it makes men favor you. So we have to keep it pretty." Giselle sat up on her elbows, and Aster returned to straddle her once more. She dressed the small slit, rubbed in the ointment to ensure there'd be no scar.

"Even if I had a hundred scars across my face\I'd still be pretty," said Giselle, braggadocio her armor, her only armor. "Come on. Back to the game," she said, the adhesive in place.

"What is Husband supposed to do now?" Aster asked.

Giselle's tongue swiped across the surface of her bottom lip slickly. "He holds Wife down and then *goes*."

"Goes where?"

Giselle rolled her eyes. "Just move around. You know."

"Like so?" asked Aster.

"Yes."

Husband rubbed against Wife and so on and all that, stopping only when he heard Aint Melusine on the other side of the hatch, bidding the girls, "Quit fooling around like little children. There are chores to do before Reveille, and the others have already begun."

Aster hoisted herself up, sat at the edge of the bed.

"Why'd you stop?" asked Giselle.

"This is childish, and you heard Ainy, I have to go do my chores."

"Aint Melusine won't care if you skip yours. I'll do them for you. Okay? We still got awhile yet before work shifts."

"No. I would like to check on the status of my plants," Aster said. She worked to breed, hybridize, and otherwise corrupt the florae in her botanarium, and as such, sought their company. They were her progeny, and she their mother. The wreath dragons remained of particular interest, stalky stems rising up a most deep shade of green. The parent plants, a tinny wreath and a corliss, produced hearty offspring, already surpassing their parentage. Aster hoped in time the fruit would produce an effective taste-concealing enzyme.

Giselle pouted, lips poked out like a keloid scar, but when Aster said, "We will play later," Giselle smiled, and so did Aster, and at the time it'd felt so right and like everything would always be good between them.

They were sisters, in spirit if not in blood, and in blood if not in spirit. They did not share direct ancestry, but like all humankind, possessed a genetic link that went back, back, back for generations, all the way to the Great Lifehouse. Back to a time when *house* connoted a specific breed of domicile rather than loosely calling to mind some vague notion with no visual referent.

"A house is like the tents women sleep in out in the Field Decks sometimes during harvest," Giselle had explained the very first time they'd played.

"So the point of the game is to pretend to sleep in the Field Decks?" Aster asked.

"No, the point is we act like a family. A real live family."

Aster liked to think of Giselle as her sister, her twin. She pretended they once inhabited the same womb. Hot and warm and pressed together inside their mother. A single zygote halved.

Aster and Giselle both turned fifteen within a month of each other and switched from playing house to doing theater. Had more dignity to it. They were adults now.

Girls and women who lived in their corridor plopped mattresses on top of each other to watch them perform, stacks of six, then stacks of four, then stacks of two, so everybody who came could see the stage. They did it in the Scullery, the biggest cabin except for the galley kitchen next door, which was too narrow to put on a proper play.

Wife stumbled onto stage, chest stuffed with balled-up knickers, and Husband handed her an old medicine bottle. Giselle unscrewed the cap and breathed in the contents dramatically. "Oh, what marvelous perfume," she cried. Pressing the package to her chest, she sighed in that way the women down on Q deck never did, but seemed common enough up on D, E, F, G. Women in Quarry Wing, where they lived, sighed too, but it had a different sound to it. Heavy and deep and quickly disguised as the opening notes of a dirgy lullaby. "Thank you, Archibald," said Giselle. "Thank you truly."

"Here—allow me to apply the fragrance to your bosom,"

Aster said, her speech still occasionally unsteady. What she'd meant to relay was Husband's desire to apply a dab of perfume from the jugular notch of Wife's sternum bone down to her *umbilicus*—navel. Belly button.

Different sorts of words belonged to different sorts of occasions, and Aster had not yet matched which went where. It was like what Aint Melusine was always saying, that Aster was *one who looked sideways,* or *one who saw through the corner of her eyes.* When you saw the world sideways, you couldn't always get a proper handle on things.

"How about we put the perfume on my neck instead?" Giselle suggested, and unbuttoned her collar. "It's too cold for the girls to be out and about and jiggling and all that noise," she added, her natural way of speaking slipping through the charade.

"No. That is not sufficient. If I wished it to go on your neck, I would have said so, but I would like it to go on your bosom," said Husband—not Aster—a distinction she wished maintained for the official record.

"My sweet," said Giselle in a wispy falsetto, a butchered rendering of upperdeck accents, "I think it's best we put the perfume on my neck, or my wrist. It's freezing."

"I am the husband and therefore I say what is best or not best." She raised her hand up, but unsure what to do with it, she let it flop limply back to her side. Giselle mouthed silently, *Come on. Don't ruin everything.* So Aster ripped Giselle's shirt open, no great challenge, as they'd done this performance before and had intentionally sewed the buttons back on loosely.

Smudges of black shoe polish and rouge covered Giselle's chest, made to resemble the aftereffects of aggressive suction, as in the case of a sexual encounter.

"It's not what you think," said Giselle, cowering, pulling at the lapels of her shirt in an attempt to conceal her exposed body. She dipped her fingers into a nearby pail of water and smeared liquid along her cheeks. Tears.

"What I think is that you've given yourself to another, like a wh-whore," said Aster.

"Love, you know me, you know I'd never be unfaithful to you."

Aster grabbed the bottle of perfume from Giselle and threw it against the wall. Glass exploded into fragmented crystals, and the audience gasped, some women pressing their palms to their mouths to suppress screams.

"Women like you are the reason we're stuck in this glorified soup can. How many times did you"—Aster paused for effect—"fuck him? Each time you went on your knees, that's another year added to our journey. Was it one time? Two? Fifty? . . . Fifty years. Fifty more years at least until *Matilda* reaches the Promised Land. You've made this Gulf of Sin. You've made it!" Aster sometimes liked to imagine her words were true, that all the bad things she'd ever done formed the fabric of the cosmos. *The Gulf of Sin*. Like the Sovereign said. Even though she knew science. Space was not sin. It was a vacuum. It was nothingness.

"Archibald, try to understand, please, love," Giselle begged.

Archibald did not understand. He took off his belt, folded it in half, and went at Giselle's back. Though they'd layered cardboard under her blouse earlier, Giselle called out and screamed and then whimpered and then whined and then squeaked, squeaked, squeaked, until an endless silence rocked the audience into applause as Giselle took her fake last breaths.

Aster's heart thumped, like it always did, but she noticed it more so now. "Giselle? Giselle?"

"Yeah?" she answered, resurrecting from the fake-dead to take a bow.

But Aster had nothing to ask, just longed to disrupt the silence.

Things were always going wrong back then. One day, Giselle got pregnant. She'd forgotten to take the tincture Aster made for her, so when an upperdeck man had her, a not-yet-a-baby grew inside her belly.

"Aster, come," said Aint Melusine, shaking her awake. "Dress nice and wipe the dirt off your face and try not to look so insolent."

It was barely morning, only four o'clock. The other girls slept soundly in their cots. At five, guards would come to wake them for headcount. That meant Aster, Giselle, and Ainy had an hour to do their business before returning back to quarters.

Giselle slumped against the hatch, wearing her best outfit: a cornflower-blue frock, long-sleeved, with a smart white collar. Black stockings. Brown shoes that were not so beat up as the other pair she owned. "I don't want to go," she said.

"You wish to keep your offspring?" Aster asked.

"No—just. I don't want to go. I want to wake up and have it be over."

"It will be fine," said Aster. It was the sort of thing she'd heard others say in similar circumstances, and she hoped the adage applied now.

Aster stumbled in the low light, pulled blue tweed trousers over her long johns.

"Do something with that hair," said Aint Melusine.

So Aster fixed it into a thick flat braid and put on a cap. "Sufficient?"

"Hardly," Aint Melusine said. "But it'll have to do."

Aster spun the handwheel to open the hatch, and Giselle reached out and grabbed her by the wrist. "Can't the man come to me to do it?"

"We don't have time for this, child," Ainy said. Then she muttered something in patois, difficult to translate, but meaning something close to, *Fretting is for people who can afford to fret.*

"Why can't you do it, Aster?" Giselle asked. "You're always going on about being a great scientist and all the things you can make. So can't you create something that will make it go away?"

"I know of nothing that wouldn't hurt you too," Aster said.

"Then let me get hurt. Let me get so sick I almost die. I'd rather that than go. Please don't make me. They will get me and they will hurt me." Giselle turned to Ainy, clutching her shirt.

"You know I will carry you kicking and screaming if need be," said Aint Melusine. She pressed her palms over Giselle's, squeezed, then pushed them away. Aster went to her med-kit, removed the bottle she'd given Giselle before, on those occasions her braveness left her and she could not leave the cabin.

At the time, in those days, still an adolescent, Aster thought Giselle's cowardice an expression of hypervigilance, a logical but inflated reaction to *Matilda*'s dangers. After curfew especially, the guards who patrolled the corridors embraced lawlessness—one of those words that didn't mean what it meant. *Lawlessness* suggested the laws forbade such violations. They did not.

Though her surroundings amplified her fears, Aster knew now, years later, that Giselle's phobias and anxieties breeched into the territory of psychosis: a paranoia difficult to identify because so many of Giselle's concerns made sense.

"Take one spoonful," Aster had said, handing Giselle the medicine. Giselle swallowed the viscous, tangy liquid.

"Ready?" Ainy asked, already in the corridor.

Thirty seconds passed before Giselle ventured a step.

"See? My tough little woman," said Ainy.

Giselle did not appear heartened, but the medicine restored some of her cocksureness. She walked head up, behind Aster, Ainy's arm wrapped tight around her. Should anyone see them, they looked innocent enough. A grandmother and her grandbabies. Out past curfew, yes, but not for anything nefarious. This was what they'd say. Aster hoped it would work.

When they completed their upward journey, Giselle fingered the fabric of her frock so that the skirt bunched up and more of her legs were visible, revealing scratches on her skin where she sometimes picked at herself. They'd arrived at their middeck destination, and Aster straightened before knocking in the code they'd been instructed to use. Three taps in quick succession—a lone tap, then two taps.

The sound of the lock undogging, the creak of the spinning wheel, and finally the whine of the hatch opening. They entered the small cabin of a middeck woman with white skin and graying hair. "You're late. He's waiting for you." She spoke in Middle, so Melusine and Giselle couldn't quite understand, though Aster translated for them.

"Do you have the required payment?" the woman asked.

"Yes, and you will receive it following the successful completion of the service," Aster replied. She looked about the finely decorated cabin for the man they'd come to see. The middeck woman stalled by putting on water for tea. It wasn't until the rose leaves were steeping in hot water that he appeared from behind a curtain: the Surgeon. His eyes scanned briefly over Melusine, Giselle, and Aster.

"Heavens' grace upon you," he said in the Low dialect, and unlike the other upperdeckers Aster had thus far met in her life, he possessed no discernible accent. Still, Aster tensed upon hearing it. The precision of his vowels and the overpronunciation of his consonants gave the musical language a strange rigidity.

Where she'd expected a kindly, ineffectual, elderly white man was instead an imposing young anomaly. His black hair shined with multiple coats of pomade. Thick, heavy eyebrows, hairs curling coarsely at the sharp arches. Pale skin but with a definite olive-brown undertone. Brown eyes and dilated pupils. He was little more than a boy, no more than five years her senior—twenty, twenty-one, if she was being generous. His presence was that of someone much older.

"Heavens' grace upon you too, sir," said Ainy and Giselle.

Aster offered no greeting. She noted the small silver rings that pierced the round edges of his ears. Nine on either side. Prayer rings, for the recitation of the Heavenly Litany. The sight of them sent Aster's heartbeat awry. She didn't like religion because religion didn't like her, often treating her cruelly. She crossed her hands behind her back, clasping them tightly so she wouldn't fidget. "Do you consider yourself very devout?" she asked him, knowing the question was a non sequitur, not caring because she needed to investigate.

The Surgeon tilted his head to the side, squinted. "You mean, am I devout to my patients? Of course. Yes. I provide a service, and it's my duty to maintain a certain level of care and professionalism." The words themselves were mundane, no different than the ones a shoe salesman might use to describe his trade; but beneath the content of his speech crackled a tone of self-conscious indignation. Even Aster, who frequently missed tonal shifts altogether, heard it.

"You have misunderstood the question," she said. "What I meant was, are you devout to God?"

That seemed to perplex the Surgeon even more than the first version of the question, but he answered, "Yes."

Aster turned to Ainy and Giselle, jutted her head to the entryway. "We must leave."

"What?" said Giselle, but had no problem moving toward the hatch.

Aint Melusine grabbed her by the shoulder and jerked her back. "Excuse me, Aster, but you're the child here. That means you don't bark orders. I do the telling, and you do the listening," she said.

"It's a trap," said Aster.

Giselle sidled up close behind Aster, either for protection or to intimate a sentiment of I-told-you-so. Aster had not considered the legitimacy of Giselle's concerns, knowing how prone she was to anxiety. Rumors of Matildans advertising abortion services falsely, only to turn in anyone who sought those services to the Guard, circulated the lowdecks.

"This isn't a trap," said the middeck woman whose suite they occupied. "You expect me to dog the hatch and pull out a knife and hold you hostage until the Guard arrives? You're being dramatic, and wasting my time."

"Enough," Melusine said. "You think you know everything, but you don't. The next time I have to remind you your place, you get hit, and it's gonna knock you out, and you're gonna wake up with a busted lip and a broken tooth. And maybe then you'll think twice before talking."

Which seemed a curious thing for Ainy to say because in actuality, Aster always thought *thrice* before talking, having said the wrong thing too many times. "I was only try—"

"Don't interrupt me. I was the one to seek Theo out. Me. You don't trust your Ainy to mind all her p's and q's? Like she's not the one who feeds you and clothes you? Like I'm some provincial who can't tell real gold from paint?"

"Theo?" Aster said, and glanced over to the Surgeon, who stood stiffly, face placid and unperturbed by the goings-on. "You know this man?"

"I wouldn't bring her to someone I didn't," said Ainy.

Aster looked again at the rings on the man's ears, licked her lips.

"Are we all ready, then?" the Surgeon—Theo—asked.

He pulled back the same curtain from which he'd emerged. "There is room for only two of you."

Ainy made to go, but Giselle reached for Aster and clung. "Please, Aint Melusine? I want Aster," she said.

"Fine." Ainy limped to a lush velvet couch with pristine wood feet.

The Surgeon led them behind the partition, where there was a brown leather recliner. "Sit."

Giselle plopped down, moved the lever on the side so that the footrest popped up.

"Would you like a sedative?" he asked. "It is very mild, and it will calm you, which will help relax your muscles and make all of this go more smoothly."

"Already had some," Giselle said. "Aster gave me something real good before we left Quarry Wing."

The Surgeon's gaze flashed to Aster. "You gave her poppyserum?"

"No," said Aster. "Absolutely not."

"Alcohol, then?"

"All I gave her was a small dosage of anxiolytic, a benzodiazepine to be specific, which I synthesized myself. Traveling in the corridors can be dangerous. I did what was necessary so that we could keep our appointment."

The Surgeon turned on a faucet and stuck his hands beneath, skin reddening from the heat of the water. After he rolled his cuffs up to his elbows, he soaped himself, lather turning his black hair white. "You synthesized your own benzodiazepine? That's very impressive."

"It wasn't difficult," said Aster.

In truth, she'd not synthesized anything at all, only dissolved pills she'd stolen from an upperdeck woman into an herbal solution that heightened the calming effects of the drug. She'd tried to make it herself, her burgeoning interest in alchematics being what it was, but the books she found confused and then upset her. She hardly knew yet how to solve stoichiometric equations, let alone how to carry out nucleophilic substitution.

"You're a healer?" asked the Surgeon.

"An alchematician."

"An *aspiring* alchematician. She couldn't even figure out what to give me to take care of this," said Giselle, patting her lower abdomen.

The Surgeon pointed to a stool, and Aster sat, watching him as he worked. He didn't speak, and though only a few cubits separated them, Aster felt that to touch his hand she'd have to first journey across a gulf the width of the universe itself, which she understood from her studies of physics was constantly expanding.

"Do you need help?" asked Aster.

"No," he said, so she took out her flip pad and wrote, drawing detailed diagrams of each tool he used, writing notes about his process. She wanted to say, *Like your job is so hard*, but the measured movements of his hands were a sight to behold, and as she watched her own grasp a pen, she saw only how, in comparison to his, they seemed big and stumbling.

Afterward, when it was done, Giselle wobbled on uncertain feet out to the main room in the cabin. She and Ainy leaned up against each other. Aster handed the middeck woman the agreed-upon payment: a bundle of freshly spun kashmir wool, dyed a rich shade of violet.

As they gathered to leave, Aster saw the Surgeon without the white coat. His crisply starched shirt gleamed the brightest white. The triangle knot of his tie was centered just so. He was effeminate in a way she hadn't noticed before in his doctor attire. Maybe it was how clean shaven he was, when many men on *Matilda* preferred a dash of stubble—more had beards. It was a sign of youth, folly, and girlishness not to have a beard, and it was surprising that a highdeck man had gotten away with having such a smooth face.

"Which deck do you need to get back to, Ms. Melusine?" Theo asked.

"Q. Quarry Wing."

The middeck woman lived on M, which meant a homeward sojourn of four stories.

"We'll make it if we hurry," Aster said.

"Does it look like we're in any position to hurry?" Aint Melusine snapped.

"Perhaps we could stay here. We'd miss headcounts, but we could explain that away later," said Giselle.

The middeck woman shook her head. "My husband works for the Guard. His shift ends soon. We're cutting it close as is."

The Surgeon tidied the other section of the cabin, folding up the partition neatly into a canvas carrying case. Tools lay in an even row across the shelf, to be packed up into his medicine bag. He had nothing to worry about. Upperdeck men could travel freely despite the hour.

"If you'd told us your husband was a guard, we'd have made arrangements to meet Theo somewhere else," said Aint Melusine.

"Had you been on time, it wouldn't be an issue," countered the middeck woman. She closed her eyes, released a whistled breath through pinched lips. "Please. Leave."

I'm no saint, Ainy always said. But Aster knew better. Only Melusine could unknot the tangles in old skeins of yarn like it was nothing.

"How much time we got?" Giselle asked, Ainy's arm slung over her shoulder.

"Nine minutes." Aster stood one pace ahead of them, but to their side, so she could see them clutched together in her peripheral vision.

"Is that enough time?" asked Giselle.

"Not likely."

Giselle held tighter to Aint Melusine.

"We'd be fine for time if you hadn't held us up," said Ainy.

Aster hushed them, index finger pressed to her lips. "I heard something."

They approached the staircase with light feet. "Seven minutes," Aster whispered at the foot of O deck. "We'll cut through Ocean Wing here. Fewer guards." She held her breath, but could still smell the must. Women here left their boots outside their cabins. Every third bulb flickered half-dead in the ceiling, dimly lighting their way.

"Five minutes till headcount," said Giselle.

"Four," Aster corrected.

They walked single file, bodies diagonal, to fit down the maintenance stairwell. Beyond the walls, Aster heard the sound of guards coming on to morning shift. They stomped down the main steps in their thick-soled combat boots. Then—"*All residents of P deck, Q deck, and R deck—awake! All residents of P deck, Q deck, and R deck—awake! Headcounts to commence. Any residents found outside of their quarters will be seized without hesitation, including any women who have temporary housing in the wings designated for pregnancy and child rearing.*"

"I must leave you two here," Aster said, peeking through the glass of the door that led to the corridor.

"That's the exact opposite of what you got to do. Stay with us," said Giselle.

"I will cause a distraction at the end of Quince Wing so that you two can make it safely back. It is a simple matter. One caught is better than three caught."

"What about zero caught? Isn't that best of all?" Giselle said.

"What is best of all is often not physically possible. I will be fine."

"There's no good reason for you to play sacrificial lamb," said Ainy. "What are you playing at?"

"I'm playing the odds—which state that most mornings two guards stand on either side of Quarry to catch last-minute sneak-ins."

"But what about missing headcount?" asked Giselle.

"I will suffer the consequences."

"Aster . . ." said Ainy.

"It is done. Go."

Aster smashed the temperature gauge and the alert bell rang. Moments later, guards ran toward her, but she stood firm, hands resting atop her head in surrender. She squeezed her eyes shut and waited for them to do whatever they wished to do. "Grab her," one said.

They barked orders at each other she couldn't make out and pushed her along the passageway. She landed against a wall, palms out, wrist twisting upon impact. Her fingers spread out before her like five rivers on a map, ending abruptly, leading nowhere. There was no stopping it, this violent requisitioning of her person, and she let them drag her up several decks to the interrogation room. She opened her eyes and colored dots appeared in her vision. In her periphery, she swore she saw Death curtsy. Guards rarely got so violent that women died, but it seemed they were experts at toeing that line, making you think, *This is it.*

"Sit down," said one of the guards, throwing her into a metal-walled room. Aster sat on the provided stool. "Hands out." She complied. He cuffed her hands to a bar on the table and told her to wait before leaving her in the room alone. After several minutes the hatch opened again and two men entered, one in a maroon uniform, the other wearing a long white coat: the Surgeon. Aster focused on the rhythmic inhale and exhale of oxygen, felt her lungs fill then subsequently empty.

"Good morning," Theo said. He and the uniformed guard

took a seat across from her. He looked at her for four seconds—Aster counted—perhaps trying to tell her something with his eyes. His expression revealed nothing, or if it did, Aster did not know what.

"Do you want to tell us why you were out after curfew, found vandalizing Matildan property, with forged passes in your pocket?" the uniformed guard asked.

"No."

He slammed her wrists harder onto the table and tightened the cuffs. Aster closed her eyes but didn't call out as she felt the hairline fracture on the outward bulge of her radius.

"Did that hurt, poppet? I bet you'd like me to loosen those," said the guard. Aster opened her eyes and watched him. His placard read, *Officer Ivsik.*

"Poppet?" she said. Sweetie, sweet, sweets, sweetling, dear, dearie, dearest, pumpkin, dumpling, biscuit, griddle-cake, cornbread, munchkin, love, duck, flower, rose, blossom, petal, and *poppet.* "Is that a variety of flower? A miniature poppy?" She thought herself quite versed in florae, but poppet—that was new.

The Surgeon, not Ivsik, was the one to answer her. "Poppet is a bastardization of the word *puppet*—historically used as a term of endearment for young children, because of their doll-like stature—but has expanded in scope."

"I am not a puppet," said Aster.

Theo nodded. "It's not the term I would've chosen for you." He cast a glance toward Ivsik. "Officer, I will speak with our detainee alone. Dismissed."

Ivsik nodded curtly and saluted. "Yes, General," he said as he exited.

"I can remove those for you," said the Surgeon, gesturing to the cuffs then reaching into a pocket of his white coat.

"General?" Aster said.

"I know *Surgeon* is a morbid moniker, but in reality it's

simply shorthand for *Surgeon General*. That is its main usage, anyway." His hands hesitated near hers for several seconds before he slipped a key into the lock of her cuffs and released her.

"I didn't realize you were a member of the Sovereignty's Guard, let alone in such a high position." Aster rubbed her wrists, which were red where the shackles had been.

"We didn't meet under circumstances that allowed for small talk. There's a lot you don't realize about me, and our association has been brief enough that I haven't had an opportunity to prove your assumptions about me false." He sat with his hands crossed in front of him on the table, fingers arranged evenly, purposefully.

Aster reached into her pocket and removed a bottle of aloe, rubbed the juice over her wrists.

"I didn't plan this, Aster. When I received word that someone of your description had been seized, I understood what happened and came to you to help. I can only do that if you trust me, however."

Aint Melusine trusted him. He had performed his duty remarkably well only an hour ago. Had he intended harm, he could've done so under much less convoluted means. "I . . . I am willing to place my trust in you at this moment."

"Then please answer all of these questions very carefully." He removed a pad from the breast pocket of his white coat. "Are you a rebel against the Sovereignty?"

"No," said Aster.

"Then why did you damage the ship?"

"Because—"

"I said answer carefully."

Aster searched for the right answer, the careful answer, but like so often with people, she had no idea what he was after.

"Isn't it true that you didn't damage the gauge at all? You

saw someone else commit the act, but didn't get a good look at their face, having arrived at the scene late?"

She tapped her fingers against the table and stared at Theo. "That is . . . not true."

"Do you know what a lie is?" he asked.

She paused in case this was a trick question. "Yes." It was like her games with Giselle. House. But those lies she had time to rehearse, and still she often messed up.

"Now is the time to lie, Aster. Do you understand?"

"I understand." She did, but that didn't mean she'd be able to perform. She would disappoint him.

"Come, now, we must get this: You didn't smash the gauge. You were going to the head. The one in Quarry Wing is flooded. Isn't that right?"

"That's right." It was.

"That's when you saw someone commit the vandalism. When you understood what was going on, you tried to apprehend the delinquent, but you heard the guard coming and were afraid. Under no circumstance were you returning from a clandestine and illegal procedure in Mist Wing, and you haven't seen me before."

Aster took a breath and repeated the story for practice, like learning her lines: "I tried to apprehend the delinquent, but I heard watchmen coming and got afraid. Under no circumstance was I returning from a clandestine and illegal procedure in Mist Wing, and I've never seen the Surgeon before . . . Was that all right?"

She could tell that it was not by the way he bit his lower lip.

"Not quite. Don't say that last bit. When you are saying your lie, you must remember to not reveal your true actions. That's all I meant."

She expected a reprimand but his criticism was far gentler than Giselle's ever was. She tried not to give him too much credit for it. People were so often mean that when they weren't, there was a tendency to bestow sainthood upon them. Aster did not reward common decency with her affection.

"Do you think you've got it?" asked Theo.

"Yes. I didn't break the glass. Someone else did. I was just out of my cabin looking for a toilet."

"That's what I assumed. Come." The Surgeon stood up and gestured for Aster to follow. "I have to restrain you again."

She placed her hands in front of her, and he slid the cuffs on loosely. When his fingertips brushed against her, they were nearly as cold as the metal that encircled her wrists.

Outside the hatch, in another small room, waited another guard, this one high in rank judging by the silver medals pinned to his wool maroon jacket. *Captain Lieutenant Smith.* He shook the Surgeon's hand warmly. "Did you find out anything useful, lad?"

Theo pulled away from the handshake. "I believe this young woman was in the wrong place at the wrong time."

"*Young woman,*" Captain Lieutenant Smith repeated. "That's a generous title."

The man appraised her. Aster looked at him right on, didn't let her eyes wander aimlessly away like she wanted them to do.

"Yet you were still out past curfew, weren't you?" he asked.

"I was."

"Address me properly."

"I was, sir," Aster said. "Captain Lieutenant Smith."

"You may refer to me as Lieutenant."

"I was, Lieutenant, sir." She couldn't remember which question she was meant to be answering.

"And do you know what *Lieutenant* means, pigeon?"

"It means—I do not know. It is a rank in the Guard. You are Captain Lieutenant?"

He smiled, as she'd given the answer he wanted. This was

always the case when people asked if you knew what something meant. They didn't want you to know it. They wanted to be able to explain it themselves, to prove themselves bearers of esoteric knowledge. Of course, Aster knew that *lieu* meant *place*, as in, *in lieu of, in place of,* and *tenant* meant *holds*, as in, *a tenant of Crow Wing,* or, *one who holds a lease for quarters on C deck.* *Lieutenant,* then, meant *placeholder.* Usually referring to a leader. He held the place of the captain when the captain was incapacitated. Second in command. Next in line.

"It means second only to God Himself," said Lieutenant. "It's the name my father gave me, and his father gave him. We remember that God is above us, and on the earthly plains we are to do His bidding."

Aster didn't nod, because she felt his definition took some liberties.

"Do you understand what I'm getting at?" asked Lieutenant. She didn't.

"You're out past curfew, which is against the law, and *Matilda*'s laws are the Heavens' laws. When I don't enforce *Matilda*'s laws," he said, "I'm not enforcing God's laws, and that is a great sin."

Aster turned her gaze but a few millimeters to the right, so she could watch for a sign from the Surgeon about what she should say, how she should respond. He gave none. He seemed more frightened of the man than she was. She noticed how far away he stood.

"I was visiting the Su—a doctor. My stomach was aching and I needed to use the bathroom," she said, her stories getting jumbled because she was a terrible liar, and why hadn't the Surgeon just been the one to explain?

"Your place is in your cabin. Headcount assures we keep accurate records of work shifts."

"She apologized profusely to me for breaking with order," said the Surgeon.

"She'll still have to be punished. Five days in the brigbox, no food, but I will allow you eight ounces of water per twelve hours. Fair?"

It took her seven seconds to say, "Yes."

"Then it's settled. You won't be tempted to dally again, will you?"

What she wanted to say was, *I will kill you in your sleep. Would that be considered dallying?* But it was a threat she knew very well she couldn't follow up on, and saying it aloud would only get her beaten, regardless of the fleeting thrill it might bring.

"Answer me," he said.

She nodded her head fiercely. "I will not be tempted to dally again, no sir."

"You should be honored. Punishment is a gift from the Heavens. A chance for us to right our wrongs and narrow the Gulf of Sin."

He switched from Middle to High as he spoke through his radio device, contacting someone to come escort her to her cell. Theo gave her a look—which she couldn't read, exactly, but she knew it meant that she shouldn't reveal that she spoke High.

"I would like to propose alternative punishment," said the Surgeon.

"Yes?" Lieutenant brushed a fleck of lint off the collar of his white shirt, straightened a pin that had twisted on the lapel of his uniform jacket.

"Since Worstan's retirement, I've found myself in need of a servant with some medical background, someone to complete the less glamorous tasks associated with my work. Scrubbing down operating rooms, handling bodies, filing, et cetera."

Lieutenant clipped his radio back to his belt. "You don't think that's too lenient?"

"I thought as much, which is why I didn't suggest it until now. But I'm reconsidering," said Theo.

"Explain."

"Though it's not as exacting a consequence as the brig-box, if she were to work under me over a long period of time, she might develop a stronger sense of respect for duty. I, of course, would dole out corporal punishment as I see fit. Frequent exposure to my methods will ensure greater adherence to the laws so necessary to keep *Matilda* functioning as smoothly as it does."

Lieutenant paused to consider the Surgeon's words, head leaned back. "I will allow it if you can promise me constant vigilance against your inner softness. You are the hands of God. You do His work. But I am His head. It's your nature as a doctor to coddle, but I must be the disciplinarian. In other words, I am the husband, you are the wife." He laughed, and Aster shivered. She couldn't imagine what he found worthy of laughter.

Lieutenant stared at her for a long while, then bid his adieu, but it was not the last time she'd be seeing him. He would oversee every day she spent in that brig. He would read her verses and give her sermons. For years after, he watched her, and though he never laid a physical hand on her, he stood by and ordered others to do just that.

For now, though, at the moment, he was nothing more than a curious, cruel man, no crueler than any other she'd met.

Aster had skimmed each article until she found his name. The newspapers, which Ainy kept to insulate and fill blankets, dated back decades, and it took hours of sifting to find anything worthwhile.

The Matilda Morning Herald

A Boy with Heart
by Graeme R. Porter

C and D deck are abuzz with rumors of "the boy genius," as he is called among the Matildan medical elite. Yesterday evening, at 21:03 hours, Theo Smith successfully performed cardial replacement surgery on Sovereign Nicolaeus, using an artificial heart of his own design. The human body produces enough heat energy to power the mechanical heart, which is fashioned from repurposed tyranium alloy and medical-grade plastic.

The expected shelf life of the tin heart is six harvest years. Previous models lasted a maximum of seven hundred days.

Smith is thirteen years old and the child of former Sovereign Sedvar Smith. He made headlines one year ago when he single-handedly ended the W deck polio epidemic, creating a vaccine out of the virus itself, putting himself in harm's way and becoming ill in the process.

"He saved the Sovereign, and for that I'm grateful," says George Cate, Chief Overseer of Matilda's Field Decks and food distribution. "I fear that his would-be successors might be too heathenistic in their governance of this great ship."

The political ramifications have caused a halt to the emergency appointments that were set to take place in five days.

Minister of Medicine and soon-to-be Surgeon General James Fitz is less optimistic. "That we even allowed the honored Sovereign into the hands of a child of such questionable background is unthinkable. I am grateful that things have turned out fine for now, but I question what this means for the future. Young Theo said visions from the Heavens guided his invention. Can we trust that?"

The answer to that question is a resounding yes. Upperdeckers polled agreed that the Heavens chose Theo Smith to be their hands in the earthly plains. The Society for Traditional Values—which spearheaded last growing season's campaign to decrease food rations to the lowerdecks—has already begun to call Smith "the Surgeon," a reference to the scriptural verse that alludes to one of Almighty God's epithets.

When Sovereign Nicolaeus gave a speech over the intercom this morning, even skeptics changed their tune. Regardless of the controversy surrounding him, Theo Smith has made himself a place in upperdeck society.

Giselle said, "Unfair," when Aster opened the envelope. Inside were a pass and a handwritten note.

Aster,

I don't intend to beat you or harm you physically in any way. Keeping up appearances. I spoke with Ms. Melusine. She shared with me your interest in medicine. If it's what you wish, I may be of some help to you, though I know you already must have many great teachers in Quarry Wing and beyond.

However, if you're up to it, please be in my office at 20:00 in two days, after your day shift is complete and you've had supper. You should have read two hundred pages of the first book on the list I've attached, which you can obtain in the N deck Archives. So we can have something to discuss. Your pass will allow you access. I expect to see you. If not, well wishes.

The Surgeon

"What's it say?" asked Giselle.

"Nothing really."

Giselle grabbed the letter and the pass. "Tell me, or I'll burn the pass."

"He will just issue me another one," said Aster, and slipped her feet into her boots.

"Where you going?"

"To the Archives, and then to my botanarium, to read."

"How dismal," said Giselle, setting a sock doll she'd been playing with to the side. "Sneak with me to the kitchens and we can play Queen and King and have a great feast to celebrate our union or something and clean it all up before Ainy even knows we've messed with her stash of butter. And don't worry, I'll do all the actual work. You can do kingly things like boss me around while I fry up some crescent pies."

"I'd prefer to use my free time before curfew to read," Aster responded.

"We could do school, then. You can be the teacher and I'll be the student, and I'll let you write as much as you want, and everything you tell me to do I'll do."

Aster tied the laces of her shoes.

"I am too old to play school, when I could be attending school for real. I'm leaving now. Dream of us playing Queen and King if you must, as long as in your dream world you still do all the work. Dream Aster is as averse to cooking as Awake Aster."

Giselle picked up her sock doll, ripped the floral-print skirt off the soft body. "Fine then." She climbed into her bunk, undid her hair from a thick braid. The loose coils bloomed outward from her face like the petals of a flower. Aster recalled the bigness of it, even now, though Giselle had long since cut her hair into a sensible, feminine bob.

"Are you angry with me?" Aster had asked.

"Yes," said Giselle.

"Will you forgive me for causing you upset?"

Giselle sighed. "I don't forgive. I'm too petty."

"But I will see you later, sister?"

Aster said *sister* because she knew sisters could not choose to unsister themselves when their lives diverged dramatically. Friends who hated each other were no longer friends. Sisters who hated each other remained sisters, despite long silences, feuds, and deliberate misunderstandings.

"Aye, I'll see you later," said Giselle.

A decade is not such a long time, Aint Melusine would say. Days disappeared into Concept, Facts/Fictions, Theoreticals,

Events That Once Occurred but Might as Well Have Happened to Someone Else for How Unreal and Faraway They Feel.

It had been 3,611 days since that last time Aster and Giselle played house, pretend games their strange solace, feigning they were family.

XV

Aster checked the time. It wasn't yet 19:00, so she had just over an hour. She hurried down to her botanarium, gathering materials. Giselle had asked her to do something, anything, and she had no choice but to try. They were sisters. What happened to Giselle had been Aster's fault. Giselle should've stayed in the Shuttle Bay, but Aster had made her come down. This new set of traumas would fling Giselle further into her grief-borne madness.

Aster flipped open cabinets, removing this and that ingredient. The bombs she'd made in her youth had been effective but small. More akin to firecrackers. They had also taken meticulous care to create. She fumbled a bottle of alcohol and it dropped to the ground. She was in no state to be working with explosives. She put down the jars of nitroglycerin she'd planned on using. They were small amounts in tablet form for her heart disease patients, but she figured if she crushed them all up together . . .

She didn't have the time and she didn't have the knowhow. Aster paced around her botanarium, looking for something. She didn't know what, not until she tripped right over it. She didn't know if it would change anything, but she had to try it.

Aster got together what she needed and ran as fast as she could updeck. She couldn't go to E deck alone, but Giselle had already told her how to do it—through Theo.

A man waited at the centerdeck staircase standing guard. Aster handed him her pass before he asked for it. He examined it carefully and motioned to hand it back, but held onto it for several seconds as she tried to grab it.

"Sir?" She imagined the second hand on a clock ticking quickly forward. He released his grip and she took the little wax-sealed card. She'd never seen a guard standing watch here, and she knew it was Lieutenant's doing.

She went to see Theo in his Goosefoot clinic in the same dirty clothes she'd been in last night. Men and women stared at her as she passed through the corridors. When one lady asked her if she might see about fixing the air cooler in her cabin since it was getting terribly overhot, Aster did not reply.

G deck was mercantile. There were hardly any personal quarters, and the passageways stretched wide and open, with booths set up for selling sugarcane that Pippi or maybe Giselle had harvested. In addition to the Surgeon, there were other doctors, their names posted over hatches. Still early, there was little chatter, but Aster distinctly overheard the word *coronation* from a prim-looking man in a very clean suit. The brass buttons on his jacket shined.

"Excuse me," someone called to Aster. He appeared ready to ask her something.

"Excuse you," she said, and walked past him until she reached Theo's office, one of several he worked in.

There was a small bell attached to the frame of the hatch, and she rang it. When no answer came, she rang it again. A third time—again, no response—and she grabbed the latch and pulled. Theo's office was nothing like his study. Instead of shelves and shelves of books, instead of bright globes of light, there was a pervading dimness. A few chairs lined the wall. There was a door inside the cabin—not metal like a hatch, but made of the same wood as the chairs.

"Theo," she called out, and knocked on the door. "Theo, it's Aster. It's an emergency."

"Wait one moment," he said. "I'm with a—"

But now that she knew he was there, she opened the un-locked door.

"I'm going to ask you never to do that again," he said. A clear mask covered his face, two utensils in his hands as he leaned over a man on a table.

"It's an emergency."

He looked her up and down, taking in her sorry state. "One second," he said.

The man on the table mumbled a few words, and the Surgeon removed the metal prongs from his mouth. "What in God's name is going on?" the man said, sitting up, forcing Theo to push away the light globe hanging on a small crane. Before Theo could interfere, Aster reached into her medicine belt and removed a syringe, stabbed it into the patient's neck. Almost instantaneously, his eyes fell shut.

"Brandt?" Theo said, and patted the man's cheek, then went to feel his pulse. "What did you give him?"

"He'll be fine. Tell me, can you take me to E deck?"

Theo removed the white gloves from his fingers, went over to a pale of water, and dipped his hands in. "The coronation?"

"Aye."

"We need to get you cleaned up. Tell me what happened to you. Are you all right? Are you hurt?"

"Stiff. Sore. Not hurt. Please, can we hurry?"

Theo nodded, directed her to one of the patient rooms. "Wash yourself up in there. I will think of something."

She nodded, and began undressing even before he'd fully walked out, her sweaty shirt over her head, her long johns at her knees. She went to the sink and guzzled water directly from the tap, filling her belly until she wanted to puke. It was sweet and cold and she could not get enough. There was no toothbrush or paste, so she washed her mouth out with soap. She preferred the taste of it to the guard's piss, the acerbic bite of detergent cleaning her out, burning. She rubbed the bar of soap against her teeth, used a cloth napkin to wipe them clean. After her mouth felt fresh, she drank more water.

She scrubbed herself with the cold water and some liquid hand soap because it smelled of lemon. Thick glops of it ran over her knees and down to her feet, her belly, her chest and shoulders, and she massaged it in with her hands.

"Are you finished?" Theo called, knocking lightly.

"Leave me." She wasn't finished, or near it. She reached into one of the cabinets and got out an old box filled with amber vials of isopropyl alcohol. Expensive. Hard to find. She emptied them out one by one over herself, even over her shorn hair, until she smelled like medicine. Until she was a sterile thing no more sexual than a pair of sanitized scissors. That sharp too.

"I have sent someone for clothes," Theo said through the door. She could tell he was not himself because he didn't usually keep nagging after she explicitly told him to leave her.

"I would like a towel."

"Of course, Aster, one moment."

Theo returned with the towel after several seconds, held it to her through a crack in the door.

Aster was about to tell him not to bother, that he could come in and see her naked and shaking and wet, because she didn't care, and she thought of Giselle and that man Warner, and of past times, and thought it might not be such a bad thing to separate body from self—even though self was tied up in body, made of body, made of cells, hormones, chemicals. At the last second she changed her mind. Covered her chilly, wet arms with her hands and jogged to the door to grab the towel. "Thank you," she said.

"Clothes are waiting for you outside. We shall sneak you to E deck as a man. All right? My uncle can't know you're there. In general, you'll stand out less. Understand?"

"Understand."

The alcohol left her skin dry and rough. She scraped her finger through the ashy white of leftover soap flakes. Her medicine belt was strewn over the exam table and she reached for the all-purpose salve inside. Slicked herself up with it. She shined. She was a brand-new coin.

Aster examined her new self in the mirror and said, "I make a very dainty man."

She looked nothing, nothing at all, like the man she hoped she'd look like, one of those burly, rough-faced types who walked the passageways of *Matilda* like a conquistador, each step a flag in the nonexistent soil.

But Theo's intervention was not completely unsuccessful. The garments were the fanciest she'd ever worn: dark-green tweed slacks that fit close to her legs, tapering into her ankles, a button-up shirt dyed a rich, lavish purple, a plaid vest, burgundy tie, and a jacket to match the trousers. The clothes fit like they were made for her, wide in the hips and ass and shoulders, but fitted at her waist. Aster didn't know where Theo acquired them, but she was glad that he had. She looked neither male nor female, but if one were to pick—and people so did like to pick—they would choose male, of that she was certain.

Theo grabbed Aster's shoulders and turned her toward him. "Not dainty—stately. Well-to-do. You make a fine young gentleman, if I do say so myself." He pointed to a chair. "Now for the hair."

"*What* for the hair?" Aster slid her fingers into the mass of bends and turns and folds.

"It'll need to go." Theo glanced to the clock on the wall, and Aster did the same.

"Men can have hair like this," Aster said. With only thirty minutes to spare before the shift, she didn't have time for a haircut. As much as she wished to stay here with the Surgeon, being clever.

"They can, but they don't." He gestured again to his chair. "When you argue, you waste time. You asked for my help, did you not?"

"Unless my internal glossaelia is incorrect, *help* does not mean *haircut*," she said.

"Don't snark me. I'll just take a bit off the top and shave the sides. That will be very handsome."

"The amount of enjoyment you are getting out of this seems incongruous with the objective level of fun there is to be had. Is this your secret passion, Theo? Surgeon General by day, barber by night?"

He rolled his eyes and waved her over. "If I could have my way, you wouldn't be going to this at all. Since you're set on it, I'll do all that I can to help you avoid trouble."

Aster finally walked over and sat, removed her watch from her medicine belt, not trusting Theo's clock. "Do it fast or I'll become angry." She bit her lip waiting for the sound of snipping scissors.

"Not an effective threat considering you spend a great deal of your time with me angry. It'd be no different than the status quo." Theo set the guard on the buzzer and began to work, first using scissors to shorten the length to something manageable.

"I don't want to be one of those bald-headed boys who look like they had no mothers to comb and oil them proper."

"I'll leave you some length," said Theo. "Now quiet."

Knotted, kinked hair fell to Aster's lap in ugly clumps. She gripped the arms of the chair, refusing to confront the image in the mirror.

"You think I would hurt you?" he asked.

She thought about that question, working through the possibilities, and realized the answer was no; she did not be-

lieve he would hurt her. There was no one else she felt that
way about. Not even Ainy. "No," she answered.

"Then breathe. It will look fine. You will be fine, *little nervous one*," he said in Low. "I will be there looking after you. You
won't be alone."

He ran the buzzer over the sides of her hair, leaving zigzag
puffs at the top in a common style.

"Still not enough," he said. "Your bones are sharp, wom-
anly. I have to go shorter than normal to offset it." He clipped
the top until there was only an inch. The razor tickled against
her scalp, as did the brush against the back of her neck,
sweeping little hairs away.

"Done?"

He handed her a mirror. "You look very handsome."

Aster ventured a peek. "Fine," she said, then slid out of
the chair and headed toward the hatch. "Let's go." Before she
entered the corridor, however, she remembered she needed
shoes.

"For you." Theo handed her a pair of wingtips, beautiful
but in need of a shine. She emptied the contents of a small
box onto the shoes. Using her old shirt, she massaged the ink
into the leather, dabbed coconut oil onto the toes, and rubbed
until they shined black as throat.

"Are you quite ready?" asked Theo.

"Aye."

"Don't look so happy with yourself."

"But I am happy with myself," Aster said. The haircut,
contrary to her initial fear, had unlatched and freed her. She
ran her fingers over the neatly shorn strands. It was lovely and
exquisite. She wanted to barrel headfirst into everyone, to cut
them open with her parietal and frontal bones, and let them
know there was only the slightest trace of skin and hair separating their soft bodies from her skull. The illusion of cotton
was gone. They should be afraid. They would be split in two.

Aster was obsessed with bifurcation. Wholes were foreign to her. Halves made more sense. A split nucleus could end *Matilda*'s tiny universe. She wanted to be the knife. She wanted to be knived.

XVI

Opulent: *adj., extravagant, overdone, rich.*[1]

As in: second helpings of maize pudding, hot water from the tap, flannel bedding, walnut butter. Vocabulary lessons weren't a part of every Quarry Wingers upbringing, but Melusine insisted Aster memorize every word in her tattered copy of a thin dictionary. Word, definition, example.

Aster continued the exercise into adulthood, the boundaries of words ever-shifting, the need to understand their confines paramount. *Blood* meant/could mean: cell-dense plasma, life, kinship, disease. *Medicine* meant/could mean: healing serums, both literal and metaphorical, soup, pills, cure. *Family* meant: to be determined. There were some words that meant everything and others that meant nothing. *love baby god death.*

As Aster now entered E deck for the first time at the Surgeon's side, word-meanings evolved once more, her previous definitions not surviving to the age of reproduction, their genes obsoleting themselves out of existence, suited no longer to *Matilda*'s particular ecology. *Opulent* was not a second helping of supper at all, but bronze statues of weeping angels, dresses so grand and full of fabric they quite easily could be sewed into five or even six dresses.

She'd been to the updecks before, of course, but never to E. It was the deck reserved for occasions.

"Stop dawdling," Theo said. "When you gawk, you draw attention to yourself."

Aster ascended the large, carpeted steps, so clean she wanted to undress and lie in the dark blue fibers. She dragged her hand along the bannister, surprised that when she examined her fingers, there was no dust, only the faint smell of lemon and orange. "Opulent," she said. "Opulent means no lint. Opulent, no lint."

Theo grabbed her gently by the elbow and pulled her along. "Please do not leave my side. Is that understood?"

"It is understood," she said.

"You agree to obey while we are up here? It's the only way I'll carry on with this."

She wanted to put her face against his cheek, calm him. That was what her Aint Melusine did for her when she worked herself into a state. "I agree," she said.

They walked together through Egret Wing, Eastern, and Emerald, on a somewhat tangled course, hopefully toward Evening Star, but who could really say? The Surgeon only had a vague sense of the layout, and it showed. She knew he'd been here before, forced to attend functions, but Theo's reputation for hermitry was well-founded, and he was rarely required to appear at gatherings and events.

A passerby stopped them. "Can I help you?" he asked, but his attitude conveyed skepticism rather than an earnest desire to aid. It surprised Aster how few people knew the Surgeon's face. His name, they recognized. Even his voice from occasional announcements on the loudspeakers. His likeness appeared regularly in the *Matilda Morning Herald*, but it was the same one over and over and over, from when he was a boy, twelve or thirteen. Black-and-white. Cloudy.

"You can help us, yes," said Theo. "My assistant and I have been called to the coronation. Might you lead us to it?"

Aster wished Theo would give the man his name and title. That would speed things along. His modesty did not allow for it, though, even in these desperate moments. Aster thought to blurt it out, to speak it: *This is him! The Surgeon! The man you all worship, more than the Sovereign himself! Your precious Hands of the*

Heavens! He cures disease! He had visions as a child! And look at him, isn't he beautiful?

"You've got a pass, I assume?" the man said. "For you and your boy?"

"I do not require a pass," he replied. It was the most prideful thing she'd ever heard him say. He must've seen Aster reach for her medicine belt, because he grabbed her arm and squeezed hard. He would not have her syringing this man as well. "Here is my identification card." He handed the man a thin sheet of two-by-four-inch metal, his color picture emblazoned on the right, his details on the left atop the emblem of the Sovereignty.

Name: Theophilus Isaac Smith
Prof: Surgeon General of the Sovereignty
Rank: General, Sovereignty's Guard
Residence: G Deck, Grass Wing, G-01
DOB: Precise Day Unknown, Harvest Year 300

"If you could please direct us quickly," said Theo,

"You're—you're the Surgeon?" said the man. "I imagined you to be—grander." He squinted, looked Theo up and down. Next, he examined the ID, waved the paper-thin metal into the light until the holographic seal shimmered brilliantly, a ringed planet surrounded by what appeared to be seven suns, but was actually the same sun, moved, then moved again, then moved again.

"You've caught me on a bad day." Theo slicked his hand over his sparse black hair, but doing so did nothing to tame the cowlicks.

"If you're the Surgeon, as you claim, then I'd like for you to remove my kidney, right here, right now. Can you do that for me?"

The Surgeon could do no such thing, of course. Such a

procedure would take more than an hour. The coronation was in less than half an hour.

After a pause, the man laughed boomingly, throwing his head back. "I am joking, yes? Even God's chosen can take a joke?"

"Of course." Theo laughed as well. A lying laugh.

"Now let me show you to it," the man said. "Evening Star awaits us."

Melusine, who used to work in the highdecks as a nurse, described E deck as everybody doing nothing very slowly. Aster didn't disagree.

"You think it's all right to bring him to this?" the man asked. He looked like a Villem, so in her head, Aster began to call him that. "A coronation is a very holy event. Of course, who am I to school you on what's holy?" Villem laughed again. "What's your name, boy?"

Aster stared ahead, kept her hands stuffed into the pockets of her trousers so as not to slap her thighs nervously. "Aster," she said.

"Aster? What a peculiar name for a boy," said Villem.

"He's named for his mother," said Theo, "as is the custom on his deck when the mother passes in childbirth."

Theo's fibs possessed a suaveness Aster's lacked.

"Are we almost there?" she asked, quickening her pace.

Villem smiled at her, threw his arm around her shoulders. She wanted to bite his pale hand dangling at her chest, finger almost touching her nipple. "You're excited," he said. "It's good to see one of your sort so invested in the political goings-on. I know life on Matilda isn't always fair, but we all agree some sacrifice is in order, and we must maintain a level of decorum if we're to survive this voyage." He patted her back, and she tried not to tense.

Chuckling, he pulled her into his embrace, strange, alien affection scaling off his skin. They were not comrades, and yet he treated her with such camaraderie.

Villem showed them to Evening Star's entryway. "Mind you, everyone is always late. I wouldn't worry about missing anything. This is my third coronation."

"Do you know any specifics on the protocol?" Theo asked. "I was only notified last minute. What will actually happen?"

"We were all only notified last minute. There tend to be weeks of deliberation before a new sovereign takes the helm. I suppose you'd be too young to remember how much time there was between your father and Nicolaeus. The blackouts have the Sovereignty in a right state, don't they? They have faith that the new sovereign, whomever it might be, will return things to their previous glory."

Aster tugged at the tail of Theo's jacket, Villem's hand still at her waist.

"Sorry, General, but don't we need to go? Villem, you've been kind. Goodbye," Aster said, wrangling out of his grip and pulling Theo forward. When the man followed them through the double doors, Aster made sure to walk briskly toward the crowd to lose him.

Evening Star was a magnificent ballroom. Portside, there was only stained glass, large windows that covered end to end in every direction, looking out onto Baby. Her light made the colors so vibrant.

The ceiling seemed to stretch infinitely high. "So much light," Aster said, though for once, it wasn't a bother. The walls were not rusted bronze, but some strange plaster material, painted a pale, creamy white and engraved with intricate loops, points, twists, patterns. Everything was wood—the floors, the fixtures, the furniture, the window frames, the doors. Pews, like at temple, circled the room around a center platform. "What now?" she asked, surveying her surroundings.

Theo searched the room just as frantically. "Up here, you're Aston, by the by. We can't expect that everyone here will be as stupid as—Villem."

"Oh, I think we can expect it," she said, glancing about. "We *should* expect it."

Theo made a raspy sound in the back of a throat, then laughed softly. "That was funny, Aston. I'm impressed."

Men and women filled the seats, speaking hurriedly. Curiosity warped their faces into uncomfortable frowns. A young man, black like Aster, lingered over her for a long moment. She squinted her eyes to see if she knew him, but his face held no meaning. The shape of the eyes, the bumps in the nose, and the burgundy in the lips coalesced into a fine enough face, but not one with which Aster was familiar.

"Do you know that man?" Theo asked.

Aster shook her head. "Should I take care of him?"

"Was that another joke, Aston? I believe you're on fire. Though I highly doubt that would end well. He's stymied trying to determine your gender. If you ignore him, he'll move on. No need for violence."

"But I could be very discreet," she said.

Theo laughed again, this time more vigorously. She wondered if it was nervousness, because he rarely laughed, let alone so freely. "Aston, you don't have a discreet bone in your body."

"A discreet bone?"

"It's nothing, never mind."

In the corner, Aster spotted a brown woman in a head wrap. She wore a long white dress, a chain around her ankle attached to a weight. That was the only way lowdeck women got this high up.

"I am going to speak to Reginald. He's a Council member and will know what's going on." Theo pointed ahead to a finely dressed fellow in spectacles, his gray beard long and excessive.

"All right," she said. "But you must explain the *discreet bone*. It's not nothing. You said it. Tell me what it means."

"It means you are not discreet. To say that you don't have a discreet bone is to say you have nothing in your body that predisposes you toward discretion. It is not in your nature. Not in your bones."

Aster straightened her back and shoulders as they approached the center of the grand hall. These last few days she was always straightening, bending, looping, whipping left at the last possible moment, only to realize she'd meant to go right. "I hate nature," she said.

"And yet nature's rather indifferent to you," Theo replied. "Are you ready?"

Inhaling deeply, Aster summoned what strength she had. "No, but I will do what needs doing."

"I find it useful to remember that everyone here has the power to kill you with impunity. Your own sense of self-preservation and survival should direct your behavior appropriately. Follow my lead."

She let him move two paces in front of her as they approached the bearded, bespectacled man. Theo moved confidently. Aster homed in on the rhythm of his steps, tried to mimic the hop of his hips. Even in her fine clothes, Aster felt a foreign species. Gold engulfed her: the embroidery on the handkerchiefs, the watches, the necklaces, the flecks in the servants' eyes. Opulence for days.

The grandiosity of it all got Aster to imagining a different sort of life, one in which a man named Aston and a man named Theo were lovers. The World Fair for the Society of Astromic Physiomaticians was to be held in Evening Star; the topic: Undermining Infinite Time Loops Using the First Three Laws of Transcurviogetics. Aston and Theo were the fanciest men in attendance. They drank fermented libations. A scientist named Patrocles gave a presentation on how in order to change their natures, universes must collide into other universes, creating a new, third universe with otherworldly physiomatic constraints. Being in the camp of the aviotologists, Theo would call it hogwash, but Aston would listen attentively and hiss at Theo to be quiet as he made jokes under his breath about Patrocles's mustache actually being the thing that was under otherworldly physiomatic constraints.

Different worlds, worlds opposite the one in which Aster lived, teased and beckoned her. She had to remind herself that those worlds were not possible. Aston was not Aston, but Aster, and Theo was not an aviotologist, but the Surgeon.

She followed Theo and tried to focus on the here and now, the mass of bodies surrounding her, what she might say or might not say as they finally reached the important-looking man.

"Excuse me, Sergeant," Theo said.

The man turned to the both of them, straight-faced, his eyes the cruelest blue. Seeing him up close, Aster realized she knew him. Pockmarks dented his translucent skin, and his cheekbones rose high. He wore a black jacket over his shirt, ribbons and medals at the top right corner. He was Sergeant Warner, only dressed up proper now. Under the soap and oil, Aster could still smell Giselle on him, and her body slipped into mild dysfunction. She tried to count each thump of her heart, but swore it only beat the one time, a solid, thunderous clap. She stared at his pomegranate lips. If he recognized her, he said nothing. But how could he not? Shorter hair and a new outfit were hardly a facial reconstruction. That was how *nothing* she was to him, to all of them. He could stare her in the face and beat her backside with a cane, and then forget. She turned to leave.

"Aston," Theo called.

"Theo," she replied, but continued to walk.

Aster wandered the slowly gathering crowd, turning left when she saw a group of women sipping coffee, then weaving through a row of semifilled pews. She tripped over a woman's leather bag, apologized, and moved on. Off to the side, she saw a stack of neatly wrapped boxes, some in beautifully decorated paper, others in gold tissue paper.

"Those offerings are for the new sovereign, boy. To welcome him to the throne. Don't go getting any ideas. I know your lot have sticky fingers."

Aster ignored the woman and walked toward the stack. There was finally a place she could do what she'd planned back in the botanarium. The woman was now turned away from her, conversing with others. When Aster was satisfied no one else was watching her, she removed her own gift for the Sovereign from the leather medicine bag she carried and set it down next to the others. Those boxes were surely filled with fine wine and spirits, silks, brandy cakes. Aster's was filled with Flick's frozen foot, freshly gathered from the botanarium. She had written and attached a note that said, *Now that you are sovereign, please consider reevaluating the atmosphere controls in the lowerdecks.*

Something in the water must have made her do it. Alcohol or some other inebriant known for its ability to lower inhibitions. Or the ghost of her mother had inspired her. A collective frustration letting itself out all at once. It was not quite the same as setting everything ablaze, as Giselle had suggested Aster do, but as she left the amputated foot for Lieutenant, she had the distinct feeling she was committing an act of self-immolation.

PART III

PHYLOGENY

XVII

Melusine Hopwood

It's morning time and I'm on my way updeck to teach Abe his letters, Lord help me. Here's what I do: Put uncooked corn grits into a little pan (a waste of grits but his mother say children learn best when they can touch and feel). Next, I draw the letter with my pointer into the grits nice and big so he can see. Erase. Then he got to copy it from memory, drag his itty-bitty index finger through the granules. If he don't get it at first, I show him again. We up to letter M. He can spell some. Bib. Feed. Gab.

Bell is his favorite word. He draws the letters into the dried grits, says the word out loud, then likes to ring the little bell his father keeps on the desk. He's almost three harvest years old. Quiet. Sometimes his father hit him, so he's afraid to speak, laugh, cry. He always up for saying *bell*, though.

I wish I could say I loved him, because he might be better off if one person doted on him proper, but I don't. He make me tired and bored, and I'd rather be doing almost anything than playing with him. They say there's nothing like watching a child's face light up as they learn something new, but the folks who say that is lying. Children are fine enough, just not my favorite.

At 07:00 exactly I tap the little buzzer next to the cabin hatch. The white woman let me in. She cleans and cooks but isn't a servant like me. She gets paid a little something for her effort.

Say the white woman: "Morning, Ms. Melusine." I don't know her name.

Say I: "Morning."

"Abe isn't feeling so well today, so his mother is letting him out of his studies."

Say I: "I'll go report to my wing then."

That's not true. Like any good woman, I'm a liar. I'm going back to my cabin to sleep, and if I play it right, my overseer won't ever know.

I'm already on my way into the corridor but the white woman call after me. Say her: "The mistress wants you to stay the full three hours and watch over Abe anyway. He doesn't like his nanny as much as he likes you. He gets afussed when he doesn't see you or when his schedule is interrupted."

I sigh, but what can be done? I should feel lucky that I'm here and not somewhere worse.

It's not common for a lowdeck woman to tutor an upperdeck boy. A proper schoolmaster, a fine man, should be in charge of the boy's learning. But the mistress don't respect men very much and say a young child's place is with a motherly type. For some reason, people think I'm a motherly type. Because I'm brown and dowdy. She got her husband to hire a lowdeck woman who knew her letters. To play meema. It's not my favorite type of work, but it's better than normal shift, like washing pots and tilling fields, and it doesn't hurt my joints so bad. It isn't my first nanny job, and I suppose it won't be my last.

Say Abe when I walk into his room: "Ainy." They still keep him in a crib. He smile a little when he see me. He missing a canine tooth. He look like a sweet mongrel wolf.

I pick him up and hold him. He rests his head against my shoulder. His breath smells like cocoa milk. His skin is too hot, fever. I almost call out, *Silly white woman! Come here!* But catch myself in time.

Say I: "Miss, where his mother?"

The white woman come into the room, dust cloth still in her hand. "What was that, Melusine?"

"Where Abe's mother?"

"The salon, I think."

The salon is where the rich women go to drink coffee and tea, to eat biscuits and lemon cake, and talk about important matters like *why this* and *why that*, *but did you ever imagine such and such?*

I let Abe down because my joints hurt too much to carry him, but slide my hand around his, which is hot and sweaty. He's in footies, the little buttons running down the side of his legs all the way up to the collar. It's thick, almost like fleeced wool, and ivory-colored, darker and more yellow than his pale, pale skin.

Say the white woman: "He's shivering."

I nod my head. No way he should be so cold in that one-piece he got on.

I lay him on the velvet sofa, and he don't protest. The white woman and me get him out of his footies, take off his diaper. There are tiny little red rashes on his bum, back, thighs. Could be scabies. I wrap a fresh prefold around him, pin it secure.

Say I: "Go strip his bed, miss."

She nod and do what I say. She a good woman. I like her. I wish I could remember her name.

Say I to Abe: "We're going to get you fixed up good, *weewa*, okay?"

He's too lethargic to cry or whine, but he smile up at me. I suppose it should melt my heart.

I unbutton the top of my dress, pick up the boy, and press him almost-naked to me, then settle a blanket over his back as I bounce him. We skin to skin. His shivering go down a little, but he still cold. Say I: "Hush now, *babwa*," although he already hush as can be. Like the little mouse in my favorite story. Who build a house under a little girl's bed, with old colored pencils, shoelaces. All the other little mice want to get in on it, but they loud as can be. So little mouse teaches them how to be quiet. How to scurry. And they build a mouse village beneath the little girl's bed, and she never know about it.

My sweet, perfect one—Aster—she quiet like that too. Used to be she never spoke a word. But even now when she talks, it's quiet, like she never sure the words she's using is the right words. All her words is the right words to my mind, though sometime she get smart with me, back-talking and all that, but every word out her mouth I love because so what if it makes me angry, I like to hear her. I like to know what's on her mind. Sometimes I think what she says is foolish, but I say foolish things sometimes too. It's a woman's way.

Abe almost as quiet as my Aster.

Say the white woman when she come back into the room: "I stripped his cot, got his little stuffed toys too. Now what?"

Say I: "Get his mother."

I hold Abe close to me and rock him gentle, say: "You look like an animal, all those red spots all over you. You been talking to my Aster, haven't you? She gave you one of her serums?"

Say Abe: "Momma." I know he don't mean me. He's calling for the mistress. Hattie.

Say I: "She'll be here soon."

"Momma." He look at me as he say it this time. That's what make me put him down, lay him on the sofa, cover him with that blanket. He don't reach for me, but he look at me and moan with all the passion of a child wanting their caretaker. I sigh, put a hand on his forehead, but don't pick him up again.

It's best not to call me *Mama, Meema, Mother, Nana*. Ainy is all right because it sounds just close enough to a real name that I forget it means *great-aunt*.

When I look after upperdeck children and they call me *nanny*, I nip their ears, right there in front of their fathers, and say, "Do I call you *little beast brat?* No. I call you your name." The fathers don't mind it because they remember their mean nannies fondly.

Mothers tolerate my meanness less. They're always threatened. I am old now, but even when I was young I was not the prettiest thing. But they acted like I was some hot little toy that was going to lure their husbands away. And I wanted to tell them, *Honey, I don't want to be here. Your husband looks like boiled cabbage smeared with cream cheese. If I could be in my room smoking a pipe by my lonesome, I would be much happier. But no, I am here cleaning your infant's nasty, nasty spit-up. Luring your husband away is the last thing on my mind.*

I'm not the maternal type. Lullabies bore me. The idea of a child hanging off my breast, using me for sustenance, makes me very angry for some reason. Probably because I am always angry about everything. I am like a gramophone and the volume's too loud, and you can't find the off button, and all you can do is cover your ears until the end of the record. My head is too filled with stories. Children think because I can spin a good tale that I can be gentle. I can't be.

I had a son once. They took him away. Sometimes I think I might have let him eat from my breast because he had that sort of handsome face most babies lack. One time, I pressed the bottom of his foot to my cheek, and would you believe it was so small that when the heel was at my chin, his big toe did not even reach up to my nose? I am glad most nights they robbed him from me, when they saw he was white as a lamb and could pass, because I would be a bad mother. I am not always so good with children.

I had three little sisters and I disliked them all. Their diapers smelled and if ever I was babysitting, I would let them cry and get rash because I hated so much having to get close

230 * An Unkindness of Ghosts

to their thingies to wipe them clean. I only wanted to clean myself. Get washed up, comb my hair into cute little pigtails, put on a nice dress, and then draw or paint or play dice with the older boys. I don't like to take care of other people.

My meema always asked, "Would you look after your sisters while I go see about a man who has pretty, wavy hair?"

"No," I would say. And my mother was so frail that when I protested like this she didn't slap me like she should've. Didn't try to get me in line. Instead she'd tell me how: okay, she'd work out other arrangements, and so my three little sisters would go to stay with this upperdeck woman who was a schoolteacher and had a mission to make all the little dark lowdeckers into readers. So they could read about the Heavens and the Promised Land and so they could memorize prayers. She'd tell my baby sisters that if they read and said their prayers and obeyed the Sovereignty, *Matilda*'s journey to the Heavens would be made sure. She taught this with such fervency that she must've actually believed it. What a sad thing. Nothing is more sad than a person who believes in something that's so clearly not true.

Now Abe say: "Momma. Momma. Momma," peering up at me.

I hear the hatch open, which means the white woman went to get the mistress, and she's arrived.

She slide off her jacket, hang it on a hook. Say her: "Melusine, what is it?"

Say the white woman: "He got a fev—"

"I was talking to Melusine. Lucy, get us some ice water." *Lucy*. That's the maid's name.

Say I: "Fever. These red rashes. Could be scabies, maybe. He real tired."

Hattie come and feel her son's head, sit on the couch next to him, move him so his head is in her lap. Abe wedges his fat thumb between his lips and starts to suck. His black hair is up and away, pressed out where it should be pressed down.

The white woman, Lucy, come back to the room with a cup of ice water and a rag. Mistress Hattie dip the cloth in to the water, then ring it out over Abe's forehead.

Say I: "Can I use your telegraph, missus?"

Mistress nods and shows me to it. I type a message for Theo. Tell him to get my Aster. That boy is real sick. I know he'll come to see after the child himself, but he'll get Aster too. I like seeing her face, and I missed her this morning. She's always off somewhere, and it's nothing like she was when she was little, her little fist balled into my skirts always tryna stay close, hanging onto my every word like it was from a god.

I'm not maternal but that doesn't mean I don't love. I love Aster. I love all the girls and women I look after. It is hard to be in somebody's presence for so long and not develop something like love. I don't have romantic feelings. I never fell in love with a person the way princesses falls in love with princes. I never wanted to be with nobody in bed. Aster, though, my love for her is—it's malignant. And if I try to chop it off, all the bits of love will spread everywhere else and infect me worse.

It's a whole hour before Theo come. I love him also. He's the son they took away from me. I can't help but feel something strong for him.

Say I: "I had Lucy strip the sheets."

Theo nod. "Please, Ms. Lucy, will you pull his clothing too? Clean and unclean. They'll need to be sent to the wash."

"Yes sir, of course." She never seen the Surgeon before, clear by the way she become nervous and flighty all the sudden, her voice getting more fancy. Even Mistress Hattie is suddenly shy.

Theo begin his examination of Abe, listen to his heart, look at his red rashes, swab inside his nose. He smear the cotton onto a little glass slide.

"Melusine?"

It hurt when he call me that instead of Ainy, even though I know he don't mean a thing by it. Theo never been the type to use sweet names. When he was little he called his father by his rank and surname. He is as handsome now as he was when he was a little one. I think it's the dark in him. He'd make any mother proud.

I used to think he was like me. Urgeless. I don't have desires for coupling like others do. It made sense that he could've inherited that from me. But I get now it's all about his religion. What he thinks he should and shouldn't do. I don't know where he got it from, his devotion. Not from me. Not from his father. I think it's true what they say, though, that he is touched by the Heavens. When he was three he could read books grown men couldn't understand. Not a late bloomer like my Aster.

His father beat him, and when I tried to stop it, he beat me too. He called Theo *sissy* because Theo was small and only liked to read and listen to stories. He called him *worthless* and a word I don't like to say that starts with a *f* and rhymes with the word for fly larva. The same kind of names folks would later come to call my Aster, though not exact.

Say Theo: "Melusine?"

Say I: "What?"

"Would you please send a message to the I deck nursery letting them know I wish to see their roster for the last week?"

Abe's mother pats his head, says: "I'd never send him there. Weekday mornings he's with Melusine. Afternoons he's with his nanny. Evenings starting at three he's with me." Abe sucks away at his thumb. His eyes are closed now and he snores.

"Are there any other public places he's been?" asks Theo.

Say I: "Yesterday I took him to the Field Decks. When he

get low, I take him there so he can get some sunshine. Picks him right up."

Say Hattie: "Melusine, you should've taken him to the promenade. I would've allowed it." The part she leave out is that she think the Field Decks are filled with my filthy kind, and that's where he caught whatever sickness he got.

"I'm not welcome on the promenade," say I.

The mistress give me a look, like she sorry, then go back to patting Abe's head. "Please, tell me, what's wrong with him, Surgeon?"

Say Theo: "I'll investigate the sample I took, but I can say with much certainty that it's a staph infection." He push a thermometer into Abe's ear, press a button so the reading stay recorded into the machine. "I assure you, Miss Hattie, he will be fine, but I would like to start him on medication as soon as I've identified the strain of the bacteria."

Say I to Hattie: "Sorry, miss. I understand if you want to let me go." I hope she do.

Say Theo: "It is unlikely that he caught the infection during his time with you in the Field Decks. I only asked where he spent time out of the cabin to ascertain whether he might have given the infection to others."

He already done with the examination, and Aster isn't here. As he's putting away his things, and the mistress is carrying Abe back to the crib, Theo start talking to me. "I told her I'd write her a pass to join me," he say, like he know what I'm thinking before I say it.

"And?"

"She said she's trying to keep her nose to the ground, though not in so many words."

Say I: "It's not like her to avoid trouble."

Theo nod. "I think Lieutenant's ascension has a lot of us very frightened."

Say I: "No. It's something more specific than that that got

her all worried. She been asking me all kind of questions."

I look at him so we eye to eye. So maybe he can know that he is my son, that I was more than just his nanny. For the better part of a harvest year I swathed him in my skin and muscle. He look just like me except for his pallor. I wish I could say I was the one who taught him his fine manners, but that's all him. He was born the most loving, kindest soul, and stayed that way, the very opposite of me.

Say Theo: "I'm sure Aster will inform us the full breadth of what's on her mind when she's ready to."

I sit. I can't stand for more than a few minutes these days. Say I: "Does she tell you things? Like how a lover would? Maybe she tell you more than me." I am fishing like a nosey old woman. They spend all their time together, and I do be wondering. I'm a old gossip. I got to get my stories from somewhere.

Theo fluster the slightest bit, then say: "We have developed a good working rapport."

When he leave, I go to check on Abe. He asleep. Hattie is humming him a song, leaned over his cradle. Say I: "If you need me, I'll be washing up his sheets and all that."

"Oh, Melusine, you don't need to do that. Come here. You can stay."

I don't want to stay. I'd rather scald my hands scrubbing Abe's dirty bedding, even if it make my knuckles swell as big as the wild strawberries that grow in the Field Decks.

Say I: "How about I go to the Archives, miss? I could pick up Abe some new picture books. I'm allowed as long as you write me up a pass."

Hattie smile. "Oh, that's a splendid idea.

Once there, I show my pass to the man working the front desk, and he nod perfunctory-like. He used to seeing me here for years, since when I used to get books for Aster when she was nothing but a little thing. He put up a fuss my first few visits back then, accusing her of smudging the books with dirt and ripping pages out. My boy Theo had to shut his protests down. At ten years old, he took me by his hand and pulled me into the stacks. He told that librarian man that he was to give me no more trouble.

"Sign in," he say now, not glancing up. I reckon I can't be gone long before Hattie put up a fuss. It's not enough time for a full search, but enough to find the books I'm looking for and stash them in my bag. I scrawl my name onto the sheet of cream paper and mark 2-N.55, the physics branch.

Well, it ain't picture books for Abe. I'm a good liar.

Aster been asking all sorts of questions. Her mind else-where. I know she and Giselle up to something. I only want to help. I need only show her that I can.

The science stacks ain't as nice as all that, more akin to the lowdecks than anything. Long, narrow aisles, barely the width of a person.

Poor, poor books. Lonely pages bound in lonely leather, their only company the occasional louse. They exist only to be read, and yet with no one there to read them, they might as well not have been bornt at all. I run my fingers along the spines of the books I can reach. I do it to affirm them. To let them know I'm a lover of stories, even stories about alchemat-ics or biology and other true things.

The catalog say the Archives contain three books on dis-tortion balloons and one where it was the main topic. None of them are here, all four checked out. A small gap in the shelves where they ought to be.

I make do and gather up some of the more general books. My eyes ain't used to reading in this dark light, the typeface small. Flipping through the index, I find distortion balloon re-ferred to on pages 8, 323, and 411-5 in a textbook on advanced topics in astromatics. When I flip through to the right sec-tions, there's only the rough edges marking where someone's done torn out the pages.

I go right up to that front desk man and say, "Excuse me, sir. Sir?"

Say him: "What?" Dried spit is all caked into the corner of his lips, white, flakey. He got the look of a man who died, come back to life, and is bitter about being among the living again. His gray beard isn't trimmed a lick. Messy as all hell.

Say I: "You got some records of who checks out which books?"

"Name?"

Say I: "Huh?"

"Of the book you are looking for."

"*Theoretical Models of Distortion Systems for Light-Speed Travel*," say I, just picking one out of a hat.

He—somewhat begrudgingly, I can't help but note—stand from his chair and go to the shelf behind his desk. He pick up the fifth volume from the left, a thick blue tome. He let the book thud loudly on his desk and say, "It is all in alphabetical order, assuming you know what that means."

I find a little nook to work in. I'm not alone in the Archives, but the stacks is big enough that when I find the right corner to tuck myself away in, I can make myself all cozy.

I scan the catalog looking for the title and find it about halfway through the book. Unless there a error in recordkeeping, the book is currently in the possession of a man named Seamus Ludnecki—or it had been twenty-five damn years ago.

It don't escape my notice that the day it was checked out is during the year my Aster was born. I fount something I can give her. Something to make her grateful and look at me how she did when she was my sweet little one.

XVIII

Aster received the summons to appear in Sovereign Lieutenant's office as she was readying herself for sleep, not
long after she'd been introduced to her newfound ob-
session, Seamus Ludnecki. Ainy had given her the name and
told her about the curiously missing books she'd found in the
Archives.

The notice arrived by way of a guard seconds before Aster
was to take a long lie-in. It was Sunday, her one day off from
shift. *ASTER TO REPORT TO O-0211 IMMEDIATELY UPON RISK
OF LOSING PRIVILEGES*, the notice read.

She rushed her way up the main stairs to O, didn't bother
to avoid contact with the guards. As soon as they saw the
summons signed *Lieutenant*, they pushed her along her way,
told her to hurry up.

"Sovereign?" she said when she reached his hatch, pressing the button to activate the comm speaker. No one lived in
Osage Wing, all of it offices, storage, break cabins for guards
who worked the lowdecks. There was a buzz, then the hatch
opened.

"Enter," said Lieutenant.

It was odd to think she was in the presence of the head
of *Matilda*. This man believed himself second to God, but he
occupied such a modest office. She stepped inside, forcing her
gaze to his, refusing to bow down her head despite wanting
to. Aster barely recalled him. It had been a couple of years
since she'd last seen his face.

His light-brown eyes, brunet hair, and straight nose did

nothing to ring the bell. He had blotched and purple skin, suggesting the passing of time—because that was something she would have noticed then, and remembered. Age discolored things. Left them too pale or alternatively too saturated. Eyes fading to washed-out nothingness, while the skin beneath was the brightest shade of purple.

"May I sit?" she asked, eyeing the chair across from him at the desk.

"I've just had that cleaned, actually, and would prefer you not," he said. "You understand."

She answered immediately, without a moment's hesitation so he wouldn't know his comments stung: "That is very well. I prefer to stand anyway."

His smile had a tiredness to it, but was genuine, Aster thought. He had no reason to fake it. He'd gotten everything he ever wanted. "You've grown since last I saw you." Lieutenant tilted his head as he examined her with a casual but unblinking gaze. "You are not as unpretty as one might've expected you'd turn out, little pigeon."

"I am surprised you remember with such specificity the details of my person, given our meetings have been so brief and quite some time ago."

"I do not forget sins committed against the Heavens, Aster," he said. "You are still at it, it seems."

"I have been called an aberration before."

"Aberration. Yes. I like that word. Your High accent is flawless, by the way. You speak it as well as my wife, and she is of the finest upperdeck stock. A true lady."

"My time under the Surgeon's employ has refined my tongue," she said, though she'd always spoken High, for as long as she could remember. Long before she could speak, she listened, absorbed the sounds people made, mimicked them as best she could.

"Indeed." Lieutenant stood, grabbed a flask from the shelf,

and unscrewed the cap. The scent of bitter coffee wafted toward her as he filled a mug with the black liquid. "The Surgeon is a very good man, Aster. One of the best. Chosen by the Heavens to be their hands in this plane of existence. But he has a certain soft spot, shall we call it, when it comes to you. Which is no matter. No man is perfect, and he's not the first to seek relations with a lowdeck woman. I suppose there's something about your lot that heats his blood. Your animalian nature, I presume."

Aster clasped her hands behind her back, so tight that it hurt and with such force that if she held on any tighter, she'd break her own fingers. "Theo and I are not—"

"And yet you are on a first-name basis. Don't deny it. It's pointless, and your lies only widen the great gulf. I find it strange that the Surgeon fixated on you above all others, but then all men have their proclivities, and who am I to judge? My problem is your obvious exploitation of his weakness to have your way aboard this ship. That will not do at all."

Aster reached for her goggles, wanted to slide them from her forehead over her eyes. She didn't have them, forgetting them in the rush to meet Lieutenant.

"What do you have to say for yourself?" He leaned his elbows on his desk, chin rested on his fist.

"I do not know how you reached the conclusion that the Surgeon and I are engaged in a relationship of a sexual nature, but I can assure you our dealings are entirely platonic," she replied, carefully modulating her tone so that it did not come out defensive.

"Your sort can't help but to lie. It's a sickness."

"I'm not lying. And I would not seduce or take advantage of the Surgeon in the manner you suggest. Even if I were to try—and I wouldn't—he is too good to ever succumb." She had feelings, but she had not and would not act on them, not so long as Theo didn't want her to.

"Even those whose faith in the Heavens is unending have their moral failings. I certainly do," said Lieutenant, clipped, short.

"Maybe the Surgeon is of stronger faith than you, because he would never carry on an affair the way you've described."

Lieutenant's eyes narrowed into sharp darts. The muscles in his neck and throat contracted as he swallowed. He was a subtle man, small gestures and fine movements, and if Aster had blinked, she'd have missed the way his teeth grit and clenched, visible only for the minute twitch in his cheek. "Apologize," he said.

Aster let her head drop forward like a sack of something dead. "I am sorry," she said, hating herself as much as she had when she was a child and couldn't figure out how to speak. "I am sorry. I am sorry. I am sorry. I didn't mean that. Of course you are of unwavering faith and of course you are good, and compared to me you are practically God and I am filth. Forgive me." She hadn't rehearsed these lines, and they weren't pretend. She couldn't have faked contrition if she'd tried because she'd never been a good liar. Aster meant each pathetic panting plea for mercy. "I am sorry," she said once again. She couldn't take any more pain. She still felt the bruises on her back from last night.

Her groveling seemed to amuse him. He poured himself more coffee. There were the beginnings of a smile on his face. "And are you sorry about the little present you left me?" he asked, cool again, his feathers smoothed back into silken elegance.

"It was—it was supposed to be a reminder that the cold has real consequences. Flick was just a child," she said, unsure now why she'd left the foot for him. It had been a meaningless gesture.

"Of course the cold has real consequences. If it didn't, I wouldn't have done it," he said.

"Consequences for what? What did that child do that made her deserve that? What did I ever do to you but break curfew a few times? I do not understand your reasoning. I am trying to, but I cannot."

"Of course not. You can't see the big picture, only the petty, small, meaningless pleasures and pains of your tiny lives. Mating and drinking and carrying on no better than the draft horses who stubbornly refuse to work when they've got a sore ankle." Lieutenant's lips snarled. "We have a purpose. *Matilda* has a purpose. We are on God's path, and we mustn't stray. It has been centuries, and it will be centuries more. All we can do is live well. Live good, according to the Heavens' will."

Aster wondered if it was a speech he'd given before. The tirade had a practiced fury to it. She imagined him in front a mirror, wrinkling his eyebrows at just the right angle, widening his eyes at the climax of the diatribe to signal his intensity. Lieutenant was a man who would not let himself be misunderstood.

"What is my punishment, sir?"

She saw from the way his face fell into a disappointed frown that it was not the response he expected. "I can offer you no real punishment. You've had countless opportunities to mend your ways." Lieutenant took another sip of coffee, sucking air between his teeth because it was still too hot to drink smoothly. "You were confused about my intentions, and now I have clarified them. That was my only wish. Think of this as clearing the air."

"Then I am dismissed?"

"Yes, pigeon," he said, and she turned to leave without another word. When she grasped the handle of the hatch, he called out to her: "Pigeon?"

"Yes sir?" She did not turn to face him.

"It's a kindness that there are few mirrors in the lowdecks—

for your own sakes. You'd kill yourselves if you knew, if you were faced with your faces over and over again. As it is, I don't know how you stand to walk through the corridors among yourselves, seeing what you see."

Aster kept her face to the door as she listened.

"I have six pit bulls, the same shade of brown as you, a dark burned-maple color. And they are graceful, fierce, beautiful creatures. How is it that a four-legged beast with a snout for a nose, that doesn't bathe itself—how is it more beautiful than you? Where is the fairness in that?"

Aster could not answer his question because she did not accept his initial premise.

"More than anything, I pity you. We try to tame you, but there is no taming vermin. Tell me, how would you feel if a mouse joined you at the supper table without explanation, without apology? Would you not recoil? Would you not chase it away and lay traps for it? Often, a mouse will lose a limb in a glue trap. And is it not for the best?"

He seemed to be done now, and Aster thanked the Heavens for that. There is a breed of mouse that existed in the old place," she said. "Spiny mouse. *Acomys spinosissimus*. They could regrow entire limbs after losing them. I read about them in the Archives."

"Hmm," said Lieutenant. "Dismissed."

She left quickly and shut the hatch before her, not wishing him to call out to her again.

Lieutenant was not a merciful man. Any leniency he gave was so he would have something to take away later. She didn't know what her punishment would be, but it was certainly coming.

XIX

Lieutenant hadn't been sovereign long, but he'd already changed Q deck. He made the women walk in lines. He ordered raids on their cabins. He deemed the food they ate unhealthy, and switched them from meals of spicy meat stews to simple broths and hot cereals. He hadn't yet instituted a uniform on Q, but there were rumors that he had on W.

Aster supposed the newly imposed rigidity was what made everyone so excited when they were told to report to the Field Decks during what had become their newly required devotion hour. A spot of sun appealed more than religious recitations and quiet, mindful prayer.

"Are you coming?" Aster asked Giselle.

The rest of the women were already on their way. Quarry Wing was mostly empty but for the two of them.

"I'm tired," said Giselle from where she lay prone on her bed. She'd barely moved from it since the night in the brig-box. Several guards had tried to rouse her for shifts, but she could not be moved. Their threats of punishment did nothing but make her shrink more into herself. A priest had declared her too ill for work, though her illness was in her mind, not her body.

"I don't want to leave you here alone," said Aster.

Giselle had grown more and more suicidal, and every time Aster said goodbye, she wondered if it was the last time. She'd made this happen. She'd brought this.

"It's not safe out there," said Giselle. "I'm not safe in this." She gestured to her nightgown, but then Aster realized she meant her body. "I need a new one. I gotta shed the old one so I can get a new one."

"Will you eat some of the fruit I brought you?" Aster asked. Giselle continued to stare blankly at the wall. "Did you see I brought you some more of Lune's journals to read? I know how much fun you have picking through them."

Giselle didn't respond.

Sighing, Aster put on her hat. "I'll be back as soon as I can." She was glad she'd moved the rifle to the botanarium. She'd also taken to keeping all of her serums and medical blades in a locked box.

Aster caught up with her bunkmates as they made their way to the Field Decks. They'd be gathering in the potato field. Aster realized when she got there that it was because it was so flat, perfect for a large gathering. It was mostly Quarry Wing that was there, though there were some Aster didn't recognize. They were crowded around a large stage set in the middle with a single chair on it.

Out of nowhere, she felt him grab her hand, his fingers twined with hers, cold and soft. She knew from the feel of the palm that it was Theo. "We must go," he said, and pulled her toward the corridor, only stopping when she pulled back.

"What are you doing here?" she asked, as surprised as she was glad. She hadn't seen him since the day she'd abandoned him in Evening Star.

"You can't see this," he said. His hair was ruffled and his shirt sleeves were rolled up. He'd been searching for her through the crowd, who knew for how long. "For once, trust me. We must hurry."

"You hurry. Leave me here alone if you must, but I'm not going anywhere." She removed her hand from his grip, dreading a return to her cabin, to Lieutenant's newly enforced drudgery. She'd not had a single moment to go to the Shuttle

Bay. She could no longer get passes to travel freely. She'd barely made it to her botanarium.

"Listen to me," he said.

"No." She turned to get lost in the crowd.

He grabbed her hand again, this time clutching over her fingers from the outside instead of intertwining them. "Come with me, now. That is not a request. It is an order from a general to a civilian. Heed what I say, Aster."

She'd never heard him raise his voice like that, not ever, certainly not at her. The way he said her name, like it was a swear word. "Do not speak to me like that ever again."

He closed his eyes, squeezing them tight so the lids wrinkled, his fingers still cluthing hers. "Forgive me. Please, please forgive me. But we must go. I can't let you see this."

A small group of people watched them curiously, some pointing to the Surgeon with confusion in their eyes. They were trying to place who he was. Aster slipped away in the moment Theo wasn't paying attention.

The crowd hushed as Lieutenant held up his hand, taking the stage.

"On behalf of the Sovereignty, and by extension the Will of the Heavens, and your fellow passengers of His Sovereign's ship *Matilda*, I ask that you maintain composure as we herald in a new age. The wrath of the Guard falls heavily and appropriately, and it is for this reason that today we are responsible for carrying a life from this world into the next, where the Judges will punish her according to her wrongdoings. With humble hearts, we say—" and the crowd joined him in chorus, "*Hallelujah. Blessed be.*"

"It's an execution," someone said. Mumbles and cries filled the audience of onlookers. They'd been summoned here to watch someone die.

"Silence," Lieutenant called.

Theo spotted Aster and weaved his way back toward her.

"Please. There is still a chance for us to leave. I promise you this is nothing you need or want to see."

"What is it? Who is it? Just tell me," Aster said, whispering as quietly as she could.

"Once I tell you, it can't be untold, and you will want it untold. I am begging you with every bone in my body to come with me. I will do whatever you ask of me, and I mean it. You are my new master, not the Heavens, if you leave with me at once." He knelt in front of her, as in prayer.

"What is it, Theo? Just tell me what it is."

In the very next moment, she found out. The person Lieutenant led out in chains to be executed was Flick. They made them walk on their still-healing little leg, blood coming through the bandages, their wails so loud that at that moment Aster knew gods weren't real, because if they were, they'd end this now. All of humankind. A snap of the fingers.

"My God, she's only a baby," someone said not far from Aster, as two guards pushed the cuffed executionee along.

"I do not understand," said Aster.

She tried to move but Theo held her still. He gripped her hand hard and squeezed over and over. She squeezed back in an alternating rhythm.

"This is my punishment," said Aster.

"This is not your fault. It's not too late for us leave."

"It is. It is my fault." Aster tried again to move away, only to be thwarted once more by the strength of Theo's hands over her thighs, holding her there as he knelt. "I have not yet made them their new foot."

Lieutenant read the charges out loud to the gathered crowd, and they were minor, so minor, almost nothing. Insubordination. Talking back to a guard. A full circle of guards surrounded the stage, all of them armed with batons. Some had cans of gas, which they would not hesitate to release onto the lowdeckers if anyone tried to stop the proceedings.

"Under the previous regime you lived in a fantasy of wickedness and sin. Today you will learn this is what it takes to appease the Heavens."

"What's happening? I'm sorry if I did something wrong," Flick cried out. "Where is my great-meema? She will explain."

One of the guards cuffed the child's ankles to a chair, strapped their arms.

"Aster, do not leave from this spot, do you hear me?"

"Aye."

"Please, Aster. Swear to me."

"I swear to you. I swear to you. I swear to you," she said, wanting to say it more, but stopping herself.

"You swear what?"

"I swear to you I will not leave from this spot."

The Surgeon squeezed her shoulder, then jogged on his limp leg toward Lieutenant and Flick.

"Do not do this, Uncle. It is not the Heavens' will. Such a thing as this is beyond even God's brutality," Aster heard him say. Flick continued to cry, their face soaked with tears.

"It is time you stopped being a woman about these things," said Lieutenant.

A young man held a silver case. Aster knew there were syringes inside.

This was the moment where Aster should stand, say, *Take me instead.* But she couldn't speak. She watched silently as a doctor slid a needle into Flick's arm. She watched silently as Flick died. She was not one of the crowd members who tried to storm the stage, but she got caught in the spray of gas all the same. As she felt her body hit the floor, she hoped she wouldn't wake up.

The day Aster learned to speak, eight years old, Aint Melusine was doing a puppet show for a group of girls about Little Silver—so named for the stripe of shimmering gray in her otherwise dark hair. She had six elder sisters, all married to the king, and Silver was next in line. Not wishing to marry him, Little Silver rode to the swamplands, where the water waifs lived, and sat herself upon the muddy bank, saying, "As I am not to marry the king until I turn fourteen and am declared a woman, make me remain thirteen forever."

A rousing murmur from the swamps—and it was settled. Little Silver should go back to her village, but they would grant her request on the eve of her fourteenth birthday, which would give them time to learn the magic necessary to do what she bid.

"This story is boring," Giselle had interrupted. She sat on an overturned basket of freshly folded laundry.

"Shut up," said Ainy, and Aster was glad for it, as she wasn't in the mood for Giselle's back-talking that night. Aint Melusine snapped a long, thin branch over Giselle's forearm, and waved it as a warning to anyone else who thought to say something smart. Then she carried on with the tale.

"Now, on a warm, summer evening —"

"What's that?" a little girl named Nella asked.

Aster knew all about it. Summer was when—well, first, to understand, you had to know that a long time ago there was the Great Lifehouse. It twirled and twirled like a ballerina, trying to impress the Great Star. One twirl was equal to a day. One dance, which was lots of twirls added together, was equal to a year. The year had four quarters, and when the Great Star shined greatest and longest (its way of telling the Great Lifehouse she favored it), that was known as the summer quarter.

"Aster, you got something you want to say?" Aint Melusine had asked from up on her stool.

Aster rocked, bit her lip, stared at the little puppet theater Ainy was using to act out the story for the children.

"Come on then. Say it. Just open up your mouth and say a sentence."

Aster had hummed a gurgled, low-pitched noise, and Nella began to laugh. She got nipped with Aint Melusine's switch, little welts appearing on her arm.

"Do I laugh at you even though your face is ugly as sin?" Ainy had asked Nella, and hit her again with the branch, till Nella started to cry. "I asked you a question."

"No, ma'am," said Nella.

"It's not right to make fun of someone for the way the Heavens made them. Do the stars laugh at the planets? The bee at the sunflower? And so forth? Huh, child? No. So stop taking joy in the plights of others. Like the bad men. You a bad man?" She had clutched the switch so that her pink palms turned white.

"I ain't," Nella said.

"You sure?"

"I'm sure. I ain't like them. I'm nothing like them." She'd stopped crying by now. Her chest puffed out like the breast of a hen.

"So what do you say?" asked Ainy.

Nella regarded Aster with wet eyes. "What's the point of saying sorry? She's too dumb to understand, anyway."

So Aint Melusine beat her full on, right on her bare bum in front everybody. Nella's drawers bagged around her knees, and her shirt hiked up, and it was like all the choked silences inside Aster unchoked themselves at once.

"No," she said between smacks.

Attention shifted from Ainy and Nella to Aster. One of the older girls, Junebug, had to restart the braid she'd been working on in Mae's hair.

"I knew you was always faking it," said Giselle, "to get out of reciting verses."

Aster, satisfied that her utterance had achieved its desired goals—Ainy had, indeed, stopped beating Nella—spoke again: "Please cover her, as she clearly doesn't wish to be so exposed, and it's impolite to make someone be naked."

Ainy held fast to the switch, but helped Nella off her lap. "Get dressed," she said. Nella pulled up her drawers, stockings, and skirt, readjusted her blouse. She ran out the cabin, pushing past the others.

"Now, for the rest of the story," Ainy had said.

But Aster was too busy touching her lips, clicking her teeth together, understanding that the next time someone wanted her to do something she'd rather not, she would say, *I do not wish to*, and it would be so. Was that what Little Silver did after her visit to the water waifs? Did she visit the king? Did she tell him she wasn't going to marry him? Did he say, *Okay?*

These were the questions of a child. Adult Aster would never wonder such foolish things.

XX

Aster took to keeping what free time she had in her botanarium, in the company of plants. There was comfort in their spindly branches. She'd made them. She knew which were dethorned and which were not, which could poison with a single prick or cure cancer with a taste. Ever meticulous, she tried to predict with ever increasing accuracy which seeds would germinate and which would never take to living. In her notebook, she recorded size, shape, color, mothering plants, temperature, soil condition, position in the pot. And though she managed to make 90 percent of her plants turn from seed to seedling, there was always the one or two that lay dead. She dipped her fingers into the soft mud, dug one such seed out, and placed it in a jar which held similar dead-end seeds. It should not make her sad, but it did, ever occasionally.

That was the way of things—to live, and then to have their offspring live, and so on, for all time, as it was in the beginning and would be until the end of days. And everything connected, back to the very first thing that ever was, and to the last thing that ever would be.

She heard someone at the hatch. "Who is it?"

"Your Ainy."

"I don't wish to see you. I don't want to see anyone," Aster said, returning to her ledger, marking in ink which seed failed to sprout. She wrote hard enough that the nib of her pen poked through the paper, a blob of dark blue where the number 3 should be.

"Aster, open this hatch right now."

Aster blew air over a cup of tea, even though it was already cool. Her breath made the rose-colored liquid ripple. This was the fourth cup she'd poured herself in the last couple hours, and the fourth she'd let go cold without a single sip. A plate of lukewarm fried eggs sat next to the tea, the runny yolk having solidified now.

"Aster? Baby?"

She poked her fork into her egg, then laid her pen down before opening the hatch.

"You need to come home. There's still an hour before curfew and you got patients to see," Ainy said, leaning heavily on her cane as she walked.

Aster sprayed the leaves of the xanthe plant with a solution of water and blood meal. "No. I need to work." The green leaves of her florae dripped with water, and the smell of it was crisp, sweet, clean.

"Heard about Flick, that little T-decker," said Ainy.

Everyone had, as Lieutenant wanted. Every newspaper, article announcement, radio broadcast mentioned the execution of an insubordinate lowdeck child named Flick—an act that secured Lieutenant's reputation as the hard ruler that would get Matilda back in shape. *Tough on immorality. Unshakable. Wrathful as God Himself. God's second. God's lieutenant. If the Surgeon is our ship's mother, Lieutenant is its father.*

Aster closed the notebook she'd left open on her desk and returned it to the shelves in the section labeled, *Ge*, for *Germination*. Finished with that task, she woud start afresh on something else, naming her plants according to the principles of the ancient languages she was studying.

"Aster, talk to me. Your bunkmates are worried. You've not spoken to them in days. Giselle is in a state."

"An interesting euphemism. Giselle is only doing what we all should. Giving up."

"She needs you."

"To do what? I can do nothing for her, and even if I did, who's to say Lieutenant wouldn't take it all way? Murder her too, in front of a crowd of bewildered cowards?"

"No, to be her doctor, said Aunt Melusine. "That's what you are, aren't you, child?"

"Stop calling me that! I'm not a child. I know you mean it affectionately, but all I hear is condescension and disrespect." Nightmarish visions of Lieutenant's thin, pursed lips washed through her. In them, he was mouthing the word *pigeon*. "I am not a child. I cannot be told to mind and be quiet," Aster said, willfully ignoring the fact that Lieutenant had proved the opposite quite true.

Ainy lifted her cane a few inches, then slammed it back onto the floor with a thud. "I can't talk to you when you're in one of your moods."

"The mourning of a child's murder is not *one of my moods*, so please do not dismiss it thus." Aint Melusine was as bad as Aster, perhaps worse, at knowing how to talk to people when they were hurting. People's unhappiness unnerved her. Ainy was empathetic but emotionally incompetent. Aster had learned that well as a child.

"You right. I know," Ainy said. "I just meant, there's a lot of us who stop going on at the very moment you do. I ain't a soft woman, but I've witnessed my fair share of unspeakable loss."

In that moment, Aster realized how little she knew about her Aint Melusine. All she had were her stories, which she mined for scraps of the woman's past.

Aster sat at her desk and faced away from Melusine. She would go through each drawing in her sketchbook, list its properties, the common name she used for it, and make up a scientific name based on its characteristics and family name.

"I know you feel ganged up on by life at the moment, As—"

"Ganged up on? This is not a game of red rover and I've gotten picked last. A child is dead because of me. I was thoughtless. I believed I could fight someone and I couldn't, and now Flick is dead. Who is next? Naveed? You? Anyone I touch, Lieutenant will come after."

Aint Melusine staggered to a stool and tried to sit, but it was too high for her, and she ended up leaning awkwardly. "Come back to Quarry. Home will make you feel better. It always does."

"Quarry is not my home. I am homeless. We are all homeless. We are the very definition of homeless. We are vagrants in Lieutenant's kingdom."

"Everyone does a little worse without you there."

"I don't care! Let them do worse! Let them die!" Aster threw her pencil to the floor, slammed her sketchbook shut, but it did not make a satisfying sound. She tried to pull herself in, to find the calm that came from her internal world: quiet, rhythms, beats, patterns. She inhaled a breath, then spoke quietly but decisively: "Maybe all the ghosts were doing was telling me to join them."

Melusine snapped her cane against the counter, so hard Aster heard the wood crack. "Do not pity yourself. We live in the dredges of a stinking ship long abandoned by the Heavens." She looked up to the silver ceiling, then back down to where she found nothing but the claws of plant stems. "We pray only to *Matilda*. And ourselves. I'm only myself. I wish I could protect you from everything that's after you, but where would I even begin? Maybe we all should've bornt ourselves in another time, another place. You keep thinking there's a reason for everything, 'cause you can figure some out. There ain't. All the bad that's happened to you, it was never about you. It was about *them*. You can't blame yourself. It's sad, so very sad, and maybe if I were a different woman I'd weep like a little baby. Maybe I want to weep. Maybe if I wept people would feel sorry for me and do nice things for me."

Aster prepared yet another cup of tea, pouring not-quite-boiling water over loose purple leaves. The blend was supposed to be calming, but she was far past a state tea could remedy. "I don't believe anything you say. It's all a fiction you spin like the spider gods."

Melusine coughed hoarsely, as if to prove her frailty, and said, "Light me my pipe, you ungrateful child." She removed it from an invisible pocket in her long skirt, held it out.

Aster had the matches right beside her, but she didn't reach for them. They were not always so easy to come by, and she did not want to waste what few she had so that Ainy could fill her lungs with particles of burned tobacco. "I want to forget everything," she said.

Especially the way Flick called for their great-grandmother with that strange, childish naïveté. One need only call for their meema—she would explain all. After meemas got involved, matters always had a way of working out. It was no different than Aster's search for Lune. Stupid, so very stupid.

Aster watched the dandelion roots drying on the line, smaller and less complicated than she was, genetically, but possessing the ability to locate and destroy cancerous cells where Aster herself could not. Her skin itched. She wanted it to fall off so she could be just bones—hard, blunt edges.

"What can I do for you, Aster?" asked Melusine, quieter now. Her eyes swirled with rheum, bluish gray, but the tiny pupils pricked like lancets.

"You can get out," said Aster. This was her only sanctuary.

Ainy gripped her cane, turned, and left.

Lieutenant continued to lurk the lowdecks in spirit if not in corporeal form, every day another new restriction. Quarry Wingers scarfed lackluster meals, then hurried to their cabins for much-needed sleep—if they could sleep. Guards were posted at every turn, their numbers much greater than usual. Lieutenant had turned the lowdecks into an effective military state.

Aster kept her head down as she returned to her cabin for curfew. She wanted at least to tend to Giselle's physical condition. When she reached her turn, she saw one of the guards bark at a little girl Aster believed was called Selah. It was her birthday. She was laughing and playing with her new present, a jump rope, skipping it down the passageway. The guard grabbed her midjump and she fell back. Everyone cleared the corridor.

"Surprised to see you here a whole fifteen minutes before headcount," said Pippi when Aster slipped through the hatch. She and Mabel lay together in the bunk, listening to the radio. It was nothing but a crackle, but there was always an underground show sometime in the hour before bed. Aster admired their bravery as well as their craftiness. She didn't know where they hid it that it didn't get confiscated in the raids. It was a big and bulky thing.

"Your Highness has decided to grace us with her presence," said Vivian. "Where you been? With your companion, the Surgeon?"

Giselle didn't join in. She sat in the corner on a rug, fiddling with a doll with black button eyes. She played with her dolls a lot these days, sometimes trying to light them aflame with a match. She rarely spoke.

"Have you been having a go with him? I was certain you was a dyke like that lot over there," Vivian said, pointing to Mabel and Pippi, "but I suppose you learn something new every day."

Instead of slinking off, like she probably should have, or like Vivian expected her to, Aster backhanded Vivian so hard she stumbled into the iron wall, her head snapping against the bolt. Then Aster made herself into a hammer, rammed forward, and head-butted Vivian, forehead to nose bones.

"Aster!" Mabel yelled. Pippi sat up helplessly, pressed back against the wall at the sight of the blood. Giselle looked on with eyes shocked open.

Aster hated them all. She wiped off the blood from her forehead. She glanced back at Vivian, with the intention of saying something quite biting, but couldn't think of anything. So she got into her bed, pulled the covers up over herself, and stared above at the rusty blankness. She touched the metal and it was cold. Maybe *Matilda* had been a girl once. Maybe she was a giant. Maybe she froze to death in the vacuum of space, and they hollowed her out and put stuff inside her, and that was why she was so cold. A giant empty girl alone in the Heavens with only tiny colonists to keep her company, prattling about stupidly.

Early the next morning, Aster slid her key card through the lock of Theo's office hatch, didn't bother to knock or warn him of her entry. He was in his U deck clinic, one of the few places Aster still had access to. She was now banned from all but a few lowerdecks.

Theo sat behind his desk, his tie loosened about his neck, rubbing his eyes, which were red. Were she not absolutely certain that he was a teetotaler, she'd have thought he'd had a drink. He was not a disheveled man.

"You know I don't prefer it when you walk in without announcing yourself first. I could've been indecent."

"You're too godly to ever be indecent," she said. "You were born clothed. Without urges. A veritable eunuch." She meant the words harshly but they slipped right past him. Perhaps he was too tired to be offended by her childish attempts at insults. Regretful, she decided to apologize, but he spoke before she could.

"I wasn't expecting you. Are you allowed to be here?"

"I still have half an hour until I've got to be ready for shift," she said.

"You're certain? Lieutenant has specific guards watching you."

"Believe me, I know. How could I not?"

"Of course," said Theo. "I just . . . I worry. My days and my nights are filled with it. I fear for you. You mean so . . . You should leave here. Right now. If Uncle knows that we're talking, he will only come down on you harder. I forbid it. I order you, please go. Believe me when I say I have your best interests at heart."

"I am the only one who gets to decide what is in my best interest. Not you, Theo. The fact that you have been given arbitrary power over me does not mean that you should exert that power when it suits you."

"Do I have no moral responsibility to protect you?"

"I don't know. I don't worry about those kinds of things."

This was one of those moments where Theo wasn't Theo, but the Surgeon, obsessed with what was right and what was wrong, what he *should* do. It was no way to live, constantly on the edge of existential crisis, prostrating himself at the throne of ideological purity.

"Where does that leave me?" he asked. "How do I both protect you and respect your autonomy? What if you are a danger to yourself?"

"Short of suicidal ideation, it is my right to be a danger to myself." Even if she had thoughts of self-murder, it was still her life.

"How am I supposed to distinguish between your reck-lessness and your occasional seeming death wish? I spoke to your Ainy and—"

"You spoke to Aint Melusine about me?"

"I was concerned for you after everything that happened. You didn't speak to me after. I had no idea how you were doing. What would you have me do? Pretend not to care about you? Not think about you? I wish I could. I wish I could *not* think about you."

Again, Aster was confused as she was as a child, unable to interpret the people around her. Their bodies, their behaviors, their actions spoke in a tongue with too many tenses, moods, and declensions, all the verbs irregular.

"The next time I am worried after your emotional state, I'll go visit your dear Uncle Lieutenant. What do you think about that? Would you appreciate it?"

He clasped his fingers together, his thumbs tapping against his desk. "I said go—now go. I don't want to see you anymore."

"I thought we were—" Aster started, but she didn't finish. The truth was, she didn't think *friends* was a very good word to describe their relationship. The feelings she had for Theo were not the same as the ones she had for Mabel, Pippi, or even Giselle. She sometimes thought Theo's feelings for her were similarly inclined.

"You thought we were what? What do you delude yourself into thinking you are to me?" The force of his words cracked through the air like a whip.

The laces of her shoes had at some point become untied, and she let the dirty string drag against the floor as she walked out of the room.

XXI

The story of the Raven's house went two ways, and Aster didn't know which she liked best. The first, Ainy told like so:

Raven returned home after many years of flying about, only to find that the tree of his boyhood had been cut down. The wood that made up the trunk of the great oak had been transformed into the planks of a cottage.

As Raven flew closer, he saw smoke rising from the chimney of the cottage and smelled what he thought was stew cooking. He went up to the door and pecked at it with his beak. "Who's there?" said a voice from inside. "It's me, Raven." Then a man opened the door. He saw Raven and began to salivate. His stew needed meat. "Come inside," he said to Raven. Raven entered. "Aha!" the man said, and he went after the bird with a hatchet. But Raven said, "No, no. That's a silly way to eat me." The man dropped his axe. "Oh?" Raven perched on the top of the fireplace and began to speak: "If you kill me and cook me up, I will be tough and stringy, breaking your teeth. You must have me alive, uncooked."

So the man sprinkled salt, rosemary, lemon pepper, and cayenne onto the Raven and swallowed him up whole in one gulp. Once inside the stomach, Raven began flying about the man's body, pecking away, chewing up important parts, until the man died in great agony.

Raven flew up the canal of the man's throat and escaped by way of the mouth. He fixed himself a bowl of stew. He thought about how it was good to be back home. The End.

Aster likened herself to Raven in this story, Lieutenant to the man. If only she could get inside of him. Cannibalize his insides and reclaim her place. It wasn't a pretty story, not like the other version, which went like so:

When Raven came home, he saw that his woman was inside the house with another man, cooking the good-for-nothing some stew. "That's my stew," Raven said. "You only cook *me* stew." His woman said, "There, there, Raven. It's not so important who eats the stew but who's in it. Because what's in it will soon be a part of me." That's when the good-for-nothing man said, "I want to go in the stew then." But Raven flew in front of him and dove into the pot of scalding-hot broth, boiling himself alive. To prove he was most important, the good-for-nothing man followed Raven into the stew, boiling himself alive as well. The woman enjoyed her stew and thought how nice it was to be at home."

In stories, girls were brave and played tricks, and won. Aster wanted to be one of those girls. She wanted to be like Giselle, who'd put a bullet in that guard's head with no more difficulty than she'd brush a knot out of her hair. She wanted to be like Lune. This sadness ringing through her, resonant and unending like the repeated clang of two cymbals, tired her.

Everyone in Quarry Wing stayed out Aster's way, and it was Frannie from R deck, either Ravine Wing or River if Aster remembered right, who finally got through to her. "Oy, the Surgeon told me to give this to you," she said, handing Aster an envelope. They passed each other on the way to shifts. Frannie often played messenger woman. She had a lot of contacts and a wide network of friends, lovers, and people who owed her favors, making her perfect for delivering post.

Aster waited until after shift to read Theo's letter, doing it in the kitchens while meals of watery porridge were being prepared. She leaned up against the counter, trying to hide from the gaze of watchful guards in the corridors. Here, she felt a little less under scrutiny than she did when out in the wing or in her quarters.

With steady fingers, she broke the seal, pulled the folded letter out of the envelope, and read:

Dearest Aster (and that you are, I swear it, more dear to me than any other),

I'm writing so that I might clarify my intentions regarding our meeting. You won't pick up your radio. You will not agree to see me. My hope is that your sheer love for the written word will compel you to read.

Uncle frightens me. He has since I was very young, and though I am sometimes, shamefully, thankful that his affection for me often saved me from the ire of my father, my chief feelings for him are those of absolute disdain. He knows that I hold you in the utmost regard. He is jealous. He is possessive of me. Any time you and I are together, it is fuel for this jealousy, which he will take out against you until he eventually feels the need to remove you from the picture entirely.

I acted out in fear, in anger, to drive you away, and I regret it. There is something I wish to discuss with you, which I can't put in paper lest we both be in danger. I believe it will be of great interest to you, however, and this is my way of making it up to you for my callous behavior.

Kind regards,
Theo

He'd written the letter in Q, and it was amusing to see his proper, updeck way of speaking in a language known for its informality. Aster wished he'd told her this before. She didn't know why people were so indirect.

✳ ✳ ✳

Theo—the Surgeon, or Surgeon General Smith as he was called by his students—led a seminar on neurophysiology with eleven upperdeck men and one middeck man twice a week, and today Aster had been invited. That was what he'd meant to discuss with her in person. She would not be going as herself; she'd be attending as Aston.

He rescheduled the seminar to the evening so that she could attend. It began fifteen minutes after her shift. Today there'd be discussion on the pathology of neurodisease, and Aster put away some of her anger and sadness to make way for curiosity. She'd never been in a real school setting, and she looked forward to it. It was a break from Lieutenant, from Lune, from Ainy, from Giselle, from all the troubles troubling her.

"Are you nervous?" asked Theo when he came to collect her. He examined her up and down in her Aston attire.

"I'm fine," she said. "I should be the one asking you."

He shrugged his shoulders and gathered papers and folders into a brown suitcase. "I would rather worry while we're together than be worrying while apart from you. I really am sorry about those things I said to you in anger and fear."

She didn't want to forgive him yet. "We will be late if we don't leave soon, no?"

Theo nodded and pulled on a wool sports jacket over his shirt. Aster opened the hatch for him, held it with the side of her hip as he went through. Tall, Theo had to duck, but he made even that look graceful.

They climbed the stairs to G deck, strolled a lingering path from Gosling to Granite. Aster jogged to the glass observatory, the Field Decks visible below them through glass, so, so beautiful. Green. Dotted with color. Wild and fragrant.

"Come, Aster," said Theo, touching her on the shoulder.

"Yes, sorry."

He guided her around the corner into Gorge Wing, quiet

and empty save for one young man running off to a class. He slipped into a cabin at the very end of the corridor. Gorge, along with Gully and Game Hen, were reserved for schooling. "Remember, you are here to observe and enjoy the lesson, but I think it's best you not participate."

Aster was there under the pretense of being the Surgeon's teaching assistant. She sat outside the circle of desks and took notes.

"Surgeon Smith?" the lone middeck man said. He asked the most questions, raising his hand uncertainly every five minutes.

"Yes, Mr. Ludnecki, what is it?"

Aster looked up, spilling ink from her well onto her notes.

"You said that pain disorders qualify as neurodysfunction, but what is the difference between neurological and psychological pain?" asked Ludnecki. "Both have chemical components, do they not?"

Aster rushed silently from her chair to the desk where Theo had set his bags. She dug inside his leather tote as the class continued its conversation.

"Excuse me, sir? Do you realize your boy is rifling through your things?" asked one of the upperdeck men. Hardly a man. A lad, not quite full-grown yet, with an awkwardness to his skinny limbs.

"Didn't you say you wished me to take attendance?" said Aster. She hoped her High tongue impressed the boy who had called her out.

Theo shot her a confused glance but did not protest. He was still trying to weave his way back into her good graces. "The roster is in the outside pocket," he said.

She found the off-white envelope and pulled out a sheet of paper, then started reading out the names: *"Evans, Clark?"*

"Surgeon, do we really have to do this?"

"Quentin, Harry?"

"Present."

When Aster made it to *Ludnecki*, she was disappointed to find out it was not *her* Ludnecki. "*Ludnecki, Cassidy?*"

"Um, yes. That's me." Cassidy, the middeck fellow with light-brown skin and hair gelled back, put a finger into the air.

"Very well," said Aster, and returned to her chair.

"Wait, you didn't call me," said someone Aster didn't care about. In her mind he was a *William*, *Peter*, or *Steven*. Something handsome but tired. "Boy, could you check the list? The name's Timothy Walton."

"We'll sort it later," said the Surgeon. "Please, everyone, back to the discussion."

Aster took the roster sheet and circled the name again and again, caught up in the silky sway of her pen against the paper. Seamus Ludnecki, not Cassidy, was the man who'd checked out the books Ainy had meant steal, but the surname was uncommon, not one Aster had heard before. Surely Seamus was a brother of Cassidy's? She underlined Cassidy's information. He lived on L deck, Laurel Wing. Aster knew it was a sign from Lune. The time for grieving had passed. Now was the season of searching.

Aster stayed in disguise as she made her way to Cassidy's cabin. "L-31, L-31, L-31," Aster said aloud, squinting as she looked at the hand-drawn map someone sold for each deck, copied from blueprints, with notes about which guards lurked where. According to said map, she should be there, but she was in Lark Wing. Definitely wrong.

"Excuse me. I am looking for Laurel Wing," she said to a woman fiddling with an instrument in the corridor, restringing, it looked like. Her eyebrow was cocked and her mouth hung open as she wrapped the metal wire around a knob.

"Sure, dove, Laurel Wing's not far. You got to make it over to starboard side, though," the woman said.

"The map specified port."

"Someone switched Laurel and Lark around ages ago, long before I was born, so I can't tell you why. You can cut through Lemon Tree Wing, then turn right at the fork, and you're there once you get to the end of that passageway."

"Thank you." Aster had seen patients on L deck before, but didn't know it as well as some of the other middeck levels. Mostly families lived here, like on M. Some folks worked a mandated shift, but others had normal trades. Shoemakers and watchmakers.

She reached Laurel fifteen minutes later, found L-31 roughly where it should be. "Hello," she called from outside the hatch. There was no speaker to buzz. "Hello?" she called out again. "The Surgeon sent me."

Beyond the door, there was the shuffling of papers, the thud of something hitting the floor. "One moment," Cassidy said. He opened the hatch, his face falling when he recognized her. "You."

"And you. Cassidy Ludnecki."

He tried to shut the hatch but Aster was too quick, slipping into his cabin just as the metal was about to smash her hand.

"You don't belong here," said Cassidy. In Theo's seminar he'd been reticent, timid, and nervously enthusiastic. Now he was cocky and cavalier.

"I wouldn't be here if it weren't important."

"You're only a little twit when it's something important, then? I won't say it again: you need to get out." Cassidy loosened his tie and pulled the loop over his head, tossed it onto his cot, then unbuttoned his collar. Sweat dripped from under his chin down his neck, making the black hair there coil. Aster watched him disrobe, and she felt something she could only characterize as . . . distant disappointment. Not the sort of upset that ruined days, but a generic and faraway disillusionment that spoke to her acceptance of a mediocre status quo.

"It's been my observation that you middles can go a number of ways," Aster said. "Everyone I've met thus far on L has been very kind. I thought you might be too."

"Kindness is unnecessarily glorified," he responded, his voice a mix of world-weariness and irritation. Too angry to be sad and vice versa.

"Sometimes it is, yes." Sometimes it wasn't. "You must know what it's like to be talked down to as the only middecker in the Surgeon's class. But you call me a twit. Why?"

"Because that's what you are." Cassidy popped open a can of peach juice, guzzled it. Peach Jimmy. A thick, fizzy beverage popular among lowdeckers. Old, old, old, from when *Matilda* left the Lifehouse. A decade ago someone went through the remaining few boxes to copy the recipe—got something pretty close to it and repackaged the new version in the old cans. Aster could taste the carbonated, sticky sweetness on her tongue just watching Cassidy tip the can back and drain those last few drops. She could hardly ever find it. Last harvest year, she'd discovered a whole crate of the old ones, unwrapped, in a random P deck storage crate, tucked among mops, orange-scented cleaner, and moldy oats. "Do you want some? I can cut open the can for you and you can lick the inside, like a dog."

Twit, now *dog*, and she'd heard much worse so many times that she did not care, could not care. She didn't need much. Didn't need to be adored and loved and called nice things. All she wished for was perfunctory respect paid to the fact that she was, indeed, alive. Real, breathing, thinking, movable parts and all.

"You are mean because inside you're tiny. So tiny you cannot hold up the weight of your own body. You must inflate your ego just to fill the skin. You float around like a helium balloon. Blown up and bloated and gassy and empty."

She went to his desk, from where he'd pulled out the Peach Jimmy, and got one for herself. She popped it open and took a long sip, not finishing it. Then she opened each of the three that remained, repeating the same behavior. One sip from each.

"What do you think you're doing?" he snapped.

"Whatever I want." She took another long drink from the first can until it was about halfway empty, then poured the remainder on top of his pillow.

"Stop that right now!"

Cassidy grabbed her arm and jerked her away from the remaining cans, but she was too close. She pulled out of his grip and succeeded in toppling one of the mostly filled cans with the tip of her finger. The thick juice gathered into a puddle over the papers on his desk. She hoped they were all very important and very irreplaceable.

"Are you daft?" he said.

Yes.

He sighed angrily. "Why are you doing this to me?"

Aster thought he might cry out like they did in plays she'd read: *Woe! Lo! Why have the Heavens forsaken their child?* She took pity on this weak-boned middeck boy and told him the purpose of her visit: "I'm here because I need to know how to find your brother Seamus."

His grip tightened on her arm. "What did you say?" The edges of his hairline frayed into curls from sweat. He was a nervous man, he lived a nervous life, and he'd die young, of a heart attack, most likely. Stress rewired the body, and most likely his had already effectively been transformed on the inside into byways, crossways, tunnels, and bridges of overstimulating hormones. The heart couldn't handle it.

A small coffee stain blemished his shirt, apparent now that

his blazer was unbuttoned. His shoes, Aster saw, were worn and gray. At some point they'd been black, but that point was many, many years ago.

"How do you know about Seamus?" His voice cracked the way young teenage boys often did. He began pacing the cabin. Aster remembered the frequency of questions he'd asked at the Surgeon's seminar, and now she wondered whether that had been a manifestation of his restless intensity.

"Twenty-five years ago a man named Seamus Ludnecki checked out a book I need," she said. "I can't imagine there are many other Ludneckis around."

His lips moved to form a response, then stilled. Then he smiled. "You are relentless, *yongwa*."

"Aye. You speak the Low pidgin?"

"No, of course not."

"You called me *yongwa*. Not even the Surgeon calls me that, and he speaks Low like a native."

"It's just something I overheard once. Had a nurse who used it," Cassidy said.

"Your accent was perfect."

"You could detect my accent with a single word?"

"Yes."

And now more of it made sense. Like the Peach Jimmy, considered a lowbrow drink by even those as high as N deck. And the age of his shoes.

"Well then, you're mistaken. I was born on L. I'd have no reason to speak Low."

Aster switched to a pidgin dialect used up and down the lowdecks, not particular to a deck, side of ship, or corridor. It was the language guards used to speak to them in. "Why are you lying to me? You are growing flustered, I can tell. You pace and pace and pace."

"I can't understand you when you speak that heathen tongue," Seamus replied in Middle.

"Aye, you can, *lywa awo deni sylf*." Lying one who denies himself. "*Betraya na ver*." Truth betrayer. "Who are you, Seamus Ludnecki of L deck? Something tells me you are not from Laurel Wing. Should I call the Surgeon and let him know?" Aster showed her two-way radio to make the point. "Aston to Theo," she said into the speaking piece, glad that she remembered at the last second that she was still in disguise.

A crackly pause, then the Surgeon's voice: "Here. What do you need?"

"I am presently with your student, Cassidy Lu—"

Cassidy reached for the radio, but she pulled it away before he could get his hands on it. "Talk later, Theo. If I a die, the man who did it lives in L-31. Goodbye." She cut the transmission.

"Look, it's not what you think it is, whatever ridiculous scenario you've cooked up in your brain." Cassidy flopped onto his cot, worked his feet out of his shoes. Soon, he'd run out of appropriate garments to take off as an expression of his nerves, and would be naked.

"Do you or do you not speak Low?"

After a moment, he looked at her intently and nodded his head once. "I do—though that was the first time in a very long while. You unsettled me, *yongwa*, broke my rhythm."

She asked him where he was really from, and he said R deck, just one level below her. He'd taken over the identity of a middeck man who'd passed away. "It was Seamus who offered me the papers, said his brother had died and there was no reason why a good identity should go to waste. We'd met once during a shift. I wanted to be a doctor more than anything, so I took the offer, no questions asked. I got my own cabin. Got out of work shifts—well, I still have to do two a week, but not like before. That was two years ago."

"No one noticed the change?" asked Aster.

"If they did, they didn't care," Cassidy said.

"Are you still in touch with Seamus?"

A hesitation. "I'm not."

"Are you fibbing to me again, *lywa*?"

"You are persistent."

"It is important," she said. "I believe this book may help me find my mother. I have long thought her dead, but now have reason to believe I was wrong."

Cassidy seemed softer now, and she wondered if his earlier behavior was his affectation of an upperdeck manner he had developed. "Chasing missing mothers is a losing game, *yongwa*. Quit now."

"It's foolish to ignore the dead," she said.

Cassidy watched her carefully. "Then I say, be foolish."

XXII

It was the nature of a thing to want to know its creator, so that it could know itself. That was what Aster craved, to be able to peer into herself and see more than what *Matilda* had made her. She'd chosen her path, and that path led her to Seamus. It had taken some prodding, but Cassidy told her where to find him. She hadn't yet met him in person, but they'd traded written correspondence. His missives were short but polite, and tonight she'd be seeing him face to face.

Seamus worked three twelve-hour evening shifts a week in *Matilda*'s Bowels. Aster decided she'd exploit her new boyish facade one more time to sneak in to meet him. It wasn't necessary, but she liked to do it, to pretend she was a man. It wasn't the boy part that attracted her. It was the lying part. It was becoming someone else. Her old mistakes were gone because that person didn't exist. She could learn how to be brave again in a foreign skin.

The task of shoveling waste into the funnels to be processed into usable materials was an indignity generally reserved for lowdeck men, though it was a big job, and some middeckers had to do it too. Everything in the ship emptied here, the toilets, uneaten food. Fat pipes fed their contents into large cylinders, emptied by the workers into processing churns. Everything down here was like a furnace, hot and stinking.

Aster worked while she waited here for Seamus. As she scooped spoiled lettuce into a wheelbarrow, a man with freckles and greasy hair charged into her with his shoulder, snorting, calling her *cocklet*. She didn't like the feel of his body brushing against hers, even if it was only for a moment. It made her remember all the things she didn't want to remember. She didn't like skin on hers, unless it was certain skin. Ainy's skin, or Mabel's skin, or Pippi's, or Giselle's. Or Theo's.

"Look at that little soft boy," someone said.

All eyes turned to Aster. Men chewed the insides of their cheeks then spit, the wads landing near her boots.

"He's got fancy clothes like a proper nancy."

"*Girlyboy,*" one sang in mock falsetto.

"Leave him alone. Back to work," the overseer called, barely looking up from a status report he was filling out.

"We're just having a bit of fun," said a man. "Or are you a girlyboy too, Sergeant? You want us to look away while you have a go with Aston?"

"I said shut it, or I'll break your fucking nose. Today's not the day to piss me off." The overseer didn't have to get up to make his point, because several of the men returned to their tasks.

"Fine. I'll leave the girlyboy to his work. But look at the way he walks," the man said, laughing. "His poor bumhole's probably sore. Sergeant, why don't you kiss it for him to make it better?"

Aster knew these insults weren't meant for her. She was playing a part. They hurt anyway. They hurt because of the people they were meant to target, and they hurt for all the ways she'd been targeted in the past. With everyone insisting it was true, it was hard to believe she was any good at all.

She felt Lieutenant was right about her. She didn't understand, but when she thought about herself, she was repulsed. Aster was a vile fiend, a dyke, uglier than a dog. She was other things too, more dreadful things, things that were not so easy to say or admit. A bevy of parts cast off secondhand, to be used up by whomever had need.

Memory wrapped its rope around her neck until she couldn't breathe. Her vision was spotty and gray. She was a child again. She was three and four and six and nine at the same time. She was sitting on a guard's lap, and she was kneeling and she was lying on her back. She was begging for her Ainy. She was thighs, knees, bellies, groaning, buttocks, ejaculate.

If she vomited, it was her own weak stomach. Ainy always said she was an awful, picky eater, couldn't hold a single thing down as a baby. Nothing was anything to cry about.

Memories could not be unmemoried, only shuffled so as not to be in the forefront of things. Surrounded by men, they all resurfaced at once.

Aster threw down her shovel and walked to the water cooler, bumping into her shipmates, purposefully throwing them off their course. She was someone else here. She had to remember that. They didn't know all the ways she'd been made into to a trembling mess. They didn't know she wasn't strong.

Ahead of her, there was a man with a scar across his eye, the lid pinched shut with mutilated tissue. He hadn't been among the group of men who made fun of her before. He smiled when he saw her, one section of his face contorting. His good eye widened, threatening her. Aster did not avert her gaze as their proximity increased, nor did she inhale a steeling breath.

Scar-man stalked up, lorded his height over her. He smelled sweet, like he'd just come from the showers—and that was just another reason to hate him, that he thought any amount of washing could ever make him clean. He pushed his chest into her, but she was prepared. Her feet stretched wide and anchored her in place. "What do you want?" she said.

"You're a child. You don't belong here. I don't work side by side with babies. It's an insult, you simpering cunt."

Men dropped their tools to watch the exchange. Instead of scolding them, the overseer simply observed, hanging back. "Maybe I am a cunt. Does that mean you want to fuck me?" she asked, speaking in the manner the men had before. Laughter exploded around her.

"What did you just say to me?"

"That you want to fuck me. Is that what you like? Fucking girlyboys?" She channeled old games of house. She channeled theater. Listen, then repeat. Listen, then repeat. That was all it took to pretend well. What was a person's self but carefully articulated mimicry?

"You're dead." He pushed Aster into a large metal vat. Her skull slammed against a metal knob, and she shook her head to shoo off the pain. His cocky grin revealed twisted, graying teeth. "I will gut you." As he sized her up, no doubt under-estimating her strength, she took advantage. She pushed out of the vat, screamed, and went for him. She took the steel toe of her brand-new boot and cracked it into his knee as hard as she could. The man tumbled down, groaning. His voice was like a hog's, simultaneously guttural and squealing. He tried to stand up, but Aster knew she'd broken his knee.

She took her boot to his other knee, to his thigh, to his groin, to his stomach, her movements quick so that he could never get the better of her. She hit every part of him over and over until she felt hands around her waist, pulling her back. So she went at that man too. Nobody could touch her unless she said they could.

"Calm down," someone said. The man turned her around, moving his hands from her waist to her shoulders. It wasn't anyone she recognized. "Come on, son," he said. "It's all right now. It's okay, it's okay."

His affirmations inflamed the wound. Things were no more all right now than they'd ever been. She writhed, hoping her fury was enough to outgun him.

"Let it pass," he said.

"No," she cried out, but her body began to heed his words anyway, her heartbeat slowing. She relaxed into his grip.

"I'm here," he said.

"Nobody's allowed to touch me. Nobody's allowed to call me names. I'm alive," she sobbed out. "I'm alive."

"You are. You're here, and it's going to be all right. It's over." His eyes were on her, examining.

"It's never over." She turned and launched a wad of spit at Scar's wilted body. A couple of others saw to him.

"You're going to get yourself killed, acting like that," the man said. He wore a knit cap that covered his ears, the brown of it milky and murky compared to the rich brown of his skin. She knew then that this was Seamus. He'd told her he'd be wearing a cap.

"I didn't mean for you to see me like this," she said quietly.

He nodded his head. "I don't think any different of you."

She struggled to catch her breath. "I don't want them to see me crying." She wasn't certain she would, but she didn't know what to expect of herself at the moment. She wasn't stable. She felt her emotions were as wobbly as Giselle's.

"I know a place we can go. Aster, that's your real name, right?" he asked, quiet. He was nothing like Cassidy. Aster supposed it was because they weren't really siblings.

"Yes, but I'm Aston here."

She wiped her sweaty brow with her jacket, not like a proper girlyboy would do, but she had no handkerchief. Scarman groaned on the floor. "You'll think twice before touching me again, won't you?" she called over, but Seamus led her away.

"Leave him," he said. "You already won it, right?" It didn't feel like she'd won anything.

Two men helped Scar to his feet. "You're a little shit," one of them said to her. He had velvety golden skin and thick eyebrows that met in the middle. His voice was as pretty as his face, which held dark eyes, a sculpted nose, and pursed, angry lips.

Seamus slung his arm around her shoulder, pulling her in close, away from Scar and his entourage, ducking into another aisle of the Bowels so they were alone. "You were a terror in there. Haven't you heard you're not supposed to kick a man while he's down?"

"Whoever said that?" Aster asked, because no, she'd never heard that. That was the best time to kick a man, that was what Melusine had taught her.

"God or somebody said it."

"Which god?"

"The big one," Seamus said, shrugging.

Aster leaned back against a metal column. Her heels rubbed up and down against the back of her boots and were starting to blister. She slumped against the column until she flopped onto her butt, pulling her knees into her chest.

"Don't you believe in God?" Seamus asked. He sat down next to her, his eyebrows raised.

"I believe in unseen things," she replied, imagining the billions of atoms floating around her.

Seamus nodded. "Your mother did too. Believed in a world off this ship. She got me to believe it too. She thought she'd found a home for us and that she could fly *Matilda* to it. I'm not a scientific-minded person, but she seemed so sure that I believed it." There was a somberness in his aura. Lune had given him hope, then taken it away.

"My mother's mother, my grandmother, used to tell me something her mother's mother used to tell her. A fact they passed down," Seamus said. "Landside, the sun was bright and heavy on her back; it tickled her skin and woke her when she lay too long on the dirt. The rays touched you, hot beams of light and heat that stroked your skin like a meema's hand against her baby. Bright and yellow and sometimes white. Not like that Baby Sun that grows the food—but thick in color like turmeric or soured milk. That's what she said. And she would douse me with kisses and warm breath and say, *This is how my nanny told me it was, and this is how you'll tell your grandbabies it is.*"

Aster tried to feel it for herself, what it would be like for a star to spray plasmic light onto her. She could almost access it, a memory etched in her organelles, in the golden hairs that lived on her dark skin, in the shade of the dandelion flowers that poked from the greens she picked and ate.

"Were you my mother's companion?" Aster asked.

"No."

Aster let the breath rush from her lungs and out her mouth in a tidal swoosh, her limbs loosening. "Who were you to her?"

"A man who could be of service. Little more than that, I'm afraid. I work in identities, trading them whenever a mid-decker dies. Lune threatened to expose me unless I helped her." He laughed.

"Help her how?" asked Aster.

"Get her books from the Archives. Sneak into some gent's quarters to get plans and blueprints. Help her with the shuttles."

"You've been up there?"

"Not since the day you were born," he said, standing up. "Come on. Let's go to the break room. Get something to eat. Stories are best shared over meals." He reached his hand out to help her stand, and she took it.

The mess was a large cabin with rows of tables, where a woman served food from a pot of something brown and bubbling. Aster missed the meals Ainy could no longer make under Lieutenant's new rules. Just last month, they'd be gathering suet, cornmeal, salt, and pumpkin flour into little balls, dumplings they'd steam in a spicy broth of duck and greens, the water thick from chicken feet and pepper paste.

"Try to eat a least a little of it," said Seamus. "Shoveling like you were is hard work."

Aster stared blankly at her soup.

"One bite," he pressed. The bigness of her earlier man-nishness was nowhere now. Short-lived. All that was left were the taunts, and the crack of Scar's knee, and the past swooping in, an unkindness of ghosts. Her old life had pos-sessed her, strengthening her, but like everything, used her up and then was done. She scooped some of the broth into her mouth, swallowed.

"What did she need your help with the shuttles for?"

"Fixing them up, working my connections to see about getting fuel, testing to see how many could fit in a single one. She was planning an escape, far as I could tell, though I don't know where the hell to."

"And then?" asked Aster.

"And then nothing. One day I never heard from her again. I'm sorry I don't have more to tell you. I brought the books though, like you asked." He passed her a heavy duffel.

Aster wondered if Lune had taken one of the shuttles to see what she could find. Perhaps she thought she could do better than *Matilda*'s computers. "What was she like? Was she nice?"

"Nice enough, though not the first word I'd use to describe her. Smart as a whip, sharp-tongued. She was a lowdecker but had a lot of upperdeck ways, in my humble opinion. I reckon she went through one of the reform education programs they used to have. Lune was fine, well-spoken. She charmed peo-ple. Always knew just what to say." Seamus grabbed a shaker of pepper and sprinkled it into his bowl, followed by the salt and some red sauce in a jar. "You look just like her, you know. When I saw you in that fight, I knew you were who I was supposed to be meeting. The last time I saw her was so many years ago, but when I glimpsed your face, it was like being back in that moment two decades ago."

Seamus ate up his food with vigor, and Aster had a sense he was doing it more for her than him, giving her a chance to absorb the information. When he stood to get himself seconds, she closed her eyes and tapped her fingers against the tabletop. She wasn't sure why she'd bothered.

"Marlowe is staring at you," said Seamus when he returned.

"Who?"

"Look."

Aster turned to where Seamus gestured, saw the man from earlier with the perfect skin and the perfect eyes and the perfect lips, his thick black eyebrows knit together, the man who'd helped Scar up back in the Bowels.

"I have to go," Aster said, abandoning her tray.

"That's what he wants. He's trying to goad you into another fight. Stay. Sit. Eat. Be calm. You got to stick by me, okay?"

"I can't stay here," she said, glancing around at the men as they ate. There were about forty of them, or more. She didn't know how she'd missed them before. She started to move away.

"As—" Seamus called. She heard him get up to follow after her, but she was already ahead of him, and unless he jumped over the table, she had an advantage. "Wait!"

"Thank you again for everything," she said, grabbing on to what she could to steady herself—one man's shoulder, a table, a wall.

She hustled through the mess until she reached the corridor. There, she could finally breathe. All she had to do was make it back to the Bowels, where she'd be under the gaze of the overseer. She looked left, then right, realized she'd been so busy letting Seamus lead her that she did not remember which way it was. She picked left and hoped for the best.

"You've reached a dead end," Aster heard behind her, and even though she knew she shouldn't, she turned.

"Please leave me alone," she said.

"Like you left Ty alone? A doctor just looked at his leg. Said he might not walk right again."

Aster thought, *Good.*

Marlowe walked up and grabbed her by the neck, his hand forcing her windpipe shut. "Sick of pricks like you thinking you can treat us like that. Who told you? Give me a name, and I might spare you."

He loosened his grip on her neck, but Aster still felt like she couldn't breathe, her clavicular muscles bruised and sore. "I don't know what you speak of," she mumbled. "I assaulted Scar-man because otherwise he would've assaulted me."

"Scar-man? Say his fucking name." Marlowe pushed his palms into Aster's chest.

"Ty."

"Did you know that he got that scar from a fucker just like you, some pansy-ass kid trying to prove himself, came right up behind him, jumped on his back, and sliced a razor across his face? Said faggots were half-people, so he should only have half a face. Is that what you think?"

She shook her head but had trouble saying the word aloud. The absurdity of it, that anyone could think she had a vendetta against Ty for being with another man when it was mostly women Aster longed after.

He slapped her hard across the jaw, knocking her to the floor. Half her face disappeared in an instant, like Ty's, numb, the nerves dying off.

"Take off your trousers," he said.

Aster hadn't put on her salve today. She'd never had the chance. She tried to gather herself up, but her eyes watered, obscuring her vision. She tried to crawl away. "You misunderstood," she said, in a voice that was chopped and choked.

"Shut up. You talk again and you're dead. Trousers off, now." Marlowe reached into his back pocket, revealing a large knife with a serrated edge. "I just have to decide whether I'm going to cut off your balls and let you bleed out, or sew you back up."

Aster forced her eyes shut, and she rocked on the ground. In her fantasies, she always said to them, *I could rip you up. I could kill you. I could kill you so many times.* And the men would say, *Go on and try.* And Aster would, and she'd bite them and scratch them all over, hard enough so that she broke off pieces of their bodies. And the men would say, getting the better of her, *Cry mercy, girl*, and she'd say, *You cry mercy! You cry mercy! Cry mercy, and maybe I will grant it to you! But heed, I am not a merciful god!*

She hardly felt Marlowe cut the fly of her trousers, then through the cotton fabric of her briefs. But she registered his shocked gasp, his pulling back.

Aster's eyes darted open. Marlowe stood over her. She gulped, tried to pull up her slacks, but they were shredded at the top, ruined, her underwear and thighs exposed.

Marlowe unbuttoned himself, let his trousers fall to the floor. Stepping out of them, he kicked them to Aster and stood there in long johns. Aster put on the new slacks over her ripped ones.

"Who are you?" he asked.

She was going to respond, *Aster*, but then that seemed like a lie too. Orphaned and feral, she didn't deserve a name.

XXIII

It would be foolish to say that the mutiny that led to the massacre of hundreds, their limp bodies lying across *Matilda*'s corridors, began with Aster, who after all was only a woman, a small and largely unliked woman, whose heart was no more prone to thoughts of violence than any other who'd endured the decades of trauma that characterize all who lived in the lowdecks. She was stubborn and recalcitrant, but so were many. Like any tidal matter, a mutiny only had a middle.

The night in question, the night a storyteller might falsely call the beginning, *Matilda* percussed. Aster couldn't shut away the ship's metallic effervescence as she traveled back to her quarters from the Bowels, so instead she fed off the resultant overstimulation. There were worse things than being a motherless child. Without a past, Aster was boundless. She could metamorphose. She could be a shiny, magnificent version of herself.

She'd had a chance to read through the books Seamus had given her, and though she couldn't understand every detail in the marginalia notes, she understood enough. That was all one could do with the past—be satisfied with half-answers, take the rest on faith. Combined with the notes Aster had absorbed from the Shuttle Bay and Lune's journals, the astromatics began to make vague sense, as did what her mother was trying to do in her last days. She wanted to set *Matilda* on a different path. Aster recalled the passage that had stymied her so much when she first read it:

After using the lavatory, I see the H deck guard in front of me. I stare into his dark pupils, unafraid. I will not run from him, nor will I indulge his protective instincts by seeking to move past him. So what if he apprehends me? Pushes me backward? All he has done is saved me a bit of time on my journey, so I might be returned to my quarters more quickly.

After night headcount, Aster lit a candle and stood at the center of the cabin. Knowing no other way to put it, she said, "I'm going to save us all." Pippi, Mabel, and Giselle all turned to her at once. Vivian, of course, was absent, having moved after Aster broke her nose.

Aster made eye contact with each of her bunkmates to assure them she had very much meant to say aloud what she did. She was not going mad. She'd already gone mad and had remained that way ever after.

"Save us from what?" asked Mabel.

"What are you on about?" asked Pippi.

Aster held tightly to a book called *Space Compression and Relativity: Methodologies.* "My mother had a way off the ship," Aster said.

Giselle slid onto the floor with her blankets. "You figured it out?" she asked. It had been days since she'd said so many words or expressed as much interest.

"Not all the way," Aster admitted, "but I am close. I need you all. Ghosts talk in riddles and metaphors. Those have never been my strong suit."

"Well, that's the truth," said Pippi.

Mabel put on her glasses and lit more candles. She placed a pipe under the handwheel to keep out guards doing night raids. "What are you and Giselle even talking about?" she asked.

Aster began, rather arbitrarily, because all beginnings are arbitrary, with the blackouts twenty-five years ago. "During her work investigation on Baby, she discovered a Shuttle Bay and the controls to Matilda's navigation systems."

"The Gods navigate Matilda," said Pippi.

"In a fashion, yes. Computing consoles run on an autopiloting program. The ship is moving constantly forward, and when the system detects an obstruction, it diverts itself. That diversion is what causes the blackouts. She's a big ship. She's got a lot of momentum. It takes a lot of energy to change her course. She gets that energy from Baby."

"So twenty-five years ago, there was an obstacle?" said Pippi.

"Yes. Something called an anomaly in the Heavens, best described as a bottomless pit pulling everything in its reach inescapably toward it. In my studies, I have seen it referred to as a black hole, God's throat, well of despair, gravitational nexus, camera obscura." In Lune's notebooks as *his dark pupils.*

"Sounds like something best avoided," said Mabel.

"That's what the automatic piloting system concluded. My mother, however, disagreed."

"She wanted to send us *into* the bottomless pit?" asked Pippi. "She was mad as you."

Aster shook her head. "Look," she said, flipping open the astromatics textbook to the passage she'd marked, long ago highlighted by Lune. *"Though less relevant in contemporary astronautical design, which tends to be based on space compression and use of distortion fields,"* Aster read aloud, *"we'd be remiss to skip the topic of gravitational propulsion altogether. Travel at relativistic speeds obsoletes the need to use a planet's gravity to accelerate vessels traveling the Heavens, but every engineer should be familiar with the calculations involved in this area of orbital mechanics. There are rare moments when gravitational propulsion and space compression can be used in tandem."*

Pippi groaned, but Giselle and Mabel listened raptly.

"I am not sure if I know how to explain except to say that my mother wished to navigate Matilda around the anomaly.

The autopilot sought to avoid it completely, but she wanted to get the ship closer to it so it would be pulled into its orbit and reverse direction as it spun around it."

Giselle pushed her short bangs back off her face and spoke quietly: "The H deck guard, pushing her back."

"Exactly," said Aster.

"Back to what?" Mabel asked.

"The Great Lifehouse," said Aster and Giselle in unison.

"But why would she do that? I don't understand. What's the point? So we can fly for three centuries *backward*? And for what? So that when *Matilda* finally stops, we're on the doorstep of a dead planet?"

"Mabel's right," said Pippi. Losing interest, she crawled back into bed.

"Ain't y'all even listening?" Giselle said. "Mabel, I don't have half your book smarts, but I heard the word *accelerate* in that thing Aster read. That means go faster, yeah? Lune whipped us round and sped us up." Aster wouldn't have used those exact words, but Giselle was right. Lune used the gravity of the black hole to propel *Matilda* faster.

"So you're finally talking. I guess you feel better now," Pippi said.

"Giselle is correct," said Aster. "From what I can understand of her mathematics, Lune believed she could reduce the journey so that it was much shorter than our initial three hundred–odd years—a single year."

"Seems your mother is about as good at math as me then," said Giselle.

Aster snorted. "I do believe that was a joke. It's good to see you make them again."

Giselle shrugged. "Don't be fooled. I'm far from cured."

"Still. It is good," said Aster. "It's pained me to see you in such agony."

"Aster, are you trying to have a heart-to-heart?" asked

Pippi. This land of feelings and tender moments was the sort of thing at which Pippi excelled. At the very mention of emotions, her indifference became enthusiasm. "I'm glad that you're opening up," she added, taking on a lofty air. It was as if she'd somehow stopped time, brushed her baby hairs down with fresh grease, changed into a clean frock, and smeared rouge onto her cheeks, restarting time only when she was about to take her rightful place as queen of cabin Q-10010.

"So if her math was wrong and it didn't take one year, how long?" asked Mabel, but then she answered her own question: "Twenty-five years. Of course."

Aster went to take a seat on her cot. "I don't know for sure, but I think the autonavigation system is slowing the ship down as we approach the Great Lifehouse, preparing *Matilda* for orbit." She had remembered Ainy's explanation of motion with the ball. If you set it to rolling, it took an outside force to change its direction. That was what had happened twenty-five years ago when *Matilda* sought to avoid the black hole.

Objects also required an outside force to slow down. As *Matilda* approached the Great Lifehouse, she drew on energy from Baby to set her brakes. Aster had figured this out without help from Lune's notes. Sovereign Nicolaeus helped her make the connection.

Every sovereign had been exposed to siluminium, by way of the private glass observatory Giselle had described in his chambers, but something about the start of the blackouts made it worse for Nicolaeus. Aster believed it was the ship slowing down. The siluminium underwent a special reaction to allow *Matilda* to travel at velocities approaching lightspeed, and that reaction stopped when the ship had to come to a halt. Whatever the change, it had been disastrous for Nicolaeus, making the siluminium unstable in his body.

Alternatively, the pulsing electromagnets that activated the blackouts and helped slow the ship might have affected the siluminium. Aster had nursed a number of theories, but what was most important was that Lune's connection to Nicolaeus was incidental. She was thankful this small link had set her on the path to discovery, but the two had been exposed to the liquid independently. It was unlikely the siluminium caused Lune's death, and Aster still didn't know where her mother had gone and why—and if she died, of what.

"So slamming the brakes caused this wave of blackouts," said Mabel. She'd begun scribbling notes into her journal.

"As far as I know, we are the only ones who know about this. We have to act now that we have this unique tactical advantage."

"What do you need us to do?" Mabel asked.

"Giselle, are you well enough to leave the cabin?"

"Possibly. I don't . . . I don't know."

"What if it involves getting your rifle back for a short time?" said Aster.

"Then definitely. I am ready," Giselle replied, perking up.

Aster remembered the resourcefulness of the Tide Wingers, their magical starjars made with difficult-to-come-by materials. She asked Giselle if she could bring them the rifle and request they fashion more bullets for it. "They'll need the gun, though, so they can see how to make them."

"I can do it," Giselle said. She seemed happy to give up possession of the rifle if it went into making more of its juju.

"What are you planning exactly?" Pippi asked.

"I want to be prepared. I want us to be able to defend ourselves. I want you to be able to defend Mabel," said Aster, knowing this would convince Pippi it was the right course of action.

"I can defend her. I *will* defend her." Pippi scooted closer to her love.

"I need something from you too, Mabel," said Aster.

"Anything. I'd rather return to a dead planet than spend another day under Sovereign Lieutenant."

Lune had made the same wager. Though three hundred years had passed on *Matilda*, considering the relativistic speeds, more than one thousand years had passed on the Great Lifehouse. Maybe life had started anew there after whatever disaster had reduced it to ruins.

"Spread the news," Aster said. "Not everything. I want people to be ready for a change. Do you still know people who can work the loudspeakers?"

"Aye, of course."

"Good. Here is what we need to do." Aster doled out instructions. There was still much to put in order, but they were on their way.

XXIV

The hand-pie Aster bought smelled promising, but once unwrapped, it lost any and all appeal. She took a bite and found the crust dry and crumbly, the meat gamey, flavorless. After a second and third bite, no improvement. Suppressing a disgusted shiver, she lay the barely eaten morsel on a piece of foil, thought longingly of Quarry Wing's kitchen. Tuesdays, before the new diet restrictions, Melusine boiled plantains, stirred the starchy flesh with salt, scallions, cilantro, onion, bits of pork skin, scooped the mixture into pancake-sized patties, and fried them. Pippi said the dish was too rich, too meaty, and too salty, but plantain dumpling was one of the few foods Aster enjoyed without caveats. For all G deck's loveliness, there was a distinct lack of good cooking.

Aster removed a pen from her belt and uncapped it, drew squiggles in an empty notebook. Working with Theo again had many benefits, but the abundance of clean paper made it most worthwhile. Flipping to a new page, she composed a color-coded to-do list, red ink corresponding to tasks of utmost importance, blue ink corresponding to tasks of midlevel importance, and green ink corresponding to tasks she wanted to do, but couldn't until she'd completed the red and blue tasks. She needed to ask Seamus if he still knew how to operate the launch pad.

"What language are you writing in?" Theo asked, moving up behind her so that he could peer over her shoulder. His shadow obscured her writing.

"Q," said Aster, realizing, quite suddenly, that this was not a proper name for a language.

"You invented a personal alphabet then?"

"It's the standard alphabet," Aster said, comparing the letters in her notebook to those of the documents spread over the desk. She supposed her print differed significantly from theirs.

"And you're able to read that?" Theo asked.

Aster knew that her messy scrawl wouldn't win any handwriting awards, but then she hadn't submitted it to a handwriting contest, had she? She didn't care. "I can't read it at all, but writing it down helps me remember. I usually recall what I've written before I even try to make sense of the letters."

"You've taken notes for me that look much better than that," he said.

Aster lifted her shoulders up then let them fall. She was fond of words, but Theo should know by now they didn't come easily to her. "I suppose when I am writing something for you I put in more considerable effort, but it's exhausting and extremely slow going. When I write for myself, I don't bother."

"You've never told me this before. Had you, I would've done something about it."

"I have learned how to hide my weaknesses well." That was the secret to surviving.

"Give me a moment," said Theo, but instead of going into his exam room, he opened the main hatch and entered Goosefoot Wing. A second passed, then another. It made her nervous being here without him. She was playing Aston, but it wouldn't fool anyone who knew her face well, certainly not Lieutenant.

When Theo returned, Aster was about finished with her to-do list. Theo carried a large black case. The leather was grayed and worn in places, bits of skin nicked out of it, edges curled up. He sat it in front of her.

"A black box," said Aster.

"A gift," he countered.

"You bought it just now?"

"I retrieved it from my quarters. Open it, please."

"I do like gifts." Aster stood so that she could reach the top of the case. She unsnapped the brassy buckles that were speckled with rust. "A machine," she said. She ran her fingers along the buttons, punched them, relishing the clicking sounds. It was shiny, freshly oiled, nothing at all like the case. There were no scratches or impurities. Emblazoned across the top was beautiful gold lettering, though Aster was not familiar with the tongue. "A very beautiful machine."

"It's a typewriter," said Theo. The size of his smile was amusing.

"You are very giddy. You'd think it was you who'd just been gifted a machine."

"A typewriter," he said, correcting her again.

"I know what it is. Of course I know what it is. But the fact that it's a machine interests me more than its particular function. I like machines very much." Her microscope, pocket watches, radio, radiolabe.

"I'm giving it to you because your writing is abysmal. I bid you use it." He gestured to her to-do list.

"No. I believe you are trying to woo me. Sorry, but I am unwooable."

He snorted.

"Don't scoff at me. Gifts mean affection. Do they not?"

"I meant only to make your job easier," he said. "It's all set up if you want to try it."

Aster poked around, experimenting with the keyboard. She loaded the typewriter with paper and began to write.

theo lovvs A s T E R with alll his hart.

The keys were sticky. She removed the paper from the feed, folded it into a plane, and threw it so it glided toward Theo's desk. Theo scribbled a note on the back of the plane and flew it back to her.

Theo giveth. Theo taketh way.

Aster slid a blank sheet of paper into the typewriter and typed another note.

Theo woud not taketh the machine from one he is trying to wooeth.

"Aster, our next appointment is in ten minutes, and it might be nice if when our patient arrives you aren't throwing paper airplanes."

They traded notes like these frequently, but the typewriter added a layer of novelty. It felt nice to engage in mindless fun. Aster didn't consider herself flirtatious, or one to entertain casual dalliances, but all she could do was kill time until she figured out how to reverse *Matilda*'s redirect. Theo hadn't offered any ideas and said the science of it was too much like God's stuff to even fathom getting involved. He encouraged her to worry about fixing the Sovereignty before fixing *Matilda*. It was as good a plan as any, and Mabel and Giselle were busy doing their parts.

She should be back in Quarry Wing helping them, but curiously she was freer in the upperdecks. The guards Lieutenant had watching her didn't know she was here. She could read Lune's notebooks without interruption.

When it came time to head home for headcount that night, Aster was not ready. She walked with Theo down the corridor to the steps, but then told him she'd forgotten something in his office—and not to wait up for her, as she had a key and could go retrieve it herself without worry. He nodded assent, though he looked suspicious.

She hid under the desk, as she knew several women came to clean the place in the after-hours. Upon hearing the hatch snap shut, she emerged from under the desk. Dark, cold, and deserted, Theo's office resembled a prison at night. The metal walls creaked an accordion yawn. What had hours before been a lobby bustling with middeck gentry was now a tomb. Lemon-scented disinfectant sterilized every surface, and the chemicals skidded uncomfortably down the skin of Aster's throat.

Cabin G-1001, and the objects therein, reeked of loneliness. It wasn't the office she'd longed for after all, but Theo's company, and he was gone. She tried to think of a course back to Quarry Wing, but couldn't. The passageways, pipes, chutes, and abandoned corridors that were usually so clear appeared blurry in her mind. She couldn't recall if the vent in Gully Wing dead-ended or led to a fork—and if there was such a fork, whether the chute down to S deck was on the left side or the right. At this hour, she'd be caught and punished if caught alone in the corridors.

Aster tiptoed into the exam room and shut the door behind her, dogged it. Aches in her body made themselves known all at once. She curled into Theo's mechanical chair. Atop the tray table next to her lay a row of surgical devices: vascular occluders, retractors, scalpels, drill bits. She studied the display, remembered that the C-shaped silicone device was necessary to block compromised blood vessels. The metallic sheen of lancets and forceps dulled as Aster drifted sleepward. She now felt, inexplicably, safe.

When a whisper woke her sometime later, particles of breath hot on her outer ear, she shivered and forced her eyes open. Crusted with rheum, her lids stuck to her waterline.

"Giselle?" she asked, but that wasn't right. She wasn't in Quarry.

"Aster, I'm sorry." The voice came at her more loudly this time. It was Theo, and his palm squeezed her shoulder.

"What is it?" she asked, stretching herself up. The back of the exam chair inclined, but only just, and she maneuvered into a sitting position.

"He knows you're here." Aster noticed the tininess of his voice. It cracked with pain.

Fuzzy-headed, Aster understood only half of what he said. His words had shocked her awake, but she had yet to catch up to their meaning. She glanced to the door, which was closed, the shelf she'd wedged beneath the nob broken and on the floor. The exam room, for sterility's sake, contained no vents, hidden compartments. The cabinets were too small to hold her.

"Is he coming for me?" she asked, swinging her legs out of the chair and sliding to the floor.

"His guards are already here, beyond that door," he said. "I'm so sorry. I don't know what to do."

Escape impossible, Aster cleaned herself off as well as she could. She wiped her eyes and the creases of her lips. Without asking, she went to the sink and splashed cold running water onto her face, massaged the skin with her fingertips. Then she scooped some of it into her mouth. Knocking on the door roused her from her ministrations.

"Now, Surgeon, or we'll break it down," they called.

"Aster, you must come," said Theo, holding out his hand. She did not take it, but went to open the door herself.

"Apologize, apologize, apologize. Apologize profusely. And lie," he said. "Please."

She didn't answer him.

Four guards stood in the lobby, none of whom Aster had seen before. Except for one, they had dark-brown eyes. Three stood in formation, their arms folded behind them. The leader, one with squinted eyes, high, square cheekbones that frightened Aster with their strength, and sand-colored hair, presented a pair of cuffs. "I wouldn't resist, if I were you," he stated.

Aster turned and let the guard clasp the metal over her wrist, much too tightly so that her fingers buzzed.

"Theo," she said, or tried to say, the words hiccupping out of her mouth in a syncopated mess.

The blow from the guard dulled Aster's senses. When they reached the top of the stairs, pushing her toward a hatch, she struggled to read the words on the cabin door. She narrowed her eyes, brought the calligraphic letters into focus: *Interrogation—D-00.*

Her breathing descended into a fit of erratic gasps, and she jerked out of the guard's hold with a yelp. He tightened his grip on the back of her neck, fingers drilling into her levator scapulae and sternocleidomastoid. "What does a girl as ugly as you need with a face?" he asked, then tore his knife across her cheek, chin to temple. Aster was no stranger to extraordinary pain, but she screamed as loudly as she had when she'd received her first blow as a child, the sting of the cut spreading over her entire face. She cried out again, sound trickling from her lips halfheartedly. "You try something again, and it'll be an ear," he said, knife pressed against her hairline, cold. She dared not shiver.

Another guard keyed open the door, shoving Aster inside. Her feet dragged. The room was tiny, seven by seven meters, even tinier for the imposing presence of Lieutenant, who sat with one leg crossed over the other, eyes on his wristwatch. "About time, gentleman," he said.

A single lightbulb hung down over a wooden table. The guards dragged her to a stool across from him, uncuffed her, only to recuff her to the table. Aster stretched her fingers, wiggled them, but her wrists were locked firmly in place, bound in metal.

"Leave us," Lieutenant said, calm. The guards saluted and filed out, the one with the knife slipping his blade back into its sheath.

Sweat trickled down Aster's neck. Her face bled, but chained to the table, she could do nothing about it. She made note of a metal toolbox on the table, the name *Sovereign Lieutenant Smith* written in marker at the bottom; above, *Please ask before borrowing*.

Lieutenant drew his hands into a pyramid. "You know why you're here today?"

"I'm sorry I missed headcount," said Aster, maintaining what she hoped was a contrite tone.

"I have expectations for every citizen of *Matilda*, and you continue to fail to meet those expectations."

Aster laid her sweating palms on the surface of the table, sat straight and unmoving like a metal beam. "What are you going to do to me?"

"Nothing you won't survive," he said. Lieutenant opened the toolbox, the lid obscuring the contents from her view. He removed a hammer from within. Aster watched as he grabbed the handle in his fist, began to gesture his arms flamboyantly, shaking the hammer into the air. "You're a—what's the word you used when we last spoke? An *aberration*. I'd thought I'd made myself quite clear at that meeting, yet you are still playing by your own rules."

Aster tapped her feet on the floor, right foot then left foot. The room was uncomfortably hot. Her shirt, wet with sweat, stuck to her heavily.

"I'd thought you a smart woman. Now, I'm not so sure. Or perhaps you have no conscience . . . Did you feel shame when you found out about Flick?"

Aster felt her lips tremble at the sound of their name.

"It is you who killed her, Aster. Do you understand that?"

Aster remained silent.

"Answer me." Lieutenant rested his chin on the metal of the hammer.

"Yes," she whispered, curled her hands into a fist.

"I spoke to her before we led her out onto the block. A sweet child. A good child. You may rest assured knowing that she is safe now on the Other Side, embraced by the Celestial Shores," he said. "Her death could've meant something, yet you dishonor her memory by continuing to be insubordinate and incorrigible."

Aster's eyes flicked to Lieutenant's. She studied the rims of his irises and the diameter of his pupils, looked and looked for a secret, or a key, a cipher, but found the same bits of anatomy present in any eye—cornea, sclera, lens. Her own facade of calm was failing, wobbling on its arthritic knees. Lieutenant's practiced ease showed no signs of imminent dissolution.

"This could be over, Aster, right now. You tell me you're sorry, and it's done. Forgotten. Say it, Aster. Say it, and Flick's death isn't meaningless. Say it, and beg forgiveness."

Aster knew he lied. This could never be over. "No," she said.

"Say it!" he barked. "Say it, and mean it."

"I'm not sorry. I'm not sorry. I'm not sorry."

"Enough," Lieutenant said.

"Why are you doing this? Please tell me so I can understand. What do you want me to apologize for? Being alive? Breathing? I can't help it that I exist. If my presence hurts you so much, end me. Snap my neck and be done with it."

"You'd like that, wouldn't you? An easy end to your pathetic existence. You think you're a martyr? To be a martyr you must have a cause, you stupid, stupid naive girl. It does not end with you. It does not end with me. The Sovereignty is forever because the Gulf of Sin is forever. We were yesterday, and we will be tomorrow. One uppity lowdeck cunt cannot change that." He massaged his palm, pinched the flesh with the index finger and thumb of his other hand, working out some invisible strain. "It does, however, require maintenance. And that is why you are here."

Before Aster could hitch a breath or beg for reconsideration, Lieutenant raised the hammer and smashed it over her right hand in three different spots, with enough force to crack the underlying bones.

XXV

ittle Silver, so named for the strip of shimmering gray in her otherwise black hair, had six elder sisters, all of whom were married to the king. The king had acquired much wealth through a variety of business endeavors, and he felt entitled to the world and all that was in it simply because much of the world and much of what was in it already belonged to him. Thirty-six wives, swaths of land stretching from the swamps in the north to the gulf in the south, an estate of considerable size, another estate of even more considerable size, and yet still another estate larger than the other two combined.

This is where Little Silver worked the kitchens, saved from marriage to the chieftain for her young age. Yet she would not be such an age much longer, as was the nature of things. Little Silver walked northward for many days until she reached the place where the water waifs lived, and sat herself upon the muddy bank, saying, "Make me forever young, so I do not have to marry the king."

A rousing murmur from the swamps—and it was settled. Little Silver should go back to her village, but they would grant her request on the eve of her fourteenth birthday, which would give them time to learn the magic necessary to do what she bid.

A warm summer evening, one of Silver's sisters came to her, chanting: "*Little Silver, Little Silver, hair painted ghost. You are the earthly vessel for our heavenly host.*" She continued: "I no longer wish to be enslaved as the king's wife, and I request the counsel of the spirits in your communion. What say they?"

Little Silver said, "Eldest Sister, I have communed with the spirits, and it is their opinion that you must kill the king, lest live life his slave." Little Silver had not really communed with the spirits. The streak of white in her hair was not a mark from the netherworld, as her sisters and the villagers believed, but the result of her first encounter with the water waifs, their strange faces scaring her not quite dead. But she knew that if her sister killed the king, she'd be spared from being his seventh wife, even without the waifs' help.

"How do I kill the king, Little Silver?" her sister asked.

"Here, you must find a way to feed him these." Little Silver gave her herbs she'd picked in the village outskirts.

That night, the eldest sister sprinkled the herbs into her husband's tea, waiting patiently in bed for him to die. "Wife, let us kiss," he said. And so she kissed him, knowing it would be the last time, and therefore not minding it as much as she had previously. Little Silver's sister proved herself much more sensitive to the poison leaves than the king, however, and died as soon as their lips touched, falling back into the sheets, a warm heap. Yet the king was unaffected, less sensitive to the poison than she.

The next day, another of Silver's sisters came to her.

"Little Silver, Little Silver, hair painted ghost. You are the earthly vessel for our heavenly host." She continued: "The king has killed our eldest sister, and I fear that I am next. I request the counsel of the spirits in your communion. What say they?"

Little Silver said, "I have communed with the spirits, and it is their opinion that you must kill the king, lest you die as well." Silver gave her herbs much, much stronger than the last. That night, when the sister prepared tea for her husband, she died from simply touching the leaves.

And so it went with Little Silver's four other sisters as well. One dying from simply smelling the tea, another from looking upon it, another from being in the same vicinity, and the last from even thinking about it. So the king decided to make Silver his bride now, rather than waiting till her birthday, out of other wives and therefore very lonely.

Little Silver had to ride to the swamps to escape, seeking the counsel of the water waifs. The king, also on horseback, rode after her, only a few paces behind. Silver kicked her horse's side and said, "Gyup, gyup!" spurring it to move more swiftly. She could hear the stomping hooves of the king's stallion behind her, and Silver gripped her mare's mane.

The waifs did not appear when first she arrived, so she jumped into the swamps to escape from the king, leaving her silver pony behind. She swam and swam, but the water was too murky and too vast and too filled with beastly creatures, and she drowned straight quick.

Keeping true to their promise to keep her young forever, so she might be free, the waifs used all the power inside themselves to make Little Silver into a ghost, draining themselves until they were weak and brittle and dissolved into the water like so many dead before.

Little Silver sat perched on a tiny little island in the middle of the swamp, too afraid from having drowned before to leave her place. To keep herself company in the dark, she hummed, rousing the attention of the king, who had been searching for her onshore.

"Little Silver, are you ready to end this foolishness?"

"Aye," she said.

He jumped in after her, leaving his white pony behind. The chieftain swam and swam, but the water was too murky and too vast and too filled with beastly creatures, and he drowned straight quick, dissolving into the water just as the water waifs had done, and like so many dead before.

It was a grim sort of tale but one that used to give Aster much comfort. A poison so strong that the mere scent of it leveled an entire castle? Perfection. That the king escaped its power was a fluke of the narrative.

She used to think that. But Aster understood now that kings don't die. Even when they do, they have sons, and those sons have sons, and so on. Was that what Lieutenant meant? *The Sovereignty is forever.*

She awoke in her botanarium alone. The alert bell rang and she ignored it. Eventually, she used her good hand to rip it from the wall, the force of which jostled her right hand into a fit of agonizing throbs. Time got mixed up, lost, confused. She measured hours in pain. When she needed to inject more poppyserum into her neck, she figured four hours had passed. Had it been a day? Half a day? Two guards had led her in chains back to Q, the ship still dark in the early morning. Somehow she'd made it here, epinephrine doing what her normal self could not.

Aster's brain felt fogged, the serum slowing her thought processes into a slow drawl. It hurt, and she didn't want it to hurt.

Next to her, where she lay in a self-made den beneath a desk, sat the leather bag filled with some of her medical instruments. She'd grabbed it to use as a pillow, the leather thick enough to provide cushion. Inside was a large knife, larger than that of the guard who'd mangled her face. Resolved, she picked it up and stumbled to a chair.

She unfastened her suspenders, the movement taking her twice as long as usual with only the one hand, and used them to tie her wrist to the arm of the chair where she sat. With the knife in her left hand, her bad arm locked in place, she started to bear down with the blade.

Aster shivered. She knew that she had to be quick, a quick swipe just past the styloid process. She'd performed amputations before. It would hurt, but no more than what she was feeling now, the unfathomable aching in her metacarpals.

"Aster?"

She heard banging against the hatch.

"Are you in there? Aster. It's Theo. Please let me in."

"Go away," she said, the blade still in her left hand.

"You know I know how to override the lock," said Theo.

"I also know that you won't do it," she said.

"You think you know me so well?"

"I do."

Then nothing, not another sound.

"So? Go ahead. Override the lock. Do it," she said.

Aster hated how weak her voice sounded, longed for her monotone back. The pain in her hand radiated outward and everywhere, affecting her vocals.

"Aster, please let me in," he said.

She loosened the tie she'd made with her suspenders and stood, hand limp and resting at her belly. "I told you that you wouldn't bust in." She undogged the lock and opened the hatch, turning away before he could get a good look at the guard's and Lieutenant's handiwork.

"Thank you," he said, reaching for her shoulder. She felt the pressure of the squeeze and jerked away, the movement sending a pang to her fingers.

"Turn around."

"No."

"Please, Aster. Let me see your face."

"Why? So you can dry my tears? I'm not crying."

There was a whistling sound as Theo sucked in air through pursed lips.

"Please don't say sorry," Aster said.

He started to speak then stopped. "Please look at me."

Aster went back to her chair, turned to sit, and finally faced him.

"Aster," he said.

She'd not bothered to bandage the gash on her face. It would need stitches, a wound like that, the way it split the side of her face open. She could feel it tingling all raw and exposed.

"You should have come to me after," he said, and the words faltered when he glanced down at her hand.

"I wouldn't want to interrupt your and Lieutenant's private time," she responded, not knowing whether she meant it sincerely or sarcastically. Her right mind was somewhere else, in its place a bitter, angry, lashing mass. She fiddled with the dangling elastic of her suspenders. "I regret saying that."

"I forgive you. I deserved it. I am as angry with myself as you are at me for letting them take you."

"You're an ascetic. You are always angry with yourself. And you didn't deserve it."

"May I look at your hand?" he asked, already kneeling down in front of her. She moved her arm from her stomach to reveal the scope of the injury. Theo did not react but to close his eyes for a few moments too long.

"I will fix it. You know I will," he said.

"I hope so. It feels very—tender," she said, and Theo smiled at her understatement.

"You took something for the pain?"

"I took many things for the pain."

Theo laughed, and though he still appeared too pale in the face and veiny under the eyes, a lightness seemed to wash through him. "I meant it when I said you should have come to me. Or called on your radio. I'd have walked straight to your cabin and escorted you updeck."

"Without a pass?"

"Goddamn a pass."

Aster shivered, a tremor of pain in her knuckles, and Theo reached out to sweep a finger against the hot skin of her right hand. The faintest of touches. She hardly felt it, not through the haze of poppyserum.

"This is not sustainable, this thing between Lieutenant and you. This hatred he has. And I know you. You will not become some silent, sweet thing, no matter how many bones he breaks. You will get hurt again. You have already been hurt so much. It is not Lieutenant, it is—"

"Kings. Lots of kings. Kings for days," she said.

He nodded in understanding. "It is the kingdom itself. Any kingdom."

"Then what do we do?"

"What is necessary. I will make what choices I need to make." His hands couldn't seem to sort themselves out. They moved from his hair down to his sides, into the pockets of his trousers, and back out again.

Aster rested her cheek against her knee, scrunched up her face as she considered his hypothesis. "I am too uncomfortable to do what's necessary," she said.

"You need a proper bed—not that God-awful pallet of blankets. Come to my quarters. Let me fix your hand."

There was a hole in the knee of Aster's trousers and she could see through to the scab on her skin. She picked the brown and black bits off with her good hand until it shined pale pink. "Your quarters?"

"I know it's not proper. If you'd prefer, we could return to my office. I just thought you might—"

"No. Your quarters are fine. I thought there might be a Book verse against that. *There shan't be any Asters past dark.*" He smiled at her attempt at humor, for which she was grateful.

"Come. We will walk together," he said.

"And if we run into a guard?"

"Then I will kill him, Aster, should they wish to report you to the Sovereign. I will kill him regardless. I will kill him for being a potential threat. It is really that simple. I should have killed those men who came for you before. I didn't because I lacked faith. I have prayed on the matter and am feeling resolved."

He held out his hand, and she took it, used him as leverage to pull herself up. Theo removed his jacket, tied it around her shoulder to make a sling, a little cradle for her broken hand.

She awoke in his bed. The mattress was the size of three low-deck cots pushed together. Thick blankets covered her, so heavy that she thought upon opening her eyes she'd find Theo on top of her.

Aster turned her head and saw him sitting at the edge of the bed, a book in his hand. He closed it and set it on the bed-side table. There was a stain on the cover, brown. Coffee or tea? Iodine? It was unlike him to spill, and she surmised she'd been the cause of it in her earlier poppyserum haze.

Aster raised her right hand and saw the cast. There was black calligraphic writing on the white gauze. *Beneath lies Aster's hand.* The tips of her fingers peaked out from the cast, the nails bitten to the quick. She smelled the residue of antiseptic gel spread across them.

"How is your pain level?" Theo asked.

"Nearly nonexistent," she said. She knew he'd used the ultrasound to locate the nerves and inject anesthetic into only that particular area—something she could never do for her patients because how would one lug an ultrasound machine down to the lowdecks? The precision required to insert the needle just so, also not Aster's specialty. Big cuts—those she could do.

"Shall we test it?" he asked, and reached out toward her wrapped hand. She nodded, and he pinched the tip of her exposed thumb. "How was that?"

She watched the way his fingers brushed her nail, like he was afraid to touch her skin. "I feel it, but no pain, Surgeon."

The use of his title must've reminded him of something, because he drew his hand away. He'd changed out of his doctor ensemble into fitted forest-green trousers and a silky button-down. She liked the way he dressed when he was alone. The coal around his eyes. His touch was always soft as mango butter, but among the general populace he forced himself into an odd directness. "You are an anomaly of a man," she said.

"Perhaps because I'm not a man at all." He sat closer now. The sheets wrinkled as he scooted himself toward her.

"Aye. You gender-malcontent. You otherling," she said, the fog of anesthesia wearing off. She could see him clearly now. The curl of his lashes. The white flecks of skin over his dry lips. "Me too. I am a boy and a girl and a witch all wrapped into one very strange, flimsy, indecisive body. Do you think my body couldn't decide what it wanted to be?"

"I think it doesn't matter because we get to decide what our bodies are or are not," he answered.

Aster sat up, and Theo helped her prop two pillows beneath her head. "Is that so? Then I am magic. I say it, therefore it is true," she said.

"It is true. You are a very rare magic, Aster. Don't you know that?"

She felt his eyes on hers even as she stared off into his cabin. She'd never been here before. Despite the large bed, everything else was basic. A small wooden desk. A chest of clothing. She knew the sparseness was because he'd given the rest away.

"I enjoy it when you give me hyperbolic compliments," she said, and she tried to face him, to look at him eye to eye as was expected, but could not. His eyes were too much. She settled her gaze on his ears and the rings on them.

"Aster?"

"Please do not tell me to look at you." She still hated to

look people in the eye, and she did not wish this moment between them ruined by that anxiety.

"I wasn't going to."

"Then what?"

"I . . . care for you very much."

"I've often thought so," said Aster.

The sound he made was part laugh, part sigh, and he reached his hand up to touch her face and she leaned her cheek into it. He pressed a kiss to her forehead, then over each eyelid. "Is this all right?"

She didn't trust herself at the moment not to mess up a nonverbal gesture, so instead of nodding vigorously like she wanted to, she said, "Yes. It is all right."

He kissed her left cheek, then the right one, his lips against the newly stitched cut. It prickled but did not hurt, and she moved her face so that she could kiss him on the mouth. She knew how to kiss, had done so before, but the newness of Theo turned her lips into cautious, trembling things.

He moved onto his side so they were lying next to each other, Aster on her back, Theo propped on one elbow as he scraped his teeth against her bottom lip and slid his tongue against hers.

Aster, occasionally, through no will of her own, worried she wasn't pretty enough, and why? Pretty was a strange thing to concern oneself over. Pretty was subjective and fallacious. Pretty couldn't be replicated in a lab. She, as much as anyone, enjoyed the prismatic sweep of amaranth in bloom and the geography of animalian bodies. Yet when applied to people, it didn't jive with her that pretty was meant for some and not others. More pressingly, it didn't jive with Aster that some days she wanted to be one of those folks who was prettier than the other folks. It was like wanting to be more vanadium-based, or wanting to have orange-pigmented skin—arbitrary, bizarre, pointless. Still, she wanted it, and Theo made her feel like it was already so.

"I do not wish to be penetrated," Aster said, his hand near her thigh.

He nodded his head, his heavy breaths hot against her neck.

He didn't unbutton her shirt or otherwise slowly undress her as he moved downward, laying kisses to her stomach over the fabric of her top. His fingers fumbled briefly with the button and zipper on her bottoms, then pulled the lot of it, underwear and all, down to her knees. He rubbed his cheek against her thigh, lingering there for several seconds until she felt his face move between her legs.

Aster could not think in words at the moment. Only in sensation. The feel of his tongue and the scratch, scratch, scratch of his stubble, which she'd never thought she'd feel, as under normal circumstances he shaved his face relentlessly.

She dressed as he slept, finding her trousers balled up at the foot of the bed under covers. Aster grabbed briefs from his chest of drawers and a clean shirt. A flannel she'd never seen him wear but smelled strongly of the incense he burned when he prayed.

Dear Theo, she wrote on a pad of paper once ready to leave, *I am off to the Shuttle Bay.* Deciding the note not suitably warm, she added: *You are not unpleasant to look at when you sleep. Love, Aster.*

Dune Wing was empty. No guards patrolled here. Aster dragged her feet along the carpeted corridor, purposefully tracked mud from her boots into the intricate arabesque designs. The passageway was wide—the span of several men. The doors, wood—not the metal hatches she was used to—

were widely spaced, revealing that the quarters inside were extraordinarily large.

She traveled up to C, B, then A, and where the staircase abruptly ended, she jumped to reach the hidden entryway she'd discovered, letting the built-in ladder swing down. She closed it after climbing up, then headed toward the bay.

PART IV

ASTROMATICS

XXVI

Giselle Nwaku

The most important thing to know about me is that I have an extremely nice bum, the type you'd like to smack, spank, grab hold of, lick, bite. It's a bum that will be passed down in stories.

So what happened was Giselle's bum.

Once upon a time there was Giselle's bum.

Brer Boar saved the world from Giselle's bum.

It's be-all, end-all bum.

Melusine says my ego is as big as my ass, and she's right.

If Aster were inclined to look, she'd say, *Your buttocks require further study,* which is her way of saying, *I creamed my knickers.*

I should probably talk about more wholesome things, like knitting or biscuit making, but the very thought of it makes my pineal gland secrete melatonin into my system. *Pineal gland. Melatonin.* Sleep stuff. Regulates your rhythms and all that. The glories of knowing Aster! She talks a lot, and when I'm not ignoring her, I pick up this and that.

I'm a bad, bad girl (sultry pouty face), and I need to be punished. There are those who feel shame for what's been done to them, who call themselves *bad* for that reason, but I feel no shame. I feel no shame for what's been done to me, and I feel no shame for what I've done. Once, Mabel and Pippi heard stories about this subdeck woman, Wailing Creek Wing I think, who sold her younger sister to this man who lived in the uppers, to, you know, do the type of things that's been done to all of us. They fussed and lamented like old grannies.

"Oh, I'd never do some shit like that!" Pippi said.

It's cruel, but I'd do it, wouldn't feel that bad about it. Stuff was done to me, and I'm all right, so it stands to reason the girl would be all right. I'm not destroyed. It's not possible to be destroyed.

Sevri o'lem mol'yesheka ris ner.

That's how you say *hello* in the language of my kin. *Sevri* means *to dip bread*. *O'lem* means *with all* or *together*. *Mol'yesheka* means *into a common pot*, and *ris ner* means *let us*.

Let's dip our bread into a common pot.

It used to be one of the only things I could say, till Aster taught me how to speak it proper. We acted like we were so grown that year, me eleven, I think. But we were babies. We still played dress-up. I dolled myself up until I looked like a queen, and she'd turn herself into a little gentleman. "Wash the clothes whilst I smoke my pipe!" Aster would say. She was great at pretend games because she was an excellent copycat.

"Yes, honey," I'd say, then take a fake bundle of clothes to a wooden barrel and stick them inside.

"I require supper!" Aster would say.

By now, I was the fed-up wife, and I'd say, "Cook your own damn supper, fool, if you so damn hungry!"

Then Aster would say, "This is the part where I hit you, but I don't wish to hit you."

And I would say, "Are you sure? You can if you want."

Her nappy-ass hair stuck out in a halo around her face, those wiry strands that had escaped the confines of her ribboned ponytail. "I'll do it, to preserve the integrity of the game," she'd say. "But I'll do it gently."

I would cross my hands over my chest and say, "No, do it hard."

She would. One time she smacked me so roughly I fell back onto Giovanna's (a girl who used to bunk with us) cot.

Then Aster came on top of me, her thighs straddling my hips.

"What do I do now?" she asked.

I don't remember what I did exactly, probably swallowed heavily and licked my lips. I instructed her, "Now you take out your penis and put it in me and go in and out."

"I don't have a penis," she said.

"Then just kind of move about, like they do."

Then we rubbed our bits together through our clothing until we were spent.

Aster snuck into the Archives and found a book called *A Practical Dictionary of Ifrek*.

"This is your language," she said. It predated Q. "Do you wish to know it?"

"If it's *my* language, then I already know it, don't I?"

"Then why do you only say the same five words? I'm tired of those five words." She foisted the dictionary against my chest. Her hands were orange, stained from turmeric, and some of the yellowy spice had rubbed onto the pages. That was the year Melusine tried to teach her to cook, but Aster could barely dress herself then, let alone fold butter into dough, heat palm oil until it turned the most delicious shade of pink-orange.

In my language, there is no word for I. To even come close, you must say, *E'tesh'lem vereme pri'lus*, which means, *This one here who is apart from all*. It's the way we say *lonely* and *alone*. It's the way we say *outsider*. It's the way we say *weak*.

Everyone always wonders about *I love you*. In Ifrek you say, *Mev o'tem*, or, *We are together*.

"How do you say, *I'm tired?*" people ask.

"*Ek'erb nal veesh ly*. The time for rest is upon us."

Back to my bum. I thought Aster would be in her botanarium because that's where she always is, and I wanted to say—I don't know—*Sorry, thank you, I hate you*, etc. But she's not here and I am waiting. Shaking my bum to pass the time. I think of myself as a fairie in a wood. When I was wee I used to hop around in the Maple Wood wishing to be stolen away by a changeling. I would give them a very good deal. I wouldn't even have to become fay. They could change places with me rather than kill me, and I'd be all right with that. I'd flop my arms and jump about looking foolish, anything to catch their attention.

It's 09:00. Aster didn't come to bed last night, so I figured she was here, but there's no sign she slept here. Her bedroll is tucked neatly under the wooden desk. I guess she left early, so I turn on a record and wiggle my hips, twist and turn, curve my body as seductively as I can.

With no one to watch, it's not as fun, so I cut off the music, tap my fingers along the wood of the player, trying to think of what to do. Sighing, I flop onto a stool, pick my way into the top drawer of Aster's desk, and look at her notes. Her handwriting is foul, but I've seen it enough times to be able to muddle through it.

I flip a few pages until I get to something that actually looks interesting, a crumpled page with print scattered strangely on the page. Like it had been folded into a paper airplane. Her handwriting is actually legible for once:

> *do you think of me at night?*
> *I am a religious man.*
> *religiously devoted to me.*
> *so you are a god?*
> *aye.*
> *That would explain the curious hold you have over me.*

Something between the Surgeon and Aster, then. It's all very tame and dull, so I scrunch it into a ball and throw it into the bin, then I kick the bin so the contents scatter onto the floor: tissues, old slides, leaf clippings.

I'm a very physical person. I like to touch and be touched. I like to tear things apart when somebody gives me the chance. Sometimes it's like I can't help it, then I think, no, I could help it, I could hold it back, like a sneeze. But it feels so much more satisfying to say the cruelest thing, to hurt, to harm. I wish I was better, but I'm not, and so there's nothing to do but love who I am.

I wanted to help Aster because I know what it feels like to have something bad in your bones that you can't get out, something deep.

It's like brain surgery. The doctors can't remove the tumor without lobotomizing you, so you wait to die, sick, but yourself. That's all we've got—ourselves. We don't even have history. We don't even have family. I barely remember my mother's face. She died giving birth to my little sibling Emile. And what of *her* mother? And hers? What of the fathers? What of the origin of our kind? Aster is an alchematician and studies these things. She knows the way all life connects because she researches and researches. She throws herself into it like I throw myself into fucking, like if done hard enough we can discover the One True Mother, and she will cradle us in her breasts and rock us the way we were never rocked. Our mothers—not just me and Aster's, but all of ours—were so rough and cold. They'd sooner pump milk out their breasts and feed it to their infants from a cup than feel those wee lips against their nipples. I understand.

It's ten and she's still not back. I take a big gallon bottle labeled, *Mirobyl Netoxate*, and empty it onto the soil of her beloved xanthemum plants. Nothing happens, so I grab them by their bases and uproot them.

A scalpel sits perfectly straight in a metal tray, and it's infuriating, how Aster takes the time to make her tools line up just so, but can't bother to be on time. I could be luxuriating in a bath somewhere. I could be reading a book about ladies and gentlemen, about a dandy man who is frosty on the outside but hot with passion on the inside.

I take the scalpel and rip it through the roots of the xanthemum plants, snipping each one until they're in coarse, woody shreds. It looks like kindling for a fire, and I get the most perfect idea in my head.

Little fires, like for having a smoke, are all right, so I keep matches hidden in the pockets of my skirt for when I need a quick moment with the tobacco pipe. I take one out, flip it against the matchbook, then set the little flame atop the plant roots. They catch light quickly. There are so many papers to burn, to keep the fire ablaze, so I crumple them into balls one by one and burn them. Charts, pages and pages and pages of notes, thick folders smoldering to black.

The stools are lined up around a table perfectly symmetrical, spaced evenly apart. It's easy to bang them into the walls and break off the wooden legs. The fire bursts to new heights as I feed in the wood pieces.

Calmly, I walk to the thermofilter, use Aster's code to override the purification system, closing the vents so as not to smoke up the whole ship. Aster knows everything about *Matilda*. She could've long since destroyed it, flipped a switch and cut off our oxygen supply. Maybe she should've.

I take my flask from thigh holster and spread its contents all around, over the plants, over the books of reports and research.

I take special care to get ethanol alcohol on her mother's papers, getting them good and soaked and set. Smoke rushes my lungs through my mouth and nose, and I sit in a corner and wait for everything to burn, myself included. I know I will be reborn.

There was a time Aster and I stopped speaking for a year, when she started working with the Surgeon. Melusine was always saying Aster was so smart, so bright, so special, so this, so that, like she was an angel incarnate. Maybe she was, and maybe I'm a little devil, but that's all right too.

It's just that I'm so angry, for all these reasons, for all these reasons I can't help.

I don't believe in the Heavens, I don't believe in Hell, so when I wake up to unfamiliar voices I know it means that I'm still alive and that my half-assed suicide attempt didn't bear its intended fruit. As with all things, you get out of it what you put into it.

I inhale, but all I feel is burning. I start to cough so hard I hurl up bile onto myself.

"I'm going to shift you to your side, if that's all right," I hear, a voice that reminds me of my father's, though I've never heard my father speak. It's God talking, or something, a soothing voice that doesn't soothe me at all because it's impossible to soothe an unsoothable thing like myself.

Squeezing my body into a rod, I prepare to be touched by overly decorous and kind hands. He seizes me by the shoulders and hips, grasp so gentle as to barely be felt, and flips me until I'm lying comfortably. I throw up again, but this time the mess lands on the floor instead of on me. I don't know why, but I'm not thankful. I'm never thankful. I want to be, I do, but all I feel is this annoyance that won't stop. Every nice thing that anyone could ever think to do to me leaves me feeling enraged. It's like, too little too late, buddy. *Kill yourself and get out my way, that is the kindest thing you could do at the moment.*

Tears and the sensation of stinging make me hesitant to open my eyes, but when I finally do, it's the Surgeon standing before me. I see I've thrown up on him too, his lab coat yellow, and I'm not sorry.

"My throat feels like it has a urinary tract infection," I say, or rather choke out pathetically between hoarse half-sobs.

"You've inhaled a lot of smoke," he says.

"Yeah," I say, but then wonder if it's not clever enough for him, and add on, "You're quite the detective," in my most posh voice.

"Can't you sedate her? The Sovereign won't stand for all that cheekiness," says a second voice. Through inflamed eyes, I see that there are a number of strange faces, all in the uniform of the Guard.

The Surgeon hands me a cup of water I'm too thirsty to refuse. My gulps are loud, wet, obnoxious, and I don't care. The liquid cools my sooty mouth and throbbing *esophagus*. That's Aster's favorite word, and I get it. Like all words that describe the body, there's a strangeness to it. For fun sometimes, I imagine Aster talking dirty using such vocabulary. *Shoot your come down my esophagus.* She hates it when I talk like this, because it reminds her of how different she is, and more than that, how we all notice that difference. But I keep doing it. I like making her mad. I like making her feel embarrassed and humiliated. I get pleasure from it, even if I know later I will feel so bad it makes me nauseous. I don't know what's wrong with me. I have this compulsion to hurt, and I try and try to stop it, but I never do.

"Guards, you're dismissed," says the Surgeon.

"We've got direct orders from the Sovereign on this one," says a man with pinky-white skin and graying hair. Everything about him is repulsive, his sniveling voice and button nose and wide, shock-stricken eyes.

"You have direct orders from me to stop talking," I say, and I try to get up. It's only then I realize one of my wrists is cuffed to the side of the cot. "What is this? What did I do?" I ask, but I know what I've done. There are so many sins on my register.

The same sandy-haired guard comes toward me with a hand wrapped around his baton, and I wonder if he realizes how incredibly phallic the whole thing looks! "Come closer and I'll bite off your dick," I say, but I wouldn't. I've never bitten a man's bits, unless he specifically asked me to *use teeth*. I'm compliant. Easy. Tell me what you want done, and I'll do it without protest. People think me a fighter, but I'm the opposite, really, when it comes to the bed. If people want to have me, they'll have me. There's nothing to be done.

"You will give me and the girl fifteen minutes, and that is an order. I'm very sure the Sovereign will understand. Get out now," the Surgeon says, placing himself between me and the other guards, all four of them.

There's a hum of understanding among the four, and one says, "As long as I get fifteen minutes next, sir," like it's the cleverest thing he could've said, rather than the dumbest. They're bumbling idiots, the whole lot of them, and I'm glad I'm not too incapacitated by smoke to roll my eyes.

The guards funnel out the hatch, and one gives me a backward glance. I don't feel afraid. I don't remember the last time I felt afraid.

"We don't have much time," says the Surgeon.

"What's happening?" I ask, and then correct myself. "What happened?" He gives me another glass of water, which I devour. Everything upward of my stomach aches and burns, but I can speak clearly now.

"I discovered you in the lab, unconscious, and brought you to safety," he says. "Obviously, we were discovered in the corridor. Your attempts to seal the smoke into the botanarium weren't successful."

"Fuckwit," I say. "You should've left me."

He nods, and it's not the reaction I was expecting, his sage face struck with remorse. "I overrode the locks because I thought you were Aster. Believe me, had I known it was you, I wouldn't have bothered." His tone implies insult, but I know him too well for all that. His lips shake, actually shake, and I know there's something he's hiding.

"You would've left me to die?"

"I believe that would've been the merciful route."

"What do you mean?" But I know perfectly well what he means. I'm boarding the same train Flick did.

"An execution," says the Surgeon. "Sovereign's order. This time, it's for the whole ship to see."

I gesture for another glass of water, and he fills my cup from the pitcher. "Does Aster know?" I ask.

"I will contact her by radio shortly. She wouldn't let any harm befall you."

I bite my lip and close my eyes and imagine the unusual cadence of her voice. "When Aster sets her mind to something, it's as good as done." My voice isn't as firm as I'd like it. Water splashes on my fingers. The glass almost slips from my hand, but the Surgeon catches it. "You and Aster are together?" I nod, and now he's the one to almost drop the cup. "She's more delicate than you'd think," I say. She's glass. I'm glass. We're all glass, busted up, unrecognizable from our original selves. We walk around in fragments. It's a circus act. "She's my kin," I say. "I think our fifteen minutes are up."

"Keep faith," he says, walking toward the hatch. "Aster is limitlessly resourceful."

She is.

Maybe she'll save me. Maybe I want to be saved.

XXVII

Aster received the news about Giselle via two-way. "Are you there?" Theo asked through coarse static.

"Aye," she said, "I'm in Alpha. I've figured out how to plot courses into the shuttles, but only one of them has fuel. Of course, that's the one with the password lock. I don't know if I'll be able to get more from the manufacturing plant without Lieutenant finding out, but I may be able to crack the code with a bit of time."

Aster chose the route for the shuttles based on her mother's disguised star map, the blue dot in the center of the chemical models. She knew that was the Great Lifehouse.

More and more of Lune's notes about the navigation systems made sense. In the control room Aster familiarized herself with the manuals explaining the computing consoles. One of them compiled data about potential habitable planets using sensors in *Matilda*'s external systems. The printouts from Lune's time looked so grim, nothing habitable for light-year upon light-year upon light-year, it was no wonder she'd chosen to flip the ship around, where she knew, at least, there was an end in sight.

"You've not been to your botanarium yet, have you?" Theo asked through the radio.

"Not in a few days, actually," said Aster, sitting on top of the *Fleeting*, legs dangling.

"Right. You left me to go straight to the Shuttle Bay?"

"Yes."

She heard him breathe heavily over the transmission. "There's no effective preamble I can give, and so I'll give none.

Your botanarium is gone, Aster." His syllables were rushed and slurred together. "Giselle set fire to it." The transmission ended abruptly, a silent emptiness in its place.

"I didn't hear you correctly. Repeat."

"I think you did, and I'm sorry to say that's not the worst news yet. Aster, are you still there?"

She was already on her way to the lowdecks, dread urging her to action. Was it gone, or going? Still ablaze?

"Aster, please, I need to hear you say you're still there, still aware, still focused."

"Here, aware, focused," she said. Indeed, she walked purposeful steps down the secret staircase, sliding through the slim hatch, not bothering to reset the screws.

"He's going to kill her," said Theo.

"You mean that I am going to kill her."

"Aster."

"This is Lieutenant's doing?"

"Welcome to the New Regime," Theo said.

"I'll be in touch shortly," said Aster, cutting off the transmission.

Aster ran her fingers along the walls of her laboratory, peels of cakey black falling to the floor in papery rinds, the texture calling to mind recently shed snakeskin. Archimedes, the fourteen-year-old tree Aster grew from seed, lay in a pile on the floor. She remembered him as a weak-kneed sapling, yellow leaves, failure to thrive—the right mixture of cool air and low light, a feeding solution of water, bone gristle, duck eggshells keeping him alive. Sounds stirred him into vigor. The recordings Aster used to learn to speak proper helped Archimedes too. His stems turned a lush shade of dark green, as rich as maple leaves. He grew tall, spread his shoots around the laboratory with colonizing force, emanating the sweetest, crispest smell.

Her mother's lab notebooks, the curiously tiny print, almost microscopic, carefully color-coded, the detailed diagrams labeled with neat script, burned up to nothing. Maps, so many maps, of the stars and the galaxy and of places Aster would never understand, the last in the universe, gone.

Everything she'd ever held dear had been housed in this botanarium. There'd be no forgiveness this time. It was one thing to destroy a person, but to destroy their work was a sacrilege Aster couldn't easily forget. All that was left of a person's life was recorded on paper, in annals, in almanacs, in the physical items they produced. To end that was to end their history, their present, their future.

Without her notes, without a laboratory, Aster could do little but thrash open each of Theo's cabinets, raid their contents for something, anything at all, that might work. Brown glass bottles with cork stoppers broke against the floor: larium coltate, ammonium brislyhide, silver dilectide, all of it useless. Anesthesia would do the trick, lure her into a comatose state, slacken her heart into a slow, syrupy waltz.

With Theo's help Aster could, for all intents and purposes, kill Giselle, pump oxygen artificially through her body to sustain her organs, then revive her at the right moment.

That required equipment, devices, a team of healers. She needed something straightforward and elegantly simple, and then the solution occurred to her. A concentrated dose of poppyserum would slow her respiratory functions and heart rate, enough to fool the Sovereign. As the Surgeon General, Theo would be the one to declare death. When it was time to move the body to the morgue, and they were clear of oversight, Aster could inject her with enough adrenaline to awaken her body's system. It was far from a perfect plan. On the converse, the scheme carried with it a number of risks.

Aster fumbled through her keys until she found the right

one, inserted it into the cabinet where Theo kept his narcotics. She squinted at the vials until she found two labeled, *Dihydromorphinone*. It would have to do. The time on the big grandfather clock read 22:00 till. She didn't have much time. Aster tucked the two bottles into her medicine belt and ran faster than she'd ever had reason to before.

She needed to get in touch with Seamus before meeting Theo. Mabel too. And the Tide Wingers. The time had come.

Matildans gathered in the corridors around the loudspeakers, making passage difficult. Though those in the lowdecks were already used to Lieutenant's reign of terror, a state-sanctioned, ship-wide execution was a novelty. Their ears turned to the wood-cased speakers. Husbands and wives held hands. J deck teemed with a diverse cross section of *Matilda*'s inhabitants. Lowdeckers, laborers who rarely had a rotation out of the fields, lowborns who'd managed to marry into a measure of success, merchants, poor professionals. Aster dodged through all of them with not so much as an *excuse me*. The execution was to be held in the Maple Wood Clearing, a particularly cruel choice. To inject a girl's veins with poisons in the same space folks gathered to worship their gods indicated a hatred Aster couldn't fathom.

She worked her way both downward and toward the center of *Matilda*, sprinting through Lagoon Wing, Laurel, Locust, Lark, Lightning. She had only ten minutes now. She hoisted herself up onto the bannister and slid down three flights of stairs to M deck, finally. Here, too, Matildans milled anxiously, gathered around the double-paneled hatch that led to Maple Wood.

Aside from narrowed eyes and a few heavy breaths, they appeared calm. Aster recognized their expressions as ones of resignation. She'd cultivated such a face herself, a refusal to react because reacting never helped a damn thing, often made it worse.

"Move," she said to a skinny, dark man with woolen white hair. He looked ready to start something, but by the time he turned to face her, she'd moved past him.

The hatch was open so that people could peek through, and Aster saw him. "Theo!" she called out, entering. She had minutes to spare, enough to slip him the poppyserum covertly.

In what was becoming a predictable pattern, a guard grabbed her by the arm harshly and pulled. "We're at capacity, no more people. And that's *General* to you. Show the Surgeon some respect." A murmur of commotion played out up ahead, through the thicket of stunted trees, but Aster couldn't see.

"Leave her, she belongs to me," said Theo. His voice came out a barely contained roar. It frightened Aster, almost, to see the man she most associated with equanimity so visibly infuriated. "My assistant. She's here to clean up any mess there may be, Sovereign's orders." Maple trees twelve meters tall rose above them in a thick, short canopy, blocking out Baby's rays, giving Theo a dark look. Shadow painted his face into fearsome lines. He was not putting on a show for the guard. His rage poured from him genuinely.

"Teach her some manners," said the guard, shoving Aster toward Theo. The look he gave her, the way he poked his lips out in a mock kiss, said he didn't believe Aster to be Theo's assistant, but his whore. His assumption didn't bother her. Say it were true—there was no shame in it. She didn't understand the smug, knowing way he eyed her.

People like this guard tried so hard to make Aster feel lesser, but some days, like today, it didn't work, because she saw clearly how superior she was.

She walked at Theo's side to Maple Wood Clearing. His

gait was longer than hers, and he moved at a steady clip, but Aster kept up, explaining her plan.

"I don't know if it'll work," he said as they approached the Clearing.

"I don't know if it'll work either," she replied. "That's the nature of a plan."

"And do you have a Plan B, Aster?"

"Yes. Plan B is you don't do it. You refuse. You can refuse."

He reached to grab her hand, but Aster pulled away. "I'll do what I can," he said. "Be safe."

They reached the Clearing, a hundred or more lowdeckers in a thatch surrounding a large platform, two meters tall, ten wide in every direction, wooden steps surrounding them. Aster wondered who'd built it, if they knew who and what it was for, if their palms blistered as they sawed the wood.

Silver poles situated at five-meter intervals held up a plastic awning, with the purpose of providing shade for the Sovereignty. Sixteen guards flanked the platform on either side, snapping at lowdeckers to be quiet and to stand back, commands followed with little complaint. They had no desire to be here. They had no desire to witness this tragedy at close range. They were here as victims of unfortunate timing, workers harvesting maple at the worst possible hour.

Aster saw that above the Clearing, even more lowdeckers watched through the glass, their eyes discernibly sad even from this distance. Made to watch, they would share this burden together.

"Aster," Mabel called. She was coughing. She'd run to get here.

"Did you get everything sorted?" Aster asked.

"I think," Mabel said, out of breath. "The Tide Wingers have a surprise for you too." She lifted her skirt and revealed a rifle, but it was different than the one that belonged to Sovereign Nicolaeus. That one had signs of wear. Divots. Markings. Initials carved in. This one was shiny and brand new, much simpler in design. It seemed the Tide Wingers' reputation for resourcefulness wasn't overstated. They'd done more than make new bullets—they'd made new guns. Aster imagined they'd used copper piping already available behind their walls for the barrel. "There's twenty in all. They're passing them out now. Do you want this one?"

Aster shook her head. "You keep it. Protect yourself. Protect Pippi and Ainy." After this mess, she hoped she'd see Mabel again.

"Give me the poppyserum now," said Theo.

Aster slipped him the vials. "Will they strap her to that?" she asked, pointing to a chair on the crude wooden stage. Leather belts draped over the arms, the color so richly brown it appeared burgundy.

"Likely," said Theo.

"You are being unusually terse. You don't think you can do it?"

Before he could reply, the Clearing settled into an uneasy silence. Aster heard the sound of clanking metal and shifted to see two guards leading a manacled Giselle into the Clearing, ankles chained with only a foot of give between them, wrists the same. Dark patches turned her eyes into dull spheres. Black, wavy hair hung from her scalp in bedraggled sheaves. Her skin, set off by undertones of olive, looked a sickly, sallow green. Following her were four more guards towing something large and heavy, hidden beneath a veil. Aster gazed upon it with squinted eyes, but had no idea what it was.

The two guards pushed Giselle along. In nothing but a slip and her work boots, she didn't look her twenty-five years. She had all the smallness of perpetual childhood, but none of the innocence.

The Sovereign funneled in last, took his place to the left of the platform. The guards held Giselle off to the side, while the others hauled the concealed object up to the center of the stage. Lieutenant turned to those men and made a gesture with his hands. At the signal, they pulled away the veil.

A single cohesive and alarmed gasp filled the Clearing. Under the fabric was a gallows. Hurried and hushed conversation gripped the crowd once more.

The Sovereign sidled up to Theo and whispered, "You'll forgive the lack of notice, but your services are not needed after all. I thought such an event required more flare."

Theo kept his face neutral. "Little says flare like a hanging."

Lieutenant smiled and tilted his head to the right. "You should feel relieved. I know firsthand how weakhearted you can be when it comes to young girls." He pointed his head to Aster. "Isn't that right, Aster? I'm sure the two of you have learned your lesson on that front, and I know you both appreciated my mercy."

"Of course, Sovereign," Theo replied. "Your mercy as well as your restraint prove boundless."

Aster recited *Philosophia Botanica*, paid Sovereign Lieutenant no mind. The verses, methodical and orderly, rendered in perfect iambs, provided her the steadiness she needed. If Giselle was to die by hanging, then their plan had failed before it had begun. What use was there in feeling despair? It was her own fault to have thought the best-case scenario an actual possibility.

There were specters who lived at the edges of Aster's vision, fat-mouthed gorgons with elephantine teeth. Their braids protruded squid-like under the large brims of their straw hats. Holes dotted their dungarees. They chewed tobacco and jerky and bone gristle. Gunpowder trickled from their wounds. Whenever Aster turned to get a better glimpse, they were gone, perpetual inhabitants of the margins. That was how she understood hope, nothing to get too invested in.

"Sovereign," said Theo, "I understand you desire a spectacle, but too much of a scene may rouse rage rather than fear. I beg you reconsider the injection. You could even leave the gallows here, as a warning."

Lieutenant made a sound in his throat only slightly more dignified than a snort. "And girl, what do you think?" he asked, not exactly a rhetorical question, but not one for which he was genuinely interested in her answer.

"I think you're sadistic and wish to see a hanging, and therefore there'll be a hanging," said Aster. She wished herself brave enough to look up into his eyes, but she kept her focus downward, head bowed respectfully.

"Not sadistic, ruthless. There's a difference. Otherwise, an astute observation," he said, then returned his attention to the gathering. "On behalf of the Sovereignty, the Will of the Heavens, and your fellow passengers of His Sovereign's ship *Matilda*, it is my honor and privilege to announce the heralding in of a new and better age. It is for that reason we join together today to carry a life from this world into the next, where she will be judged accordingly. With humble hearts, we say—" and the crowd called out in unison, just as they had with Flick, "*Hallelujah. Blessed be.*"

When Lieutenant read the full name of the accused aloud, he pronounced it with an unexpected combination of grandeur and solemnity. "Giselle Nwaku," he said, reading from a small piece of paper.

"That isn't my name, that'll never again be my name!" Giselle screamed, pulling against her chains. Several took a cautious step backward, faced with the viciousness of her tone. Those who knew her nodded their heads, unshaken.

"You disrespect your forbearers, and by extension the Heavens, by forsaking your own name?" said Lieutenant.

"It isn't my name! My name's Devil now!" she cried out. "And I'll kill you all, I swear it, if not in this life, the next."

One of the guards kicked her up to the platform and she fell to her knees on the steps.

A woman with hanging skin stuck her nipple into the mouth of a toddler who refused to be soothed, but his wails were no match for Giselle's shrieks.

The same guard grabbed Giselle by the scruff of her neck to push her forward, but she surprised him, turning and head-butting his nose, blood spraying. Aster saw that this was her chance. "Giselle," she called out, "catch!" Aster slid her blade from its sheath in her boot and tossed it over to Giselle. She didn't catch it. It bounced against her chest, tumbling over her chains before falling to the ground.

Giselle scurried after it, having gotten the jump on her guards. Several others clambered after her, and though she was slowed down by the shackles, her determination made her unstoppable.

"Do it! Kill them all!" yelled an older woman in the crowd.

"Aye, do it!" yelled another.

"Devil! Devil! Devil!" cried others, taking several seconds to find a uniform rhythm.

Aster knew that the world in which Giselle slew every one of these men, Lieutenant included, did not exist, that one half-crazed woman could do only so much. Still, she found herself shouting, "Spare none! No clemency!"

Giselle—Devil—got her hands on the knife, flipped the blade open, and stood, jutting it out to five guards who circled around her. "I will haunt you," she said, then took the blade and stabbed it into her own stomach.

Aster choked back a startled scream. Giselle, forever defiant. She'd not let them take her, not when she could so easily take herself. Gasps dominoed their way through the Clearing. Devil slumped backward on the platform, limp-limbed.

"Quiet now," Lieutenant said, his fearsome demeanor forcing everyone into compliance. He walked up the steps to her body. Aster heard Giselle's squeaky wheezes. Lieutenant lifted his foot and set the bottom of his boot on the tip of the knife handle, pressing down. He shifted left and right, driving the metal jaggedly through her.

She howled, and if souls were real, that was the moment Giselle's abandoned ship. What a small thing she had asked for, to be left alone, to be allowed the solace of her own atoms. The only cocks she wanted inside her were the ones she requested, the only hands on her body the ones she begged to have touching her, the only knife in her gut the one she lodged there herself.

Aster felt Theo grab her from behind, but she wrangled out of his grip and ran to Giselle's body.

"Stop her!" shouted one of the guards, but it was Lieutenant who said, "Let her have her moment. It is done."

Sweat and blood had turned Giselle's slip translucent, and it showed her breasts, stomach, and legs, the triangular thatch of hair covering her pubis. She was naked before the world.

"Aster?" she said, her voice a simpering croak.

"Devil," Aster answered.

"I'm going to die?"

"Aye."

"Then promise me you won't remember me fondly. Promise me you'll blame yourself," said Giselle. Words left hurriedly from her lips, whisper-quiet.

"Aye, I will," said Aster. "I can't help but do so."

"I want to be the chip on your shoulder. Fifty years from now, you'll think of me with a sodden heart. Promise me, promise me I'll be the mean wench ghost who drives you mad. Don't be happy. When people say, *She'd want you to be happy*, know better."

"Aye, aye, yes, yes," Aster nodded.

"Aster?" said Giselle, eyes fluttering spastically, tears pooling in the corners of her eyes before spilling onto her cheeks. The thick black ink from her eyelashes smeared onto her lids.

"What is it? Whatever you'd like me to say, I'll say it. I'll say it one thousand times. I'll swear you any oath you want."

Aster begged Giselle to say more, but she didn't. Her spiteful eyes had gone dead. When Aster bowed her head, laid her cheek against her chest, she could hear no beating heart. She placed her ear to Devil's lips to listen for the sound of flimsy breaths, was rewarded with only silence.

She crawled to Giselle's wellies, removed them from her narrow, scabbed feet. The audience murmured, and Aster spit on the toes, took the hem of her shirt, and rubbed them into some semblance of shininess.

"All right. Enough," Lieutenant said.

A guard hit Aster across the back with a baton two times. She wept not for the pain, but for Giselle. Wretch that she was, she'd disregard Giselle's dying wish. Aster would remember her quite fondly, indeed.

The guard struck her again, and the pain was immense. He had a heavy hand. Aster tried to imagine herself someplace else, but she couldn't. She was here, in a field splattered with blood that didn't belong to her. Giselle lay lifeless. Her lips were chapped and caked with white.

A heavy sadness settled upon Aster, and she remembered again that she was nothing, a puppet. Unpleasant memories bobbed upward to the forefront. Unsoft hands, splintered wooden spoons, how she hated everyone.

Aster felt another bash from the baton as she sat crumpled on her knees.

"You cease your savagery this instant or be killed without mercy," warned Theo, voice cool with measured fury. His gaze bore into the man beating Aster, teeth bared. The expression he wore revealed determination, and none of the disquiet he likely felt. Theo, like Aster, was a man of rules. Order offered him solemnity. A disruption to the system was a disruption to his sense of calm.

The guard did not drop his baton. Aster flinched in anticipation when she saw him draw it over his head. But the blow never came. Midstrike, he stumbled to the ground, the baton along with him. He clutched his neck, which had been pierced with a dart. The poison meant for Giselle had found its way into the guard's veins. Mind bleary from pain, it took Aster several seconds to understand what was happening. Theo had a tranquilizer gun.

A fresh set of shocked gasps emanated from the crowd. Aster glanced toward the commotion, and were she not in so much pain, she'd have risen up. Finished with Aster's attacker, Theo stood with the tranquilizer aimed at Lieutenant.

"I can't let you carry on in this manner," he said. "It's not right, and I can't tolerate it. Not anymore." Members of the Guard kept to their places, unaccustomed to such momentous betrayal and therefore unschooled in the proper response. Their beloved Surgeon, the Meticulous Hand of God, was poised to shoot five hundred milliliters of cortalviss into the newly appointed sovereign. Stunned into stillness, they watched, bludgeons and batons at the ready.

None stood as stationary as Sovereign Lieutenant himself. "You defy the Guard? You defy me?" he asked. Incredulity didn't suit him at all. Shock tinged his characteristically baritone voice into an unintimidating whine. "You're a liar and a traitor," he said, a single squinted eye revealing intense apprehension.

In his dark burgundy uniform, the brass buttons shining under Baby's oppressive light, he appeared waifish and weak. His wide shoulders and sturdy frame did nothing to negate the image, nor did his hands tightened into powerful fists. Aster realized his power never came from his sternness, but from his knowing calm. Theo's sneak attack had stolen that from him.

"To think I served by you, broke bread with you, called you Brother in Battle," Lieuteant continued. "You are less than nothing, less than dead, less than never having been born, a disgusting, filthy turncoat who no one could ever trust. A man without loyalties is a man without a soul. Do you think yourself brave? Noble? Honorable?" He posed these questions not rhetorically, but as a man hungry for answers

Sensing the desperate curiosity in Lieutenant's inquiry, Theo responded in earnest, the tranquilizer gun still poised in his arms, prepared with another dosage of cortalviss. "I am not after honor, Uncle. My righteous anger could never undo the bad that's been done here today. But I can kill you, and in doing so, prevent similar tragedies."

Lieutenant stared hard at his nephew, lost for words. Silently, he called for his guards with the snap of his fingers, but Aster charged forward. With all her woman-might she barreled into the guard nearest Theo, jumping upon him before he could react. She set her forearm across his throat, pushed so hard his windpipe crushed.

She heard the wind-like snap of Theo pulling the trigger of the dart gun. When she looked up she saw the needle had landed in Lieutenant's eye. He would die in minutes.

Three guards seized Theo, and with that, the riot began. Lowdeckers rushed the guards. Weaponless, they were weak, but they made up for it with volume. The bravest, or foolhardiest, attacked straightaway. The more reticent hovered around the perimeter execution-black, shouting violently in moral support, pushing away the guards who tried to quiet them.

A woman Aster's age or a little older, with long, reddish-brown hair and wide shoulders, snagged the scarf off her own head, leaped up behind one of the guards, and strangled him. Her gently sloped muscles pulsed as the skin pulled taut over them. She twisted the cloth around his neck with abandon.

It was a sight, truly. Aster had always been interested in the ways bodies lived, and the ways they didn't, and there was an artistry to the science of suffocation. Without oxygen to sustain its biological, anatomical, and physiological processes, the body withered into blackness, and that was that. This brought on a definitive and visible shift in the status quo.

The guard's face brightened to an unappealing shade of eggplant. He whimpered wet, ineffectual breaths as the brown-haired woman pilfered the life from him like it was nothing but a goldpiece in a rich man's pocket. Others of his rank dashed to save him, only to be hindered by enraged civilians.

A family of four demonstrated godlike lack of mercy—a mother and another mother, a son whose voice had not yet deepened, and a daughter with only the hint of breasts. When a guard accosted one of the mothers, the two children ("Yella and Ajax!" their parents called out) grabbed hold of a guard's ankles. They yanked until he toppled to the ground, his head cracking against the base of a maple tree. Yella grabbed the bludgeon from the man's belt, held it over her shoulder ready to swing, body shaking. Ajax looked near vomiting. He leaned against the trunk of the tree, eyes closed. Aster could see that he was praying. The volume of the horde made it difficult to hear his exact phrasing, but she knew that he prayed not for forgiveness for what he'd done, but for ruthlessness, so that he might do it again to another.

Another watchman grabbed one of the mothers by the arm, hit her stomach with his bludgeon so hard she keeled to the grass after a single strike. Ajax ran toward him, though he had not a weapon. His meema, not the one on the ground but the other, shouted, "No Ajax, no!" because she saw what Aster noticed out of the corner of her eye: a different guard approaching, this one with a curved blade as big as an arm. He sliced it through Ajax's gut. The boy cried out, then fell.

The guard sliced through him again. Ajax died.

Aster felt Theo's slender arms wrap around her from behind. He pulled her from the fray, fifteen meters out from the maple tree where Ajax only seconds ago prayed, right by the hot creek. He removed his shirt, ripped and torn from his altercation, dipped it in the water. "May I?" he asked, gesturing to the hem of her shirt. Aster whispered assent, then he pulled the fabric up. Near them, a mad mob declared war, and here he was, pressing a hot compress over her bruised spine.

"They're going to kill you, then me," Aster said.

He nodded, then wet the cloth again. "I don't wish it, but it's likely so."

"You killed Lieutenant," she said.

"I did."

"I wanted to be the one to do it. I wanted him to die by my doing."

"I know," he said. "But so did I."

Aster stood, her back sore but not debilitatingly painful. With a great amount of effort, she took a step, and then another, forcing her body into a straight line. The urge to bend and bow threatened her posture, but her will was strong. "I am taking Giselle with me in one of the shuttles," she said. She couldn't leave Giselle's body here to be broken down and repurposed, or defiled.

"I'll provide whatever assistance I can. We need to move." Theo checked the time on his wristwatch, turned toward the mass of rioters growing ever closer to their sanctuary. Giselle's body appeared protected up on the wooden stage, but it would be difficult for Aster to work her way there.

The loudspeakers popped on at once, a burly but posh voice coming through. *"Matildans . . ."* the announcement began. Mabel had really done it. This was a prerecorded message impersonating a member of the Sovereignty's Council, informing everyone to move portside so starboard would be clear for Aster to go up to the Shuttle Bay. Seamus would be there, waiting for her. *"Matildans, this is Lieutenant Governor Wilkins Beauregard, Lieutenant Governor to the Sovereign and current commander of Matilda. The Guard requires the presence of all military personnel to Errol Wing immediately to handle a disturbance. Those guards not present will be sanctioned. Civilians, remain calm."*

The announcement played in a loop. The real Wilkins Beauregard was no doubt quite bewildered and enraged to be impersonated so skillfully.

The rebellion moved outward, into the fields, becoming more diluted. As the guards still living departed, lowdeckers laid down their arms, circling around Aster to offer aid. It was a bloody sight. Aster couldn't imagine what it looked like in the corridors where Mabel had distributed the rifles.

She turned toward the platform. Giselle's body appeared oddly angelic. "I must get her."

"You two," Theo said to a couple of stragglers who'd deserted the fight, "can you fashion some sort of stretcher?"

Nodding, they toppled the main viewing tent, tearing out a large square of sturdy synthetic fabric. They tied the ends to some poles, and the whole thing took less than ten minutes. People approached, weeping and carrying on, offering Giselle kisses. They laid their jumpers and jackets on her for cover. One woman removed an ivory decorative comb from her own hair and slid it into Giselle's.

"You will come with me," said Aster, "in another of the shuttles. We can figure out the fuel. I can siphon some from the one I plan to use." She knew it didn't make sense.

"There are people here that need my help. You will be back. It's no matter."

"What if I meet whatever fate my mother did? What if I disappear forever? What if I am wrong?"

"Then I will come after you," said Theo, and though his words were impossibly romantic, they heartened Aster.

With no time for extended goodbyes, she carried the body with help from one of the men who'd built the stretcher. Her muscles strained under the weight. Skin popped and blistered on her palms. In death as in life, Giselle liked to make things difficult. Sweat-slicked fingers made it hard to keep hold of the metal rods. Aster gripped more firmly, but doing so only exacerbated the problem.

"You good?" the man asked.

"Aye," said Aster.

"You sure?"

"I'm sure." She wasn't. Her previous surge of adrenaline could only sustain her so long.

They hobbled with the stretcher out of the field and into the corridor, a small crowd rallying behind them. Waiting at the foot of the stairs to the next deck was Melusine, standing next to a wheelchair. "Sit her here, boy," she said to the man.

Melusine's declaration was a welcome relief. Aster helped him lower Giselle to the ground and began to hoist her into the chair.

"Not her, this one," said Melusine. She grabbed Aster's wrist and pulled her toward the chair. "For once, do not fight me, child. Trust that I know. I have lived long and I know."

The man took her other arm, guided her gently. "I got you," he said. Aster had no choice but to sit.

"Who's got Giselle?"

"Be quiet, rest, and don't concern yourself," said Melusine.

Four men from the crowd lifted the wheelchair into the air, carrying it like a throne. They hoisted her up the stairs. Aster saw Melusine bend down to Giselle, but she was too weak to carry her. Instead, she snapped at another man to pick her up. He lifted her up with ease, and as they traveled up the decks, flight to flight, Aster was reminded of a funeral processional, like the one given to Sovereign Nicolaeus.

When they came upon several guards, the processional

overpowered them. Unhindered, they marched. It felt nice to rest. Aster was spent and used up but surrounded by kin. She felt moved to give a speech upon reaching the threshold of Alpha. Bodies crammed the narrow corridor and stairway. Expectant gazes beseeched her to speak.

"My name is Aster of Quarry and this is a eulogy," she began, then waited for everyone to hush. A eulogy was a tribute to the dead, in which the speaker spoke thoughtfully about the deceased. Aster felt prepared to do thus. "Giselle was a person with myriad psychological disturbances, the logical outcome of the trauma she suffered. I estimate she experienced ninety-one events that could be described as intense trauma, but data is scarce and inconclusive. She had a short list of likes and a very long list of dislikes. She was very difficult. She was very mean and abusive. I wish she wasn't dead, but the amount of blood loss she sustained as a result of a knife wound to her lower abdomen made dying an inevitability. May her soul finally be at peace." She didn't wait for those gathered to respond, she simply gestured for the men to carry her upward.

"May your days be unburdened, Aster," Ainy said, the traditional farewell before a long absence.

"And may yours," Aster replied, the words causing a pang of longing.

The mob burst through the wall with ease, using only the force of their own bodies.

Aster pressed her fingers over the keys of the keypad to the *Fleeting*. She typed A-S-T-E-R, but nothing happened. Next, she tried L-U-N-E. "Think, think," she said. She scanned her memory of Lune's notebooks. She wished she could flip through them, but they were all gone now. Except—

Aster unclipped her radiolabe and took off its backing. She removed her mother's goodbye note.

Aster, dear. Achingly, sorrowfully, tearfully, regretfully, angrily, I leave you. I am sorry.

She read it over and over, trying to see it with Giselle's eyes, which were always so good at picking out patterns that weren't there. Aster read the words out loud, enjoying their cadence. *"Aster, dear. Achingly, sorrowfully, tearfully, regretfully, angrily, I leave you."* She repeated the phrase, her tongue sliding over the consonants neatly.

She typed once more into the keypad. *A-D A-S-T-R-A. To the stars.* It had been right there all along. With several clicks and a vibrant hiss, the two doors lifted open and up.

Inside, there were bones, a human skeleton lying on its side in the backseat holding a medicine kit. Aster jolted backward. "Meema," she said.

Seamus gasped. Aster saw the makings of a tear in his left eye, felt her own forming. She shouldn't be surprised Lune had been here all along. She was a mechanic, after all. She hadn't flown off into the sky. She'd gone to make repairs.

Lune had needed to fix the dent in *Matilda*'s hull to restore the eidolon pumps to full functionality to make sure the reverse around the anomaly would work. What had been non-critical damage became critical the moment Lune planned to interfere with the ship so momentously.

Aster breathed in, attempting to steady her palsying nerves. Lune knew she would die making the repairs, unable to survive exposure to the compression field's radiation outside the ship. Aster was thankful she'd had the strength to navigate back into *Matilda* even if she was too sick to even stumble back out of the shuttle.

Voices from above rang out, two guards making their way down the metal stairs onto the Shuttle Bay.

"Quick, get her in," said Aster.

Seamus helped Giselle into a seat, pulled the safety harness down, and buckled it between her legs. "I'll take care of them," he said. "You're not going to have much time. Be ready to launch when I let open the airlock."

Aster nodded, focused on the dashboard of the shuttle, forcing herself to remember every detail of her mother's meticulous diagrams, disguised in her lab notes as charts, stoichiometric equations.

Aster checked the air supply, logged in the number of passengers, clicked the view-screen dial two spaces to the left so the digitized version displayed an electronic representation of what lay beyond the window. Suddenly, temperature, humidity, and other atmospheric readings appeared on the glass, accompanied by a star map showing Aster where she was in space.

Guards banged on the glass, which meant Seamus had effectively sealed them off on the other side. Soon he would open the airlock, and Aster would need to be ready.

She turned the dial to log the flight plan, and a gray screen appeared.

Enter Passcode.

Aster pressed in *AD ASTRA.*

The screen refreshed to reveal the same text: *Enter Passcode.*

Aster tried the same letters, alternating between capital and lowercase, skipping the space and then keeping the space.

You have reached your maximum number of attempts.

The monitor turned to black. Aster jammed her fingers into the keys, turned the dial again and again, but the screen remained blank. "Fuck, fuck," she mumbled, and mashed the fleshy part of her fist into the display. Outside, an alarm sounded, the sixty-second warning for the airlock. She had to navigate to the tracks of the launching pad. The high-pitched ring of it hurt Aster's ears. She could override the shutdown if she reset the system. She pulled the power lever into neutral, knowing if she turned it all the way off, it would take too long to boot the ship's life-support systems back up in time for the release of the airlock. After ten seconds, she pushed it back on to full energy. When she prepared to log the flight plan, the original message appeared: *Enter Passcode.*

"Think like a ghost," she said aloud.

Seconds to spare, she hoped her instinct was right. *A-D T-E-R-R-A-M*, Aster typed.

Flight plan loaded, read the display. *Press right foot pedal to engage directive.*

Unprepared for the whoosh of oxygen rushing into space, carrying the *Fleeting* along with it, Aster's head slammed backward. Yet she managed to press the pedal before succumbing to unconsciousness. "*Ad terram*," she said. "To Earth."

XXVIII

Aster squinted to observe her surroundings, but sediment coated the shuttle's windows. Through the dirty glass, she could make out only smears of blue. She used her hands to check herself for injuries. The safety straps cut into her shoulders, collarbone, chest, and ribs, and she pressed the red button to release them. They sprung back into the seat, leaving bruises in their stead beneath her clothes.

From the corner of her eye, Aster noticed movement, and she turned to see Giselle's head lolling downward, chin bopping her chest. For the briefest of moments, Aster believed, fanatically believed, that Giselle had nodded off to sleep.

"Wake up," she said, immediately realizing her mistake.

The screen displayed numbers she didn't understand, but that didn't matter. Her mother's journals supplied what information she needed, and Aster did not hesitate to click the hatch of the shuttle open. When she inhaled, sweetly scented air, so cold, brushed her face and lips, drying the sweat on her forehead and neck.

Certainly, these lands before her were what the Sovereignty referred to as the Heavens, a perfect tangled mess of plant life so large, so big, so colossal, it equaled one hundred *Matildas*. She stepped out into the tall grasses, tawny shoots reaching up to her shoulders like stalks of amaranth. She grabbed one and sniffed, then sneezed.

"It seems I have died along with you, Giselle, and we've been spirited away to the Heavenly Lands," she said, and her voice must've startled creatures in the surroundings. She heard a flurry of wispy sounds and turned to see the largest trees she'd ever encountered, a whole bundle of them, stretching left and right as far as she could see, a most intense shade of green.

The blue was, it turned out, space, the cosmos from which she'd come. And there, in the distance, was its star, a hot pink circle. It put poor Baby to shame.

Aster didn't know what tragedy had befallen this place, but time seemed to have erased it. Though 325 years had passed on *Matilda*, a thousand had passed here.

A murder of crows, more than fifty, swooped downward toward a point in the distance. Never having seen so many birds before, Aster stalked toward them, leaving Giselle behind.

More than half the crows cawed and flew away, but those who remained stared at her curiously, their bulbous eyes fixed to her, unafraid.

Aster returned to the shuttle, climbing into the back with Lune's skeleton. The urge to pull away from the grotesque sight nagged at her, but the desire to touch was stronger. She drew a finger along the chin, the broken teeth, up to the cheekbone, stopping before she reached the eye sockets.

Lune's clothes were intact, a dark-green jacket, very soft, and leggings made of hide. Aster removed the jacket, her movements gentle so as not to break the skeleton apart. She smelled the fabric of the coat, expecting the odor to be foul, but time had washed the stink away and it smelled only of wool. No hint of her mother, or her mother's scent, remained.

Beside the skeleton sat a basket, a knitted ivory blanket inside. Aster roved her fingers over the soft stitches, then pressed it to her cheek. As an infant, she'd lain in here, probably only for minutes before being forced from her swaddling.

Aster carried her mother's bones in the basket outside and set them on the ground. She got on her hands and knees and dug. The ground was soft and damp, the dirt pliable, the grasses with shallow enough roots to upend with ease. She moved maniacally, scooping earth into her hands and throwing it to her sides, her breath fast and her chest burning. Arms numb, fingers numb, she could not bring herself to stop, not until she'd dug a hole one meter deep.

She placed her mother inside first, covered her with the blanket. It was harder, much harder, to lay Giselle to join her, and though Aster's muscles hurt, she held her in her arms for many minutes, kissing her cheek and nuzzling her face into Giselle's hair, and whispering "Sorry" into her ear, and that it was she, not Aster, who was the reason they'd found this place.

Aster lay down in the black dirt, the granules cooler than the coolest sheets on *Matilda*. Sadness twisted up inside her, like a rope or maybe like a snake or maybe like a rosary. Whatever it was, this gangly sorrow, it had tied itself around Aster's vertebrae and would remain quite a long while.

She felt sentimental. She felt superstitious. She felt like she could cry and catch her tears in a magic vial, pour the tears over Giselle's face, and resurrect her. But Aster was too dehydrated to weep, and even if she weren't, the water would do nothing but wet Giselle's dead, indifferent face, then evaporate. Repositioning Giselle's fingers so they were interlaced with her own, Aster rested beside her. Water was not good for such times as this, insubstantial as it was. But dirt, dirt would do. They were sheathed in it.

Acknowledgments

First and foremost on any thank you list is my family, who've always supported, nurtured, and encouraged my strangeness, which is part and parcel with my creativity. I am especially grateful to my grandmother, Elizabeth Humble, whose love of cryptograms and crosswords helped cultivate my love of language. Thank you to my Aint Goldy, my Aint Pauline, my Aint Florence, my Madear, my Aunt Lisa, my Aunt Cathy, my Aunt Karlene, and to my most enthusiastic and dedicated supporter, my mother. Thank you to my father, who has embarrassed me too many times with his endless belief in my greatness, and thank you to my partner, for whom there will never be adequate words.

I could have never written this book without the help of my various writing teachers, especially Adam Johnson, Elizabeth McCracken, and Jim Crace. All of my gratitude to the Michener Center for Writers, where *An Unkindness of Ghosts* was born.

Lastly, thank you to Laura Zats, who believed in me and believed in my book, who is endlessly patient with me, and who made all of this possible.